IRISES FOR ALAN
LOVE AND FAITH, LOST AND FOUND

ROBERT PAGANO

MaJuLi Publishing

D1452431

MaJuLi Publishing LLC
4607 Library Rd,Ste 220-1027
Bethel Park, PA 15102
MaJuLiPublishing@gmail.com

This book is a work of fiction. A story that actually happened in another universe on a world with certain characters, settings, and events similar to Earth's. The author has used these similarities fictitiously, naming things familiar to readers in this world to create an engaging experience. Otherwise, any resemblance to actual persons, living or dead, or actual places or events on this planet is purely coincidental.

Any opinions, statements or perspectives in this novel, which are controversial, inaccurate, or insensitive, are solely the fault of the characters herein and the author. Apologies extended.

Book Layout: ©2017 BookDesignTemplates.com
Cover Design: bespokebookcovers.com/
Figures: Media Elements via Canva.com: ©"chalkboard" by narloch-liberra; "Chalk Pi Symbol" by by cheradie (Adie) from CSGA Designs; "Chalkboard Texture Background" by stux from pixabay; "Hand Drawn Line" by moonnoon; "Red Thin Arrow Straight Arrow Pointing Right" by SkildLabs from SkildLabsvia; "semi circle line arc" by Axio Design from Rotaru Virgiliu's Images; Ripple circles: "Hand Drawn Basic Abstract Shape" by sparkelstroke;"Rock Stone Gravel Pebble" by siluetstrip: Via Canva.com

Irises for Alan/ Robert Pagano-- 1st ed.
ISBN: 979-8-9869407-0-0

Dedication
To my children: Matt, Justin and Lindsay, who have been, and will always be, a part of my universe and my inspiration.

The Brain is just the weight of God -
– Emily Dickinson 1863

At heart I feel free, yet if the total amount of energy in the universe never changes, wouldn't that destroy free will?
– Emilie du Châtelet circa 1740

Iris

Noun

1) a thin, pigmented membrane composed of muscle fibers, located behind the cornea, which gives the eye color and has an aperture (pupil) that adjusts to light.

2) a flower, typically with delicate, purple tongue-shaped leaves.

3) a rainbow.

Greek Mythology
The goddess of the rainbow, who acted as a messenger of the gods.

PROLOGUE

When Alan brought some interesting information to my attention two years ago, I urged him to write about how he came to his unusual viewpoint. I knew there was something important in what he had learned and encouraged him to share it. He asked me to contribute, and we agreed to write a story with fictitious characters so no one would be harassed or accused of admitting to any crime. That is how this book came about.

It's not unusual to see nature, as I do, composed of opposing forces that tug at us through life. To see everything in terms of Yin and Yang. Some would argue that our experiences and choices are not always black and white, that sometimes they are gray. But isn't gray just finer points of black and white? Alan's friend, John, taught him this lesson, and it was in such a binary framework that Alan discovered something unexpected. At times we can be awestruck by the nature of a world where something came from nothing, and light was brought forth from darkness. Ever since the animate sprung from the inanimate, there has been a dance between the poles of opposites and, like the characters in Alan's narrative, each of us struggles with life and death, knowledge and ignorance, courage and fear, love and hate, faith and doubt, moral and immoral.

This is Alan's story and shortly I will let him tell it in his own words. But I wanted the reader to be aware that there is a part of this story that Alan could not tell: the part played by an antagonist that Alan was unaware of for a time. Until the paths of two people cross, they appear to be traveling on separate lines, each drawn through their own unique space. Each unknown to the other, until their lines intersect and the illusion of separateness shatters.

Alan and his friends had no idea that there was an inchoate threat growing in their town. While Alan was an adolescent, a poisonous seed had been planted there. Its tendrils sprouting with deadly intent, but wearing a disguise of normalcy. It originated in the form of a father and son. The boy was a celebrated athlete in the town's public high school. His name was Bellcon.

You will find scenes about Bellcon that I have inserted in chronological order to keep you informed. I spared no effort to keep these accounts accurate. Speaking at first with a few contacts, I developed a list of everyone who could provide some insight. I tracked down and interviewed everyone who knew him, from classmates in New Jersey to neighbors in his home town of Dargton and acquaintances in California, including his uncle the police officer in L.A. I spoke with his high school principal and coach, the local police, and a military sergeant. I also searched public records. Finally, I was able to speak with Bellcon's mother and father. His mother was blunt, unforgiving, and critical. His father enjoyed bragging about a ruthlessness that he shared with his son. He seemed to know what was going through the boy's mind on various occasions. It's uncanny, but the boy must have confided in his father and his father was proud of his boy's cunning.

Admittedly, I used information from my interviews in a creative way. I wrote Bellcon's story from an omniscient point of view— having added a few fictitious scenes to fill in small gaps in the boy's past and speculating at times about what people were thinking— but I suspect I'm not far off. If anything, the story I tell underplays the boy's nature.

In a way, the differences between Bellcon and Alan highlight the binary world we live in. But the amazing twist to this story is what Alan and his friends created out of black and white.

I hope you will be as inspired by this tale as I have been.

Now let's hear from Alan.

(Rev) James MacKristin, December 2014

CHAPTER 1

One Saturday in the summer of 1963, the year Tim and I would be starting fourth grade, I rode my bike to his house to ask him to join the altar boys. If you were riding on my handlebars, you might have been surprised to see so many nearly identical Cape Cod houses. You certainly wouldn't have thought you'd find the diverse townspeople of Forrest Creek, N.J. living in carbon-copy homes. Yet we did share a kinship that defied understanding until you realized that the early settlers here—Irish, Italian, Polish, German, Slav and other immigrants, working as laborers or craftsman (yes there were a smattering of professionals)—wanted to jettison their cultural identities. To forget the homelands that reminded them of famine, poverty and persecution. They wanted to be as American as these cloned Cape Cods, and they had a determination to survive. Their ambitions created a neighborhood of individuals either driven to help one another, or defiant, combative, and sometimes self-destructive. That's why, as a child who knew these people, it was urgent that I convince Tim to join the altar boys with me. It was for his own protection. Protection from his father and the bullies in school, but, more so, protection from himself.

I was nine years old, Tim was already ten. He had been held back one year. School wasn't his thing, he said. As I rode my bike to his house, the sun nearly burnt the skin off my arms. I found refuge waiting on the shaded front steps of his brick Cape Cod. We had planned to ride bikes over to the superhighway construction site in town. There, we could drive down steep hills, around berms, over dirt pile jumps and through huge concrete storm drains.

Tim's father was in one of his rages. "Get this god-damned shit out of here!" he roared. Something smashed against a wall. "Now clean it up!" Five minutes later, Tim raced out the front door. His spindly limbs and large face looked like an animated stick figure in a panic. "Come on!" he shouted. His father stomped and growled behind him in hot pursuit, his paunch bobbing as he ran. He was the size of a N.Y. Giants offensive guard and looked ridiculous chasing such a small boy. I know what he would have done if he caught my friend. I'd seen it before.

Speeding away on our bikes, I fantasized that when I got older, I'd come back and beat the shit out of that ass-hole.

"Why's your father always trying to kill you?" I asked. Tim was never one to offer much.

"He ain't."

"Is so. I saw him hit you last week, when he was yellin' at your mom. You got that black and blue on your back. What's with him?"

Tim sounded guilty. "I just didn't listen 's all. Didn't do what he told me."

I thought about my father, Michael. His toughness was forged in childhood by the misfortunes of his family.

"Your grandfather," he told me, "came to this country from south London in 1921, after world war one, during a depression in England. The clothes on his back were all he had." I never met either of his parents, but I pieced together enough of the stories that were retold on holidays.

Grandpa settled in Bethlehem, Pennsylvania. There, he met a Frenchman who lived in a garage with his daughter and a bicycle, his only real possession. Grandpa and the Frenchman did odd jobs and used the bike to shuttle messages and documents between local industry magnates. They made five cents for each delivery. "Your grandfather fell in love with the Frenchman's daughter," Dad said.

He married her *one year* after coming to America. I couldn't help wonder: what were these two thinking—who didn't have a dime between them—deciding to get married and have my father? I thought they were dumb, but I watched Dad when he told this part of the story. Face relaxed, eyebrows and the corners of his mouth turned up, he glowed with admiration.

Grandpa's only bit of luck was getting to know some people at the steel mill while doing deliveries. He eventually landed a good job there. From here the story goes downhill. "When I was eleven your grandma contracted polio, and two years later grandpa was killed at work trying to save another steel worker when a furnace exploded. It was 1935, in the middle of the Great Depression." Dad would tell this part of the story with his chin up and a smile on his face. I'm sure he was proud of his dad, but this part always made me sad.

Grandma wore leg braces and used crutches. I imagined loud clanging thumps as she struggled in her tiny apartment going from the bathroom to the kitchen, calling for Michael to lend a supportive arm or to go pick up some groceries. She worked at home as a secretary, but did not make enough to keep *one* person alive. So, Michael got up at four a.m. to work mornings and weekends at a bakery, until he finished high school. (The baker let him take home bread or rolls that were not sold the previous day.)

My father never made a big deal about winning a full scholarship to Cornell or continuing to work nights through college to send some money home. What I found intimidating was that he played Rugby at Cornell. There are pictures in his bedroom. He wore number seven. If you saw his narrow-eyed, clenched-jaw face when he was solving some problem with a slide rule, or even washing the car, you'd know he probably bulldozed over would be tacklers and flattened opposing ball carriers.

Dad was a sophomore the year Pearl Harbor was bombed, and the year before he got his degree in electrical engineering, grandma died. Natural causes, they said. She was young. After graduating, Michael enlisted.

Although it had been years since Dad served in World War II, he still thought of himself as a paratrooper. His bootcamp friend Jules described him as fearless. Dad was not as big as Tim's dad, but he was straight as an oak trunk, with a square jaw and body, penetrating brown eyes, and crew-cut, black hair. If it came to a fight between our fathers, I wouldn't put my money on Tim's. Comparing the two fathers in my mind made me wonder if, one day, my father would snap and beat me. He sure didn't seem to like that I was friendly with Father Curtain, and that I faithfully attended church and Sunday school. Dad was a fervent atheist. Once I overheard my parents arguing.

"Your son has different beliefs, Michael. I understand your war experiences shaped yours. I respect your beliefs, you respect mine. It's the same with Alan, right?"

"But he's always talking about that priest, what if he decides to be one?"

"There are worse things he could be."

"Marie, don't you see? He's big for his age and really bright, he could do so much in the *real* world. Can't we just discourage religion a little and push him more towards sports, academics?"

"Let's respect his choice and see where it goes, OK, dear?"

My mother was like that. Tolerant, understanding, convincing. That's partly why she was so popular. She knew just about everyone in our town and I believe they'd all come running if she needed help. People wanted to be near her, on her side. If Tim's mother was like Marie, the whole community of Forrest Creek would come down on her husband like a hammer.

You think I'm being partial? I mean, her being my mother. Of course I am. She's the only person on Earth who would jump in front of a speeding truck to save me. But what I'm getting at is the *community* loved her. Not just for the reasons you might think. Sure, she did a lot of charity work and stuff at the church. She met tons of people. But Mom was different. I'm not sure what it was, but when she walked into a room, everyone noticed. They seemed pulled by some invisible gravitational force to revolve around her, like planets happily orbiting the Sun. She was pretty, but that wasn't it. It wasn't just those arresting blue eyes, the spirals of long brown hair, or the slender frame and strong, confident posture. There was something that extended even through her lean arms and smooth graceful hands. When her fingers danced on the keys of our living room piano, guests were mesmerized.

Anyway, I'll bet Tim wished his mom was like Marie, but he had no one to protect him at home. Tim and his mother were equally terrorized. That's why, as we rode our bikes over to the construction site, I thought about suggesting that we become altar boys. Tim needed protection. Not just from his father and the bigger boys at school, who picked on him relentlessly. He was also a threat to himself. Tim had a dark side. He was quiet. I did most of the talking, but when he spoke, it was often about leaving home, or wondering what heaven was like. Being altar boys, I figured, might get God, or at least Father Curtain, to back him up.

Our parish priest, Father Curtain, was like a favorite uncle to me. In Sunday school he told us Bible stories filled with swashbuckling heroes—Christians who God had endowed with superpowers. I was hooked, believing that certain individuals could conjure plagues to humble pharaohs, part seas, or raise the dead. I wanted to be one of those individuals. Priests had powers too. I was sure Father Curtain was a man who could protect Tim. Maybe I could even get the bishop involved. Bishops were probably even more powerful than priests. Father Curtain and the bishop had a close relationship with Mother. This was in part because she ran our church's fund raisers and was a lead in the *St. Peter's Players*, a troupe that performed religious stories to entertain parishioners.

The bishop, though, had a special relationship with Mother. A bond of trust. I didn't know until I was older that the bishop's niece, who attended my elementary school, became pregnant in eighth grade. Before she began showing, and until she delivered, she "went on a retreat," sparing the bishop's family embarrassment. My mother had to juggle her day job as counselor and music teacher at Forrest Creek High School, in order to discretely tutor the girl at home. The bishop was indebted.

I had thought about becoming an altar boy for a while and wanted to do it with a friend. Rich was too busy. And Tom was too much of a free spirit. He was totally into his drums and guitar, often fantasizing about smoking pot. That's why we called him *Hip*. Besides, he loved to challenge every religious idea that came up. I knew Tim was the right guy, and this was the right moment.

When we arrived at the construction site, we drove up a steep dirt hill that would become a highway overpass. Just before we tilted our bikes to plunge down into multiple construction site hazards, I said, "Hey Tim, why don't we become altar boys?"

He frowned for a minute, in deep thought. "Why's that?"

"It'll be like a club. You and me. We'll ask Father Curtain. You like him, don't you?"

"I guess."

"We'd have to learn Latin. It's like a secret code. Maybe we'll have like a Bible adventure someday."

Tim smiled. "Yeah. Hey, think being an altar boy'd get me into heaven when I die? What do you think heaven's like?"

"Will you stop with dying all the time?" I asked, annoyed and unnerved how Tim flirted with his own death. I had no rejoinder, other than: "Race you down. Set, *go!*"

Our bikes flew down the steep narrow paths, jerking and jumping over rocks and dirt piles, flying through giant concrete tubes awaiting burial, across the wide, flat scraped earth that would transport future travelers to parts unknown.

CHAPTER 2

Within two weeks I had started a new religious routine with my best friend. Kneeling in the sanctuary behind the altar on Sundays, Tim and I wore red cassocks under white surplices. Dressed like twins, we looked inseparable, and we were. Father Curtain stood between us. He sang the Latin phrases, and when Tim didn't know the response, I'd call it out, louder than usual, to cover for him. Our mysterious words echoed through the nave, as if our voices had spiritual counterparts.

The vestments, majestic architecture, deep mysteries of faith and the power of priests, which all came together in the Mass, amazed me. At each Mass, when the priest declared, *Hoc est enim corpus meum,* transforming bread and wine into flesh and blood, I wanted to be a priest more than anything else. What could possibly be better? To have that power, while at the same time dedicating your life to understanding God and helping the less fortunate. That was something I was sure was in my destiny. It would make my mother and grandmother proud. It might throw my father into a rage, but I was becoming more convinced at each service that I wanted to be a priest. If a blowout with my father was coming, so be it. God would be on *my* side.

Three months passed. Things kept getting better: school was fun, being an active part of the Mass was uplifting, my dad became somewhat distanced, Tim began talking more. Then disaster struck. On Friday afternoon, November 22, 1963, our teacher, Sister Michelle, was called out of our room. A few minutes later she came back in. Her hand was over her mouth and it looked like her eyes were red. A tinny voice crackled into our classroom over the old PA system. "Today..." Pause. Microphone clicking off and on several times. "There will be early dismissal." The principal's voice wavered. She cleared her throat. There was another pause. "In observance..." She said nothing else. Sister Michelle told us President Kennedy had been assassinated. Then she began to cry. After that announcement, Tim became withdrawn and kept his face in his hands. He'd mutely shake his head when we tried to speak to him.

We were sent home early. Some of my classmates, teachers, and my bus driver were crying. The high school also ended the day early, and I found my mother at home, her eyes reddened.

"Why would someone do that?" I asked. "What do we do now?" A void had formed in the world so large, it threatened to suck in everything: me, the rest of North America, perhaps the world.

"Alan, there is evil in the world. Bad things happen. We pray. Put our faith in God. Things will go on. We will all get through this."

We hugged and talked for a while. I knew what I had to do. I called Tim. I was relieved that he answered the phone. "Hey, Tim. Listen. We've got to do the Mass on Sunday."

"I was just gonna call you. Could you do it alone?"

"Come on, Tim, remember Father Curtain says getting into heaven is all about helping people. This is our chance. People need us. They're going to need to go to church this Sunday more than ever."

"Maybe."

"Come on, man. This is big. Everyone's scared. We can help them. We all need to put our faith in God."

"Uh."

"Tim, I need you there. Both of us. To help one another. To help Father Curtain. To help the people."

"I guess so."

"Promise?"

"Oh, OK."

I hung up and thought of my father. He had no faith, no God. I wondered how he would handle this tragedy. But then, he'd gotten through a world war.

Tim and I were assigned the six thirty a.m. Mass. We showed up at the usual time, changed in the same sacristy, put on the traditional acolyte vestments, and got ready to repeat a ritual that had not really changed for hundreds of years. Yet something was very different. Since the assassination, people seemed to have lost their bearings, as if they were sailors on a ship at sea one night when the stars vanished. Tim had become more remote.

Father Curtain came into the sacristy. "Sit down, boys."

We sat in the small wooden chairs.

"This is a difficult time. We've lost our president. Our leader. A Catholic. We wonder, who will guide us now, protect us?" He looked at Tim. "We must have faith in God, for He has always led us. He will protect you. I will protect you, and the church will protect you. We may not always understand the ways of God, but He does love us and his plan will become clear one day. Will you believe in what I'm saying? Alan? Tim?"

Tim and I looked at each other. Tim's expression brightened a bit. We nodded.

The priest smiled, "Good. Because I need you behind the altar today showing your faith. The parishioners need you to give them strength." I wondered if Father Curtain planned a miracle, because there was no way two kids were going to help a church full of grieving adults. Tim and I must have looked skeptical because the priest added, "That's right, they need *you*. You will help them if you believe in what I'm telling you."

The pews were full, which was unusual for the early Mass. The dead silence was punctuated by occasional coughs. Faces in the crowd were pale, expressionless. Some sat slumped, others were fidgeting.

During the service Tim's posture straightened. His Latin responses were louder than usual. I looked out at the congregation and saw the same metamorphosis. A wave of reassurance spread across their anxious faces. The change was something miraculous. Then came my favorite part of the service. Bread and wine to flesh and blood: *Hoc est enim corpus meum.*

Kneeing on the altar steps, looking up at the priest, I was overwhelmed. The darkened Gothic church, its majestic architecture creating the impression that God maintained the world, the transformation of bread and wine into flesh and blood ("the transubstantiation"), the change in Tim and the parishioners in the face of utter tragedy. Father Curtain had created that change with a spiritual power that flowed through him and the church from God.

When the priest descended the stairs to read from the Gospel, Tim and I stood. My face and head began to tingle. I wondered if I was being called by God, if the burning around my head was the aureole depicted in religious paintings and whether others could see it. I looked at my mother in her first-row seat. She smiled approvingly but unaware.

By Thanksgiving I decided I would be a priest. All I could think about was how I would be able to change people. If someone was poisoning himself with alcohol, as a priest, I would learn how to channel the spirit of God, like an antidote, through me to them. If someone lost the vital force to stay alive and planned suicide, I would be the wire carrying a current from God, ordained to recharge them with God's love. It was exciting and I wanted to share that decision with everyone, especially my family. So, I planned to make the big announcement at Thanksgiving dinner.

On Thanksgiving Day, Grace, my grandmother and only living grandparent, was there. She usually came to our house and helped prepare the feast. I called her *Ona* because when I was learning to talk, I couldn't pronounce the *N* in Nona. When we took our seats around the holiday dinner table, my mother proudly asked me to lead the prayers. My father looked like he was tolerating the bad behavior of the neighbors' children.

When I finished the prayer, I said, "I've decided to become a priest!"

Mother and Ona, the two Catholics, brightened and took turns singing praises: "Alan, that's wonderful. Oh, you'll make a great priest! Maybe a cardinal someday! Or pope!" They asked enthusiastically when I decided and if Father Curtain knew.

When their exhilaration died down, Dad, the atheist, said with disdain, "A priest? You're serious?"

"Yes," I replied, a bit surprised by his frankness. I must have believed that the women's approval would have tempered his reaction. It didn't. He pressed on.

"You have a sharp mind, son. You could be an engineer, a doctor, a lawyer. Make a difference in the world. Why keep your head in the clouds?"

"I want to know God and teach others. I know you don't believe, but He called me. I might save souls. Wouldn't that make a difference?"

"Saving souls. That's the problem," Michael groaned. "Death being glorified. What about life? You can save *lives*, Alan. No one is certain about afterlives."

Grace stiffened in her chair, my mother's mouth began to open.

I bolted up from my seat, face burning. "Why are you always telling me what to do?" I blurted. Frustrated, and afraid I'd curse or insult him, I left the food untouched and went to my room.

There was an emotional war going on in me that pitted hostility toward my father against the recoil of sinning: *Thou shalt honor thy father.* My decision to become a priest had laid bare the differences between my parents. My father, Michael, was rigid in his thinking, an atheist, ex-paratrooper, and brilliant engineer. My mother, Marie, had a tolerant soul. She was a devout Catholic, accomplished pianist, a counselor and music teacher at the high school. These differences, which ironically must have created the opposite poles of attraction, now became battle lines as I sat in my room and overheard the unfamiliar raised voices of their argument.

"I don't believe what you just said to your son, Michael!"

"Marie, the boy is brilliant. What do all his teachers tell us. He's exceptional, the work comes easy to him. And look at him, he's nine for heaven's sake! He's going to be big, strong."

"What's your point?"

"He has so much promise. He could make a big difference in the world. I respect your religion, but a priest?"

"I don't see how you're respecting *our* religion, and *you* have no choice. Alan can choose to be a priest, or not. I'll support him one hundred percent." Her words warmed me, my anger receded. I wanted to go back and hug her.

My father replied in a low voice. It was hard to hear. What I heard sounded like, "a course for fight." I heard the front door open and close. I'm sure he retreated unconvinced.

Later, Ona came to my room. Her hair was white, her skin wrinkled, but in her voice and posture there was a power about her, a strength that defied age. She was an older version of my mother. "Your mother and father are very different," she said. "I never thought they'd marry. Did I ever tell you how they met?" I waited. "It was at the roadside stand your mother and I set up to sell vegetables and make some extra money for her to go to college. She was finishing high school. Your dad was on a long car ride and happened to stop. Must have been love at first sight." She laughed, sounding like she was clearing her throat, as my mother entered the room.

Mom said, "Yes it was," and smiled.

"I wish you hadn't met him," I grumbled.

CHAPTER 3

It took the rest of the school year and the summer until the world became familiar again. By that time I was old enough to realize that life was a dance between good and bad times.

In the fall of 1964, during the second week of fifth grade, I knew something dangerous was coming when a fairly typical event took a fateful turn. Sister Whipney, who we called *the Whip,* walked out of our classroom for a minute. We ate lunch at our desks. Suddenly, Jerome, a big oaf in our class, reached over to my friend's desk and slammed his fat hand on Rich's tangerine, squashing it. I wasn't surprised. He'd been intimidating kids for years. Rich stood. "Jerry, you're a fucking idiot." With dark, angry eyes, and braces gleaming, he cocked his arm, ready to bean Jerome with the dripping orange mass.

"*Richard! Sit down!*" The Whip was back.

Rich sat, mumbling, "OK man. OK." He glared at Jerry.

Hip (a.k.a. Tom) and I walked over to Rich as the class filed outside for recess. "Jerry the jerk off. That kid's such a douche bag!" Hip said. "I gotta take a leak, then let's get that scumbag." He took off.

I patted Rich on the back. "Jerry's just a jerk. Don't get yourself into trouble." Rich grinned, holding what was lunch fruit a few minutes earlier, now garbage.

Rich gave a quick mean laugh, saying, "Tah-ha, I'm not done with this orange yet. Hey, can you come over Saturday? I wanted to show you some cool stuff I got from my dad and his friend."

We stepped out of the school building into a clear sunny day. We looked out over the large blacktop, which was our playground during the week. On Sundays the asphalt field became the adjoining church's parking lot. I did not see Tim anywhere. Usually, he stood alone watching other kids play dodgeball or whatever.

There was some commotion at the far end of the playground, so Rich and I headed over. A small mob of kids was chanting something. As we got closer, we heard, "*Weakling. Weakling. Weakling.*" Jerry and a cluster of his roughneck friends had surrounded Tim. Tim was cringing, Jerry leaning into him. Suddenly, Tim whirled around and slapped Jerry's face. The mob gave a collective, "Ooooou!" Then Jerry punched Tim, and Tim fell down.

"Hey!" I yelled and ran over to help my friend up. His lip was already swollen and bleeding. I looked up at Jerome. "I'm gonna break your damn neck, you moron!"

Tim grabbed my pant leg. "*Don't,* Alan. The Whip." He was pointing through the crowd at a nun walking briskly toward us. She had an instinct for finding misbehavior and a reputation for dealing harshly with perpetrators. Wearing a black and white habit, she was an angry penguin with boney fingers.

From somewhere behind me an orange blur whizzed past my right ear. It glanced off Jerome's shoulder and walloped the Whip right in the face, colliding with her cheek with a splat. I turned and saw Rich running at Jerome. Obviously, he'd missed his target. Did he know he hit Sister? I thought he was doomed. But Rich had realized what happened. He knew the Whip could not see where the soggy tangerine had come from. He ran up to Jerome. "What did you do! Why'd you throw that tangerine at Sister?"

Hip saw what happened when he came outside. He ran over to Jerome and played along, laughing. "Holy Jeeze, Jerome, why'd you do that?"

The nun was momentarily stunned. She gaped at Jerome. Drops of sparkling orange liquid ran down her face. Her expression suddenly revealed the demon that she was. "*Jerome!*" she bellowed, her eyes aflame and her mouth contorted into a wolfish snarl. She stomped over, grabbed his ear, and headed for the principal's office. Jerome protested, "*Ow!* I didn't do it. It wasn't me!" Hip walked away alongside them, taunting Jerome. "You're in deep doo-doo, man. You'll probably be expelled!"

Rich walked over to me and Tim. "That kid's stupider than he looks." He looked at Tim, "You definitely need to come over my house with Alan Saturday. I got some stuff you could use." Rich told us about his dad's friend, a semi-pro boxer whose nickname was *Lumps.* The guy was retired and gave Rich a bunch of boxing equipment. They set it up in Rich's basement, converting it into a gym. Lumps offered to give Rich and his friends lessons. Tim looked skeptical. I was all in. This was just the kind of athletic pursuit I needed. When my father implored me to play football, I had refused. I would have liked to, but he had to learn to accept what *I* wanted to do.

I tried to convince Tim. "Come on Tim. Some boxing lessons? You ain't always gonna be skinny. You could punch Jerry out instead of giving him a slap. Maybe we could punch out your old man."

Tim wasn't buying it. "Yeah, right."

Rich and I talked him into it.

On Saturday, I got to Rich's just as Tim pulled his bike into the driveway. He set it down on the grass and walked up the stairs, "OK Rich. Where's this gym you got?"

"Downstairs, dickheads. Come on."

When we got to the bottom of the stairs, I saw that Rich and Lumps had transformed the basement. Lumps must have hung an old black leather heavy bag from chains attached to a steel ceiling beam, because Rich could never have lifted it. Lumps also donated a bench press, surrounded by racks full of weights, which was set in the center of the room. Rich had installed a speed bag in a far corner and covered the walls with posters that either had instructions for proper weight training or pictures of famous boxers. Rich smiled as Tim and I wandered around the room admiring the equipment. I jabbed at the heavy bag and was disappointed when it barely moved. Tim struggled with a ten-pound barbell.

Lumps clattered down the stairs. "Hey guys! How do you like Rich's gym?" He wasn't as big as I imagined, though he looked solid. His red hair was short and close-cropped above a pockmarked face and flattened nose, which gave him an air of intimidation, but he seemed friendly.

"Pretty cool," I said. Tim nodded.

Lumps sized us up. "I can make you guys champs! That is, if you're willing to help each other out. Are you?"

The three of us nodded. "Sure are," Rich said. "What do we have to do?"

Lumps picked a jump rope up off a chair. "First I'm going to show you how to start using all this stuff correctly. We'll set up stations, like working on the jump rope, then weights, then the heavy bag and so on. You'll work hard at each station for five minutes, then go to the next one. I want you to work hard through all the stations three times. As you guys get tougher, I'm going to make you work harder and add some drills. The last thing we'll do is box."

And so our boxing careers began as all childhood challenges do—with us awkwardly trying to figure out what the hell we were doing.

CHAPTER 4

Jerome and his parents were unable to convince our principal that he did not throw the fruit at Sister Whipney. My mother was good friends with our principal and learned that what saved Jerome from expulsion was how distressed he and his parents were about the matter. This led to a compromise of sorts: All the parties agreed that Jerome would never *intend* to hit a teacher with a crushed tangerine or any other projectile for that matter. So, considering the charges, the boy got off easy with a one-week suspension. But he was told one more incident and he'd be expelled. That kept Jerome and his dumb friends lying low for the rest of the year.

Tim and I enjoyed the increasingly tough workouts at Rich's under Lump's tutelage, which continued into the slow, sweet summer that followed. On a blazing Friday afternoon in August 1965, I got home and found Mother sitting under the large crabapple tree at our picnic table in the backyard with another woman and a young girl. The two women were laughing and carrying on like old friends. On the table, Mother had set out glasses and a pitcher of lemonade.

"Hi, Alan!" Mom called out in a happy high pitch. "Come over. I want to introduce you."

I walked over to the table. The woman stood. She was tall, thin, wore a short, light-colored dress, and had short, black hair highlighting exotic, dark almond-shaped eyes. When she smiled, it made me want to smile back.

"Alan, this is Ada."

"Hi," I said.

"Hello, Alan, a pleasure to meet you," Ada said with a mysterious accent. She extended her hand towards the girl who looked a bit younger than me. "My daughter, Emilie."

The girl sat looking at me. Sunlight filtered through the tree casting bright and dark figures, which danced across her face. Her pure skin was like a scrim, the silhouettes creating an alluring story of shadow puppetry against a backdrop of soft brown hair. Her eyes flashed a golden color when they met the daylight at certain angles. I couldn't look away. She smiled. I nodded.

My mother said, "Come sit down. Ada just moved into town and was looking for a piano teacher, but she was telling me an interesting story about how her family came to America."

I sat across from Ada. I wondered where they were from. I never met any kid with Emilie's confident stare, and her mother's first language was clearly not English.

"Well, you see," Ada began, looking between my mother and me, "we were living in Paris and moved to Cairo, Egypt for my husband David's business. He's an international banker and opened an office there. Unfortunately, we were swept up in the conflict that happened when the Egyptian government took control of the Suez Canal from the British and French. Fighting began. The British even bombed Cairo, where David ran his business."

My mother's eyebrows shot up. "Oh my goodness!"

Ada looked at her reassuringly. "None of us was injured, but the Egyptian president was very suspicious of immigrants and began to arrest and expel the Jews and foreigners." Ada turned to me. "We are Jewish. My husband got a call from a friend who told him he was on a list to be arrested."

"Geeze, what happened?" I asked.

Ada laughed nervously. "Well, I can almost laugh about it now. We were preparing to leave the country when Egyptian security forces took David hostage. To get him released, they made me sign papers that gave everything we had, *everything,* to the Egyptian government. Then we were put on a plane and flown back to Paris. We decided to come to America. One of our Jewish organizations helped us get settled in New York City, where we lived for a few years. Then, David got a good job, we decided to move out of the city, and here we are!"

Marie and Ada chattered away like best of friends for a little while, then my mother took her into the house for her first piano lesson. I sat with Emilie, who hadn't said a word.

"Were you scared?" I asked her. "I mean gettin' bombed an' all?"

She continued looking at me. "No. I was just a baby." She did not have an accent. Her voice was smooth and low.

"Your mom's got an accent. Does she speak another language?"

"She speaks French, Arabic, and Italian."

"Wow!"

"I speak French too."

"Cool. Where you going to school?" I asked.

"At the public school. The one with the baseball field. Our house is a few blocks from there. I can walk to school. Where do you go to school?"

"I'm at St. Peter's. I take a bus, but I could walk. It's about a mile. What grade you in?"

"Starting fifth. What grade are you in?"

"I'll be in sixth, but my friend Rich's sister's in your grade at the public school. Her name's Stephanie."

Emilie sat up and brightened at this information. "Maybe she'll be in my class!"

"Yeah. Hey, maybe I could introduce you to Stephanie before school starts."

Emilie smiled. "That would be nice!"

I noticed a funny feeling in my chest. That summer I'd get that same feeling on occasion. It would happen at times when Ada came for her piano lessons and brought Emilie along. I'd be talking with Emilie, her eyes would shimmer in gold or she would make that smile, and there was that feeling.

*****

On his first day back at school, the Bellcon boy swaggered through the junior high school's doors in the isolated,

midwestern town of Dargton with a demeanor of owner-
ship uncharacteristic for a thirteen-year-old eighth grader.
It was a Monday morning, ten minutes before classes were
to begin. Anyone could tell you that he loved being big
and strong for his age and practiced being intimidating
with his posture, his contentious way of communicating,
and the stare from his dark, unblinking eyes. When he saw
Debbie walking towards him in the otherwise empty hallway, he smiled as she hesitated and began to turn away.

"Hold up Deb. You're looking good today."

"Stay away from me you bastard." She trembled.

"Come on! Didn't we have fun Saturday night?"

"I told you to stop!" she said, voice quaking. Then in a
harsh, loud whisper, "You...you raped me!"

The boy closed in on her and grabbed her arm. *"Don't
you ever repeat that."* When she cowered, he smiled and
released her. "Look, I know you enjoyed it, and you know
you enjoyed it. You don't have to put on an act to protect
your reputation. I'm not going to say anything."

Debbie spun around and began walking away. "They already know, and they know what you did!" She began to
cry. "They'll arrest you. I hope you rot in jail."

When he moved towards her, she ran down the hall.
He strutted confidently to his next class.

There were reasons the small rural town tolerated the
boy's behavior. His father, Frank Bellcon, was an influen-
tial lawyer with deep connections throughout the state to
judicial and law enforcement officials. He had a reputation
for being a real S.O.B. Stories circulated in the town about

his turbulent family life and divorce. (In one story the Bellcon boy had actually assaulted his own mother.)

The reach of Frank Bellcon became painfully obvious to Kurt Shepard—a rising Dargton star slated to run in the state's senate primary race—when his good friend and principal of the junior high school called. He told Kurt that a few parents claimed a fourteen-year-old girl was raped by one of the other students. Shepard called the chief of police to inquire about an investigation. In response, Kurt got a call from Frank.

"Mr. Shepard, Frank Bellcon."

"Hi Frank. Please call me Kurt. What can I do for you?" he said.

"You can cease any effort to ruin my son's and my family's reputation."

Shepard was no stranger to confrontation. He was a wealthy businessman who built a successful construction company fighting for contracts and political allies throughout the state. "Frank," Kurt said, "I'm sure you'd want your son's name to be cleared of these rape charges. If he didn't do it, what's the harm of investigating?"

"As far as I'm aware no one has charged my son with rape. And you, of all people, should understand baseless allegations and rumors."

Shepard paused. There were rumors ten years earlier that he had an affair with his foreign housekeeper. What no one guessed was that he had an illegitimate daughter with her. But, before she began showing, the housekeeper had returned to her home country, and no one could prove anything. If proof of this could somehow become public knowledge, it would devastate his family, his business and his political ambitions. But there was no proof. Was there? "Sorry Frank," he said, "I'm not sure I catch your drift."

"I'm sure," Frank responded, "that as a political candidate you've heard the saying 'cash has no fingerprints.' But you and I know that's not true for cash bank deposit records, especially when accompanied by photos and signed affidavits." Then, to leave no doubt, Frank added, "I'm just saying that public officials need to be careful in their *housekeeping.*"

The threat was clear. A chill went through Shepard. He understood the game and knew the value of powerful allies. "Gotcha Frank," he said, any concern for the rape of one of Dargton's children evaporating.

"Don't worry, Kurt," Frank said. "I'll send my donations to your campaign by check. No cash. All on the up an up."

Shepard was honestly grateful. "Thanks!"

And so, the Bellcon boy was tolerated until the next major incident two years later.

CHAPTER 5

On Saturday, I walked Emilie over to Rich's to introduce her to Rich's sister, Stephanie. While we walked, I asked if she had any relatives in the U.S. She didn't, but she went on to tell me some incredible story about her grandparents, who still lived in France. It sounded like they were spies or something. They worked for a group called the *Resistance* in France during WWII. The Nazis chased them all over the country, but somehow they narrowly escaped.

When we got to Rich's we found his fidgeting silhouette in the doorway at the top of the front steps. His unsettled straight black hair fluttered above brown mischievous eyes, his mouth sparkled with braces. I could see why the girls at St. Peter's school liked him. He was harmless and sweet to them. To guys, though, his sharp ribbing could be humiliating. Personally, I thought he was funny, and he seemed to have more energy than he knew what to do with. He played baseball and basketball at school, skied, and even took piano lessons from my mom, which was how we became close.

As Emilie and I ascended their steps, Rich and Stephanie appeared in the doorway. I introduced Emilie. Stephanie looked excited and invited Emilie inside.

Rich took one look at Emilie and turned on the charm. "Wow, you're the new girl in town? I'm Rich. Very nice to meet you."

He held out his hand. I grabbed it. "Come on buddy. Let's not hassle the poor girl so fast."

Emilie slipped past him and waved. Rich yanked his hand out of mine. "Douchebag. I'm just sayin' hello."

Tim rode his bike up the sidewalk.

"OK. Come on. Let's work out," I said.

Rich said, "Let's work on your manners. Oh, I get it. Don't want me to meet Emilie?"

"She's not your type."

"We'll see about that." Rich laughed. He punched a little harder than usual during our workout.

Back in school, Jerome avoided physical confrontations. He and his cronies had found a new way to torment other kids. Week after week, they doubled down on verbally taunting Tim. Rich, Hip, and I could not get them to stop. Tim began to disappear at recess and wouldn't tell anyone where he went. He wouldn't come to the phone when I called his house. In late October he stopped showing up at Rich's. At week's end, I found him at church for the Mass we were assigned. He looked like he hadn't slept and was lost in thought. Father Curtain saw him, asked if he was sick, and excused him. "Alan can do the Mass today. Go home and get some rest, son."

I noticed a bruise on Tim's neck, and I asked about it a few times. He finally told me his father was an alcoholic. The alcohol made his father violent. Tim cried a little. I'd never seen him cry. I put my arm around him and told him, "Your father's an idiot like Jerome. You can't listen to them. Come to my house later. Hey, maybe you can stay with us. I'll ask Mom. But you gotta start coming back to Rich's. We gotta get strong, OK?"

Tim was withdrawn at school the following week and couldn't be reached by phone. On a cold Friday, ending the first full week of November, I finally heard from him. I got home from school and an hour later my kitchen phone rang.

"Hello?"

"Alan?"

"Yeah, hey Tim. Where you been? Come on over."

"Alan, I just wanted to tell you, you're my best friend. You, Rich, and Hip."

"OK. Thanks. You're my best too. Come over."

"I'm sorry. I'm no good. It's no good. They're right. I'm weak. Dumb. I do everything wrong. I'm just a drag. You guys'll be better without me."

Tim's voice, strong and steady, seemed mismatched with what he was saying. I was confused. "What are you talking about? You're a great kid! Your dad's an alcoholic, a jerk. So's Jerome. Come on, Tim, come over."

"It's not just them. There's nothing. I can't. I'm going to the bridge. I just wanted to say bye."

I knew what he meant. Behind St. Peter's school, on the far side of the playground, there was a short path that went through a wooded area. It led to Forrest Creek Park. Just beyond the baseball outfield was the river. That's where an old arched walking bridge crossed the widest and most dangerous part of the waterway. Underneath, boulders created turbulent rapids. The water sounded like a jet engine. A short distance down river, it gushed past a *HAZARD!* sign, which was planted on the cusp of a low-head dam. Kids called it *the chomp* because of stories like the guy who jumped off the bridge during the Great Depression. Swept over the dam, his body was pinned in a deep rocky crevice by the powerful churning water. Trapped in the river's jaws, it was not found for a month. On occasion, some folks called this place *Suicide Bridge*.

I yelled into the phone, "*Tim, no, wait!*" I heard a click. I ran through the house, bumping into walls. "*Mom! Mom! Help!*"

She was upstairs. "Alan, what is it?"

"Tim's gonna jump off the bridge! We gotta stop him. Get the car, *now!*"

My mother had never seen me like this. I had talked about Tim before, and my mother's alter ego, the high school guidance counselor, put two and two together. She ran down the stairs, grabbed keys off the dining room table. "*Let's go!*"

We flew out the front door, jumped in her green Fiat, which sat in the driveway, and pulled into the street. St. Peter's school was about a mile away. I hoped we'd beat Tim there.

We had to slow for a girl riding her bike in the street. My mother honked. "Come on. Come on," I grumbled as we passed the bike.

We turned onto the main road leading to the school. In front of us, a large dump truck lumbered down the road. There was no way to pass him. I thumped the dashboard. "Oh no!"

"When we get to the school, you run to the bridge," my mother said. "I'm going to get the jumper cables. We might need to pull someone out of the river."

We finally got to the school and drove right to the end of the playground parking lot, near the path to the river. Both of us jumped out of the car. My mother shouted, "Go! I'll meet you there," and ran to the trunk.

I ran like crazy through the path. The bridge was forty yards away. I saw a young couple walking over the bridge. Tim's gold Sting Ray bike was lying in the grass. Then I saw Tim at the apex of the bridge, looking at the roaring water twelve feet below, then glancing at the couple, apparently waiting for them to cross. It was like he was too ashamed to jump right then and ruin their day. The couple moved out of sight. Tim began climbing over the railing.

I was afraid to call out. I raced onto the bridge. Just before I got to him, he leaned forward to fall.

"*No!*" I yelled, and lunged. Reaching my left arm out over the railing I grabbed the sleeve of Tim's jacket.

Everything went into slow motion. Tim looked up. His eyes and mouth opened to their limits, as though he were going to scream. He tried to pull his arm out of his jacket. I wouldn't let go, but I had stretched too far over the railing. We both toppled down into the hungry river.

I remember the splash and the instant chill. The river tore at us, like a bear with cold claws. I held onto the sleeve of Tim's jacket. The current yanked me down, to the left, to the right, then up over a boulder. I used all my strength to keep my head above water, gasp for a breath, before being pulled downward. I remembered a year earlier, at the New Jersey shore, being warned about rip tide, then being caught in it. No one on the beach had seen me. I swam along *with* the tide, as I was told, and was lucky to get out. Now, I tried to swim with the river current and was able to pull Tim's head above water for a moment. I gurgled, *"Swim!"*

A crooked branch stuck out of the water under the bridge. I swung my free arm around it. My head was above water. Tim's head popped up and down. He shouted, *"Go back!"*

My mother was under the bridge by the river bank fifteen feet away. She threw the jumper cables to me, "Alan, grab the cable!" I couldn't let go of Tim and I couldn't let go of the branch. The cable floated away. Mom reeled it in and threw again. My strength was being absorbed by the cold powerful river. Then one of the jumper cable handles caught on the branch. I was able to hook my right elbow over the handles. My mother had the cable wrapped around her back. She tried to walk and pull Tim and me to the river edge. But for every foot she moved us to safety, she was pulled three feet into the river. Still, she wouldn't drop the tether, and I knew she'd drown before she'd let go. When she was waist deep in the water, the pull on my left arm suddenly released. Tim had wriggled out of his jacket. I saw his head bobbing its way toward *the chomp*. A scream formed in my mind but never reached my throat. An unfamiliar wild animal's spirit had suddenly possessed me. It was focused on living.

My free arm and legs flailed wildly, powered only by an instinct for survival, reaching for stones beneath the surface to move me toward land. The torrential rush of water spouted up around me. When I could lift my head to gasp for air, I saw my mother pulling the cable, her eyes and jaw clenched with determination. My arms and legs moved more slowly, weakly. The will to struggle and crawl out of the river, to be surrounded by air, faded. Then all was calm. The water was still and ground brushed up against my chest. My mother was at the water's edge, her hands pulling at my arms, "Alan, get up! Come on, we have to get you boys to the car."

I felt numb. I could hardly stand, but getting to my feet seemed to create a little strength in my legs. Something she said sounded wrong. "What did you—?"

She pointed. "Look!"

I coughed and looked across the river where a felled old tree trunk jutted out in front of the dam. The young couple who had crossed the bridge earlier were on the other side. The woman was on land. Supported by the downed tree, the man had waded out, somehow snatched Tim before the chomp, and dragged him out of the water.

The couple crossed the bridge. The man had Tim slung over his shoulder, like a soaked beach towel. He said to

Marie, "It's freezing, we've got to get these guys warm. You have a car?"

Tim coughed and moaned. I was shocked to see him alive and shook from the thrill of witnessing a miracle. My mother began marching quickly toward the parking lot. "Please, this way."

When we got to the car Mom told me to get in the front seat. She said to the couple, "Put Tim in the back." Then to the man, "You're drenched! Please, both of you come along. The rectory is right over there, we can all get warm."

My teeth were chattering. I looked at Tim. He was pale, his lips almost blue, but he was awake, shivering, and coughed a few times. Our car pulled up to the rectory entrance. My mother flew out of the car and ran up the stairs, ringing the bell and knocking loudly on the door. A matronly, gray-haired women answered looking annoyed, "Marie? What's this all about?"

"Camilla, please get Father Curtain," my mother pleaded. "This is an emergency!"

The old woman looked at me and the man bringing Tim up the stairs. "But all of you are soaking wet!" She stood in the doorway defiantly.

Marie stepped into the doorway, her face inches from Camilla's. *"Do it now,"* she hissed.

As the woman made a fast retreat, Mother ushered us into a large sitting room with tall windows, dark drapes, and a vacant fireplace. Dripping with river water, we didn't dare sit on any of the leather chairs or upholstered couches.

Father Curtain rushed into the room wearing a white collar, black clergy shirt, and pants. "Marie!" He looked at his waterlogged guests. "What in heaven's name happened?"

He listened to a brief explanation, then the priest barked at Camilla, who stood idly in the doorway, "Get towels and blankets, and start a fire! Hurry!" He looked at the young woman. "Thank goodness you're dry. Would you be kind enough to wait in the foyer? I'm going to ask the men to take off their wet clothes." He looked at the woman's companion. "Give them to Camilla, she'll wash and dry them. Wrap yourselves in blankets for now. Marie, you can change in the bathroom around the corner."

When Camilla came back, Father Curtain said sternly, "I must ask you all not to speak to anyone about this. We don't want to stigmatize this young man's reputation. I'm going to have a talk with Tim's father. Next week, I'll deal with his classmates." The priest stormed out of the room. Tim stared at him vacantly.

When Father Curtain returned, Camilla was distributing our dry clothes. We all dressed, and father thanked the young couple for their help. They left. The priest began a long conversation, centered on Tim. Telling him that helping others is the way to heaven, explaining that now that his life had been saved, he owed it to others to help them. My mother and I chimed in, telling Tim how much we loved him and how painful it would be if we lost him. Tim's face was blank. Then, at the end, sadness spread across his face. He looked at all of us, said "Thanks," and cried.

I don't know what Father Curtain said to Tim's father that weekend, but Tim did not get hit at home afterwards. At school on Monday morning, grades five through eight were summoned to the all-purpose room and seated in the bleachers. Father Curtain gave a short sermon to us about what it meant to be Christian, and the fiery eternity that awaited kids who called each other names or hurt one another. For those without an imagination, he warned us that he was secretly deputizing some kids in the school to report back to him, and if he heard of any kids calling others names, he would see to their immediate expulsion.

From that day on, Father Curtain would find something to praise Tim about at every opportunity. In Sunday school, the priest would ask for Tim's opinion, then instruct the class on the great lesson in Tim's answer. On Sundays at Mass, Father Curtain would complement Tim on his Latin. Rich and I even began to encourage Tim during our workouts.

CHAPTER 6

Following the holidays, Ada continued to come over for piano lessons with Marie about every other week. She came alone. Sometimes she'd tell us enchanting stories about her family's experiences in other countries. I learned that she gave birth to a son, Isaac, when she arrived in America. When Isaac was two-years-old he was killed when a car jumped a curb in Manhattan. It was one of the reasons they moved out of the city. I wondered how Emilie was doing, though never got around to asking.

Then one day in May, Emilie tagged along. She looked a little different, maybe taller. I was thrilled to see her because it had been so long.

We sat at the picnic table outside and talked for an hour. The conversation was lively and musical, like we were the hands of a pianist creating harmonious, and intriguing sounds. Emilie told me funny stories about her classmates, whose personalities she could describe in extraordinary detail. I told her about Jerome and the tangerine. She laughed, and the warm feeling returned in my chest.

Ada stepped out of the house into the backyard and called, "Emilie, time to go dear." It made me nervous, which was strange. There was nothing to be afraid of.

Emilie stood with a broad grin. "It was nice talking with you." The sun hit that magic angle in her eyes.

I got up, not sure what I wanted to say. "Uh, yeah. Same here. We should talk some more. Hey, your school's sorta on my way home. Maybe I could walk home with you one day? How 'bout Friday?"

"Sure. That would be great."

I waved dumbly as she left with her mom.

On Friday afternoon I was staring at the classroom clock, wondering why the second hand was barely moving and whether the human mind could slow time. Finally, classes were dismissed. I trotted to the public school where Emilie was waiting. It was a beautiful, sunny day, so we walked slowly. It set the pace for the other times I'd walk her home.

I had never thought about girls much. They never interested me. But my walks home with Emilie were like no experiences I ever had with guy friends. For one thing, she questioned everything. "Ever wonder why the sky's blue?' I never did, until she brought it up. "You know why there are flowers?" she asked, pointing at some peonies in a yard. Then went on to explain the role of bees and pollination. The girl seemed to have an endless bank of knowledge. She said she liked the library and talked about stuff from Egyptian history to seahorses. Yeah, seahorses. Did you know that the female seahorse deposits over one thousand eggs into a pouch on the male, and the pregnant *male* seahorse delivers their young? I had no frickin' idea! No wonder this girl, one-year younger, captivated me. I never talked about this stuff with guys. They'd say I was a bookworm if I did.

Each time I walked her home was exhilarating and educational. She would bring up some interesting topic and, even if I didn't know much about it, she'd ask my opinion. (I didn't tell anyone but some Saturdays I even began going to the library. I started reading all kinds of stuff, hoping one day I could tell her something she didn't know.) But there was something else that struck me during our walks. Something about her voice. The pitch, the cadence? It was a memorable sound, like a favorite song that comes on the radio and leaves its music playing in your head.

One day she mentioned her birthday was coming up at the end of July. When I heard the date, I had to ask her, "Hey that's the day before the fair! The St. Peter's summer bazaar. I could show you around the first night. Uh, for your birthday?" She accepted.

A few weeks went by. I thought about Emilie's birthday more when I saw the carnival workers in their green and orange overalls assembling the rides and booths on the school's playground.

The night of the fair was warm, the sky was clear. I called Emilie. We planned to meet at her house and walk to St. Peter's.

"What's this fair like?" she asked.

"Oh. They set it up in the parking lot behind the school. They have rides. Ferris wheel, bumper cars, Round Up. Booths you can buy stuff and play games," I said.

She looked embarrassed. "I've never been to one."

"Really? Aww, you'll like this. My mom helps run it and fills in at some of the booths with the priests and nuns—"

"Your mom is so cool. I can't believe she'll be my counselor at the high school."

"Yeah. Hey my friends will be there. Stephanie—"

"Great! Stephanie helped me make a lot of friends at school. She's *very* popular."

Emilie wasn't kidding. When we got to the bazaar, I felt like I was with a celebrity. So many girls came up to Emilie to say hi and talk about some of the booths and rides. When one of the girls mentioned a booth with Egyptian art and jewelry, Emilie made her point it out.

I felt a little awkward getting introduced so many times. Probably because, you know girls, they'd glance at me and giggle, whisper something. Anyway, we went on bumper cars and the Round Up with Tim, Hip, Rich and Stephanie, visited the pizza booth to get pizza from my mom, and played a few games. We had a great time.

Toward the end of the evening, Stephanie took Emilie to show her a booth with glass figurines. I walked over to the Egyptian art booth. They had some jewelry on velvet trays. A small bracelet with an ornament of silver flower stems and crystal flowers caught my eye. The flowers sparkled a brilliant blue. The seller told me a story about the gem, "lapis lazuli." It was a little expensive, but I bought it.

I found Emilie walking by herself, gazing around as if she lost something. I snuck up behind her and tapped on her shoulder. I handed her the small box and grinned. "Happy birthday!"

She opened the box, picked out the bracelet and turned it over in her hands. "Oh my God, it's beautiful! Thank you. What is this flower?"

I should have known she'd ask that question. I hadn't asked the woman in the booth. I didn't have a chance to say anything, Emilie grabbed my shoulder, pulled my face down to hers, and kissed me on the corner of my lips. I'll bet she was aiming for my cheek, but I didn't know what she was doing and turned my head a little at the last moment. Boy was that embarrassing. In front of everybody! My chest burned and my heart pounded. The only females I'd kissed before were my mother and Ona. I blushed. "Thanks."

That kiss, and hanging around with Emilie, wound up teaching me about life's difficult choices, and about people who will oppose even your most admirable missions in life. You see, Emilie's never-ending interrogations made me a more curious person. I began asking more questions. That didn't bother Father Curtain. If he didn't have an answer, he'd just say, "That's a very interesting question, son. Let's think about it, shall we?" But shortly after I started seventh grade, in September 1966, Father Vinious summoned me and my mother to the school for a conference. He was perched in an imposing black leather chair. Visitors sat in wood slat folding chairs opposite his desk, a large block of authority, which discouraged dissent.

"I worry about Alan," the priest said. "Some of the questions he asks. Almost heretical."

I looked at my mother, her back straight, curls of black hair cascading over her ears. Her eyes, like mirrors that could only reflect the beholders beauty or ugliness, were now fixed on the cleric. "What questions?" she asked.

The cherubic priest's collar worked into his second chin as he spoke. "Well, like 'If Jesus did not have a father, whose genes did he have?' or, 'Why would an all-merciful God allow the holocaust?' or, 'Are murderers also made in God's likeness?'"

The priest continued, accusing me of an unhealthy carnal interest in "a young girl from the public school." The priest told my mother that he had witnessed this girl giving me a kiss at the church bazaar. He said we held hands. I don't remember that.

I was shocked. The priest exposed what, up to that time, I refused to admit to myself. I began to feel guilty about the times I jogged over to the public school to walk Emilie home. Whether I was naïve about my feelings for Emilie or in denial about committing to celibacy, the priest's indictment made it clear, it was either Emilie or priesthood. I wanted to stand up and shout denials, but the truth took my breath away. My eyes burned. Mother's hand touched mine. Then, another of what I heard some people call "Marie's small miracles" unfolded, and in her quiet commanding voice I felt the role of subordinate reverse in the room.

"So," she began, "you're accusing my son of having intelligent questions? Questions I suspect you don't have answers for."

The priest's nose blushed. "His questions are not—"

She cut him off. "And Emilie? She is a soul-mate to Alan, as her mother Ada is to me. If they love one another, well, the idea of something sinful is only in *your* mind. This wouldn't have anything to do with the girl and her family being Jewish, would it?"

"Mrs.—"

"Father, you are aware of my friendship with the bishop, aren't you?"

"Well, yes. What—"

"Let me say one last thing. If you ever so much as think another bad thought about my son, I will explain your ridiculous charges to the bishop and let him know about the surplus of wine brought to the rectory each week, which many parishioners believe far exceeds requirements for Sunday Mass. Good day, Father." She snapped out of her chair, her hand yanking me up by the arm. The priest's expression was frozen terror. We marched out of his office, leaving him to find penance to satisfy Marie's blackmail.

Holy Cow! I'd seen my mother go to bat for me before. I knew she could crush adversaries. But this was a *priest!* It was a shock. *She* was the ultimate scale of right and wrong, not the priest. But the experience was my cue that if I wanted a second chance something had to change. Thinking back, I made a terrible decision. I stopped walking Emilie home, and, when Ada came to visit, if Emilie tagged along, I acted distant, polite. Eventually Emilie stopped coming and my life changed. I thought it was a sacrifice for the church, forfeiting Emilie to reclaim a path to priesthood. Sometimes our goals blind us.

CHAPTER 7

Time passed. Nothing out of the ordinary occurred, until the unimaginable happened. On Friday December 15th, 1967, Mother was killed. I remember sitting in a winged back chair at Caughlin's Funeral Home two days later. She had been in a car accident. It took great effort for me to think. I got mixed up, believing it just couldn't be. I kept imagining she'd show up. Then I'd peek at the coffin. The waxen face, the body too small. That was not Mother, was it? Her image, bright and full of life, was so fresh in my mind. She couldn't be gone. I prayed it wasn't true. Asked God if He could give her back since she was such a faithful servant. But somehow, I knew He wouldn't. And without her I was stuck in a grim present. The future ceased to exist. My life was put in a dark suspended animation. A phrase my mother often said popped into my mind, *Faith will be your strength.* The words swirled in a cloud of unformed thoughts. Those thoughts would soon organize into a stormy acknowledgement that God *allowed* this.

I found out what happened when I got home from Rich's that Friday night. My father told me. We had to drive to the hospital. Dad cried in the car. It was the only time I ever saw him cry. For the last two days I tried to

visualized the accident, piecing together fragments overheard from hospital personnel and the police. My mother
was driving home late from work. The black Oldsmobile
had run a red light and slammed into the driver's side of
her little Fiat.

The story became even more surreal when I heard who
the reckless, drunk driver was. The coincidence was the
stuff of nightmares. It was Tim's dad! He was treated for a
broken rib and a concussion and released from the hospital. Mother was pronounced dead. How could such a horrible person still be alive and Marie dead? He wasn't even
punished for what he did. The police said it was an accident! He should have gotten a life sentence. The guy was a
drunk. For years, he beat my friend and his mother. If he
had been in jail for that, this wouldn't have happened.
What good did he ever do in the world? Why would God
let *him* live? I wasn't mad at Tim. That kid suffered. He
tried to kill himself because of that bastard. And now
Tim's father killed Mom.

I sat in the funeral parlor's largest living room of death.
My father had selected their biggest room, knowing there
would be many visitors. The spacious area was crammed
with people, bouquets of flowers, and tables of photo-
graphs. My father stood next to my chair. Ona sat across
from me. They had the proper black clothes to wear, but
my father had to buy a jacket for me. The line of mourners
stretched outside. One by one they stepped up to offer
their condolences. My father stood at attention showing
little emotion. I could hear Ona's voice, so much like my
mother's. It soothed me and somehow seemed to settle

each visitor's awkward discomfort as they offered sympathy.

I watched the procession of people and heard their stories about the guidance counselor and music teacher at Forrest Creek High School whose farm-grown wisdom and devotion to others made a difference. One after another, they recounted Marie's life-changing advice, like the mother who told Michael, "My Sandra had a boyfriend. It was just puppy love, but she was brokenhearted the way that boy treated her. Marie told my daughter, 'Boys that do not treat you special are like poorly fitting dresses. Sooner or later, you get rid of them.' That was just what she needed to hear. She did get rid of him, and she's got a better attitude about boys now."

When the last of the guests had left the room, the funeral director told us we could have some time alone with Marie before the coffin was prepared for burial. I walked up to the casket between my father and Ona. I could no longer deny what I could see. She was gone. Forever. In her absence, I began to change. The faith, which my mother promised would be reassuring in times of turmoil, fell far short. I knew that people died, sometimes unfairly or from random events. Years earlier an assassin killed our president, and the Bible told of prophets that had been killed in horrible ways for centuries. This was different. It was not like losing a president or a prophet. There was no replacement for my mother. There could be no forgiveness.

"Do you want to say a prayer?" my father asked, a hesitancy in his voice. Briefly I wondered where his stability came from if not faith. My amorphous thoughts congealed into: *God allowed this!* The calling to become a priest, to know God and teach others, was beginning to feel more like a naïve delusion. Or was the sorrow, anger, and the pain from losing a mother a test?

"Yes," I said.

CHAPTER 8

On Monday afternoon, we drove in a long motorcade to Forrest Creek Cemetery, a few miles from my house. Everyone climbed out of their cars and found places to sit or stand around the gravesite. Father Curtain began a eulogy:

"We are here to remember and be thankful for the wonderful gift of Marie's life. She strengthened our characters, illuminated our lives, and showed us how to be better Christians." His words trailed off into phrases that blended into background noise. Here was a priest I had known since kindergarten and more recently revered as a role model. His Bible stories and advice had shaped my worldview. Now, as he droned on, his words served little purpose.

I became distracted by something moving at the corner of a mausoleum fifty yards away. A small figure peered around the side then stepped behind the building. It continued to pop into view and then disappear and became a merciful distraction. Then I recognized the figure. It was Tim.

When the priest suggested that the mourners say their final goodbye to Marie, everyone filed past the casket. Some paused and touched the coffin, others laid a flower on it. My father had brought irises for each of us to lay on the coffin. They were her favorite flower, and, twice a year, on their anniversary and on her birthday, he would pick up an arrangement of irises from Ronati's florist and set them in a vase on the breakfast table.

We placed our flowers on the casket. My father began to help Ona to the car. "There are some people coming to the house for the repast," he reminded me.

I was in no mood to follow his orders, and said, "I think I'll walk for a while."

Dad stiffened, but before he could protest, Ona took her scarf and wrapped it around my neck. "This will keep you warm," she said.

"Thanks," I replied, walking off in the direction of the mausoleum. "I'll see you back at the house."

When I got to the corner of the gray granite mausoleum, I heard muffled noises from the far side of the building. A familiar gold "Sting Ray" bicycle was leaning against the wall. I walked to the end and peeked around the corner. Tim sat on the ground in an oversized coat, face in hands, crying.

I called out, "Tim?"

Tim looked up. "Oh God, I'm sorry, Alan. I'm so sorry." His voice was broken and, while he had become a much stronger person over the last few years, I worried about what guilt and sadness might do to him. I remembered his suicide attempt and the encouragement Father Curtain had given him—words that I believed kept Tim alive during his darkest time. I squatted next to him, waited for him to look at me. "Hey, man, I need your help right now."

It was like a hypnotist snapped his fingers. He stopped crying. His expression changed. "You? You need *my* help? Why? What do you want?"

"Let's walk."

Tim took his bike by the handlebars and we walked out of the cemetery.

"Let's get one thing right," I said. "No one blames you for what happened,"

"But—"

"Look, your dad's to blame. Your dad. The guy who beats you for no reason, threatens your mom. I've been there. Seen the bruises."

"He's a drunk," Tim sneered.

"Yeah, did you make him a drunk? No one's to blame for what he's done but him." My hands knotted.

Tim's eyes narrowed. He choked up. "Yeah, I'm gonna kill that son of a bitch."

I didn't realize it then, but I think that's when I first saw the change in Tim. The anger turned inside out. At that moment, he must have decided to be the assailant rather than the victim.

"Look, Tim," I said. "I don't know what to do. I'm gonna need someone to talk to."

He looked surprised. "Sure. Guess your dad won't be no help."

"Got that right."

We drifted quietly down familiar streets. Tim broke the silence. "Maybe Father Curtain could help too. He's been pretty cool since we were altar boys."

"Doubt it," I said. "I just don't know what to believe anymore."

"But you brought me to see him when I took the bridge. You both really helped me. I might not even be here ...." His voice trailed off.

I shrugged. "Yeah, but my mom. How could God?" I had to pause to fortify my voice. "I don't know."

"You still want to be a priest, don't you? You're not saying? Jeez, Alan." Tim's mouth opened, wordless. Then, he put his arm around my shoulder and persisted until I agreed we would meet with Father Curtain within the next few weeks

Walking home, I thought about Tim's question. I had thought priests were authorities about God, life after death, right and wrong. But when Father Vinious had summoned me and Mother to his office and accused me of immoral behavior, Mother had been right and he had been wrong. Mother had dedicated so much of her life to the church, to helping others. Her life had been right, and that life, being taken by a drunk in a split-second random coincidence, was not the work of an all-powerful, all-just, and all-merciful Being. I climbed my front steps, angry and confused.

When I walked through the front door, a few people were milling around the house. In the living room, a woman I recognized, who worked at the high school, stood up from the bench of the upright Steinway piano. She made her way toward me and paused to offer her sympathy. I croaked a reflexive, "Thank you."

I looked over the half wall to the dining room. There was Ada. She was hugging Ona and my father. I looked back at the orphaned piano where Mother and Ada had sat side by side many times. The powerful emotional bond that had formed between them had been obvious. With their happy voices fresh in my memory, it was unimaginable such a bond was severed permanently. It reminded me of the days when Ada brought her daughter Emilie along. At one time, I had enjoyed those visits the most.

Ada saw me and rushed over. We embraced. I thought briefly of Ada's eldest son, Isaac. She had told me that he was killed in a tragic accident. Why were good people taken from us? There was a moment when, even with her arms around me, I felt detached. The world, it seemed, had slipped away into something unfamiliar, as if I had entered a new territory and realized I had the wrong map. My assumptions had been proved wrong. My beliefs were like miscalculations.

"I'm so sorry," she said softly. "I know there is nothing anyone can really do, but your mother hoped you would accomplish great things, and faith would help."

"Thanks," I whispered. "But I don't know."

Over Ada's shoulder, I saw Emilie step through the kitchen door into the dining room. Was it years since I walked her home from school? I still remembered those walks. The sunlight defining each strand of her brown hair, revealing the soft curves of her oval face and neck, and, at rare angles, giving her eyes an unusual luminescence. The guilt of turning my back on her felt like a sin. She had grown. Her features anticipated the beautiful woman she would become. As she walked toward me, my breath froze, my lungs felt singed.

"I'm so sorry about your mom," Emilie said. "I loved her so much. I wish things like this never happened."

I could tell she had been crying. "I'm sor—" I began to say, my arms too heavy to reach for her.

Ada said, "Don't stop trying to make your dreams come true. Your mother wouldn't want that. Pray for guidance."

A few awkward moments passed. Ona, my father and I said goodnight to Ada and Emilie. Father turned to me, "We are going to Ona's for a few days. I'll call the school and ask your teachers to have your assignments ready so we can pick them up on the way out." My jaw tightened. I didn't want him telling me what to do, but I loved Ona's place. I grew up roaming the woods, running through the fields, and fishing in the river. It would be far better than facing all the condolences that would come from school-mates and teachers. So, I nodded. None of us brought up that Christmas was days away.

On Tuesday morning, I woke up disoriented. I'd had a vivid dream and was teetering between two realities. There was a giant screen in an empty field. It went as high as a ten-story building. At the foot of the screen was a small altar, where Father Curtain was performing a ser-vice. The screen turned into a mirror, filled with Mom's face, clear and animated. She was smiling, saying some-thing I couldn't hear, because it was just her reflection. Then the mirror exploded into a cloud of dust and huge slabs of glass that rained down and buried the priest. The broken pieces of glass melted into quicksilver that spread over the field. When the dust cleared, my father was there, sitting in my mother's wrecked Fiat, crying.

It's odd how dreams sometimes leave you with emotions that alter your reality. You wake from them scared, or optimistic, or angry. After all, they're just dreams. I woke with an inexplicable resentment for my father. Maybe because he seemed to be dealing with Mother's death better than I was, and he was an atheist. I had believed in the God my church taught me about, and that faith was supposed to be my strength. Yet my image of God was fading, and even the assumption that my life had meaning strained to hold up under the lens of Mother's death. What was it that fortified my father? Was he right? Was priesthood a waste of life? I resented that he made me question my beliefs and what I thought was a noble goal.

When I reached the dining room table, Ona had already made coffee and was setting out omelets and toast. My father sat at the table. He looked up. I saw pity in his eyes.

"How did you sleep?" Ona asked.

"OK," I said.

"You know, Alan, we will all miss her terribly, but we have to keep in mind what she would have wanted. What she would have wanted for you, your father, me."

"I know," I said.

"She wanted everyone to make their mark on the world and leave it a better place. And becoming a priest, it's the highest calling. We're so proud."

She said *we*. Meaning her and Marie. But Mother was dead, and I knew what my father's silence meant. He actually felt sorry for me, like I was some dumb, gullible kid heading for the disappointing realization that he was right all along. That Mother and I had been conned into believing a fairytale. Well, maybe some of the things I was taught weren't true, but I was certain there was more to heaven than just sky. One way or another, I was going to prove Michael was wrong. Whether I became a priest or not was *my* decision.

I muttered, "Yeah. I mean, yes ma'am."

"Oh, stop with the ma'am, give me a hug," Ona commanded, marching over and hugging me in my chair. I kissed her on the cheek. "You know," Ona explained, "if we keep trying to do what your mother would want us to do, if we keep our best memories of her alive, she will never leave us."

Vivid flashes from the dream rushed back. Mom *was* there. Her image on a huge mirror, reflected from a world where she must have resided still. We finished our eggs. My father, who had not spoken a word, took on his commanding tone. "You pack Ona's Oldsmobile and ride up with her."

The direct order bit into my ears like shards of glass. I wanted to yell "No," but I remained silent. I suspected the war brewing between us would come later. Besides, I wanted to talk with Ona. Her beliefs were now the counterbalance to Father's. Despite losing a daughter, she was strong *and* still had faith. How was it possible?

CHAPTER 9

Ona and I watched Michael walk to his white Ford Fairlane. Perhaps the grief we all shared showed on his face but, watching his back, I only saw him soldier on to the car and pull out of the driveway. As the car passed out of sight, I came to attention, saluted and said, "I think we've been dismissed."

Ona said, "Alan, get in the car, please."

I settled into the passenger seat next to her and became immersed in a book I took for the trip. When she reached the northbound highway, she asked, "What's that you're reading?"

"Uh, Patrick Moore. Astronomy," I answered.

"That for school?"

"No. Mom gave it to me last Christmas, cause she said my head was always in the heavens."

"You're awful interested."

"Yeah. It's got me thinking."

"Oh?"

"You know they figured out that the Earth was round, and how large it was when they didn't even have telescopes?"

"That right?"

My thoughts were racing. I said, "That Greek guy, Aristotle, knew the Earth was round because some stars could be seen in Egypt and not in Greece. That'd never happen if the Earth was flat. That's so simple. Another guy, who was a librarian in Egypt, used the position of the Sun in two different towns and a little geometry to figure the Earth was twenty-five thousand miles around. He was only off by about one hundred miles! The next chapter tells how they figured out that the planets circled the Sun. They find this stuff out just by thinking!"

"That *is* amazing!"

There was something else that struck me, so I asked, "Ona, what are thoughts anyway?"

"What do you mean, Alan?"

"I mean, you got 'em, I got 'em. They can change the world, but we can't see them or touch them."

"Yes. Hmmm."

"They're like our souls, don't you think? Maybe thoughts have something to do with souls!"

"Well, I, er—"

"They must have figured out what thoughts are. They've figured everything else out."

"Scientists may be clever, Alan, but they don't know everything."

"Well, I'm gonna find out what thoughts are, then I'll know."

"Know what?"

I answered with a question. "Ona, why's Dad an atheist?"

"I'm not the one who should explain it. I think you'll learn more if you ask him that, but he saw some terrible things in the war. Experienced terrible things."

I said, "Yeah, I'm going to ask him about it. Do you believe in God? In souls?"

"Yes, Alan, I do."

"Why, why do you think so?"

"Because I have faith."

"Oh, right. But don't you want to know for sure?"

"I do know for sure. I believe it."

"Because the church teaches it?"

"Well, yes, and so does the Bible."

"Yeah, but once the church taught the Sun went around the Earth, and they were wrong."

"Oh, I see," Ona said. "Scientists are wrong sometimes too. They're human. I'm not sure that scientific answers can replace your faith." Her eyebrows went up, her voice sounded stern. I had not said anything insulting, but her response left me feeling guilty all the same.

Ona continued. "You know, Alan, we had some desperate times. Without God's help, you and I probably wouldn't be here right now. I believe prayers got me and your mother through your grandpa's passing and the Great Depression. How else could we have survived?"

I heard the story before, but I enjoyed hearing her tell it. "What did God do to help?" I asked.

Ona sighed. Her eyes flickered like the TV did when the channels were changed. "We didn't know it was coming. Guess you never do. I remember your grandfather sitting down to supper looking worn out. I just thought, 'the

Great Depression has started, he's worked the farm, odd jobs with the railroad, sure he's tired.' But he had a cough, and I begged him to go to the doctor. Oh, he was stubborn, your grandad. The pneumonia took him quick, left your mother and I. She wasn't even in high school yet."

She paused, staring out the front windshield. I knew she wasn't seeing the road ahead or the snow-covered farms expanding in front of us and shrinking behind.

She spoke to her memory, as if I weren't sitting next to her. "How were we going to pay the mortgage? Where'd we get food, clothes? We prayed and prayed. Your mother joined a charity group at the church to help neighbors." Ona looked over at me, a twinkle in her eyes. "Then, Alan, your mother got an idea. I think God put the idea in that little girl's head. She got some secretary work from a law-yer in the town who went to our church. She made a little money and convinced me to buy a few pigs and chickens. We raised and bred those animals and used their manure to grow food crops. We traded vegetables and eggs for help working the land. We gave away a lot, canned the rest. I made the clothes. We got by. God helped us all right. He made little things go right here and there for us to make it."

It was a nice story, though I wondered, *Why don't you ask yourself how come God took Grandpa just when you needed him the most?* I stared out the window for a mo-ment, then returned to my book. Ona turned off the high-way and onto a winding county road in Northeastern Pennsylvania. Dark, heavy clouds rolled across the sky, completely blocking out the sun. A dense population of barren trees, underlined by a topcoat of snow, glided past the car window, a monotony of gray bark occasionally interrupted by a white birch or bristly evergreen.

There was a long silence. The clouds began to part. The sun illuminated patches of snow.

Just before the exit to Ona's place I said, "You know how they did it?"

"Did what?" she asked.

"Figured out that the Earth goes around the Sun. See, the planets move, the stars don't. A lot of people kept notes on the positions of the planets. They used math and finally realized that the paths of the planets were orbits that went around the Sun. That's pretty neat, don't you think?"

"Yes, Alan, they're very clever."

CHAPTER 10

Eventually we turned left, onto the half-mile dirt road that skirted one side of Ona's property. It was covered with snow, but she knew the exact path. Like her, I knew every inch of her land, from the stream, three quarters of a mile away, to the river, two miles off, which marked the boundaries. I had hiked, hunted, climbed trees and swam in the river.

To our left stretched the garden area, which a city dweller would have thought was a small farm, and where I spent many hours weeding. Ona and Mother had worked this small plot of the working farm after Grandfather died. An empty chicken coop was on the right. When Ona had chickens, I fetched their eggs and sometimes collected their droppings for garden "fertilizer." Her house was a stone's throw from the chicken coop, but the road continued another two hundred yards and ended at a pond. She pulled into a lean-to garage next to the small sun room on the side of the house.

The temperature had risen a bit, but teetered on the point of freezing. We climbed out of the car, scrunching snow loudly under our feet. Ona asked me to put our luggage in the upstairs hallway. I grabbed our bags and followed as she went to open the front door. We climbed the three front steps of her white clapboard house, to the long porch, which was framed by a white picket rail.

The temperature did not change when I stepped into the house. My breaths formed small white clouds as I clattered up the steps with two suitcases. I set them down in the hallway and looked at the framed pictures on the wall. There were photos of me, my mom, my dad and my grandparents in different combinations. Mom, young and vibrant, looked back at me from several of the photos. I wondered: *What's heaven like? Why can't we see spirits?* The images blurred, I wiped the tears from my eyes and turned away

I walked out the back door and brought in two loads of firewood from the enormous tarp covered pile stacked by her neighbor. While Ona filled and started the wood stove, I became restless and called out, "I'm going for a walk."

"But it looks like it's going to rain," she said, concerned.

"It's OK, I'll put on the rain poncho and boots."

"All right, but if you're not home by dark I'll send your father out to fetch you."

The threat quickened my heart, my throat tightened. "I won't need him to get me, I'll be back."

Once outside, slush under my sliding footfalls made the only sound breaking the winter silence. I began to jog, then run. Past the garden plot, through the treeless field and into the woods. Slipping, dodging trees, making up a game, a physical contest to sedate my grief. My eyes and nose watered. I ran hard the full two miles alongside the stream, sucking in the damp cold air, suffocating in a mask of sorrow and exertion. Where the stream met the river, I finally stopped, bent over, and planted both hands above my knees. I was panting and sweating. I looked around.

The woods on both sides of the wide river looked dead. The warm summer forest, which was bursting with life not so long ago, was, like my mother, only a memory now. Life had slipped away. Between the lush summer green and the now gray barren winter, I remembered what autumn looked like here. The ending of life a finale of perfect colors.

I thought I had my emotions under control, but I was overcome with sadness. I called out for my mother, the irrationality of it making me weak. Falling to my knees at the river's edge, I stared at my reflection. A single tear struck the water, its life expended in spreading ripples. Then, as raindrops began to join the river, I saw their expanding circular undulations intermingling, forming shapes. Faces. My mother was there. I reached out. She was gone.

When I stood, the same tingling feeling that I had one time when I was an altar boy encompassed my face, head, and hands. Perhaps it was just the blood above my shoulders obeying gravity, just the brain's inclination to see faces in random patterns, but I thought something important was happening. I watched a world being created on the surface of the river, on the surface of something deep and indifferent. There were faces I didn't recognize. The wind whispered through the trees. Voices came from the river. I thought they might be calling out the answers I was searching for, telling me where thoughts came from. A place where my mother and God were, but I couldn't make out what they were saying. Was I hallucinating?

It began to pour. Water trickled over my face. Trembling from the cold, or from the vision that made no sense, I began to jog back to Ona's. The experience at the river kindled in my brain.

CHAPTER 11

When I reached the front porch, I heard raised voices from within. They grew silent when I opened the front door. The house smelled of burning wood and baking. Ona and my father were sitting on the ladder-back chairs around the kitchen table. I walked over and reached for the bowl of cookies set between them.

"Did you leave your boots outside, young man?" Ona asked, looking up.

My mind back at the river, I managed to say, "Yes ma'am."

"I was just telling your father how Marie saved us during the Depression."

I wondered if that was all she was telling him. Would that story require the near shouting I heard? I sat down trying to sort out the faces in the river calling to me. I was barely aware of the chocolate chips melting over my tongue or the sound of my grandmother's voice telling a story.

Finally, she said, "Back then people looked out for each other. The church lifted our spirits. That's how we made it."

There was an awkward silence until my father said, "You both should be canonized, even your priest said so. People keep more to themselves these days. Shame."

"We did what we had to. You boys would do the same." She smiled.

My father looked at me. Something felt different, stirred my curiosity and nudged me out of a trance. I studied his posture and movements. They gave me the feeling that Ona had chastised him. Maybe gave him some ultimatum. When he spoke, he actually sounded amenable.

He said, "Interested in some hunting in the morning, if the weather's OK?"

Hunting usually amounted to nature walks in the woods. When I was younger, we'd take the 22-caliber rifles, which my grandfather gave us for Christmas one year, and would shoot at bottles, cans or bulls-eye targets.

I was suspicious, but heard myself say, "Yeah, OK."

On Wednesday morning, when I walked into the kitchen, the stove was crackling with a bellyful of firewood. My father sat at the kitchen table. Ona was filling his cup with coffee. I saw the familiar Ruger 10/22 rifles leaning against the wall by the kitchen back door. Dad had set a box of ammo and a few bulls-eye targets on the floor. He said, "The temperature dropped over night and it snowed some more. It's pretty cold out."

"Should we still go hunting?" I asked.

"I'll leave that up to you, but I think we'll be ok if we dress warm."

I was shocked. *Had he ever left it up to me?* "Good," I said, "I'll get some gloves and—"

"Before you go anywhere," Ona commanded, "you boys will sit and have some breakfast."

She set plates of warm buttered pancakes covered with maple syrup, along with eggs and sausage in front of us. Then, for me, a mug of hot chocolate with a melted marshmallow floating on top. My "Thank you, Ona" was an admission that there are some orders from adults you don't mind.

My father and I helped Ona clean up, and then we put on two pairs of woolen socks, gloves, wool ski hats, boots, and winter coats. We stepped out the back door cradling our rifles in our arms, muzzles pointing at the ground. Several inches of powdery snow had fallen and crunched under our boots. There were sharp prickles in my nose, as its tiny hairs froze in the cold air. Our departing breaths condensed into white clouds while we crossed the field and walked into the naked woods.

I couldn't stop thinking about my experience at the river. It seemed strangely related to what puzzled me about what thoughts were. My father might have been my antagonist, but he was smart. I decided to see if he had any explanations.

"I went to the river yesterday," I said. "Something strange happened, and I've been thinking about it."

"That must have been a cold, wet walk. What happened?" he asked.

"The rain fell on the river. There were all these ripples colliding, forming outlines of faces. I wondered if that's what happens in our heads when we recognize people or imagine stuff."

"What do you mean?"

"Well, I've been wondering what thoughts actually are. I mean, does the brain make some kind of ripples when we think? You can't cut someone's head open and see a thought, so, where are they? What are they? How do we *know* things?"

Father walked from one tree to another, tacking up the paper bullseye targets.

"When you say 'know,'" my father replied, "I think you're wondering what consciousness is, right? Awareness of things. I think that's still a mystery. Last time I remember talking about this was in college. I took a philosophy course, and we talked about a philosopher who wondered the same thing a long time ago." We both walked about one hundred yards from the targets, the adjusted range for our sites.

"Really. Who? What did he say?"

"His name was Descartes. He believed people could have two parts, a physical part and a separate mental part. It was called 'Dualism.' He believed the mental part was the soul."

My heart beat faster, I thought, *Someone proved we have a soul!* Then Dad said, "But I don't think many people believe in Dualism anymore. No one could ever explain how physical parts and mental parts could interact." He paused. "So, what does rain on the river have to do with this?"

I took aim and fired. The gunshot echoed in the woods. I hit the target just outside the bullseye. "Oh. Just that, uh, you know how the river can be as smooth as a mirror? That's how the river was. All of a sudden, raindrops hit the water. Their little ripples made faces on the surface, but I couldn't see what was under the surface. It made me wonder what's beyond the surface, underneath. Maybe we only know about the surface of the brain. We know it's doing something. Maybe making ripples, like the faces on the river. But we don't know what's below the surface. Where the faces come from. Maybe thoughts have to do with what's *underneath* the surface."

Father looked down his site, taking careful aim, then pointed his muzzle down, "I don't get what you mean. Underneath the brain?" He asked looking puzzled.

I looked out into the woods, thinking. It was like trying to describe a jigsaw puzzle from a single piece with frayed edges. "I guess I'm not sure what I mean, but I read a story about Galileo in that astronomy book. I thought about how Galileo could only see what was around him. He couldn't go beyond his surface, into space, to see that the planets went around the Sun. But he did figure it out, without going into space. So, I thought maybe we could figure out where thoughts come from. What's beneath the ripples."

When I looked at my father, he wore an expression I'd never seen. I wasn't sure if it was admiration or concern that I'd been hallucinating.

He turned, lifted his rifle, took aim, and fired. "There's something multidimensional in what you're saying, with the river and Galileo. Right? The surface of the water is two dimensional, the river is three dimensional. Interesting. I have an old book that might help you; it's called 'Flatland.'"

I said something interesting? He wanted to help me? I made a mental note of the book and stared at him in disbelief.

Emboldened by the compliment I blurted, "You don't believe in God, or souls?"

"No, Alan."

I stopped short and glared at him. "So, you think Mom's gone forever?"

"Yes."

His *yes* was cold and final, condemning my mother to an eternal void. I was stunned. "How could you just think she's gone? Like we're never gonna see her again?"

"I know what you believe, Alan. But I'm a scientist. I'd need proof souls exist."

I had wondered myself where the souls were, why we couldn't see them. Then it occurred to me. "You can't see a soul, so you don't believe in them? But you can't see a thought either, right?"

Father shook his head. I could tell he couldn't be convinced.

I said, "Yeah, well maybe a drunk killed Mom and that's all there is. We live and die, and there's no reason. I can't live in that world. Maybe there are reasons, maybe God is testing us."

My father's upper lip pursed, his eyes narrowed, "Testing us?" he asked sharply. "That's the kind of world priests live in. Look—"

His assertive atheism was a burning match, but his disdain for the priesthood was gasoline. I erupted. "See! There you go again," I said. "You can't let me find my own way. 'Alan, think this way, Alan, you need to study more, play football, don't waste your life being a priest!'" I felt my lip quiver; my fists clenched. "I'll be what I want. Even if Mom's gone, even if I'm all alone. I'm gonna find out if there are souls." My eyes burned, as if drops of acid were forming. I knew they were turning red, and I turned my back to him. "I'll be a priest if I want. No one's gonna stop me!" I wasn't sure what angered me more, my father telling me what to do, or the doubts he was raising in my own mind.

When I finally looked at him, I saw the lines around his eyes soften. "Alan," he said, "you're thirteen. I can speak with you man to man now. I only pushed you to make you strong and well educated, because I want you to be prepared for the sometimes cruel and competitive world we live in. You're in accelerated classes, doing great in school. OK, you didn't want to play sports, but son look at you, you're so athletic, and physical competition would keep you ready for anything. I thought with your physical and academic gifts you would be a star."

I felt a pang of guilt, realizing that I had refused to play school sports because he had wanted me to, and I never told him about the serious boxing workouts in Rich's basement. I focused on the target, firing another shot. The echoes louder, it struck wide of the center again.

He lifted his rifle. His aim unmoved by our disagreement, the shot near perfect. "As for being a priest, I saw what happened to people who prayed to God to save them, instead of fighting back."

"That why you don't believe in God?" I asked cynically.

His face darkened. "Your mother asked me why too. I explained that I had seen some bad things in the war. You know, Alan, you can read about these things, but it's not the same as living through them. Seeing them can convince you that men have an evil nature. If you believe that, it's tough to understand why a God would create such creatures. I guess that's why I lost faith."

His answer was like *reading* about sticking your hand in fire. Unless you actually put your hand in fire there is no suffering and no lesson learned.

"What, because bad things can happen?" I shot back, hoping he would give me a more horrifying explanation of his experiences.

"No, that's not it. She and I agreed that God could have created an imperfect world, a world of suffering and random tragic events, so we could help make some things better. She would say, 'The most perfect thing about our world is that it is imperfect.'" He saw my puzzled expression. "She meant that there is no white without black, no happiness without sadness, no pleasure without pain. Without contrasts what kind of world would it be?"

"So why did you stop believing?" I said. "I guess I still don't understand."

"It was more than accepting a broken world. I could understand that wars will happen from time to time because people are imperfect, their goals clash, they fight, even kill one another. But off the battlefield I saw, and heard stories about, how men treated other men."

"What did you see? Who told you stories? About what?" I asked. The only war experience he'd ever mentioned was the freezing cold weather.

He took a deep breath, "Jules, my college buddy, and I volunteered to be paratroopers, 101ˢᵗ Airborne Division. A colonel asked if I'd be a medic, and I was put in the 326ᵗʰ airborne medical company, trained as a medic and sent overseas in the war—" he began.

I interrupted, "Why'd they ask you to be a medic?" It didn't make sense. His degree was in electrical engineering.

"Jules asked me the same thing, 'You're an electrical engineer. You should be in RADAR or something,' he said. Like I told him, go ask the Army. Maybe if I was in the airforce. Anyway, I got sent to Belgium at the end of 1944. There was a big battle in Ardennes. The 'Battle of the Bulge' it was called. We were captured by the Germans and taken to Stalag IX-B, a POW camp, in December 1944."

"Wait, you were captured? You were taken prisoner?" I had never heard about this.

"Yes, it was a bad time." He explained how POWs tried to survive in the freezing cold weather with tattered insufficient clothing, not enough blankets, little more than a daily ration of a slice of stale bread and watery soup, how they were forced to work, hard. He told me some stories about soldiers who were beaten when they were disrespectful or even impolite, the unlucky ones who were disobedient and shot where they stood, and the massacre of

Malmedy where German soldiers machine gunned a group of unarmed American POWs.

My heart must have quickened because, with rifle shouldered, the target swayed in the site. I slowly released a deep breath and squeezed the trigger. Bullseye. The noise reverberated in the cold frozen woods. I smiled and looked at my father, but his expression was distant, apparently being drawn back to the Ardennes.

"I guess that's how people would want to treat an enemy, the soldiers that were killing their guys," I said.

"Maybe you're right. Combatants may not deserve better. I was hoping I wouldn't have to tell you the other stories. They may not convince you either, but when you're there, when you look into their eyes," he said, his voice fading into the past before returning to the present. "I met a guy, another captured American medic at the camp. We only knew each other a short time, but we became friends. He was singled out one day because he looked Jewish. He was sent to Berga, a slave labor camp. He was one of the few who survived. I met him again before we were both shipped home. He was frail, a skeleton. He told me about Berga. The prisoners were deprived animals. They would kill one another for a slice of bread. The death camps like Auschwitz, with civilians, Jewish people, families who posed no threat. The Nazi's hunted them down in Nazi controlled territories, even in Germany. Their own German Jewish citizens! Grandparents, wives, children, they crammed them into train freight cars, like animals, and sent to camps around Germany where they were starved, worked to death, killed with poison gas, shot, murdered.

Innocent people. The mountains of dead bodies. The in-humanity..."

I thought of Emilie and her family. Her grandparents barely staying one step ahead of their enemy, nearly being caught and loaded onto one of those trains. A shudder went through me. His words trailed off, and I could see a change coming over him, like an awful storm beginning to spread over the horizon. His eye's reddened and started to glaze. I was certain that the only person he had ever told this story to was my mother. He confided in me. Suddenly, on some incipient level, I understood something about him. He had become intimately aware of the unimaginable suffering of people at the hands of other human beings. How could there be a merciful God? An all-knowing, all-powerful God who loved us? What kind of God created beings in His image and likeness that would torture and murder other innocent subjects of his own creation?

I had questioned how God could make such an unfair world when my mother was randomly killed by a drunk. But he had experienced more than an unfair circumstance. He had experienced entire countries of people deliberately carrying out merciless, hateful and murderous acts. God's creation against God's creation. If there was no God of mercy or love, what kind of God was left? What would it mean if there were a God without human emotions? Actually, an eternal Being could not be human, did not have a human brain, so it made sense that He would not have human emotions. But what did that mean? I stored this question in the back of my mind with all the others.

I had been ready to fight with him, now I felt sorry for him. Sorting out whether he would be an obstacle or an ally in the future could wait. I had to do something, fast.

"I don't know if I can do this on my own," I said. "I could really use your help. I've got to find out."

His eyebrows lifted. "Find out what?"

"Find out what thoughts are, maybe what souls are. Figure out, using science, what consciousness is. The brain works on electricity, right? And you're an electrical engineer. So, will you help me?"

"You're looking to explain souls? God with science? Science is all about explaining things *without* God, Alan. One excludes the other, don't you see? I don't want you to be disappointed."

"Let me do it my way, OK, Dad? I'll do it alone if I have to, but I could sure use your help."

"All right," he said sadly, "anything I can do."

I pointed my rifle to the ground and led him out of the woods. It was enough hunting for one day.

CHAPTER 12

I had finished the astronomy book and caught up with schoolwork late Wednesday evening. When I woke up Thursday morning it was damp and overcast. Ona's house smelled like a bakery. She gave us a box with two dinners and a tin of cookies for when we got home. She promised she would come for Christmas in New Jersey, which was the tradition, but this year we agreed there would be no presents or decorations.

During the drive back, my father and I had a long talk. It was a little awkward at first, then quickly became natural. It was the longest conversation I ever had with him. It was personal. We discussed how different it would be without a mother, without a wife. We told each other how Mom would not have wanted us to restrict our lives or be depressed. I hoped my father's transformation to a normal human being would continue.

The car slipped past barren rolling hills, partly hidden under a heavy mist that was slowly evaporating in the daylight. I tried to avoid thinking about going back to school. There was only one day before the start of Christmas vacation. I focused on other things, like getting to the library before it closed for the holidays. I wanted to know why, after thousands of years, no one knew what thoughts were, what consciousness was. I needed to *know*, not just have faith, but know, if there was a place where consciousness existed outside the body. If there was a spirit world where my mother still resided. And, if there was, what kind of God would be there to welcome her? What kind of God would let a drunk take her from her loved ones? I needed answers. And I thought I knew how to find them.

Dad said, "Ada asked if she could bring us a few meals when we're settled, and if you'd be able to help her with some college project?"

"Yeah. She's going back to school. I really like Ada."

I had a flicker of anticipation about school again, and I asked myself what it would be like for my father returning to work. I said, "You do some interesting stuff at work. I'll bet you've got some pretty cool friends there. How did you get that job anyway?"

"Yeah, Bell Labs is a great place. Jules knew some people there. He told me to apply and helped me get my foot in the door."

Before we got home, Dad was explaining how teams at work were testing something called a LASER. It sounded very cool. I wanted to hear more, but as he pulled the car into the driveway, we saw Tim sitting on our curb. His bike was leaning against the tree in our front yard. By the time I opened the car door, Tim was standing next to me.

"Hey, Alan."

"Hey, Tim. You been waiting long?" I asked, walking toward the back of the car.

"Nah, school just got out."

I noticed a bruise on his left cheek, he seemed to be leaning to one side.

"Hi Tim," Dad said, coming to the back of the car. "We brought back some of Ona's chocolate chip cookies. Why don't you come in and have some?"

"Yeah, great, thanks."

"We can unload the trunk," I said.

Dad noticed Tim's awkward posture. "You sure you can carry the bags?" Tim and I nodded, so he said, "OK, I'll open the house and turn the heat up." Dad carried the box of food to the kitchen.

I handed Tim the smaller bag with books and watched him limp towards the house. I hefted the two suitcases, one in each hand. I thrust my chin out, pointing at his crooked body. "What happened? Your dad?" I asked, a warm flush of anger beginning to color my cheeks.

"Naw, that scumbag's been staying out of my way. Bet he knows what I'll do if he, uh, does anything again. It was that big oaf, Jerome."

"What? I told him I'd break his damn neck next time—"

"OK, OK. Cool it. I started it."

"You what?"

"Yeah. That fuck said something about the um, accident. I clocked him in his stupid mouth. He got a punch and a kick in, then sister broke up the fight, but you should have seen his face. That fat bloody lip!" Tim said, laughing.

I wasn't sure what to say. He had never been the aggressor. Then, changing the subject, Tim added, "Hey, maybe later we can do some training at Rich's. Lumps might be there."

I wanted to get to the library, but I figured there would still be time before dinner. "Yeah, OK, let's call Rich and see if it's OK with him." We set the bag and the suitcases down in my living room.

Tim called Rich on the telephone. Rich encouraged us to "get our butt's" over there.

We rode our bikes to Rich's house and found him waiting in the front doorway. We climbed to the top of the front steps. Rich said, "Hey, Tim. Hey, Alan. You OK? I'm sorry to hear about your mom."

"Yeah, thanks," I said.

"She was the coolest lady I ever met," Rich said, walking us into the house.

I just nodded.

When we got downstairs to the gym Rich said, "Hey, my dad got some punching mitts. Lumps was here and showed me how to use 'em. One guy puts 'em on and moves his hands around, ya know like a moving target." He handed me the mitts, and he put on some boxing gloves.

I jerked my hands randomly while Rich jabbed at the mitts. Then, in keeping our custom of motivating one another with taunts, I said, "You're punching like a sissy,"

Rich smiled and began attacking the mitts with reckless hooks and jabs.

I finished several sets of weight lifting. Then I went to work on the heavy bag, which was chained to an overhead steel beam. I was thinking about what Dad said about the POWs and the Jews, about my mother's accident. Someone, or something, needed to be punished. Maybe if I could not change the world, I would hurt it. Lost in a reverie, I was hitting the bag harder with each punch.

The punches rumbled through the house, as the bag swung out, straining its chains. I stopped when my arms felt heavy and I'd broken a sweat, oblivious to the racket I'd made. Tim and Rich were staring at me.

Rich, who normally would have said something like, "You hit like a eunuch," Just said, "Wow. Good job!"

Blood rushed to my cheeks. "Uh thanks. Hey, uh, I've gotta go, so, thanks for the workout. I'll talk to you guys tomorrow."

"OK, later," Rich said.

Tim walked up and said quietly, "Maybe we can meet with Father Curtain next week?"

"It's Christmas vacation next week. I don't think next week's good," I replied.

"Oh, yeah. OK, maybe the week after?"

"Sure, we'll work it out. See ya Tim. Thanks."

At the top of the basement stairs I ran into Stephanie, Rich's step sister. She was thin with long straight black hair, and had large brown eyes. She wore a white sweatshirt and blue jeans.

"Hi, Alan," she said. "I'm really sorry to hear about your mother. If there is anything I can do for you or your dad, you can just call. You know, I can cook a few things or run some errands."

"Yeah. OK, thanks, Steph," I said.

"You guys leaving?"

"Yeah, I wanted to get to River View library for, uh, school."

"Why go all the way there? Can't you just go in town?"

"River View has more books and stuff."

"Oh, yeah, I guess that's true. Well, OK, see you later," she smiled.

"Yeah. Hey, thanks."

I rode my bike to River View library. I asked the librarians for help and told them I wanted to learn how scientists figured things out, what problems they were working on now. I also wanted to read about Galileo and what happened to the Jews in WW II. One of the librarians, Angela, seemed thrilled with my request, like I handed her a winning lottery ticket. She suggested we make a list of books and magazines that I could work on at my own pace. She took me to the periodicals section and suggested I browse through *Popular Mechanics* while she compiled the reading list.

Before the library closed, I signed out several books from the long list that Angela had provided and said goodbye to her. I left thinking I had one day of school, then a new year started.

Friday morning, December 22nd, was cold. Sunlit cumulus clouds wandered across the sky like lost sheep, gathering at the horizon. Several inches of slushy wet snow covered the sidewalks.

Dad left for work late. He set out breakfast, squeezed my shoulder and said we should both try to make the best of the day. "Please clean off the table and put away whatever needs to be refrigerated," he added as he walked out the front door.

His "Please," made me think our relationship might be becoming less adversarial, but also reminded me that my mother would no longer be setting out breakfast, no longer leaving notes to make the bed or remember to take my lunch. Dad and I would need to fill an impossibly large gap. Things would be different.

One thing remained the same for school. I didn't have to decide what to wear. It was always a white collared shirt, gray tie emblazoned with "SPS" and gray slacks. That morning I put on a scarf, a heavy winter coat and galoshes over my shoes. I grabbed the lunch bag on the kitchen table and walked down the block, tramping through the slush.

Looking down the long sidewalk, I was afraid I'd cry at the bus stop. Since driving back from Ona's, there were moments when I wanted to cry and others when I became angry. I knew these feelings had something to do with my mother's accident. Still, I was not in control.

At the end of the street, I saw the sixth-grade girl who lived two blocks over and rode the bus. A boy I'd never seen before stood next to her. He looked thin and a little younger than me and was one or two inches shorter. I lost any impulse to cry.

The girl said, "Sorry about your mom,"

"Thanks," I said.

The brief exchange did not seem to register with the newcomer, whose wide set eyes poked out from a cocoon of winter clothing. He was staring down the street, his arms bent at ninety degrees rocking back and forth out of sync, giving the impression that he was conducting an invisible orchestra. I guessed he was shy and nervous, so I tried to ignore him.

I climbed on the bus, moved to the back with the older kids, and mumbled thanks to the whispered condolences. The new boy from my bus stop took a seat in one of the empty rows at the front. Set apart from us, he continued to act oddly. He stared straight ahead. His body moved slightly to the right and left accommodating his rocking arm movements. I thought he had some mental problem.

The bus turned onto the access road encircling St. Peter's and the boy scanned the buildings. On the right side of the road was the rectory, on the left was the church and school. Beyond the buildings the road expanded into a large parking lot that doubled as a playground. Two parallel, single-story classroom buildings— one accommodating first through sixth grade, the other seventh and eighth— were connected by a short hallway where our church was attached. My impression was that the planners believed pubescent behavior was contagious and hoped that a house of God would quarantine the older disobedient adolescents.

Through the morning, most kids just said "hi," and I was grateful that the teachers from my accelerated math and science classes skipped the condolences and just offered to stay after school if I needed help.

Everyone ate lunch, then Hip and Rich found me in the large, newly constructed, multi-purpose room between the two main buildings. Hip was thin, with straight brown hair, hazel eyes and a broad smile. He was a bit of a rebel, drawn to some defiant diversions probably because he struggled with schoolwork (years later we found out he had dyslexia). We called him "Hip" because he liked smoking pot (a jail sentence at the time, if you got caught) and was an adept drummer and guitar player. He also had a talent for tormenting me with arguments that God did not exist, but we had been friends long before that, since we were six years old.

Hip put his hand on my shoulder. "Hey man, sorry," he said. "You OK?"

"Yeah, thanks," I replied.

Rich said, "It's gonna snow tomorrow."

"Yeah, like a blizzard," Hip threw in.

Rich added, "We're thinking of some football, under the lights. Wahdahyah think?"

Tackle football in the snow? I needed a diversion. "At the office building parking lot? Yeah, sounds good. Call me before you head over."

We were heading back to class when the principal, Mrs. Burn, came up to me and told me to follow her. When we walked into her office, the boy from my bus stop was sitting on the wooden bench that rested against one wall. His head was bowed and he looked down at his feet, curling long locks of his disheveled brown hair around his left thumb and index finger. I thought, *Boy he must be in trouble.*

Mrs. Burn walked to the other side of the boy.

"Alan, I'd like you to meet John. He and his family just moved into town, near you. He'll be taking a few classes at

St. Peter's and some at the University. His parents would like him to meet other children his age."

"University?" I mumbled.

"Yes, Princeton."

The boy lifted his head. Both his and my eyebrows went up simultaneously. He stood up, almost at attention. He had a peculiar expression, a face my father would make when he was looking over a complex circuit diagram. There was something very weird about him. I didn't want to appear rude in front of the principal. I held out my hand, "I'm Alan."

John looked at it for a moment, then cautiously extended his and watched our two hands come together, as if he were an anthropologist discovering the primate that preceded humans.

"You're the boy at the bus stop," he said looking up. "You looked sad and the girl said she was sorry about your mom. Did your mother...? Oh, I'm sorry."

Now, I hadn't said anything, and I admit the mention of my mother hurt, but I began to get a little pissed off. I didn't know this kid and he didn't know me or my family. Who was he to treat me like a lower life form and then bring up my mother? And didn't Mrs. Burn tell him about the accident?

John's luminous wide-set brown eyes seemed to be assimilating all the information in the room. He smiled, "We will be friends. During the week I usually keep free time after supper between seven and eight o'clock. I'm also free on Sunday mornings. You are welcome to come over any-time." Then, without glancing at the clock behind him he added, "It's time for class." He turned, opened the door and walked into the hallway.

Friends? I wasn't sure if I felt honored or belittled. Frankly, I would have felt the same if a space ship had briefly materialized in front of me. With a stunned open mouth, I looked at Mrs. Burn.

She said simply, "I think he likes you, and I think you are going to like him. He's a genius, Alan."

When I got to the advanced English class, nine desks were arranged in a circle. Mrs. Aemilia was sitting in front of the blackboard with a textbook and notepad on her lap. The new addition to the group was John. He looked up, barely smiled and nodded, then sat gazing through the blackboard. The other five girls and two boys in the group shot furtive glances at John, obviously uncomfortable in the presence of a stranger.

Mrs. Aemilia was talking, "In particular, we were discussing how Lord Byron created meaning with the use of metaphors and similes in his poem, but now that we're all here I'd like to ask the new member of the group to say a few words about himself. John, tell us how you came to St. Peter's."

"Well," John began, "I came by bus this morning—" One of the boys and two of the girls laughed.

Mrs. Aemilia smiled and interrupted, "I guess I asked for that."

John simply continued, "My mother, father and my brother Lenny moved here because my father began a new job nearby. Now we live down the street from Alan." He looked at me and nodded. The faces, necks, and shoulders of the other kids seemed to relax. "But I may not be taking the bus every day since I have studies at another school."

Mrs. Aemilia acted as if everyone knew about John's other studies and turned the conversation back to that day's English class topic.

"Thank you, John. Now, *She Walks in Beauty* was one of Lord Byron's most celebrated works. Have you touched on Lord Byron or his poetry in any of your studies John?" she asked.

"Oh yes." He said confidently.

"Really, what can you tell us about him?"

"He was a great British romantic poet. He was briefly married to Annabella Millbanke. They had a brilliant daughter, the Countess of Lovelace, who had an amazing vision of future calculating machines. Remarkable in the 1800s. But Lord Byron was never allowed to see his daughter."

"What? Why not?" It was clear from her expression that Mrs. Aemilia had not known this.

John explained, "Lord Byron could not restrain his passions. He had many scandalous romantic relationships. When he had an affair with his half-sister, his wife Annabella threatened to destroy his reputation by revealing his licentious behavior unless he left and never returned. She banished him before his daughter was born."

It wasn't an obscene statement, just a missing puzzle piece. Still, the girls in the class sat up straighter, glancing between John and one another. The boys leaned forward in their desks, looking at each other with sly smiles, acknowledging that even Lords were, at heart, horny. Shocked, I stared and slowly closed my mouth.

Mrs. Aemilia blushed slightly. "Well John, ah, now that we have everyone's attention. Ahem, does anyone have an opinion why Lord Byron's last line in the poem praises 'a heart whose love is innocent'?"

John and I looked at one another. Everyone else's hands shot up.

At the end of the day, when the final bell rang for dismissal, hundreds of kids ran for the buses or cars waiting to take them home, excited to start the weekend and Christmas break. For me there was only an enormous emptiness anticipating the holiday without my mother.

Walking to my bus, I ran into Hip, who asked, "Hey, what's this new kid's story? Is he a nerd or what?"

"Don't know yet. He's got a funny way of shaking hands."

"I heard he got Mrs. Aemilia going."

"Yeah, he did," I said.

"Ha, cool. OK, I'll call you for football. Ya think the new kid would be interested?" Hip asked as we parted.

"Don't think so," I called out, "but I'll ask him anyway."

When I climbed on my bus, I saw that John wasn't there. It hit me how much I really wanted to talk to that kid.

*****

That Saturday morning Bellcon could be found in the company of other dedicated competitors, in a corner of the school's gym, trying to get in a workout before the snow storm. It would soon be winter break for Forrest Creek's public high school.

Even in this group of athletes, he stood out from the rest. They all worked through stations designed to enhance specific muscle groups. They spotted for one another, making sure that, as they strained to their limits, the bar bells did not drop on top of them. As Bellcon began his routine on the bench press—his large chest and huge defined arm and shoulder muscles swelling while he raised and lowered weights that far exceeded his own 215-pound frame— his two spotters looked on both amazed and envious.

Although a few of the boys in the gym were Bellcon's football teammates, and had known him for about five months, they knew surprisingly little about him. Even Stan, one of his teammates who hung out with him more than anyone else, as if they were best friends, had no idea what the boy did when he was not hanging around the school.

Bellcon was a sophomore who had transferred from another school somewhere. Tall and brawny with large, black, unblinking eyes, he showed up in the middle of a Forrest Creek's Hawk football practice in August of that year, marching behind his father across the field, to confront the head coach. It was a brief meeting:

"You coach Rendick?" his father said.

"Yeah?"

"I'm Frank Bellcon." He reached out and shook the coach's hand. "I'd like you to give my son a try on your varsity defense."

"This is not a tryout," Coach Rendick said, sizing up the boy. "If your son is a transfer he'll have to—"

"Look," Frank said, putting his hand on his son's shoulder, "you won't be doing us a favor, you'll be doing your team a favor. All I'm asking is, give him a try. You won't regret it."

Rendick paused. "Well, I guess I could sub him in at middle linebacker. Just in practice mind you. My first stringer is out for two weeks with a sprained ankle, but I'm not promising he'll play or make the team."

"Thanks," Frank said, and turning to leave added, "Oh, my son prefers to be addressed by our last name, Bellcon."

The unwelcoming stares that came with an unearned spot on the varsity team did not last long. By October, other players were soon cheering their taciturn teammate who led their team to a winning season by demolishing opposing offensive squads. The middle linebacker's helmet and body were a missile made of steel, his arms were metal clubs, and his legs were unstoppable pistons in a high-performance combustion engine. He played heedless of potential injury to himself and indifferent to his opponents' wellbeing. He had put several opposing team players in the hospital with concussions. One was a strapping offensive lineman who had flattened Rendick's prized player with a blind-sided block during a game. He agreed to meet Bellcon in a deserted parking lot after the game to "settle things up."

Even now Bellcon remained an enigma to the spotters who listened to his grunts and watched the barbell laden with weights rise and fall repeatedly, at some point being set back on its stand.

The boy on the bench knew that everyone in the school wanted to know about his past, but he would certainly not be the one to satisfy their curiosity. He had more important things to ponder. He was bored. He needed some excitement. It had been too long. Sure, he'd been the star football player, but being a star only served two purposes: the fame could be either an allure or an alibi. It could attract the people he wanted to meet or make a cop or a judge look the other way.

He had promised his father he would stay engaged in "positive" outlets, like football. But punishing other players had only partly charged his batteries. He needed a plan. The preliminary work was done. He had befriended a number of students, found out what they liked and feared, and learned about their routines and where they lived. These kids had parents, they had friends and relatives in other towns. The adults were in all sorts of professions. The more contacts he could make, the more useful information he would have.

One way he used his net of contacts to provide a simple pleasure was fishing for bullies. The bigger, the better. He would identify the bait, usually some frail-looking kid, and tell him he'd take care of his bully. Bellcon would learn the deserted places where the bully liked to pick on his prey and wait in a blind, using the bait as a lure. At the right moment the big linebacker would appear, tell the abused kid to leave, and then bludgeon and torment the brute. It was when he saw a certain look of fear and pleading on his target's face that he felt chills run through his body and a rush of pleasure wash over him.

Best of all, although the bullies were often badly injured, the community's parents and authorities usually did not pursue a vigilante who dispensed with ruffians. As the stock of bullies ran out, he found he could find pleasure in the occasional unlucky kid in a nearby town who did not cower properly. Sooner or later the guardian of the underdog would appear next to them when no one else was around. It took little convincing for them to surrender their panic-stricken expressions and begin begging, which gave Bellcon that rush that felt so good. With the boys it was a simple pleasure, with the girls it was orgasmic.

He thought about next year's incoming freshmen. The elementary school girls who would be impressed with older high school boys. They would be easy targets for the football star. But he had to be very careful with the girls. He could not risk getting caught. His father, an accomplished lawyer and fortunately his greatest ally, had made the consequences very clear. That's why he needed a plan.

CHAPTER 13

Other than the monster snow storm that hit late Saturday afternoon and some muscle aches from football late that night, Saturday passed uneventfully. On Sunday morning, Christmas eve, I phoned John. He sounded excited and invited me to come over.

I hoofed through the snow to their house at the end of the block and knocked on the door. John's father, Joe, greeted me and introduced me to his wife, Claudette, and John's little brother, Leonard or "Lenny." John's parents insisted I call them "Joe" and "Claudette". I thought it was odd that there were no Christmas decorations, but I was more surprised to find that this family looked so normal. I guess I expected some wide-eyed aliens to answer the door. Claudette looked overjoyed to see me and offered me some breakfast. I declined, and she told me that their other son was in his room, first door on the left at the top of the stairs.

I climbed the stairs, knocked and opened the door. In the center of the wall on the right was a large window flanked by two identical pine wood desks, each equipped with Luxo lamps. The other walls were covered with framed and unframed pictures and posters. To the left, behind the door, were bunk beds. My classmate sat at the desk on the far side of the room, bracketed by overstuffed bookshelves. A star chart covered the wall above his desk, and alongside it was a wood-framed black board. He said, "Hi Alan, come on in."

I walked over to his desk and saw a large piece of paper covered with precisely drawn squares, triangles and other shapes connected by many zigzagging parallel lines. It looked similar to drawings my father had brought home from work from time to time.

"Hey, what's up?" I asked.

"Nothing as much fun as this," he replied smiling and pointing to the diagram. "I'm sketching a circuit board for a calculator. It works with transistors, like the ones in your radio, only the transistors in this calculating machine are used as simple switches."

I knew a little about transistors. They were developed at Bell Labs, and my father had talked about them.

John pointed to an alignment of small circles on the diagram. "These three rows of tiny light bulbs register the numbers. The top two rows are the numbers being operated on and the bottom row indicates the solution."

"But," I asked, "where do you see the numbers?"

"Oh," he replied, "this is a binary calculating machine."

Mr. Lenard, my math teacher, had taught us about "bases" in Math and called base two "binary". Most people are familiar with base ten or "decimal," which uses ten numbers, zero through nine. If you look at a decimal number from right to left, each place value increases tenfold: ones, tens, hundreds, thousands, and so on. In base two, or binary, there are only two numbers, one and zero, and each column from right to left increases twofold: ones, twos, fours, eights, sixteens, and continuing on. So, you could write the number forty-three in decimal as 43: three ones and four tens. In base two that same number would be 101011: one one, one two, no fours, one eight, no sixteens and one thirty-two.

"So, this operates in base two?" I asked.

John looked delighted. "Yes, yes, exactly correct!" he said. "A light *on* is a one, a light *off* is a zero. Imagine the rows of lights are binary numbers."

"OK, cool," I said. Then something occurred to me. I asked, "What if the answer is part fraction, like three and a half?"

"Good question. You can have decimal points in binary. They're called "binary points." Going to the right of the binary point, the places are ½, ¼, ⅛. You see? So, three and a half would look like—" He wrote: **11.1** on the blackboard. "Binary can deal with more than simple fractions. Let me show you. Do you know the transcendental constants e and Pi?" He wrote the symbols on his blackboard: e and π.

I knew Pi. I replied, "You mean like numbers that go on forever after the decimal point without repeating?"

John's eyes sparkled. "Yes, yes, how about imaginary numbers? Or the imaginary unit 'i'?" I shook my head. He explained, "i is the square root of negative one. So, if you multiply i times itself, you get negative one."

"Whhaaat?" I said. "You can't multiply any number by itself and get a negative number. A negative times a negative is positive."

John said, "Ah, but you can if you use i. It's used in all sorts of calculations. Now, here's a little equation called Euler's identity that demonstrates just how amazing ones and zeros can be." He wrote on the blackboard:

$$e^{i\pi} + 1 = 0$$

"You can see," he said, "that one and zero can be linked to numbers with unending decimals and even the imaginary unit."

"Huh, that's weird," I said, thinking, *Crap, there's a lot I need to learn.*

"What I think is amazing," he added, "is how numbers are related to *information*. You can turn information into numbers, like when spies use coded messages or scientists use numbers to study nature. Put numbers into a computing machine with some instructions, and you can figure out all kinds of things!"

That's when it first happened, what I called John's *imagination transportation*. When he'd say something and my mind jumped to another world. This time I glimpsed a future world run by machines.

"You can think about that a little," John interjected. "Now tell me what you're working on."

"Me?" I asked, wondering, *How in hell does he know I'm working on something?* I didn't know enough about consciousness yet to discuss it, though I was tempted to get his opinion. Instead, I decided to ask him about what I'd been reading, to test what he knew. "I've been looking into why it took so long for people to figure out that the Earth circled the Sun, not the other way around. Why Galileo had such a hard time convincing people."

"OK, a good story. What have you found out so far?"

"Well, long before Galileo, people believed what Aristotle taught. Everybody knew Aristotle. He was super smart. So, when he said that the heavens were perfect and unchanging and that the sun revolved around the Earth, that's what everyone believed for over a thousand years. 'Course Galileo's problem was that the Bible said the same thing as Aristotle."

John interrupted, "I think you mean *a few* church authorities *thought* that's what the Bible said. Some church leaders agreed with Galileo."

"Well, yeah, I did read some of that. But Galileo made some pretty convincing observations with his telescope that the heavens were not unchanging and that Aristotle was wrong." I paused.

He asked, "Are you religious?"

"Well, I, uh, guess I was until recently. Why?"

"There is a lesson in this story."

"What, that the Catholic Church was wrong?" I asked.

"Well, yes. But I meant something more general, and I didn't want to say something that would offend you if you were religious. I see this natural joining. There are leaders, who are obsessed with power, and then there are most other people, who only feel they matter if they are part of a group. Rather than trouble themselves with difficult choices, the group looks to the leader to be told what to think, what to do. The groups can be religious, political, or scientific. It doesn't matter. The lesson is for each of us to resist this tendency, to develop our own moral code and take responsibility for our own actions. If we allow others to dictate what we believe and how we behave, and even to silence our questions, it will be poisonous to civilization."

I said what popped into my mind. "You mean like Hitler and the Nazis?"

"Exactly, and you gave another good example. A few church authorities demanded Galileo accept *their* interpretations of religious writings."

John sounded like he had personally suffered at the hands of a mob or something, though his references about religion bothered me. I said, a bit skeptically, "Are you saying we should make up our own commandments, ignore the lessons of the Bible?"

"Not at all. I'm saying that you should come to your own conclusions and not accept what anyone tells you without thinking, questioning, and having your own interpretation."

"But there are scholars of the Bible who get it wrong. I'm supposed to think I'll get it right?"

"Exactly."

Something felt wrong with his advice. I said defiantly, "If I shouldn't believe anyone, I guess I shouldn't believe what you tell me."

John said with a mischievous grin, "You especially shouldn't believe anything I tell you!"

The tension snapped, and both of us laughed. Until then he seemed so serious that I wasn't sure if he had ever laughed. I was surprised because his laughter had a purity that was infectious.

John told me about the sacrifices his parents made for him and his brother Lenny. Apparently, his parents moved from a small town in Virginia to New Jersey, leaving their former lives and jobs, because the two boys didn't "fit in." John said he refused to attend the school there and studied from home, which the school made a big stink about. Somehow his parents convinced Princeton University to let John take some classes there. It was just a simple solution to satisfy the kid's enthusiasm for science and math. He told me about some of his cool professors, and how much he enjoyed physics. But he added that he loved music too. I told him about St. Peter's school, warned him about Jerome and Father Vinious. John said he knew the types and learned how to avoid them. I asked him about the school in Virginia, but I could tell he didn't want to talk about it. We talked about my friends and my father.

John seemed impressed that my dad worked for Bell Labs. For some reason, maybe because the kid said he loved music, I told him some stories about when Mom taught music at the high school. We continued talking until John asked, "You know it's twenty after one?"

I hadn't paid attention to the time and didn't realize we talked for several hours. "Are you kidding?" I thought, *There's no clock in here, how the hell does he do that?* "I gotta split."

While walking home, I realized that I had missed Mass, and it was Christmas Eve. I may have scored another sin, but that Sunday I felt like I'd received a gift. John had said things that required some research and thinking to understand. It almost felt like a religious experience. Unlike any I had had at church.

CHAPTER 14

I got home to find my father sitting in front of a pile of notepads at the dining room table, catching up on work. We made some soup and grilled cheese sandwiches. I told him I had visited the new family that moved in down the street and who had a kid in my class. My guilt about missing Mass evaporated when he said, "If the weather holds, Ona will be coming in the morning for a few days."

I said, "Great. I'll help get things ready."

"Oh, and Jules will be joining us for dinner tonight. Hope you don't mind."

"Jules? That's OK. I like him. And he got you that cool job. Maybe he'll spill some good stories about you guys in college."

Dad grinned. "Guess I'd better swear him to secrecy before he comes over."

Later that evening Jules came for dinner toting a book. "This is for you," he said, holding it out.

"What is it?" I asked.

"Called *Six Easy Pieces*, by Richard Feynman. Your dad said you like to read and you're getting interested in science."

During dinner, Jules and my father were discussing how innovations, some being developed at Bell Labs, would transform the world and everyone's lives. Jules explained, "Engineers are designing electronic computing machines. They work like this." He began to draw some simple circuit diagrams to show me how transistors, working as on-off switches, could be wired together and perform logic or mathematical operations. "Think of a switch in the 'on' position as a one, and a switch in the 'off' position as a zero. The calculations would be done in binary."

When Jules paused, I said, "Yeah, the new kid down the street drew a diagram like that, a little more complicated, of a calculator he's building."

My father and Jules exchanged glances. Jules asked, "How old is this young man?"

I washed down some roasted chicken with a sip of milk, and said, "I think he's twelve. But he seems older." I took the pad that Jules had sketched on, picked up the pencil, and wrote a few characters. I spun the pad around to show them. "John showed me this equation. He said it shows how ones and zeros are related to imaginary and irrational numbers, so machines might be able to compute just about anything one day. It's just a matter of turning information into numbers."

Jules and my father stared at Euler's identity. Then they looked at each other for a few seconds. Jules cleared his throat and just said, "Interesting fella."

I dreaded Christmas without Mom. Mercifully, though, the week went quickly. There were moments of sadness on Christmas day, but at times, when Dad and Ona told stories of Christmases past that took place long before I was born, I felt my mother was close, the way you feel that, even on the darkest night, the sun has not abandoned the Earth.

The rest of the week I spent mornings reading at the library, or at home. I added Euler's identity to the topics I was interested in and plodded through Angela's endless list of books. My friends and I had more fun working out at Rich's gym. For Christmas, Rich got heavily padded vests that we could wear during workouts. We no longer needed to "pull" our punches, and sparring became more challenging.

At the end of the week, we played football in the park. Afterwards, Tim and Hip came to my house. We sat at my dining room table. I told the two of them, "I think I'm gonna go back to John's this Sunday. Last time was better than Mass. Maybe you guys can come?"

"You're going to miss Mass again?" Tim looked shocked. "On New Year's Eve?"

Hip said, "You guys didn't get into all the God baloney, did ya? I mean, I know you guys dig it, but I'll pass."

The two of them looked at me, Tom with a wrinkled nose, smelling a bad idea, and Tim with elevated eyebrows and open mouth, horrified.

"It's funny, we talked about building a computer and stuff, but I thought I learned more there than at church."

Excited, Hip said, "No shit? Hey, let's do church at John's on Sunday!"

Tim looked suspicious, and remained quiet.

"If you really want to come, I'll have to see if it's OK with John," I said.

"Cool. Do it," Hip replied. "Ask him if I can bring a joint!"

"Are you fricking crazy!" Tim said, now agitated. "*No, you can't bring a joint!*" Though he had never tried marijuana, having it around scared the crap out of him, and Hip knew it.

"I know. Just pulling your chain," he laughed.

I went to the phone and called. "A few friends of mine would like to meet you. Would it be OK if we came over Sunday morning?"

"Why do they want to meet me?" John asked.

I was surprised by the question. "I told them about our conversation last week, and they thought it sounded cool." I laughed. "Hip said it would be like having church at your place."

"Church?" he echoed, sounding a bit skeptical.

"Yeah, I told them I thought I learned more at your house than I did going to Mass, so—"

"Church at John's, hmmm." He paused. "Heh-heh, sure, bring my flock over around ten a.m., OK?"

CHAPTER 15

On Sunday morning, my friends planned on meeting up at my house, so we could all walk over to our new church. When I mentioned to my father that I planned to go over to John's later that morning, he walked into his bedroom and came out with a manila envelope and handed it to me.

"What's this?" I asked.

"It's the first part of a scientific article that Jules and I thought your new friend might find interesting. It was written by a guy at Bell Labs. It's about information. Kind of what you talked to him about last week. Ask him to let me know what he thinks about it."

When my friends got to my house, Tim looked nervous, even though he'd met his obligation by going to a very early Mass that morning. His eyes darted about, he spoke rapidly and he appeared to be trembling. Hip teased him while we walked down the street. "Are you scared or something? Look, shithead, it's not like they're a bunch of aliens over there. Let's smoke a little weed before we go in there, that'll calm you down." He pulled a neatly rolled joint from his shirt pocket.

"*Jeez-us!*" Tim's eyes went wide, his face pale. "Are you nuts? I'm not going." He turned to leave.

"Aw, come on Tim. What's your problem? I'll keep it in my pocket and smoke it on my way home, 'K?" Hip slipped the joint back into his pocket, put his arm around Tim and winked at me. Tim stayed with us, but looked more anxious.

John's parents welcomed us at the door. They seemed a bit too happy to see us. Tim fidgeted with the zipper on his coat, while we exchanged introductions. Then, John's parents led to the cellar door.

"John and Lenny are down there," Claudette said, beaming.

Walking down the stairs Tim whispered to Hip, "What're they so happy about? Hope they're not cooking up Earthlings for dinner tonight."

We could hear classical music as we descended into a spacious room that had bright square panels of light set in a suspended ceiling. In the center of the room, a large brown leather couch, a matching reclining chair, and two large ottomans surrounded a coffee table. Against the far wall, John perched on a stool at the center of a long wooden work bench that was illuminated by overhanging fluorescent tube lights. To his right were overstuffed floor-to-ceiling bookcases. The bench top was littered with tools, coils of wire, a partly assembled circuit board, and a reel-to-reel tape player that filled the room with soft stereophonic sounds. A peg board covered the wall behind the bench, and John had stocked its hooks with carefully arranged electrical components. John sat at the table, like a priest at the altar of his sanctuary.

Our new Sunday minister swiveled around in his seat and smiled. "Come on in, guys."

We walked towards the middle of the room.

"Oh my," Tim sighed. He dropped into the recliner looking pale, staring blankly at the odd scene.

"Wow!" I said, admiring the electronic equipment.

"Whoa!" said Hip, spying the large, reel to reel stereo tape player that was filling the room with classical music.

"Hope you don't mind the music," John said looking directly at Hip.

"No man, Mozart's cool."

"You recognize it?" John asked, a little surprised.

"Is that Number Three?"

"Yes, Concerto Number Three. You like classical and Mozart? What else do you like?"

Hip said, "Ah, Rock and Roll, like the Beatles, Stones, Cream, I like Jazz, Blues, Swing."

"OK, great," John said. "In the index box on top of that file cabinet is a list of music I have on tapes. You might like to browse through it." Hip grinned and headed toward the file.

I made my way to the table to see what my friend was working on. I pointed to the pegboard covered with electrical components. "Where'd you get all this stuff?"

"Before we moved, I spent some time repairing T.V.s, radios, and other electrical devices. It was just a hobby and didn't pay much. What couldn't be fixed, people donated to my collection. One guy gave me the tape player we're listening to, for fixing a bunch of things."

At the back far corner of the table I noticed a black metal tube with a cone shaped top. I pointed. "That's not a—"

"Rocket," he said, finishing the sentence.

I said, "Are you serious?"

Tim sat up in his chair, now curious. "Did you say you're building a rocket?" He walked over to the table.

Hip had head phones on and was listening to music, tapping his fingers on a file cabinet.

For ten minutes, John explained how he had built many rockets, varied the designs, experimented with different fuels and calculated the thrust each delivered. Our conversation led into speculation about space travel and the possibility of life on other planets. The little professor broke it down mathematically and was summing up when Hip walked over.

"So," John said, "considering the number of stars in all the galaxies in the visible universe, even if a very tiny fraction of them had planetary systems that could support life, you'd have to conclude that there are probably many planets out there with life forms. Some of those planets could have evolved intelligent beings with civilizations millions of years older than ours."

Tim went back to the recliner and sat down, drawing his knees up to rest his head. He became quiet, while the rest of us were engrossed in a lively discussion.

John paused. "What do you think, Tim?" he asked.

"I don't think that God made aliens," Tim said softly, though he looked like he was not so sure as he gazed into our new friend's wide set eyes. "It's not what we're taught from the Bible anyway." His voice took on an edge. "Alan thought coming here would be better than going to church. But we're not discussing the Bible. You're not a priest, and I don't get how you would know more than Father Curtain about it."

"Cool it, Tim!" Hip said. "You don't *know* there's a God, you just want to *believe* it."

Tim turned to Hip, "I don't care what you think! All I know is, what would be the point with no God, no heaven or hell? How'd my father pay for everything he's done?" He looked at John. "I don't know if you even believe in God or the Bible. Do you?"

"I have read the Bible," our new minister said calmly, as though it were a slim novelette. He moved closer to Tim. "I certainly can talk about it." Hip and I looked at one another, surprised. John continued, "But I'd much rather hear what you think about it." There was only interest in his tone, not a hint of arrogance.

"What I think about it? What *I* think? What difference does it make what I think, John? Someone who knows what the Bible says, what God says in there. They need to tell us what it means, what God wants us to do!"

John began to frown. He paused for a moment, considering Tim's statement. "I don't think so. I think that your understanding of what the Bible tells you makes all the difference. Look, Tim, if you believe that God inspired men to write the Bible, don't you think He would have the authors write in plain enough language for just about everyone to understand? To make up their own minds? Why would He take the chance of putting someone in charge of interpreting His message for the rest of us? Even leaders of the church are human and can make mistakes, or perhaps twist His meaning to make people do what *they* want, not what God wants."

Hip and I nodded in agreement, but Tim looked troubled. "What do you mean?" he asked.

"When we surrender our own decisions about what God wants us to do," John said, "when we give that authority to someone else, they can make us do anything. Things we wouldn't do if we decided on our own what God wants us to do. There are many examples in history when followers of bad religious leaders hurt, tortured, or killed innocent people."

Tim's eyes were wide with disbelief, "*What*? Are you crazy? We're talking about priests, bishops, and, uh, Father Curtain never taught anything like that. That would never happen."

"It *has* happened, Tim." John said. "The most well-known example I could give you went on for hundreds of years. It was called The Inquisition."

Hip grinned, "Yeah, Pastor John, I heard about that," he said, with a new moniker that would eventually stick.

Tim looked shocked, upset, and confused. He stood up, his cheeks a faint crimson. All he could croak out was, "I gotta get home for lunch, it's late."

John announced to everyone, "It's 1:38."

I shot a glance at my watch, it was 1:38 on the nose. There were no clocks in the room. *Holy shit*, I thought, *how does he do that*!

"I gotta split too." Hip said. "Hey, maybe we could come over next Sunday?"

Our host said, "Sure, you're all welcome to come."

Tim and Hip were headed up the steps. I said to John, "Hey, Tim just—"

"Tim's a good guy." He interrupted. "Maybe someday he'll have a stronger faith in himself." Then he turned to the table and pointed. "What's in the envelope?"

I walked to the table, picked it up, and handed it to him. "I almost forgot. My dad and his friend Jules wanted me to give this to you. They said you might enjoy it. It's about information. Some guy at Bell Labs wrote it."

"Great!" John said. He looked like a starving wolf who just came upon an easy meal.

"Yeah, Jules gave me some mind-expanding stuff too. This book called *Six easy Pieces*."

"By Feynman?"

My eyebrows went up. "Yeah, that's it. You've read it?"

Pastor John smiled, went to the bookcase, removed a small thin book and handed it to me. "This it?"

I took the book and opened the cover. "Yeah." Inside the cover was scrawled: *John, DISREGARD! and best of luck.* It was signed, *Richard P. Feynman.*

"You met this guy?" I asked, impressed.

"No," John said, "but Feynman went to Princeton. His thesis adviser was Dr Wheeler, who gave me this autographed copy when I decided to take classes there. It's a wonderful little book and has a nice simplified explanation of quantum mechanics."

"What's quantum mechanics?" I asked.

"Oh-ho," he laughed. "That would be difficult to explain until you learn a little about it. I'm studying it in my physics class at Princeton now. I heard Feynman said that while plenty of people understand Einstein's relativity, nobody understands quantum mechanics! I'll tell you what, you read chapter six in that book. It explains what's behind quantum weirdness. Next week we'll talk about it. OK?"

"Sure, sounds good. Hey, I gotta go. I'll see ya tomorrow."

"Oh, there might be a little math you're not familiar with yet in that chapter. Just ignore it and try to get a mental picture of what he's saying. I'll read the article your dad sent and let him know what I think."

I was at the foot of the stairs. I said, "OK. Oh, what does 'DISREGARD!' mean?"

John said, "The story I heard was that Feynman went into a slump after he won the Nobel. Then he realized, in order to be creative again, he had to *disregard* the way other scientists thought and how they were looking at problems."

"He won the Nobel prize?"

"Yeah, interesting fella."

Walking home I realized Pastor John had given me another gift. I was getting frustrated with one of the books that Angela the librarian gave me. Gilbert Ryle's *The Concept of Mind* seemed to repeat over and over that there was no such thing as consciousness. No "Ghost in the Machine." No sights "seen," no sounds "heard," no odors "smelled." There were no imaginings in the head that played out a person's hopes or dreams. There was only a brain working and a body behaving. At least that's the most I could make out of the author's lengthy arguments. It was depressing.

Now an anchor and chain felt lifted. I had been given the best advice and raised my arm over my head, pointing and shouting into the winter wind, "DISREGARD!"

CHAPTER 16

The new year began uneventfully. On the morning of January 2nd 1968, I opened the front door on the way to school. John was standing in the walkway. "Hi, Alan," he said, holding out a stack of papers. "Thought I'd return this as promised."

I took the papers and read the title page on top. *A Mathematical Theory of Communication*, by C.E. Shannon. John had attached some notes. I put the papers on the dining room table for dad and walked to the bus stop with John.

When I got home from school, I rode my bike to the library, returned *The Concept of Mind* and stayed awhile reading. When I got home, I pulled into the driveway just before Dad. We walked into the house together. Dad saw the papers on the table. He said, "I thought you were going to give this to your new friend yesterday?"

I looked at him blankly, "I did. He returned it this morning."

"I guess he didn't—" His words were cut short when he found the boy's attached note.

Since then I must have read that note twenty times. At first, I didn't understand it. Then, like so many things John said, it became part of how I understood everything. The note said:

My intuition was that "information" exists as patterns. Any medium that has changeable characteristics can contain patterns. Like the ones we construct to communicate information. For example, a chalk board can have numbers or letters written on it; a telegraph can arrange Morse code clicks to transmit patterns.

Interesting patterns are the ones that are connected to others. You start with one pattern and, after following some instructions to alter it, you end with another. Like using an algorithm to decipher a spy's coded message. Shannon shows that the amount of information in a message can be measured in binary units, or what they call 'bits' in the article.

You could think of the number of bits in a message as the number of yes-no questions you'd have to ask to guess the correct pattern. For example, how many bits of information are there in the string of letters: "axmdjdurbt"? The minimum number of yes-no questions you'd need to ask to guess this sequence is the number of bits it contains.

I like the idea of bits. We all know that information can be transformed from one medium to another. For instance, the ink marks (notes) on a musical score can be played on an instrument, translating the graphic pattern into vibrations in the air, into music. Can any pattern, in any medium, be translated into bits?

A pet idea of mine is converting any message into bits, a string of ones and zeros. The binary information can then be put into the on-off switches of a calculating machine with instructions, or algorithms, that will decipher the message, or give a solution to a question. We could calculate the path of a rocket or the stress on the truss of a bridge.

The most interesting patterns to me are found in nature. The arrangement of forces and matter found in the smallest and the largest things, from atoms to stars. To understand how our universe changes in time, we try to understand how one arrangement of these physical characteristics is connected to the next.

I suspect, if we are clever enough, we could get a computer to answer almost any question. Maybe a future machine will develop intelligence, operating with ones and zeros. Someday, we might be having conversations with these machines!

He ended his note simply, I'll have to think about it some more, but it's very interesting. Thanks, John.

Dad and Jules were impressed. When Dad told Jules, he just whistled and said, "We need to recruit that young man."

CHAPTER 17

On Thursday at lunchtime, Tim hustled over to me on the playground. He was jittery ever since church at John's. "Father Curtain said he'd meet with us tomorrow after school."

I looked away, a bit anxious that the priest would not be happy with what I had to say.

"Tomorrow? But—" I began, trying to think of an answer that could put off seeing the priest.

"You promised!"

"Oh, OK," I said.

Tim said, with an accusatory tone, "I want to see what *he* has to say about John,"

"Why?"

"Why? Aliens in space? Priests torturing people?"

"What's wrong with him saying that?"

"And you missed Mass. It's a sin! I don't want you to—"

"You better not say anything!" Now I was pissed.

"Cause you know I'm right? You afraid what he'll say?" Tim's face was red, his hands clenched.

I had to cool things off. I shook a finger at him. "Just don't, Tim." I turned and walked away.

Tim shouted, "You'd better be there!"

It wasn't more than two minutes later I saw everyone running to the other side of the schoolyard. Jogging over, I could see that bully Jerome standing inside a circle of kids. He looked like an angry bear, his paws circled in front of him. In one hand he held out a small white twig. "I'm telling them what you got!" He scowled, gazing down. Blood dripped from his nose.

When I got closer, I saw Tim and Hip on the ground. I was just about to lose it and knock Jerome down when I saw Tim reach back and, in one swift motion, snatch a stray brick off the ground, spring up, and smash it into the side of the boy's face. Jerome went down. Tim took the white twig from Jerome's hand and bent over to whisper something in his ear, as an approaching voice roared, "*Timothy*!" An instant later, the Whip led him away, his scalp in her hand.

I helped Hip off the ground. Baffled, I asked "What the fuck just happened?"

Hip looked horrified. He whispered. "I didn't know it was in my pocket, I swear!"

"What?"

"That joint. I pulled it out, and Tim saw it. He freaked out and grabbed it. Then Jerome took it and pushed me down. Tim told him to give it back. He wouldn't, and Tim socked him, and, and—"

"Shit! Tim has it?"

Two nuns were helping Jerome up and guiding him to the nurse.

No one at Tim's house answered my phone calls later that day. On Friday, he was nowhere to be found. The teachers wouldn't give me any information.

Jerome was back in school with a bandage on his face. He walked around looking at his feet, and I imagined his days of tormenting other kids were done.

When school finished on Friday, I went to meet with Father Curtain, because I promised my friend. I also wanted to know if he was suspended. I walked over to the rectory, climbed the ten concrete steps and knocked on the door to the vestibule. A dour-faced, gray-haired woman answered the door. "May I help you?"

"I have a meeting with Father Curtain. There's supposed to be another kid too. He show up yet?"

The matron opened the door and pointed to a box in the corner of the room. Without answering my question, she said, "You can do some good by folding those Sunday bulletins while you're waiting."

I folded five bulletins with the conspicuous sermon title *Returning to God,* then I was ushered up to the study. Shortly, Father Curtain opened the door and entered the room wearing a black cassock below a white tabbed clergy collar and a serious expression.

"First, Alan," he began, "I'm sorry about Tim. I know he has it rough at home, but we warned him several times about fighting. The other thing he had in his possession was the final straw."

"Was he suspended?"

"He was expelled, son."

"*Expelled!* What? Why?"

"Violence cannot be tolerated in this school. Tim knew what would happen if he continued fighting, and, he hit that boy with a brick for goodness' sake. I don't know if you're aware of the other thing. We could have Tim arrested, but we won't talk about that. He promised never to do it again."

I couldn't tell him Tim never touched marijuana. Besides, Tim was taking the fall for Hip. That's what I loved about him, what he would do for his friends. It was what he was beginning to do to his enemies that began to worry me. And now, with the abuse Tim received at home, I was worried how expulsion would affect him. All I said was, "But Jerome's always picking on Tim; I heard that bully's jaw wasn't even broken. And Tim's father—"

"Look, Alan, I'm sure you'll understand once you think it over. This may be the lesson Tim needs to be a better Christian. He'll be OK going to the public school, and I'm counting on you to remain his friend, to help him. All right?"

"Crap, Father. It's not right." I let slip, trying to process the information.

"Alan, you have a good friend who worries about you," the priest said. I was surprised he did not chastise me for my language. "Both of us love and want to help you in any way we can. We know you have a very hard path to walk right now." I said nothing. "I understand you missed Mass, to uh, talk about things with the new boy, John, who may not have a very flattering opinion of priests?"

I thought, *Great, thanks, Tim.*

He continued. "It's understandable that a person questions how God could allow terrible things, like what happened to your mother. You might even question whether God exists at one time or another. We all do."

I looked at him. "You?" I asked.

"Yes, I have questioned too, but with meditation and prayer we can rediscover God. We can know his Divine love for us and return that love."

The priest's soothing voice began to settle my mind when a sudden jolt of connections occurred in my brain. It straightened me in my chair. "I'm not sure God has emotions," I said.

"I know it's hard to accept your loss," Father Curtain said. "It's hard to see how this could be God's plan, but—"

I interrupted. "It's not that. It's that love is a human emotion. An eternal being, all-powerful and all-knowing would not be human."

"Is this what John told you?"

"No. It's just the truth. What I'm saying is, you said it's hard to understand *how* God could let terrible things happen. But what I have to find out is *why* He would let these things happen. What kind of a being would allow these things? Because it could not be an all-loving, all-knowing, and all-powerful Being. That makes no sense."

Father Curtain's eyebrows rose slightly. "As you said, Alan, we are human. We cannot presume to understand a supernatural being. We will never understand why terrible things happen. The Divine plan is not the human plan. There will always be mysteries that are beyond our understanding. That's why there is faith. You know what we believe as Catholics, how God brought his love into the world for us. God does love us. You do believe that, don't you?"

I thought it would be disrespectful to lie to him. "I guess I'm not sure anymore. I'm trying to figure things out. It has to all make sense for me to believe it. There can be mysteries and things I'll never understand, but how all the parts fit together, the big picture, has to make sense."

"I see," he said, and a moment later, "You are a good young man. I know this is a difficult time. I believe that your mother is with God, but her love and the love of your family, myself, and Tim are with you. The questions you have, you will need to find your own answers. I will be here to help in any way I can."

"Thank you, Father."

"If you or Tim ever want to talk, or just need some company, you just have to call. I will keep you both in my prayers. Alan, tell your dad I send my regards and will keep him and your grandmother, Grace, in my prayers as well."

CHAPTER 18

By early spring it was clear that Tim suffered no ill emotional effects being expelled from St. Peter's. He said he enjoyed the public school because it was more laid back. He bore no hard feelings toward Hip. If anything, the two of them got closer. They bantered with John and one another every Sunday morning. Tim's attitude had changed. One Saturday night, while Hip smoked a joint, Tim gestured to take a hit. He said, "I paid the price and might as well see what this is all about." He took a long drag and, exhaling, he had a coughing fit.

I noticed a physical change in Tim too. Our work outs at Rich's became more intense, and Tim punched harder. His physique underwent a metamorphosis, from skinny and vulnerable-looking to wiry featherweight. Things seemed to be coming together for him ever since he used a brick to make Jerome a more compassionate human being.

While Tim and the spring landscape noticeably changed, I felt no different. Despite pouring over books and articles from Angela, I didn't make any progress understanding consciousness. No one else appeared to have changed much either. We mostly hung out in our free time and talked about what the next year would be like, going to high school. Rich and I would have a long bus ride to Northern Catholic, an all-boys prep school. For Hip and

Tim, Forrest Creek High was an easy walk from their homes.

None of us wanted to show how anxious we were about dealing with new teachers, meeting new kids, and the rumors of various freshmen initiation rites. So, the conversations usually ended with predictions of how we'd fare with the girls we'd meet. Hip and Tim repeated some variation of: "You two might as well pledge celibacy for the next four years." Rich would counter with versions of, "Listen assholes, we've got an all-girls Catholic high school down the street from Northern. Think about it. A whole school of horny chicks who haven't seen a guy in weeks! The only thing keeping those girls from breaking out and eating us alive are the Sisters of the Sacred Snatch!"

Still undecided about priesthood, I kept serious thoughts about pledging celibacy to myself.

Sometimes Hip and Tim would beg me or Rich to sneak them into one of Northern's famous dance mixers. "Forget it," Rich would say. "Good Catholic girls don't trust jerk offs like you guys." Another round of begging would follow.

We continued to attend "church at John's," with background music that ranged from Gregorian chants to Buddy Rich's jazz. We dabbled in every topic from ancient Greek intellectuals to Eastern religions. But what really blew John away was how fascinated we had become with quantum mechanics. It started when I told John I'd read Feynman's book and John began a rudimentary explanation. Since then, Hip, and even Tim, begged for more.

At his blackboard, John drew diagrams and asked us to use our imaginations to understand how atomic-sized particles moved through space in the weird world of quantum mechanics. We learned that they did not move in the familiar fashion of rocks, baseballs or bullets. They acted like particles *and* waves. Waves that were described in an equation penned by a famous physicist named Schrodinger. I remember John's first lecture word for word.

"In order to understand how subatomic particles move through space differently than bullets," John had begun, "you have to understand *interference*. It's what happens when waves of any sort collide. Imagine a small pond of water. We place a wall across the pond separating the water into two parts." John drew a large circular pond on his blackboard, then a line cutting the figure in half. "We'll make two small openings in the middle of the wall." He used an eraser to make two small breaks in the middle of the line he drew.

"Now imagine a rock on the end of a string going up and down in the water on one side of the wall. The bobbing weight will make expanding circular waves." John drew evenly-spaced concentric circles, representing wave peaks, starting where the weight hit the water, crossing the pond until one circle met the wall. "The waves will head towards the wall but will only be able to pass through at the two holes we made." On the other side of the wall he began drawing concentric circles again, but beginning at each hole, getting larger and larger until they crossed the rest of the pond. Where the chalk-drawn arcs from each hole overlapped, they formed a crisscrossing pattern of warped rectangles on the blackboard.

"Where the waves from the two holes meet," John said, "they *add* together. So, a peak meeting a peak, makes a *larger* peak, and a trough meeting a trough forms a *deeper* trough."

Hip asked, "What happens when the highest part of one wave meets the lowest part of another?"

"They cancel each other out, the water would be flat at those points." John paused to let his lesson sink in, then he told us, "This pattern, formed by the waves coming from the two holes, is called an *interference pattern*."

My mind returned to Ona's river, when I stood by the bank and watched the rain create interference patterns on the water.

"So what does this have to do with anything?" Hip asked.

John smiled. "OK, so notice that we can draw straight lines through the crisscrossing wave peaks and troughs coming from each hole." He drew the lines he described and capped them with arrowheads, they fanned out from the two holes and crossed the pond. He drew a thick chalk line to show where the arrows were headed. It looked like this:

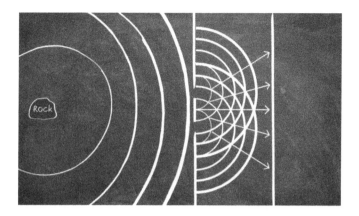

"What experiments show," John said, "is that *particles*, fired at a barrier with two holes, like the one in this diagram, will only turn up where these lines reach their destination. The pond is just an analogy. If you replace the pond and rock in this diagram with a gun firing *electrons* at a barrier with two holes in it, you get the same result. Of course, this doesn't happen with bullets. If you were firing bullets at a barrier with two holes, each bullet would go through one hole or the other. Bullets line up directly behind one of the holes."

"Hold up," Hip said. "You drew the crossing circles, the waves, spreading out from the two little holes A particle is a *solid* thing, like a very tiny bullet, isn't it? It can't spread out. So, you're just saying that when particles get really small, they will follow one of those lines? The arrows?"

"Not exactly," John replied. "Quantum mechanics is a mathematical model that correctly predicts the strange behavior of particles, like electrons. The diagram I drew illustrates what the equations tell us. We can calculate, starting with electrons being fired at a barrier with two slits, where the electrons will end up, say on a detection board. We know where the electrons start and end their journey, but we can't say what happens in between. We can't say whether any of the electrons *really* travel on any line. Actually, we can't even say which hole an electron went through, or if it went through both holes! We can only calculate where it will show up, and it *will* show up at one of the locations where the lines I've drawn meet a detection board."

This made no sense to me. I asked, "A particle might go through both holes? A single particle can act like a wave, going through both holes?"

John beamed. "Yes, that's it exactly. It's what we call a *duality*. Waves are particles and particles are waves. That is precisely what I've been describing. The wave behavior of particles can be demonstrated in the *double slit experiment*, which is what I've diagramed on the blackboard."

Hip, Tim and I looked at each other, baffled.

Tim said, "You said a particle will show up where one of the lines meets the detection board? How do you know which particle goes to which location?"

"Good question," John said. "You don't. We only know the *probability* that a single particle will show up at one of these places."

"Then what makes a particle choose the location it goes to?" I asked.

"No one knows," John said.

I said, "That's really weird." I thought, *There are designated places where an electron can go, but no one knows how the final destination is chosen?*

"Oh, it gets much weirder," John added. "If you spy on the electrons, put a sensor behind one of the holes in the barrier, you'll detect the electron going through one or the other hole, but then the interference pattern disappears, and the electrons cluster behind one of the two holes, just like bullets."

Hip blurted, "You're bullshitting us!"

"No way." Tim said.

"John," I asked, "you're telling us that the electrons go to different destinations depending on what we know?"

"Depending upon what we *can* know, or how their environment changes."

I thought through these ideas. Particles have choices. Their choices change depending on their surroundings, and we can't be sure where they'll choose to go until they're at their destination. That's what humans do. Each of my friends and I consciously chose to go to John's that morning. If the weather was different, or one of us had something better to do, we wouldn't have showed up there. And I wouldn't have known what my friends decided until they did! Although the thought shocked me, I was too embarrassed to ask John if he thought consciousness and quantum particles had something in common.

"That's crazy!" Tim said, crossing his eyes and laughing.

John replied simply, "That's reality."

CHAPTER 19

Saturday, March 30th, two weeks before Easter, it was drizzling. Dark clouds lumbered across the sky.

Despite the weather, I mounted my bike for the five-mile pilgrimage to "River View" library. I ran up the wide marble steps and slipped through the cathedral doors. Inside, I passed the long cherrywood table and chairs in the center of the ground floor. The weather darkened the overhead skylight. I grabbed the latest edition of Popular Mechanics and went up the stairs to the mezzanine. My favorite spots, the desks in nooks on the second floor, were taken, so I sat down at one of the small study tables dotting the open boundary overlooking the first floor and set down my rucksack.

I had just opened to my favorite article "An Eye on Space" when a group of girls walked in and sat down at the long table below. I recognized Rich's sister, Stephanie. I didn't know the other girls until one of them took off the hood of her rain poncho. It was Emilie.

A ray of sunlight broke through the clouds and shot through the skylight, highlighting Emilie's face and giving her eyes a golden iridescence. She sat with her back straight, head tilted, as she used her arms to make some point to the others. One hand glided gracefully while the other seemed to deftly work some unseen instrument. I imagined her playing a cello, producing music of magnificent resonance.

A powerful churning began in my abdomen. The discomfort paired with a strong urge to be near her. I wondered if it would be a sin to be alone with her, kiss her lips, her neck. Was it a sin to even think about? I worried about something Father Vinious said: "There is a beast of arousal in teenage boys, it will lead you into sin!" Was that beast stirring inside me now? Guilt drained the blood from my face and I felt lightheaded.

An hour and twenty minutes passed. The girls collected their notes, stacked their books on the table, and left the library. Emilie never looked up or looked back. Like a poem we read in English class, I felt like *Nothing Gold Can Stay.*

When I left the library, the clouds were gone. The sun was blinding. A black Ford Mustang passed by with windows open and radio blaring. I recognized the tune that wafted through the air and seemed to play on my one-sided feelings. It was Sam Cook's *Cupid.*

The brilliant spring day seemed an inappropriate change in weather.

For the next few hours, trying to remove thoughts of Emilie from my head was like trying to pour air out of an empty glass. The more I tried, the more hopeless it seemed. She was comfortably residing in my mind with no intention of leaving, unaware that a raging battle surrounded her. I knew what was wrong. The force that had motivated most of my life, my plan to become a priest, was threatened by this girl, again. Yet, like a traitor to my own aspirations, I was plotting ways to renew a friendship with Emilie. Nothing seemed workable. Every scenario seemed to have a fatal flaw.

I was looking forward to a boxing workout in the afternoon, hoping for some distraction. When I got to Rich's, Tim was on the front steps talking with Stephanie. Something seemed odd. Was it the way Stephanie's hair was combed? Tim's posture? The new screens on the storm door?

"Hi, guys," I said.

"Hi, Alan," Stephanie squealed, as usual a bit too animated. She stood up and went inside the house.

"Hey, Alan," Tim said smiling.

"What's happenin'?" I asked.

Tim fidgeted. "Uh, Stephanie and I are going out."

"Going out where?"

"Going out, going out. You know?" He laughed nervously.

My eyebrows went up. I asked a bit too loud, "*You serious?*"

"Yeah, but keep it down Alan, will ya?" Tim stood. "Come on, I like her a lot. She's a cool girl. So what if she's a year younger than us? I don't care."

More composed, I said, "Sure, you're right. She's a great kid." Then I asked the burning question, "Does Rich know?"

"Just about. She's been working on it, but she's going to tell him today while their parents are out."

I laughed, "Good idea!"

"Whada ya think? You like Stephanie, right?"

Suddenly, I had a brilliant idea. I thought, *He goes to public school now with Stephanie and Emilie. Tim and Stephanie can get me reconnected with Emilie!*

"Stephanie's great," I said, "a great girl, she may, ah, talk—"

"Talk a little fast, a little too much? I don't mind. I kinda like it."

Then from deep within the house we heard a roar. It was Rich, *"What? No fuckin way!"*

Tim turned sheepish. "I guess she told him."

"After you," I said, bowing and swinging my arm towards the door.

As soon as we stepped into the basement, Rich said, "You? Go out with my sister? The horny scumbag who wants to get in the pants of the Sacred Snatch girls? No way!"

Tim donned the padded armor vest and target mitts.

"Oh, come on, Rich," I said, "that's just talk. Think of the stuff *you* say."

"I wasn't talking about my sister."

"And neither was Tim," I shot back. "You know he's a good guy. What about all the boys in Steph's class? You like to see her going out with one of them?"

"Losers," Rich remarked while I helped him lace up the boxing gloves.

"Right," I said.

Tim pointed to his head, telling me he had an idea. He said, "Scumbag, huh? Ok shit face, let's see what you got!" He held up the mitts.

Rich was angry. He swung at the mitts ferociously and pounded the body vest. But Tim smiled, unfazed.

"I think you're getting weaker." Tim provoked Rich. "You've got nothing. Punch like a momma's boy. You a momma's boy?"

Rich was infuriated. He punched harder and faster. But Tim still smiled and moved around slowly, continuing his taunts. "Wussy. I don't even feel you. That all you got?"

Soon Rich was panting, his arms weak. Tim's mettle, acquired from his father's bare fisted beatings, earned some respect.

"Look," Tim said, "I just like Stephanie. I respect her. She's a great girl. What's your problem?"

"OK. I get it," Rich said breathing heavy. "But if I hear you're doing something, you won't have body armor to protect you."

"Yeah sure, sure," Tim smiled. "It's all good, you'll see."

A bit later Rich said, "I gotta get going, my mom signed me up for tennis lessons. I wanna grab lunch before we head out."

"Cool," Tim said. "Stephanie told me you had a lesson today. I hear Northern has a tennis team. Might be fun to play in high school."

Rich shot him a suspicious look.

"We have to go now anyway, right, Tim?" I gave Tim a look that said, *If you ever want to see Stephanie again, you'd better come with me.*

Tim got the message and said reluctantly, "Yeah, great workout, thanks."

We left Rich's and Tim asked, "What was the look for?"

I said, "I think you oughta let Rich settle on the big news for a while. Give him some time. He'll be OK with it."

"I just thought I'd hang out with Stephanie for a while."

"What? And make out?"

"What of it?" Tim grinned.

"If you hung around after Rich left, with no parents home, Rich would think...?"

Tim blushed a little. "Alan, you're the best. You saved my ass in there and you stopped me from doing something dumb." He put his arm around my shoulder.

"No problem," I said. "Maybe you'll help me with a girl someday."

With an incipient plan in mind, I decided to think things through. Did I really want to bring Emilie into my life? Give up being a priest?

Since Tim told me he was hanging around with Stephanie the next day, and John was away with his parents for the weekend, I decided to wait and consider asking Tim for help with Emilie the following Sunday. I knew where I'd find him. He had become a regular guest at John's.

CHAPTER 20

On Sunday April 7th, Tim was not at John's. He had gone to Mass with Stephanie. I was disappointed, but figured I'd talk with him over Easter vacation.

An event that occurred earlier in the week set a serious mood at John's. I knew we would be talking about it. Everyone had been shocked three days earlier when Dr Martin Luther King was assassinated. The newspapers, TV news, and conversations in schools and at dinner tables across the country tried to make sense out of what happened and to understand the implications and what it taught us about human nature.

Hip had brought up the assassination to explore the differences between self-determined and canned moral codes. One of John's favorite sermons.

"King had a personal moral code," Hip said. "He preached non-violence. He had a big following. What if they turn violent because of his assassination?"

"What do you think, Alan?" John asked.

"A lot of people followed King. There'll be plenty of very angry people. Things could get violent."

John asked Hip, "Would you blame King for the violence that followed his murder?"

"No." Hip said, sitting back in his chair.

John clasped his hands together on his lap, a preacher repeating his familiar message: "Every individual is responsible for their own actions. Letting others decide right and wrong for you, or following the crowd, is the wrong path." John looked at me "Even friends can pressure us into accepting what they think is right or wrong. It can be hard to make up your own mind."

It was the way he said it. Now I was sure he must have been wrongly accused of something. I was about to ask him when he said, "We can continue this conversation next week if you like. We have just enough time for me to explain another fascinating thing about quantum mechanics, if you're interested."

"Yeah, OK," Hip said. "Is this going to blow our minds?"

John smiled, "I think it might. It, uh, blows *my* mind. Have you ever heard of *entanglement*?"

Hip and I both said, "No."

John reached into his pocket. "OK," he began, and opened his hand to show us two large black marbles. "Imagine we could open these marbles and inside was a colored light. By experiment, we learn that each time we close, then reopen one of the marbles, its color has changed randomly to either red or blue. There is no way of knowing for sure if a marble will be red or blue until we open it."

"I know I'm gonna regret asking this," Hip said, putting his left hand over his eyes. "What's the big deal?"

John said, "If these marbles were subatomic particles, and the colored lights were certain properties of these particles, then here's what entanglement means." He walked to the blackboard and drew a solar system, labeling *Earth* and *Saturn*. "I tap the marbles together, then I give one of the marbles to Alan and he travels in a spaceship at light speed to a space station orbiting Saturn." John drew a chalk line from Earth to Saturn and wrote "1 hour" under the line. "Hip has the other marble here on Earth. Now, Hip opens his marble here on Earth. Let's say it's blue inside. Entanglement means that we can be instantly certain that when Alan opens his marble it will be red!"

John looked excited. Hip and I blinked at one another. Our faces blank.

"Don't you see," John continued, "how could they possibly be connected? They are three quarters of a billion miles apart. How could the color in the second marble be determined by the first?"

"Does the first send some kind of signal to the second?" I asked him.

"Ahhh, remember nothing can travel through space faster than light, and it would take light about one hour to get from here to Saturn. Yet observing the color in one marble *instantly* determines the color of the other. As if they were connected across hundreds of millions of miles."

I said, "Well how do we know that the marbles don't signal one another when they are close to each other. Maybe they synchronize their colors here on Earth and their internal colors freeze when they get a certain distance apart. Then no surprise."

John handed me one of the marbles. "Remember, I can open and close my marble here on Earth. Each time I reopen my marble, I cannot be certain what color it will be. It will have changed *randomly*. But, once I open *this* marble, and see the color inside, I will instantly know that your marble, near Saturn, will have the complementary color."

I asked, "How can they be connected?"

"No one really knows," John said. "Theoretically it has to do with the wave functions of the particles combining."

I had a vivid chain of thoughts. I saw the ripples from the rain drops in the river at Ona's. I remembered feeling that the ripples were like the lives of the raindrops, spreading out and intermingling with the lives of others. I thought of Martin Luther King, of all the people's lives he had permanently changed. It was like the consciousness of many people became entangled. Suddenly, I was struck again by the similarities between quantum particles and consciousness. I thought of the choices made by Reverend King, his followers, his killer, his opponents. They each had choices. Like quantum particles, their choices were set by their experience and their environment. I thought of Ona reassuring me about my mother, "If we keep our best memories of her alive, she will never leave us." An image of my mother flashed through my mind. I asked myself, *Are we all entangled somehow? Is there something in common about quantum particles and people? How strange that there could be any analogy between the two.*

"That's pretty amazing." I said.

Hip said, "Weird."

We looked at John. He grinned. "Yeah."

*****

Bellcon saw her in the Township Luncheonette on the first day of the high school's spring break. She was standing at the counter. He recognized the tall boy with dark curly hair who was speaking to her. He was a junior at the high school. The big middle linebacker thought the boy looked uninteresting and spindly.

He looked the girl up and down. Her hips, buttocks, and long legs were outlined by the fit of her blue jeans. A blue-checkered blouse accentuated her breasts. She looked hot, but he felt more attracted by something else. Maybe it was her posture. She seemed to project an uncompromising, defiant personality. Bellcon envisioned her alone, bound, gagged, and afraid. Her eyes looking up at him, helplessly. He was aroused. He thought, *I'll find out about him, and you. Then we'll meet.*

When she walked through a column of sunlight entering the store front window, he saw that her eyes flashed golden. They were unusual, but it didn't matter. When they had that pleading look, they were all the same.

CHAPTER 21

On Monday afternoon, the first day of Easter vacation, I called Tim hoping to get his help reuniting with Emilie. He had been hanging out with Stephanie a lot, but I wanted time alone with him. I suggested we take a bike ride. I knew he enjoyed the park at Garrison Mountain, where rugged trails dropped downward from a colonial stone castle at the peak. Turned out he was free for the rest of the day and excited to take the eight-mile trip.

We went right to the top of the mountain and rested at the foot of the old stone castle.

I asked, "How's it going with Stephanie?"

"Great. Thursday we were invited to a birthday party with a bunch of her girlfriends."

I thought, *perfect.* "Cool. Dad and I are going up to Ona's Friday morning for Easter. Hey, Tim, you think Steph could set me up with her friend, Emilie?"

"You mean, what, like you two go out?" His eyebrows pulled together, as if I'd given him a tough riddle to solve.

"Well, yeah."

Tim smiled broadly, "You dog. But any girl in your class would like, freak to go out with you. You want to date a younger girl too? What's up?"

"I was thinking, Steph's a great girl. Emilie's probably cool. We could double date or something."

"That's a great idea!" Tim stood up. "I'll talk to Stephanie tomorrow."

I was thrilled. The plan was going to work!

We drove down the east mountain trails, taking an occasional detour into the woods to challenge our bikes. On the ride back home, Tim said if things worked out, we could bring the girls on the trail. He made it sound like a done deal.

I felt fine until I finished supper on Thursday. Then I began to feel nervous waiting to talk to Tim. He told me he'd be home by ten p.m., so at ten minutes after ten I headed straight to the phone. After six rings I was about to hang up when Tim answered.

"Tim?" I said.

"Oh, hi, Alan. Hey, I just got back from the party. It was a little weird at first. I mean, Emilie was the only other girl I knew there. She's a real fox. The other girls ain't bad either. But sorry to report Emilie has a boyfriend."

Nausea welled up inside me. I tried to suppress it thinking, *It's better. Maybe she's another test. If I become a priest, I can't have....* The train of thought derailed. I didn't know what I wanted.

"OK," I said, "thanks for checking. Hey, I'll see you at school on Monday."

"You all right? Sound a little tired."

"Yeah, fine. Just getting ready for the trip."

"OK, see ya. Hey, say hello to your grandma for me. Bring back some of those great cookies!"

Friday morning was sunny and cool. Dollops of white fluffy clouds spread across the sky. On the ride to Ona's, Dad and I didn't talk much.

When we pulled off the highway, Dad said, "Nice day for fishing. What do you say we get busy on the chores for Ona this morning and then head out to the river this afternoon?"

"Sounds good," I said.

We drove down the long driveway, past the chicken coop, and pulled the car alongside Ona's Oldsmobile. Entering through the back door and stepping into the kitchen, we paused, enchanted by the aroma of my grandmother's baked bread. Ona materialized in the open doorway on the other side of the room. She snapped, "What are you boys standing around for? The garden needs to be turned over and that gutter needs fixing again. You still have to work for a meal around here, you know!"

She could always make you smile.

"Yes, Ma'am," Dad said.

"Oh, skip the ma'am," Ona shot back, "and you both come over here and give me a hug. Then go make the garden."

While Ona prepared chicken salad, Dad and I used pitchforks and shovels to turn over the soil and mix humus and peat across the fifteen by twenty-five-foot remnant of the old prodigious garden. We straightened the stakes and chicken-wire fence that surrounded the garden, then cleaned off and stored the tools and headed back to the kitchen.

I was still mulling the news that Emilie had a boyfriend. Ona set out the food and a pitcher of lemonade, and in my silence, she filled us in on local news.

"You know the Wallmans' daughter got married again?" she began.

"Again?" Dad asked. "That number three?"

"Yep. And Lilly's old cow had a calf, and let's see, that Johnson boy's going to leave the farm and go to college. Plans on studying accounting or something."

"Accounting could be a little risky," Dad said. "Bell Labs and other places are working on calculating machines. They will do all the number crunching in the future."

"Ahhh yes," Ona said, looking over at me. "The scientists are going to change our world! Has my scientist figured out where thoughts and ideas come from yet?"

"I'm working on it," I replied. "But I just learned something from my friend John you might find interesting." Then, so my grandmother wouldn't think I was sulking, I gave her John's simplified explanation of entanglement. It had the desired effect, flummoxing her so I could excuse myself to get the fishing gear out of the shed behind the house. I turned to look at her as I walked out the back door. Her expression changed from puzzlement to understanding. I had the strangest feeling it was not that she suddenly grasped entanglement; it was that she *knew* what was on my mind. She smiled.

My father and I carried our rods and fishing gear through the woods on the hike to the river. The fragrance of spring's first flowers mixed with the smell of composting leaves and dead branches underfoot. My father didn't say much. I caught him staring at me off and on as if he suspected I'd been replaced with an imposter. Finally, he said, "Ona thinks you have a girlfriend. True?"

I tried not to look embarrassed or surprised, but my voice stuck in my throat and I choked out, "Nawh."

"You seem a bit preoccupied," he said. "You know, head in the clouds, more than usual."

"You've always said that was my problem, right?" I said, hoping this would make him feel guilty enough to stop the interrogation.

"What I meant was—Ahhh! Don't want to talk about it? That's OK." He gave a knowing smile, like Ona's. A smile that makes you want to apologize to yourself for once believing a fairytale.

Near the river bank, we took Ona's canoe from the neighbor's shed. It was a mutually beneficial arrangement. Ona's neighbor let her use the shed and launch the canoe from his property and Ona let him and his family use the canoe. I filled the bait box with worms. We pushed the boat into the water, hopped aboard, and paddled to our favorite spot, a deep-water area cradled within a curved finger of land. The water's surface was as still as the nearly soundless air.

Happy for a moment without thoughts of Emilie, I cast my line. The small sinker and hook entered the water with a "plunk." I watched expanding circular waves transform the smooth surface and I was transported back to the day when raindrops expended their lives creating beautiful interference patterns on this river.

I thought of John's explanation of the double slit experiment, his description of the paths particles travel, and the mysterious property of "entanglement." The similarity to brain behavior was striking: the tiniest particles apparently took their circumstances into consideration and picked, from a limited number of choices, where to go. Also, after interacting with each other, they become *entangled,* a shared existence. I felt a shared existence with my mother when she was alive. She changed my mental universe as I'm sure I changed hers. Was this an entanglement of sorts? I remembered another one of John's explanations about how matter and energy were just different forms of the same thing, one could be converted to the other. I wondered, *If two particles are entangled and one of them is converted into energy, what happens to the entanglement?* I thought of my mother. *Are we still entangled, Mom?*"

Dad broke the silence.

"Any luck?"

"No," I replied. Then added, "Do you think we'll ever see Mom again?"

I caught him off guard.

"You know what I think, Alan." Seconds later he continued, "But her memory is strong. Sometimes I almost feel her presence, like she's right next to me."

"Yeah, the same thing happens to me," I said. "Sometimes in dreams. You know, I was just thinking. There's like a similarity behind how brains and quantum particles behave."

"Oh boy." Dad grinned. "That sounds hefty."

"*Heavy,* Dad. We say, 'sounds heavy.'"

"Sorry, heavy. Are you going to explain that one, because I have no idea—?"

"OK. John said that in the double slit experiment a particle's interaction with its environment creates choices for where a particle can go. Same thing for us. The way our brains decide. We didn't have to fish today, and we didn't have to come to this spot. We had choices. If the canoe had a hole in it, if there were a thunderstorm today, we would have chosen to do something else."

"Hmmm. OK. Interesting," he said.

"There's something else. Particles become entangled once they've interacted with each other. There's a connection between them, even though that connection can't be detected. We're connected with people we interact with too. There's nothing physical attaching us, but our brain's get changed, and we're connected. Like us still having thoughts about Mom. It's a crazy idea I guess."

Dad said, "It's not a crazy idea. It's just strange there could be such an analogy."

"Here's what's got me. John said matter and energy are the same thing. What happens when one of two entangled particles is converted into energy? When one of the particles isn't really in *a place* anymore?"

He thought for a moment. "You're wondering what happens to a person's consciousness when they're gone? You've certainly come up with some interesting questions."

Despite our different ideas about religion and rocky past relationship, it was becoming harder to see my father as an adversary. He was actually being supportive. Our conversations were becoming more natural.

"I'd like to get John's opinion too," I said, reeling in my line, "but he might think I'm weird or dumb."

"You know Alan, plenty of people thought Einstein's ideas were weird at first, but nobody could think you're dumb, son. I think you should discuss this idea with John. You never know who can help you with the challenges that come your way. If anyone could help solve a tough mental problem it would be him."

*****

The information Bellcon collected from his informants helped him devise an ingenious plan. Luncheonette girl, he learned, was gutsy. He heard that she had lectured her history teacher that it was wrong to say that Hitler brought the Nazis to power. She had said, "The Nazi party succeeded in Germany because no one stood up to Hitler's band of bullies. They got more violent until they took over the country." Then there was the boy who enjoyed roughing up one of her classmates. At an assembly of the entire eighth grade, she confronted him with such a raucous tongue lashing that he publicly apologized. In one of the versions of this story something she had said stuck out in Bellcon's mind. She had said, "I'll never respect a bully or a boy who does not stand up to one." *That's the key*, he thought. *That's how I get close.*

He understood that she would not be attracted to him if he just beat up some rough neck. She'd likely conclude that he was a hooligan, and that would be the end of that. But he could use the girl's boyfriend, Andrew. Andrew would never confront a goon, even if he knew his best friend, Sam, was getting his ass kicked by one. So, the plan. Bellcon would have his right-hand man, Stanley, start something with Sam while Andrew and as many students as possible were around. It would have to be clear that Sam was going to be hurt badly. That should not be too hard to stage. Stanley was big and intimidating. Maybe he could bounce Sam off a few lockers before a hero, Bellcon, waltzed up, stopped Stanley from hurting Sam, and forced Stanley to apologize.

Maybe, he thought, almost laughing to himself, *I'll save his friend's ass and, with everyone standing around, I'll ask Andrew 'What's the matter with you? Why don't you stick up for your friend?' That oughta do it!*

The plan fit with rumors circulating through the school about how Bellcon helped kids in other towns with their bullies. He smiled to himself and thought, *When the girl with the strange eyes hears how spinelessly her boyfriend acted, and how I saved poor Sam, it might be the beginning of something exciting.* He knew he could not overplay his hand. He'd have to keep himself under control for a while and not appear to be violent or intimidating with the girl. He never understood why boys acted so gently towards girls, but he knew it was how he'd have to behave if he wanted a shot at this girl.

CHAPTER 22

April 20th, 1968, was a sunny Saturday. I stuffed the notebook I was keeping about consciousness and *Six Easy Pieces* into my rucksack, wondering if I'd see Emilie at the library. When I got downstairs for breakfast, the phone rang, my father answered, spoke briefly and hung up.

"Ada asked if we could drop off the book she left here a few months ago. She's going to college part time. Doing research for a class."

I finished a mouthful of cereal. "It's that big book on ancient Egypt. Yeah, I can bring it over on the way to the library," I said, trying to sound indifferent. Mixed emotions bounced my heart around in my chest. Elation for seeing Emilie combined with dejection because she had a boyfriend. The result was distress. I put the book in my backpack and rode over to Ada's.

Across the street from Ada's, parked at the curb, was a black 1957 Chevy with mag wheels and dual chrome tail pipes. Cool. I coasted past, slowly. The driver was waiting for someone. Blaring from the radio was the repeating refrain ending the Beatles' *All You Need Is Love*. By the time I got to Ada's door, I could hear the familiar guitar notes introducing *My Girl* by the Temptations. I rang the doorbell.

Despite steeling myself for the meeting, when Emilie opened the door, I felt as exposed and unprotected as a defendant taking the witness stand. I stood dumbly.

The Temptations serenaded behind us.

The outer rims of her irises were yellow-brown with minute threads of black and red. I held Ada's book and stared, barely aware that she had said hello and asked me to come in.

Ada appeared behind her. "Oh, hi, Alan. Thanks so much for bringing the book over. Tell Alan to come upstairs, Emilie."

"I did," Emilie said and smiled. She reached out, her hand touched my elbow, a gesture reinforcing the invitation. Warm electricity radiated up my arm.

Ada ushered us up the stairs of their split-level home to the kitchen. I set my backpack on the floor and took a seat at the large kitchen table. Emilie sat across from me.

Ada stood at the stove. "Would you like some coffee or tea?"

"Sure," I said.

Ada stood staring at me for a moment, then laughed briefly. "Ha-ha, which would you like, Alan, coffee or tea?"

"Oh. Either would be fine."

Ada smiled. I prayed it wasn't that *knowing* smile.

Emilie said, "I hope you don't mind my saying we miss your mother very much. Mom and I talk about her. Her wonderful stories."

"Thanks," I said, the trance broken by the reference to my mother. "Your family has some great stories too. How you guys almost didn't make it out of Egypt. And your grandparents. Fighting in that Resistance and hunted by the Nazis?"

"Yeah, my grandparents were something else. My grandmother would say, 'Fight evil when you first see it. Your family may not get another chance.' They were lucky to survive. But their tough times actually helped my dad get started in his business."

I was puzzled. "How could your grandparents help your dad when they were hiding from the Germans?"

"Because my dad's father had contacts. They got money from rich businessmen in nearby countries to help the Jews fight the Germans. My grandfather introduced my dad to some of those contacts in Great Britain and France. That's how Dad got started in banking."

"And then," I said, "you were all thrown out of Egypt."

"Yes, but when we got here, the big banks fought over Dad because of those contacts."

I said, "It's wild how your family moved around so much."

"Well, none of them really had a choice. You know, my family could have been wiped out before I was born. One of my aunts, an uncle, and grandfather," she nodded at Ada, "were killed in Nazi extermination camps."

I was shocked. Ada had never mentioned this. I recalled what my father had told me and what I had read about the Holocaust, but now I felt closer to it. *How was it possible?* I thought.

"Emilie," Ada interrupted, setting the tea and cups on the table, "this is Alan's first visit to our home. Maybe we can talk about something less troubling?"

I said, "No. Please. I'm very interested. My father was in a German P.O.W. camp and knew someone who went to a labor camp."

Now Ada and Emilie looked shocked. They turned to gape at one another, then looked at me.

"I never knew this," Ada said. "Marie never—"

"My dad never talked about it to me until recently," I added nervously. "I hope he won't mind I told you."

"We will not bring it up again unless Michael does," Ada said. She put her hand on Emilie's shoulder. "OK? Now, please excuse me, I have to tend to a few things." Ada left the kitchen.

I said, "That's terrible about your relatives. They called them *extermination* camps?"

"My father told me it started with a movement to strengthen societies by stopping the mentally and physically handicapped from reproducing. It happened in many countries. Sterilizing unfit parents even became legal in the U.S. for a while"

"Did you say in the U.S.?"

"Yep. For a time. The plan was dropped here and other places of course. But, in Germany the Nazis began putting undesirable children to death and took this idea to its most deplorable ends, exterminating inferior *races,* executing political opponents."

"What about the Jews? Why them?"

"Hmm, there's always a scapegoat, right?"

"So Hitler blamed the Jews? For what?"

Emilie said, "Losing World War I? Anything that went bad for Germans? My grandfather said it's human nature.

Most people want to be led by someone who they think shares their deepest feelings, who can make sense out of their misery and tell them what they have to do to have a great life or have a great country."

I still had a hard time understanding this. "But a country going along with building extermination camps and killing millions of innocent people?"

Emilie looked away for a second, then looked back at me. "We don't know what's in the back of people's minds. Our neighbors, our friends. When some group feels they're being taken advantage of, they can be turned against others. Once the killing starts, even people that don't want to hurt anyone, how far will they go to save themselves? Did you know the Nazis used some prisoners to help run the death camps? The *kapos*. They abused their own people."

I asked, "You think such a thing could happen here?"

"Yes. I think it could happen anywhere."

"But the Nazis lost," I said, proposing some virtue in humanity.

Emilie said, "But millions were put to death. Too many either stayed silent or followed the leaders, let the Nazis decide right and wrong for them."

"Huh, that sounds like something my friend John would say." It was so easy talking with her. I asked, "Do you believe in God?"

"Yes," she said without hesitation.

"But with all that's happened to your family, don't you think that God should have stopped the killing, all those good people, children, parents. Where's the justice?"

"I've thought a lot about that. It was hard to have faith with what happened to my family. I read about different religions. Now, I don't think of God as a person, someone separate from the world who can stop evil. I don't think it works that way."

I sat up straighter, "Yeah, I agree. That's my problem. What kind of God would allow extermination camps? How does it make sense?"

"I think God is in everything, everywhere," Emilie said. "The Eternal One was the beginning, the rules that created it all. The rules behind the changing universe."

"But how can such a Being not care about what happens to his creation? How could He allow such evil in His rules?"

"I don't think of God as 'Him'. The *rules* are God. The laws of nature. And, every stone, every star, every person is a part of God."

"But the rules allow evil?"

"One thing that was difficult for me to understand was, like my dad says, the price for free will is suffering. If God could stop people from doing evil, they would not have free will. Right? We can't be selfish children who want it all, free will and no suffering."

"So, God is...flawed?

"Perhaps *we* see the world as broken and imperfect. But people that do bad things have a choice, don't they? And we can build shelters against the weather, discover medicines to cure diseases. We can choose to fix the things we can or pout about the imperfections. Actually, I believe the imperfections make the world more perfect."

An instant memory echoed my father's words in the woods at Ona's, *Your mother used to say that the most perfect thing about the world was that it is imperfect.* My mouth dropped open. I was dizzy. I said, "That's... that's kinda what my mom thought."

Emilie smiled. "You know, Alan, we are all just a small piece of God. Our life was lent to us. Someday we'll have to give it back. But life is a precious gift, every moment, every breath."

"I never really thought of it that way," I said.

My conversation with Father Curtain, questioning God's existence, played back in my mind. Emilie had such a different point of view. Then I remembered something my mother had said years earlier. Rebuking Father Vinious, she had called Emilie my *soulmate*. At that time, I chose a righteous path. I self-exiled from Emilie, in pursuit of religious enlightenment. Now I knew that Emilie was also devoted to understanding God. All the time we were apart, she must have struggled with the same difficult questions that troubled me. How else could you explain her coherent answers? These were not explanations she was taught. It was clear that, like me, she must have agonized over every doubt this broken world threw at her. Yes, she was my *soulmate*. It should not have surprised me. My mother knew. Yet, like a register in John's computer, the binary flip from 0 to 1— from not recognizing to recognizing this invisible connection to Emilie — changed everything. I wanted to stay and ask more questions, but when Ada returned to the kitchen, I had the feeling that Emilie and Ada had their own plans for the day.

"I hope I didn't disturb your plans today," I said. "I'm sorry I asked so many questions. Just curious."

Emilie smiled. "You didn't upset our plans. It was really nice talking with you. I hope we do it again soon."

"Yeah, great talking to you too," I said. If she hadn't had a boyfriend, and if I hadn't felt so guilty about snubbing her for years, I think I would have given up any aspiration to become a priest right then and pursued her. Instead, I climbed on my bike and headed for the library.

In thirty minutes, Emilie had given me a lot to think about. One thing she said bothered me. "We can't be selfish children who want it all." I thought, *Was the free will of a drunk worth my mother's life? Is my father being childish rejecting the existence of God because he was exposed to the horrible evil that some people do to others? I don't think so. And yet, this girl, whose relatives were victims of those atrocities, thinks God shouldn't be blamed.* She had said, "The *rules* are God, the laws of nature." The laws of nature.

My father had said, "Science is all about explaining things *without* God." Had Emilie found a way to explain God with science?

I was almost at the library. The sun began to break through the clouds. I could *see* white and blue sky, green trees, scattered purple, pink and red blossoms. I *smelled* flowers, *felt* the cool breeze, *heard* birds and an occasional car rush by.

How, I wondered, am I aware of all this? What is consciousness?

CHAPTER 23

On Sunday I got to John's a little early and, as usual, John's parents ushered me down to the basement. Descending the steps, I heard someone playing a guitar. I recognized the tune—my mother had enjoyed playing it—*Take Five*.

Sitting on a folding chair with his back to the stairway, John faced a music stand. His hand moved up and down the neck of his guitar, which stuck out to one side. I listened and began clapping when John finished. John spun around and looked at me. His head tilted to one side and he looked up as if he had forgotten something. "It's only nine minutes to ten," he said.

I thought, *How the heck does he do that?* "Yeah, I'm a little early. That OK?"

John smiled. "Sure."

"I didn't know you played guitar. You're pretty good. Play some more."

John wiped off his guitar, put it back in its case and stored it in a closet. "I'll play for you and tell you how I helped build that guitar another time. Our congregation will be here soon."

"You built that guitar?" I asked, ready to be amazed at another one of John's accomplishments.

"Helped to build it," he said. "An old musician-carpenter from my home town did most of the work. He got me really interested in the lives of trees and the properties of wood."

"Cool. I'd like to hear that story. Can I ask your opinion about a crazy idea I had?"

John sat on the couch and motioned for me to sit on the easy chair. "Shoot," he said, resting his forearms on his thighs and leaning forward.

I told John how I thought the behavior of quantum particles and human brains had similarities; how, when each comes to a decision point, they have a limited number of choices that depend on their environments. I pointed out that in each case the decision-making process cannot be observed either.

"Suppose I'm an electron," I said, "traveling towards a barrier with two slits. I can't show up just anywhere on the other side. There are only certain spots I can choose to go on the detection board. You said there is no way for an observer to know which spot I'll choose. And, if you set up a monitor to see which of the two slits I went through, my choices are changed. So my choices, as an electron, are changed by conditions around me. Right?"

"I'll go along with that for now."

"Now let's do my brain. I want to go for a bike ride one morning. There are a number of places I could go. I imagine driving over to Tim's, to the ball field, to the lake at the park, or to Garrison Mountain. I consider the weather, traffic, maybe where else I want to go that day, and I choose a destination. My circumstances determine where I go, but an observer can't predict which one I'll choose, unless I tell them." I sat back, anxiously awaiting John's answer.

"Are you saying that a particle decides or knows where it's going?"

I laughed. "No, no. It's just that brains and quantum particles acting similar in some ways just seems odd."

John's dark brown eyes narrowed, and he appeared to look past me, to a place that I could not see. "Hmmm," he said, "I'll have to think about that."

At that moment, I had no idea that many years later John would have something very interesting to offer about this "crazy idea."

Tim arrived, followed by Hip. As we talked, I noticed the difference in Tim over the last few weeks. He seemed more confident. For the last month, he had not missed a Sunday at John's, and that morning Tim had skipped his Catholic Mass. He looked like he had grown an inch or two, put on a few pounds and developed visible muscles. His father must have noticed the difference too. Aside from Father Curtain's talk with Tim's dad, I guessed there would be no more beatings. I wondered, *Did Stephanie create this difference in him?* Tim seemed genuinely happy for the first time since I had known him.

I listened to Tim, Hip, and John discuss different historical figures who risked their lives teaching the truth in the midst of social repression. As church at John's wrapped up, Tim wanted to know if it could be moral to kill someone who you thought was doing evil things. I worried that Tim was toying with the idea of killing his father.

John straightened in his chair, squeezed his eyebrows together and turned his full attention to Tim. "Why are you asking this?"

Tim said, "Just thinking. If you get rid of someone who does terrible things, isn't it a good thing? I mean, there are Bible stories, seems like lots of killing, but then there's *Thou shalt not kill.* Maybe part of that commandment was lost. Maybe it was Thou shalt not kill *unless* someone's bad or something."

"It's hard for me to imagine a moral killing," John said. "But there will always be violence. I guess killers must accept responsibility for their acts, and the judgment of society. What do you think, Alan?"

The two of them looked at me. "What?" I said, turning up my palms. I had nothing to add.

John said, "Let's talk about this another time."

None of us knew what was on Tim's mind, but silently I imagined Tim's father was part of our imperfect world. Could I blame Tim if he got rid of the guy?

CHAPTER 24

In the few remaining weeks at St. Peter's school, most of us graduating had a sense of tribal loss. The schedule and social connections that ordered the last eight years of our lives was coming to an end. It would soon be time to shed one way of life for another. We were molting. The fear of change kept our cocoons intact, while summer jobs and the great unknown of high school life threatened to tear them apart.

Just before school ended, Father Curtain asked to see me. It was a brief conversation and not what I expected.

"This sad and exciting time," he began, "comes every year, though it is a little sadder and a little more exciting this year because I've had the privilege to teach and get to know you. You are an exceptional young man. I expect to hear great things about you. I understand you are going to Northern. It's an outstanding high school. I know your mother hoped you'd go there, and she'd be very proud. I hope you find the answers that you're looking for, and please know that I will always be here for you." He opened his arms.

I hugged him. "Thank you. I won't forget our talks. I'll be back to visit for sure."

"Good luck, son."

Graduation ceremonies passed uneventfully, though a rumor circulated that Mrs. Aemilia's husband had had an affair, and when she found out, she threw him out of the house and banned him from ever seeing his daughter again. I guessed she was inspired by the story John told on his first day of school. He had explained to the class that because of Lord Byron's infidelity, his wife banished her husband and never allowed him to see his daughter, the Countess of Lovelace. I could not help think that John's minor interaction with Ms. Aemilia must have influenced her, like the behavior of a quantum particle being changed by a small alteration in its surroundings.

The next week, Rich and I went with our dads to an open house orientation at Northern Catholic high school. We shuffled around recruiting tables in the gymnasium for various sports teams and numerous clubs. The coach and a few senior players at the football table waved me over. I liked football, but I was more drawn to one-on-one competition. Since the school did not offer boxing, I drifted over to the wrestling table. I signed up for wrestling and was given a packet detailing summer strength training exercises along with a fall practice schedule.

When I turned away from the wrestling table, I was intercepted by a tall young faculty member who had apparently overheard my name. He charged up to me and held out his hand.

"I'm Father MacKristin," he said, his brown eyes twinkling and his rolling "r's" and ghostly "t's" having lost a wee bit of their native Scottish distinction. He wore a blue and white checked collared shirt with dark blue slacks.

He caught my surprised expression. I shook his hand. "I'm Alan. Sorry, I've never seen a priest dressed, uh, in regular clothes."

"I haven't taken an oath to limit my wardrobe, na' have I?" Father MacKristin laughed. "You come highly recommended, and I understand we share a deep interest in science, correct?"

I guessed that Father MacKristin was a friend of Father Curtain's. I felt a bit disoriented and thought, *A priest that wears regular clothes and is interested in science? That's pretty cool!* "Yeah," I said, "I mean yes, sir. I mean yes, Father."

Father MacKristin made a short staccato hooting laugh. "I think we're going to have some interesting discussions you and me." He patted me on the shoulder and said, "See you in the fall, Alan," and skittered off into the flock of shepherdless new students.

In the hall outside the gym, I found the table I was looking for and signed up for Math club, hoping to glean information that might help me converse with John. Walking out to our cars, Rich and I compared notes. Rich had signed up for tennis and Band. We both received fall class schedules with a list of books we were expected to read over the summer. We left with our dads, a bit excited and a bit anxious.

*****

Bellcon's Sophomore year ended with a whimper. There were no parties, no congratulations, and no commendations for academic achievement. Even his football coach was lackluster, saying only, "Don't get flabby with your time off. See you in August." A few classmates made an effort to say goodbye to him and wish him luck over vacation. Bellcon could sense their fear but acted warmly toward each of them, wondering how they might be useful in his future plans. Over all though, he was not unhappy about his commitment for the next two months.

It was made very clear that if he did not pledge to spend the summer with his aunt Lyda and uncle Don, he could expect no further legal help from his father. He had no doubt where he'd be without his father's last plea deal. He promised his father he would stay in California with his aunt and uncle until the new school year began. His uncle Don was a cop in the LA police department. He offered to get his nephew a temporary job on a construction crew. Bellcon imagined that his uncle also offered to keep his nephew out of trouble.

He's a sadistic SOB, Bellcon thought, and smiled. He looked forward to the summer passing by quickly. *Who knows*, he thought, *maybe I'll find some fresh meat, and get lucky.*

CHAPTER 25

The biggest incident over the summer happened in August, with only two weeks until school started. The groundwork was laid as Tim and I were leaving Rich's basement. Stephanie called Tim aside. I told Tim I'd see him later and left the house.

Mounting my bike, I heard, "Alan, wait up." Tim jogged over and hopped on his bike. "Hey how 'bout a trip to Garrison on Saturday?"

"Yeah. Funny, I was going to ask you if you wanted to go."

We peddled down the street. Tim said, "We'll have company. Steph wanted to come and bring a friend who's never been there." He grinned.

"OK, that's cool."

"You know her, Emilie."

My foot slipped off the pedal and dragged on the street. My bike wobbled. It was only recently that I had tamed intrusive thoughts about Emilie, and now the certainty of seeing her sent a chill through me, like a tarantula just crawled down my shirt.

"Whoa! You OK?" Tim asked, laughing.

"Yeah, yeah. Fine. Just missed a pedal," I replied, feeling flushed.

"You sure you're OK with Emilie coming? I mean, you wanted to go out with her a while back, but I can tell Steph—"

"No, it'll be fine. We'll have a good time."

"Sure?" Tim asked.

"Yeah, come on, I just missed the pedal!"

"Fucking klutz." Tim laughed and turned towards his house. "See ya Saturday. Hey, maybe you can get Emilie to dump her dumb boyfriend. But ya better practice riding your bike!"

"Up yours."

Saturday morning I woke up early without an alarm and went to the window. The sky was clear with a few brush strokes of white. I put on jeans and a white and blue cross hatched collared shirt, grabbed my backpack and went downstairs for breakfast.

My father was making coffee. "You're up early on a Saturday. Nice shirt. Going somewhere?"

"Yeah," I said, filling a thermos with ice cubes and water. "We're riding to Garrison to go on some of the trails." I took out the peanut butter to make a few sandwiches to bring.

"Ah, then you'll need a big breakfast. How about some pancakes and eggs?"

"Great!"

"Who's going along?"

I put plates and utensils down on the table, sat down, and mumbled, "Oh, uh, Tim and a couple of friends."

"Ahh, OK," Dad said. He flipped a flapjack with that knowing, annoying smile. I walked outside to strap my lunch-filled backpack to my handlebars, then returned to wolf down breakfast.

Stephanie and Tim were sitting on her front steps, their bikes and back packs lying on the lawn when I rode up.

Within a minute, Emilie was riding up the street. A blue rope bag swayed on her back. She wore blue jeans and a black T-shirt with the word "Paris" embroidered in gold above her left breast. Her gilded irises reflected the morning sun.

"Hi, Steph, Tim. Hi, Alan," she said.

I tried to look apathetic, but I could tell from the look Tim gave me, with one corner of his mouth turned up, that I looked like an over excited puppy.

Tim said, "OK, let's get going then."

Tim and I led the way with Stephanie and Emilie close behind.

Tim was chatty. "You know I'm getting along good with Rich, like we're brothers. And Steph's parents are real nice. I mean, to me they're nice. Sometimes the two of them fight and all, but they're cool with me. Hey, Steph's taking a lifeguarding class, and the whole family is renting a house down the shore. They invited me to spend a weekend!"

I couldn't remember Tim ever looking this happy. "That's great," I said.

"Yesterday we were talking about high school," Tim said. "It'll be a little weird. I think you'll be a star at wrestling. Steph wants me to join the art club. I showed her one of my drawings. She thought it was really good."

My mouth popped open, briefly at a loss for any words. "You draw?"

"Yeah, sorta." Tim mumbled. "Listen don't tell anybody OK?"

"You scumbag, you never showed me any drawings!" I yelled. I stopped my bike and started laughing. The absurdity of Tim having a talent and wanting to keep it secret seemed funny.

Tim quickly pedaled over to me and grabbed me by the back of the shirt with his left hand. He raised his right fist. "Keep your voice *down* fuckhead! You better not tell!"

I turned and held up my hands to block any incoming punches. Now the two of us were laughing. We looked back at the girls who looked at us incredulously, shaking their heads as if to say "Boys! Who can figure them out?"

We were riding on the shoulder of a busy two-lane road. At a red light we switched positions. Tim and Stephanie took the lead; I dropped back to ride next to Emilie. The radio in the car next to us was blasting Frankie Valli's *Can't Take My Eyes Off of You.*

Emilie asked, "How long have you known Tim?"

"Since first grade. He always sat alone, never talked. I was curious. Wondered if he had some great secret." I laughed. "I would get next to him at recess and lunch. I talked. He listened."

Emilie asked, "Well, did he?"

"Did he what?"

"Did he have a great secret?" she asked playfully.

"Yeah, but I had no idea. While we were altar boys things got real bad and he told me."

"What do you mean?"

I pedaled more slowly, so the distance to Tim and Stephanie increased, putting them out of earshot. "Tim's dad is an alcoholic. He used to beat Tim a lot. I think he beat Tim's mom too."

"Oh my God," Emilie said, wide-eyed and looking horrified.

"Yeah, it was bad. On top of that some kids at school would pick on Tim, make fun of him, start fights. I tried to stop it. Then he tried to kill himself. Things got a lot better when Father Curtain talked to Tim and his father."

She looked towards Tim, shaking her head, her eyes large. She was quiet for a minute, as if she were trying to imagine the suffering Tim had experienced. "There's so much more to people than you see on the surface. Stephanie said Tim would do anything for you. No wonder you're such close friends."

We rode our bikes to the castle at the top of Garrison Mountain, then we decided to split up. Tim and Stephanie rode off on the east mountain trails. Emilie and I started down the west trails. We planned to meet on the large field at the bottom of the mountain.

"It's a beautiful day," Emilie remarked, looking overhead.

The sky was clear, the sun's brightness nearly painful. "Yeah. Look at the castle. It comes to life in the sun. I can imagine lookouts in the towers and the cavalry riding out to meet the enemy."

"Definitely," Emilie replied. "And this bike path, all these wild flowers, they're so pretty. Mom would love it up here."

"I think my mom would have liked it too," I said. "It's funny, but when we talked at your house you said a few things my mother would say. And some things John said. I'd like to talk with you more about them sometime."

"Sure. But who's this John person?"

We reached the foot of the mountain. "He's this genius in my school and we—" I looked up. On the field in the distance two boys were shoving Tim back and forth. Stephanie was standing about twenty feet away. She was yelling something at a third boy, who stood in front of her with his hands up, warding her off.

Emilie followed my glance to the field ahead. She said, "Oh my—"

I felt a jolt of electricity crackle over my skin, like a short circuit knocking out my rational thinking. Other than what was happening to Tim, the world dropped away. I began pedaling furiously. I saw one boy my size push Tim over another kid who was down on all fours. Tim tumbled hard to the ground. The kid stood up laughing. Then, Tim sprang up off the ground and landed a right-left combination across the kid's jaw, followed by a left uppercut to the ribs. Tim drew his arm back to land another punch, but the big kid spun him around and pummeled him across the neck, face, and shoulders. Tim fell to the ground again and the two boys began punching and kicking him.

I wasn't thinking I'd be one against three. All I could think of was Tim getting beaten his whole life, while I could do nothing. Until now. Everything came into sharp focus, my targets seemed to move more slowly. By the time I was forty feet away I had a plan. I swung my leg over the seat of my bike, dropped it, and hit the ground running. Using a strategy I learned from Lumps in Rich's basement gym, I sprinted directly at the big goon's back, who was focused on Tim. I called out, "Hey!"

The smaller of the two thugs looked up.

"Whadda *you* want?" he said.

I continued my charge at the big kid.

He turned. "You want something, asshole?" He threw up his hands to stop me. I crouched and delivered a hard right-handed blow to the boy's left rib cage. I felt a dull snap and heard the explosion of air from the boy's lungs. His hands dropped to guard his ribs and I laid him out with a quick right-left combination. The boy dropped to the ground, groaning. It happened so fast the other two boys looked dumbfounded for an instant. Then they rushed at me. I side-stepped, so the two boys were one behind the other. I pushed the lead attacker back hard. He crashed into his comrade, and they both fell to the ground. I reached down with my left hand, grabbed one of the boys by the shirt under his neck and yanked him off the ground, pounding his stomach with my right hand. I threw him on top of the larger boy, who was still holding his side and breathing erratically.

The third boy had gotten off the ground. He had pulled a long combat knife from a sheath hidden under his pant leg. My heart raced. Behind the boy, I glimpsed Tim getting to his feet. I could see the left side of Tim's face was swollen, and his left eye was shut. Blood trickled from his nose and mouth. I was going to warn Tim about the knife, but Tim lunged forward and slammed his right fist into the boy's right kidney. The boy twisted in pain, turning towards his assailant. Tim hit him with two quick hard rights, one to the throat the other smashing the boy's nose. We watched the boy fall to the ground. Tim was on top of him. "You wanna hurt the girls? Get up you fuck." He rolled the boy over, ready to pummel him.

For a moment I stood motionless. Tim's escalating aggression surprised me, but it was my own violence that I was trying to process. The instincts, which erupted from nowhere and propelled me into combat, began to dissipate. It seemed a fog was clearing from my head.

I looked down. "*Tim!* Hold up." We both stared at the combat knife, which was partly embedded in the boy's abdomen.

"Holy shit!" Tim shrieked.

The boy moaned and clutched the blade. I reached down and pulled out the knife, wiping the blood off on the kid's shirt. I put the knife in the backpack on my bike to keep it out of the hands of the other thugs.

The girls hadn't seen the knife. They were standing over the big kid and his smaller accomplice about twenty feet away, accosting them with a hail of verbal abuse. Red-faced and eyes blazing, Emilie scolded them, "It's just so stupid. You deserve what you got. And worse is coming if you keep doing this stuff. Grow up!"

The large boy got up on one knee, splinting his broken rib, "Ah, shut up," he spat. The smaller boy helped him up. They walked over to their friend who wobbled to his feet. For someone who had just been stabbed, he moved OK. Maybe the wound was more superficial than I thought. He held his throat and abdomen. In a panicked, raspy voice he began to shout, "*Look, look what they did!*" He lifted a red palm to show a patch of blood on his shirt.

The big kid's jaw dropped, his eyebrows shot up. "Damn. Come on. Gotta get you to the hospital!" They limped quickly towards the parking lot.

"Let's get the girls out of here," I said. Tim and I looked over at Emilie and Stephanie.

Stephanie was glaring at Tim, one hand pressed against her mouth, looking shocked.

Emilie's large eyes, aflame from the adrenaline of the moment, bore into me. "You should have let me handle this," she said.

What? Hadn't I just saved the day? Was she actually upset with me? I helped Tim back to his bike.

The four of us rode home. The girls led the way.

"Thanks, Alan, I owe you one," Tim said.

Trying to build my friend's confidence, I said, "I can't believe you attacked that jerk off with the knife!"

A crooked smile spread over Tim's swollen face. "I guess I got carried away. Can you believe he fell on it!"

"Aww, looked like he'll be OK to me." As we pedaled down the street, I took the knife out from my back pack and extended the handle to Tim. "Keep it to remember today."

Tim's pupils widened a little when he saw the size of the blade. He dropped it in his back pack. "Thanks. I didn't know he was holding a knife. I guess I woulda gone after that kid even if I saw it though."

"Dangerous," I said.

"Yeah, but I promised myself I'd never let my father hit me again. I'd kill him, or he'd have to kill me. And I guess that goes for anyone trying to hurt me, or my friends now. Maybe it was wrong, but it felt good hitting that kid. Sure felt better than being hit. You know, I think Steph's pissed off. Can you believe it!"

I said, "Yeah, I think Emilie's pissed off too. Girls. I can't figure them out. But they sure brought a shitstorm of insults down on those idiots. I think we should leave it to the girls next time, they could snap the minds of any asshole like a twig!" We laughed.

As we got closer to home, Tim and I rode up to Stephanie and Emilie.

Tim said, "I'm sorry about what happened. I'm gonna go home and put some ice on my face."

Stephanie looked at his battered face, and the crusted blood under his nose. "I wish you hadn't beat up that kid, but you had to defend yourself. I'm really angry at those kids who were hitting you. What's wrong with them? Come to my house. We have ice."

"And have your brother see me like this? Whoa, I'd never live it down. No thanks. Maybe we can hang out at the park tomorrow? I don't think I'll be going to Mass."

"Yeah, sure," Stephanie replied. "And thanks. I know you and Alan tried to protect us back there." She smiled.

"Tried?" Tim said. "I think we did a pretty damn good job. And," he looked at Emilie, "think what would have happened if *he* wasn't there." He pointed his thumb at me, and began to ride off towards his house.

Stephanie called out, "See you tomorrow?"

"Yeah, the park," Tim said. Then he said a loud goodbye to me and Emilie.

I was feeling down. I thought, *I've got no chance of getting together with Emilie now. She seems pissed off, like I'm some violent punk. And I was violent.*

I wondered where the untamed emotions, the rage that directed my actions, came from. I didn't know myself. I was unfamiliar with some of the forces that could take control of me, like the beast of arousal and fantasies I'd had about Emilie. I brooded. *Who am I kidding? I can't have Emilie. Could I even be a priest with these feelings, these temptations?* I attempted to start a conversation and get a better idea of what she was thinking. "I'm sorry about the way things turned out," I said.

"It wasn't your fault," she said. "If it wasn't for you, Tim would be worse off. I just don't like violence. But I guess it's another one of those opposites we have to accept in the world. Peace and violence, free will and suffering."

I couldn't tell if she was being complimentary or disapproving. We pulled up in front of Stephanie's house. It was getting near suppertime and each of us would be expected home.

I was pretty sure I no longer had any chance with Emilie. There was no need to be guarded, so I said, "Up until that fight, I had a really great time. I mean, it was one of the best days I ever had. Thanks."

I rode down the street and called back, "See ya Steph."

Stephanie was climbing her front steps. I heard her say, "Bye Alan."

If Emilie said anything, I didn't hear it.

CHAPTER 26

The next morning I lay in bed until nine a.m., staring out the window, watching white clouds drift by. I wondered what it meant that dark emotions could take control of me. How could I not understand myself? Was I an altar boy, touched by God, called to be a priest? A brute, unaware of what triggers might unleash a violent reaction? A lecherous teenager fantasizing about a girl? I hoped going to John's would clear my mind.

By the time I made it to the dining room, my father had finished breakfast and was nearly finished with the local Sunday newspaper. "Good morning," he said. "Eggs and potatoes or cereal?"

I sat down. "Eggs sound good."

Dad got up to get the eggs and the leftover potatoes from the fridge. "Hey, I read in the paper that some police officer's kid was stabbed at Garrison Mountain yesterday. Did you hear about it?"

I froze. Guilt drawn over my face. "Uh, well, I know something happened up there. What does it say in the papers?"

"Apparently the boy who was stabbed had to go to a hospital. They're asking for any witnesses and doing an investigation."

I gulped. "Did they say what the boys were doing?"

"Said the boys were just walking through the park and got jumped. They gave police a description of the assailants. You and your friends be careful. There are hoodlums at large!"

I thought, *Damn! They jumped us! That knucklehead fell on his own knife.* I didn't think of going to the police at the time. There was no question who the bad guys were. Now I was glad we didn't. The kid's father was a cop! You think he would have believed us? Even the newspapers were making *us* out to be the criminals. If we went to the police now, they would ask why we didn't go earlier, and the stabbed boy's father would probably stick up for his son. The girls didn't see the kid fall on his knife. If they were questioned, could they say for sure that Tim didn't stab that kid? They just knew we were violent that day.

I decided to let it go. Soon this story would probably be forgotten. I made a mental note to tell Tim and the girls not to go anywhere near Garrison Mountain for the rest of the summer. I'd advise Tim to stay out of the public eye too, at least until his face healed.

I got to John's around ten a.m. He was out with his dad, but Claudette, John's mom, assured me he'd be back shortly. She invited me in and set out chocolate-chip cookies on the kitchen table. "Please help yourself. Would you like coffee or milk?"

I looked up into the familiar round face and dark eyes, the black hair with threads of gray that curled at her shoulders. "Thanks! Milk would be fine."

She delivered the glass of milk and sat across from me. "I never really had a chance to tell you how sorry Joseph and I were to hear about your mother. All we hear about in town is what a wonderful person she was."

"Thanks," I said, looking at the floor for something else to talk about.

"You know, Alan, we're so happy that you and your friends hit it off with John. Not everyone understands him."

"I imagine not." I laughed. "He's so smart. We don't understand a lot of things he talks about either."

"That's not quite what I mean. You might think that being exceptionally bright is a precious gift, and it is. But like many good things it comes with a price. John is different in other ways too. Where we came from a group of boys played some horrible tricks on John. Even while we were packing to leave, they—" she paused and stared past me, her bottom lip almost quivered. "If my husband hadn't stopped them, I don't know what—" She stopped abruptly as if something she knew took her breath away.

Claudette's expression was testimony that her son had suffered. I couldn't imagine a group of people wanting to hurt John. Why? Then the lesson John often repeated, what our congregation called his first commandment, came to mind: *Don't blindly accept what others tell you is right or wrong.* I wasn't sure what happened to John or why, but I thought about how Tim had been bullied in school and beat up on the mountain. I imagined John being beaten and felt nauseated. To erase the image I said, "John is my friend."

"And he likes you and your friends," she said. "You are all unusual. Special. You appreciate John and his gift. If it wasn't for you, I don't know how John would have been treated here. Because of you he's been accepted."

I was mystified. "Why wouldn't he be? The kid's amazing."

Claudette's tone became more urgent. She spoke rapidly. "Please think about this conversation before sharing it. I feel I can tell you—"

We heard car doors closing and voices approaching. The front door opened and in walked John, his dad, Joseph, and Hip. John gave his mother a serious look. Some unspoken warning passed between them.

Joseph put his arm on Hip's shoulder. "Look who we found in the driveway."

Claudette shooed us downstairs.

We took up our usual positions in the basement. Claudette sent Lenny down with the cookies. He set the bowl on the coffee table, took two, and ran upstairs.

The conversation weaved through a number of topics. I said nothing about what had happened at Garrison Mountain, or about the story Claudette left unfinished.

Near the end of our Sunday service, John resurrected a moral question. "What about Tim's old question? Do you think it could ever be right to kill someone?"

"Sure." Hip leaned forward. "Someone's about to kill you, you kill 'em first, right?"

"The guys in Vietnam are put in that situation." I agreed. "Either you and your guys get killed or you kill the enemy."

"Ah yes, war." John said. "So, if you're ordered to kill by superior officers, it's OK?" Hip and I looked at one another, uncomfortable.

I wondered, What's he getting at? Does he know something about Garrison, or does this have to do with what Claudette was trying to tell me? "I'm not a killer if I'm defending myself," I said, "and in a war, you're trying to defend a whole society,"

"True. But what if you don't believe the war is just?" John asked.

"Kids burn draft cards," Hip said.

John said, "Isn't it good to know there are people who decide for themselves that doing something is wrong, and would rather go to jail than do it because everyone else thinks it's right?"

"What if you believe the war *is* just?" I asked. "And what if someone on the street tries to kill you or your friend?"

"Yes," John said. "I think there is more to this answer. Let's discuss it when Tim's here next time."

I wanted to know why he brought up this question, but I got the impression it had nothing to do with what happened on Garrison Mountain. I decided to wait and hear what he had to say at our next meeting.

*****

Frank Bellcon arrived early in the morning at the Forum diner. It was hot, even for late August. He sat in a booth, waiting for officer Dunnard, enjoying the air conditioning. Confident that he would not be recognized so far from Forrest Creek, he sipped his coffee and indulged himself reminiscing, savoring each stratagem that empowered him in his new community. *I'm just better than the pack*, he thought. A scene played out in his memory from law school. A group of young law students reviewed the case of an oil magnate who murdered his daughter. Frank demonstrated a brilliant ability to distort facts and twist the legal system to exonerate the client. A woman in the group seemed disturbed.

"How do you justify these tactics?" she demanded.

"What *tactics*? This is a winning defense," Frank bragged.

"He murdered his daughter. You've muddled the facts, and these loop holes—"

"If I got the case, this is how it would go. I'd win. Doesn't the client deserve the best defense? Look, his daughter is dead. No one can bring her back. Maybe what he did was justified. Besides, winning cases, making friends in high places, that's how you're successful in this business, right?" He thought this formula for success was obvious to everyone, until he saw the look of horror on the woman's face. It was one of many reminders in his life that he was different. For some time he had struggled to understand other people, but eventually he became adept at delivering the empathetic reasoning they wanted to hear.

He consorted with people he could depend on. He had no use for friends; he needed allies. He did not want to be liked; he would rather be feared. *Yes*, he thought, *my son and I are alike. But he is young and needs to learn that using physical strength to get what he wants, if he doesn't have money and allegiance, is careless. He needs to be refined, to learn finesse.*

Frank thought of how his strategies had earned him a formidable reputation. His name circulated through the cabal of the wealthy, the upper echelons of government, and the halls of law enforcement. He was invited to golf with two judges in his county's criminal division and the captain of the Forrest Creek police force. Frank was just thinking about the police force captain when an officer walked up to the booth. As Frank had requested, a waitress set a cup of coffee in front of the officer as soon as he sat down. The two men ordered breakfast without looking at the menus. They made small talk until their plates arrived, then they ate slowly and talked quietly.

Officer Dunnard looked up from his coffee. "So you think she's just gonna roll over and play dead, huh?" His moist metallic eyes, square face and muscular neck complemented his flinty don't-bullshit-me voice.

Frank stared back, unblinking. "You'll have what you want," he answered, "a clean break, half custody of the kids, and she won't ask for alimony or a part of your pension. You only have to buy out her half of the house. If you don't believe it, why don't you check with that hotshot divorce lawyer I got for you? He's probably drawing up the papers as we speak."

Dunnard looked out the window. "I don't get it. She was gonna take everything I got. Get me kicked off the force for drinking. 'I'm gonna tear your heart out and feed it to the fishes.' Those were her words. Now I get what I want? Why?"

Frank said, "Maybe she forgives you, and wants to move on."

The cop gave a laugh that was more like a smoker's cough. "Maggie? Yeah, right. If she wants your ass, she don't stop. And she don't forget nothin', nothin'."

Frank did not want Dunnard trying to figure this one out, so he offered him a reasonable explanation. "Look, you agree it didn't work out with Maggie. You both have tempers and you're a bad drunk. That last love tap you gave her settled matters. She was understandably pissed off and said some harsh things. Now she's cooled off. She knows she'll be rid of you. She's a nurse, has a good job. She's young. She'll do OK. She'll stay in the house and be with her kids a good bit. Why should she try to fuck up your life and then always be looking over her shoulder for revenge to catch up to her?"

Frank didn't tell Dunnard the real story. How he found out that Maggie was having an affair with the mayor of Forrest Creek. He didn't mention how he couched the officer's divorce stipulations as a non-threatening appeal to Maggie. "You really don't want the mayor to be subject to an ethics investigation, disgraced and thrown out of office, do you?" Why should he tell the policeman now? This tidbit of information could be more valuable in the future. Besides, Dunnard now looked happy with the explanation Frank gave him.

"Yeah, I was already planning payback for the little lady." He smiled meanly.

"So," Frank continued, "you can get on with your life. No worries."

The cop's face relaxed. "Thanks, I don't know how you did it, but I owe you one."

Now Frank allowed his mouth to form a subtle smile. "Well officer, funny you should offer. There is a matter you may be able to help me with. You remember those kids that were assaulted at Garrison Mountain?"

"Yeah." Dunnard said, "One got stabbed. Had surgery, but lived. I know his dad. Garrison P.D. You know somethin'?"

"I've been informed that the town is investigating the crime. Somehow, they got the idea my son may have been involved. Probably because they heard he was a good fighter, and whoever assaulted those kids was good with his fists. It wasn't my son."

"It's not my jurisdiction. I mean, how would I help?"

"I thought you'd have contacts in that town," Frank said and smiled broadly, "and here you say you even know the victim's father. Find out what they know. Get me a few key people I can contact. Think you can do that?" Frank said in a challenging tone.

"Yeah, sure. I'll see what I can come up with."

"Thank you, officer," Frank said, standing up. He shook Dunnard's hand, looked at his watch and said, "If you'll excuse me. I'm late for my next appointment."

His next meeting was with a school board member. From the story Frank heard, without the proper defense,

the board member risked fines and prison time for embez-
zlement. *After all*, Frank thought, *he **is** guilty. But what's a
little thing like guilt among friends?*

CHAPTER 27

Other than the Garrison altercation, our summer vacations went by uneventfully.

John's family had worked out an accommodation with a private high school in New York called "Triune Academy." John would be shuttled between high school and Princeton University for two years and receive a high school degree. He'd spend another two years at Princeton to receive his college degree. Both schools offered him scholarships, which was important since his parents could not afford to pay for his education. John told me that he would be home on weekends and hoped that we could continue to get together.

Tim picked up a second newspaper route to make more money. He had heard about a self-defense class opening in town and joined for a membership fee that drained half of his earnings. Our boxing workouts in Rich's gym faded into childhood memories.

Rich and I talked and hung out more often. We started a program to prepare for high school sports. Early in the morning, twice a week, we climbed into Rich's father's yellow Volkswagen beetle and drove to the tennis courts at the township park. Rich gave me some brief lessons on how to fire hard serves and place return shots to catch him out of position. It took a few weeks, but I became a pretty good practice partner.

Rich also helped me with an exercise I invented. I had heard that many wrestlers had losing first seasons. I didn't plan on being one of them. I read in a library book that strong legs and back muscles were the key to a wrestler's success. So, I asked Ona to fashion a harness vest out of some old wide leather belts and showed her how I wanted a metal chain and quick links attached.

"Whatever are you going to do with this?" she asked.

I told her, "It's going to help me wrestle." She just shook her head, baffled.

I would strap on the vest, then Rich and I would fasten heavy ropes to the chain links. The other ends of the ropes were tied to the Beetle's front axle. With Rich sitting in the driver's seat, the engine turned off and the car in neutral, I pulled the car through a nearly empty parking lot, while Rich egged me on. "Mush, mush, little doggie. Come on, pull, or you'll get your weak butt pinned!"

Each session I pulled the car as far as I could. Over the course of the summer my back muscles strengthened. Rich said my legs became visibly larger.

One afternoon following our workout, I confided in Rich: "You know your sister's friend Emilie?"

Rich shot a sly look at me, "Yeah, 'member you brought her over to meet my sister and stopped me from introducing myself? I would've liked to suck faces with that one. I asked her out once. Turned me down. Believe that?" He gave a snort through his nose, annoyed.

My eyebrows went up. "You asked her out?"

"Yeah, what's that look for? What, am I too fucking ugly for her? Bet I could'a talked her into it, but—"

"But what?"

Rich frowned. "Steph told her I was 'dangerous.' Dangerous! Me?" Rich laughed. "So what? I messed around with a coupla girls in her class. They loved it! That makes me a danger to society? Plus, Emilie's got some weasel-faced high school douche bag intellectual that she's into."

"What did Emilie say when you asked her out?"

Rich looked annoyed. "Hey, Alan, which one's the good ear? This one?" He raised his voice. "*No!* she said no!"

"OK, I get it." I smiled. "But it's my turn. I've got it bad, man. I can't get her out of my head. I've never felt this way about a girl. I don't know what to do."

Rich saw I was smitten. I knew he was familiar with the look. He had helped some of our friends get past the objects of their intense adolescent desires. Over the summer, we had several discussions about Emilie. Rich turned out to be a good sounding board. One day he summarized his advice: "She's got a boyfriend right now. So get over it." He pointed to the horizon. "Do you know how many girls are out there. For chrissake, Alan, the Sacred Sacrament Academy is just down the road from our school. I'll introduce you to some great girls."

"You know some already?" I asked.

Rich laughed. "Not yet, brother, but I will after the bonfire dance mixer. It's only a few weeks away."

*****

Bellcon returned from California. It had been a very satisfying summer vacation. The swollen bruise under his left eye was still healing, but his fight with a tough construction worker had its rewards.

He had met his co-worker's daughter and niece at a union picnic. The impressionable teens were charmed by the muscular handsome stranger who explained that his father sent him to California because he had been a "bad boy." Lavished with his attention for a few days, the girls felt special. So naturally they couldn't resist the rebellious thrill that came when Bellcon asked them to meet him at a nearby deserted building and try a little cocaine he had snatched from one of his uncle's drug busts. The girls supposed it was part of the fun when Bellcon snapped pictures of them doing a few lines and acting silly. They seemed a little suspicious when the boy said they were going to play a game, and he hand-cuffed one of them to an old desk. He held up the camera and explained to the girls that they would do everything that he wanted, or the LAPD and their families would find out they were on illegal drugs.

Bellcon had pleasured himself, having his way with them for an entire month. Then one of the terrified girls ratted him out. Payback came from the stone hands of a construction worker who was also an angry father. His co-worker apparently thought justice would be better extracted from Bellcon personally, rather than notifying the police department served by the boy's uncle. Bellcon acknowledged the guy was tough, but he absorbed his punishment and doled some out too.

Anyway, he thought, it's over, and there's no arrest or police record.

Bellcon went back to school to begin another football season. For a while he would have to be satisfied intimidating the opposing players. When the schedule ended, he knew he would need a new diversion, and he knew exactly who that diversion would be.

CHAPTER 28

O nce we began high school, Rich and I lost touch with our other friends. Taking the late bus home one evening in September, because Rich had band practice and I had math club, Rich said, "Damn, I'm hungry. Can you believe all this fucking homework? I'll probably miss Johnny Carson!"

I smiled. "You work so slow you'll probably miss the bus in the morning!"

"Good one," Rich said. "I'll laugh when I think about how you get ready to do your homework, by taking an enema to get your head out of your ass."

I was actually enjoying my classes. Maybe I'm part nerd, but the teachers made advanced math and advanced biology fun, using bizarre stories to illustrate principles and giving us weird problems to solve. The best class, though, was Father MacKristin's *Science and Religion*. He was very cool. From the first day, the priest challenged all his students.

"We're going to explore how science and religion might be related," he had said. "I want each of you to think about whether science supports or refutes the existence of God. Make the strongest case you can in a two-page paper that will be due in two weeks. Then for the rest of the term you'll research and write a twenty to thirty-page paper backing up or tearing down your original idea. OK?"

In class over the next two weeks, he randomly selected students from around the room, firing questions at them, making them think, making them uncomfortable.

"Miracles? Do they show God exists?" he tested us. "Some great magicians can saw people in half, make them disappear. Could people in the past have been deceived? Are Bible descriptions just poetic fictional accounts of unusual weather or unusual outcomes based on chance, lads?"

Eventually, my classmates came to an unspoken understanding that science, which relies on observation and reproducibility, could not prove that God exists. Their discussion led them to conclude that, as a *spiritual* being, God would not have a physical manifestation. So He could not be observed. And God could not be manipulated. Even if He could, He certainly did not have to respond to experiments in any consistent way. It boiled down to: there was nothing observable or reproducible to test scientifically. That left any possible "proof" of God's existence to rely solely on unpredictable and inexplicable events. Which, it could be argued, "proved" nothing.

For two weeks, Father MacKristin had let me be an observer, absorbing the discussions and, I suspected, allowing me to form some opinions. Then, one day, he pointed at me. "What do you think, Alan? Can science lead us to God?"

I had known all along what I thought. The classroom deliberations simply made me more certain. I said confidently, "Consciousness can."

"What?" the casually dressed cleric asked, with creases deepening between his eyebrows. "What do you mean?" I said, "The key is consciousness. Without consciousness there is no omniscience and without omniscience there is no God."

It was a simple enough statement, but the priest seemed momentarily at a loss.

"We're trying to enlist science in our inquiry. There is na' scientific explanation for consciousness, is there now?"

"Exactly," I answered.

Father MacKristin grunted a laugh and said, "You're going to find a scientific explanation for consciousness? Consciousness has perplexed thinkers for thousands of years. Is that your approach?" Some of the other boys in the class snickered.

I think my face darkened and my eyes radiated a brighter blue, as my mother's eyes did when she was provoked. "Someone has to try," I said firmly. "It's one of the most reproducible experiments I know. Every evening I fall asleep, I become unconscious, and when I wake up, I'm conscious again. There must be a scientific explanation."

The teacher looked thoughtful, he began to say something, stopped, then said seriously, "You know, Alan, I think you're onto something. You just may be the guy who figures this mystery out!"

My classmates looked more impressed with my ideas after the priest's face-saving remark. A bell rang signaling a change in classes. Father MacKristin walked over to me. "Son," he said quietly, "the more I think about it, the more I like your approach. Dinnae give up."

Nearly all students at Northern Catholic, and students at other high schools from miles around, were excited about our bonfire dance mixer that kicked off the football season. There were enough tickets for all interested N.C. students and girls from the Sacred Sacrament Academy. The pecking order to obtain any surplus tickets filtered down through senior classmates, who snapped them up for their friends. This year the demand for tickets was at fever pitch, because it leaked out that there would be a battle of three well known bands. Hip, Tim and Stephanie were dying to go to this musical event, but the dance was sold out.

In preparation for this exclusive event, about thirty of our juniors and seniors formed the "Zoomers Bonfire Committee." I have no idea where that name originated, but their planning and hard work became evident the night of the dance, on the Saturday before our first game. The Zoomers had used trucks, wheelbarrows and their bare hands to transport tinder. They collected dead wood from the forest surrounding the school, donated firewood, old furniture and discarded wooden building materials to a vacant lot next to the football field. They piled it all into a fifteen-foot-high pyramid and set it on fire. The heat and light from the fire thrilled the Northern Catholic Lions (our nickname). We cheered, sang our fight song, and shouted various chants to galvanize the football team.

When the fire died down, one of the seniors, acting as a sentry, opened the school gym's backdoor and the lucky ticket holders streamed in.

Once inside, I saw that the Zoomers had transformed the darkened gym for the dance. They had collapsed the telescopic bleachers against the walls and placed accent and strobe lights on top. The lights washed the band area with changing colors, and flickered on the dance floor at random times, making the audience appear to be a sloweddown, eight-millimeter movie projection.

At the end of the gym, the bands had constructed three small stages, each equipped with a drum set and mic stands. Above the stages, they'd hung banners with each band's name: *Bit of Soul, Lighter Side of Darkness,* and *Solid Fuel.*

Enthusiastic adolescents filled the room, encircling some invisible boundary in front of the bands that left an open area for dancing. The din of a hundred conversations, the closeness of strangers, and the dizzying fragrance of miscalculated perfume and cologne was nearly overwhelming. The first band began to play, and the crowd's energy synchronized into a pulsating force.

Rich's eye was drawn to two pretty brunettes having an animated discussion.

"Hey," he said, "let me introduce you to some chicks."

I followed his gaze. "You know those girls?"

"Just come on, and don't say anything until I say your name, OK?"

I smiled, nodded, and thought, *Oh, this oughta be good.*

When Rich stood near the girls, he turned to me and, speaking loudly over the music, went into a monologue. I said nothing. "What?" Rich began, "you think she would? But if I ask her, she might just say yes because she knows who I am—What? —Of course she knows. All the high school kids recognize me." The girls could not help but overhear Rich. They were trying to figure out what exactly was going on when they heard Rich say, "She looks pretty cool, I'm going to ask her." He turned to face one of the girls, "Hi! Hey look, I know it may seem kind of forward, I mean I don't know you, but you look great and, well, let's dance! What do you say?"

The girl he spoke to smiled and shook her head. "Who are you?" she asked, looking at her friend for help. But her friend just laughed.

Rich feigned great relief. "You guys don't know me?" He turned to me, smiled and made a thumbs up sign, then turned back to the girls and said, "That's OK, in fact that's great! I'm Rich, and this is Alan." I smiled and said hi. Rich's happy-go-lucky demeanor seemed to be winning the girls over.

The gym began to vibrate to Bit of Soul's upbeat version of *Good Lovin'* by the Young Rascals.

"Come on, this song's great. Let's have some fun!" Rich exclaimed. To my surprise the girls smiled and followed Rich out onto the dance floor.

An alarm sounded in my mind: *Wait, I can't dance!* There was no time to panic. I followed Rich and the girls out on the dance floor and tried to imitate what the other boys were doing. It was obvious that I was a novice at dancing, but my partner seemed to find it funny and she started a conversation. "Your friend is crazy!" she said, laughing.

"Doesn't take that long to figure out, does it?" I said.

Slowly I relaxed, and my movements felt more in sync with the music. I noticed that most of the boys on the dance floor were doing more talking than dancing. This was especially true of Rich, who was pointing to various people in the gym and apparently joking with his partner. She was laughing to the point where she finally put one hand on Rich's shoulder and, unable to speak, wagged the other hand in front of his face, gesturing for him to stop.

When *Good Lovin'* ended, Solid Fuel immediately started to play *Do You Love Me* by The Contours.

No one left the dance floor.

By the end of the night, the pretty brunette offered me her name and phone number scribbled on a small scrap of paper. Rich had three phone numbers.

"See," Rich said as his dad drove us home, "there are lots of girls out there."

I had to admit the experience took my mind off Emilie. But when I got home my thoughts stubbornly returned to her. Those occasionally golden irises burned in my memory as though I had stared at the sun and now could not block out the image, even after closing my eyes.

As I walked into my house, the scrap of paper seemed to get heavy in my hand. I went into the kitchen and dropped it in a waste basket.

CHAPTER 29

By October there was a chill in the air. The green horizon had become a frosted tinge of yellow and orange set against a gray sky. I sorely missed socializing with some of my Forrest Creek friends, and, despite my efforts, I continued thinking about Emilie. Fortunately, my free time became more limited once wrestling practice began and "the boys," as John's mom called us, agreed to restart our Sunday morning meetings.

John's parents were delighted to see us back, and when they knew John's friends were coming over, they'd set out a tray of fresh bagels and doughnuts, which we devoured over several hours of energetic discussions. "Breakfast at John's" became our new moniker. The get-togethers were planned once or twice a month, the agenda was revitalized, and Hip brought his guitar. Sometimes Hip and John would play together.

Secluded in John's basement we talked more freely about girls, girlfriends, or our failure to strike up a relationship with someone we liked. At one meeting I even mentioned my continued interest in Emilie. That motivated Tim, and every weekend he'd invite me to the Forrest Creek Hawks' football game. "Emilie will be there," he would say, tempting me.

"Yeah, with Andy," I'd reply with resignation.

At one meeting in early November Tim's gossip gave me some hope, and a song Hip played changed the way I'd been thinking about Emilie.

Tim said, "Last time Steph and I went out with Andrew and Emilie they were arguing the whole time."

"Really?" I asked.

"Yeah. Andrew was talking about going to some law school in California. Said he'd get rich off wealthy people getting divorced because you could really milk people who are angry at one another. Boy, did that bug Emilie!"

"What did she say?"

"Haha, she looked like she was gonna puke on him. She said, 'You'd do more good in the world if you were a suppository!'"

I laughed.

Tim continued, "She told Andrew she thought about law school too. She wanted to defend the poor and volunteer in a third world country."

"Wow," I said, "that's Emilie. Doesn't sound like they've got much in common."

Later that meeting, Hip began strumming "I Will" by the Beatles. John picked up his guitar and used a glass cigar tube to improvise a slide guitar accompaniment. Hip began to sing, his practiced pitch sounded a bit like Paul McCartney.

As I listened to the words, I decided I had been foolish. Yes, I'd been violent on Garrison Mountain; yes, I had sexual fantasies about Emilie; and yes, Emilie did choose to date Andrew. So what? My violence only countered the violence of others, it accomplished something good.

Without the violent response of the Allies, could the Nazi's have been stopped? And the carnal fantasies? Rich said they were normal, and I found that practically every boy I talked to had them. Besides, my feelings for Emilie went far beyond physical attraction. Weighing all these factors, Tim's gossip and Hip's song tipped the balance, and I decided that honoring Emilie's decision to date Andrew did not mean I had to be passive. *If she got to know me better,* I thought, *maybe she'd see I'd be the best guy for her. Her soulmate.*

When we adjourned, I told Tim I'd be at the Hawks' last football game on Saturday.

On Saturday morning, I rolled out of bed and looked out the window. Wispy clouds rode over an autumn lace of trees.

I showed up at the coin toss and spotted Tim and Stephanie sitting behind the Hawks" team bench around the forty yard-line. Steph saw me and waved for me to come over. Climbing the stadium steps, I saw Emilie sitting about eight rows above Tim. She was wearing a bright blue baseball cap and a tan sweat shirt. I was a little disappointed to see her sitting so far away from Tim and Steph, but excited to see her for the first time in weeks. Above the cacophony, someone's transistor pocket radio was playing the Soul Survivor's *Expressway to Your Heart.*

"Hey man glad you came," Tim said.

"Yeah," said Stephanie, "we've got a plan for you to meet with—" She jabbed her thumb towards Emilie.

Tim added, "She always gets something from the concession stand at halftime. We'll go up, I'll introduce you to Androdoodle and say we're going to get some drinks and stuff. We'll offer to get them something."

I rolled my eyes. "OK, cool."

"Don't worry," Tim laughed, "she's probably praying that you'll come over." Tim looked over his shoulder towards Emilie and Andrew. "I don't know what she sees in that drip."

Steph said, "Shhhh!"

"What's this game lookin' like?" I said, changing the subject.

"Oh, the Knights," Tim replied, "we should beat 'em. But someone said their offense has some plays to get past our middle linebacker, who's a real brute."

I looked over at the Hawks'' bench. "I heard you guys had some crazy linebacker. Which one is he?"

"One of the team captains, number fifty-one, Bellcon, right there." Tim pointed.

"Big fella," I observed, watching the team captains jog out to the center of the field.

At the end of the first quarter the score was 0-0. I could see how the big linebacker got his reputation. His collisions with other players could be heard in the stands. He was fast, powerful, and untiring. The Knights were sending two offensive players to block number fifty-one on every play. It worked about one out of five times. The other four times I watched the big team captain dodge the blocks or just run through a blocker to flatten a running back or sack the quarterback.

When number fifty-one flattened a tight end with a signature punishing tackle, I said to Tim, "That's how I want to wrestle."

"Be like Bellcon?" Tim asked. "Watch what you wish for. I hear he's pretty weird."

"Weird?" I asked.

"Yeah. Like he beats up kids. No one knows where he came from, and he stays to himself. Only hangs out with one of the other football players who's a big jerk off."

"Yeah," Stephanie chimed in, speaking softly. "I heard he was forced to leave wherever he came from. He might have raped a girl somewhere, or killed someone!"

I squinted and looked back out on the field.

Tim interrupted Stephanie. "Those are just rumors, Steph."

I asked, "He beats up kids?" My thoughts going back to Garrison Mountain.

"Yeah," Tim said, "but the strange thing is, he only beats up bullies."

"Whaaat?" I exclaimed. "That doesn't add up."

At halftime the Hawks were winning 8-3. Their fullback had rammed the ball into the Knights'' end zone from three yards out, and they had made a two-point conversion.

Tim grabbed my elbow. "Come on, let's go see what Emilie wants." We started our way up the stands. When we reached their aisle, Tim introduced me to Emilie's boyfriend. "Hi, Em, Hey, Andrew. This is Alan, the traitor who left Forrest Creek for Northern Catholic." He threw his head back with an exaggerated laugh, and I jostled him around jokingly.

"Hi Andrew," I said and reached my hand out. We shook hands and I thought, *Enjoy your time with Emilie, it won't last much longer.* Emilie smiled, and my heart skipped a beat. I heard Tim say, "You guys want anything? We're gonna get some hot dogs."

Andrew said "No thanks," and moved closer to his girl-friend.

Emilie replied, "That's thoughtful. I'd like a pretzel and a coke please." She began to reach for her money.

I touched her arm. "No problem," I said, "we'll be right back."

As we turned to head back down the bleachers, I saw Bellcon staring at Emilie. Something about that look made my back and shoulders tighten, my heart rumble a little in my chest. Stephanie's words set off a silent alarm. *He might have raped a girl somewhere, or killed someone!* The alert triggered a memory: Emilie repeating her grand-mother's admonition, *Fight evil when you first see it; your family may not get another chance.* Emilie was not family, but she might as well have been. Despite having seen the linebacker destroy his enemies on the football field, the urge to confront him, to eliminate the danger to Emilie, surged in me.

When Bellcon jogged off to the locker room, the warn-ing bells faded and I began to relax. But, in that moment, I had changed. I recognized a controlling instinct, an im-pulse to protect people close to me; it happened with Tim on the mountain and now with Emilie. I was ready to give up my life for my friends without hesitation. I glanced at Tim and Emilie and finally acknowledged that I loved them more than I could ever love God, whom I'd never met. And while my curiosity also controlled me—I could not stop asking if science had an explanation for consciousness and a reason to believe in God or my mother's soul—I knew now I would not become a priest.

Emilie was looking at me as though trying to read my expression. I smiled at her, keeping my thoughts to myself, as I turned and descended the stadium steps with Tim.

We waited in line to get our snacks and drinks, then Tim went back to sit with Steph. I made my way back up the stands to bring Emilie her pretzel and Coke. "Here you go," I said, feeling a bit giddy when she smiled at me. Andrew looked like he was holding back a frown.

She said, "You know, Alan, my mother was asking why we haven't seen you at the house for a long time."

Something in my stomach trembled. I glanced at Andrew, who looked surprised. I said, "Ah, well, you know, starting a new school, wrestling..."

"You've been acting like a stranger," she said directly. "Promise me you will visit more often?"

I could hardly believe what I was hearing. "Yeah, sure. Tell Ada I'll see her soon."

"Oh, thank you!" Emilie said. "She'll be very happy to hear that."

I found myself sitting next to Tim, not really sure how I got there.

Tim asked, "Hey, what happened? Alan? Snap out of it! What happened?"

"She, she invited me to her house," I answered dreamily.

"Allllright!" Tim exclaimed. Stephanie looked at my face and giggled.

I could barely pay attention to the rest of the game. When the fans started to leave, I was dimly aware that the Hawks had won 19-6. I could not stop thinking about visiting Emilie and Ada. Then Emilie was standing next to me.

"Good game, don't you think?" she said to Stephanie.

Andrew stood next to Emilie. I smiled at him weakly. He turned away.

As we all walked toward the exit gate, past the pack of celebrating Hawks on the sideline, I had the feeling one of them was staring at the five of us as we left.

*****

On Sunday, Bellcon nursed some familiar aches and pains. His Hawks had beaten the Knights 19-6, and he had fun. But during the game he realized football season was over. That's why he arranged a meeting with Molly, the unattractive spindly freshman cheerleader with a crush on him. Even though he knew Molly liked him, he did not enjoy being in her company. The reason he asked to see her was because he needed information to subdue his fear, or what was at least a feeling akin to fear, the familiar emptiness that grew inside him when he was unsure where his next thrill would come from.

His uneasiness had peaked the day before when something happened at halftime that toyed with his anxiety. He had walked behind the team bench to the large Gatorade dispenser, filled a cup, raised it to his mouth, and looked into the stands. There she was. He knew her name now, Emilie. The bug-eyed girl with the hot bod. She stood out with a bright baseball cap on. Next to her was Andrew, the senior that Bellcon nicknamed "the rat" because of the boy's scraggly black hair and pointed nose. He was turning to head to the locker room when he noticed two boys converging on Emilie in the stands. One was a thin wiry kid who he thought he recognized. The other was a big kid, about his size, who he never saw before. He remembered seeing the wiry kid in a hallway during a change of classes. *Must be a freshman,* he thought, *a friend of the girl's. Looks like she'd trust him. He can be the messenger, the one to give bug-eyes the news that the rat is a coward, how he stood by and did nothing when Stan roughed up his best friend. I'll have to meet that kid. The big guy will need to be kept out of the picture.*

At the end of the game, while his teammates celebrated on the sidelines, he watched Emilie leave with her small group of friends. He knew then he would need more information, and Molly could provide it. That was the only reason he met up with her now, tried to ignore the particles of food in her braces and questioned her. He asked her about Alan, but did not learn anything useful. Then he asked, "So you know Emilie and Tim?"

"Oh yeah. I told you. I went to school with Stephanie and Emilie. Stephanie was going out with Tim, who was older. That's OK, don't you think?" she smiled, showing a mouthful of steel.

"Sure," Bellcon answered, "but Tim's father, he was the drunk guy that killed the music teacher last year?"

"Yeah," she replied. "And you know what? I heard Tim's father used to beat him and his mother when he was drunk."

"No sh— I mean, Jeeze! Tim must be a terrified little kid."

"Yeah, scared little mouse. Not like you," Molly said affectionately with a shiny stainless-steel smile.

Bellcon could not take another minute of this conversation. He'd learned enough. "Thanks, Molly," he said coldly and began to walk away.

"But you know what?" Molly persisted. "What's really weird is how Tim and Alan are such good friends. I mean, how could you be friends with the kid whose father killed your mother? That's wrong, don't you think?"

Bellcon turned, his eyes wide. "*What*?" he barked.

Molly instinctively stepped back. "I, I said, it's wrong, don't you think?"

"No, no," the large figure said in a softer tone, "I mean who's Tim's friend?"

"Oh." Molly grinned. "You know, the big kid you asked about at the game, Alan. The music teacher was Alan's mother."

Bellcon almost whispered, "No, I didn't know. They're friends?"

"Yeah, best friends," Molly answered.

"Wow, that's something," he said.

She asked, "Would you be friends with the kid whose father killed your mother?"

"You're right, Molly. That's weird. Thanks." Walking away, Bellcon thought, *I could understand that. Mothers can be a pain in the ass.* His last contact with his mother played back in his mind. He was thirteen years old. His father and mother were having one of their regular arguments.

"You don't care about anybody, do you, Frank? Not me, not your son. Even your work. You gut the plaintiffs like they're dead fish, and you fleece your defendants. It's all a game. Right?"

"Connie—" Frank tried to interject.

"No, don't give me your lawyer bullshit! You're a fucking monster. You've ignored your son except to beat him for, whatever. You've— my God, you've turned him into a monster too! He doesn't have affection for his own mother! His mother or for anyone else, for chrissake. I've had it. I'm gone."

Bellcon had listened from outside his father's study. He had understood that his mother felt distress, but he had felt no emotion. She was correct, he did not feel any affection for her. But he thought she shouldn't leave. He had stepped into the room behind her and grabbed her arm, squeezing hard. "Hey, Ma," he said.

"Don't you touch me," Connie growled. She spun and slapped him across the cheek.

The slap did not hurt that much, but for some reason he had reflexively punched her in the face. Not as hard as he could have, but hard enough that she dropped to the floor on her backside. He recalled her expression changing from fear, to incredulity, to anger. It was her look of fear that made him realize the things that gave him pleasure.

Frank watched coldly and said nothing.

She stood up and glared at her husband. "You'll pay for this. After the divorce, one day. If it's the last thing I do!"

It was when she legally changed her name back to her maiden name that her boy tried to erase his first name, the name she had given him, and asked everyone to call him Bellcon.

The next day, Frank Bellcon made another phone call to officer Dunnard. The lawyer pointed out that his son was questioned by the Garrison Township police department regarding the assault of three youths that happened in August. Apparently, Frank's son did not have a good alibi, and the police, who had no good evidence, were itching to make an arrest. Frank did not want a trial poking into his son's past. He had told his son to lay low and not do *anything* off color until the Garrison affair was settled. A resolution was becoming more urgent.

Frank asked Dunnard if he had gotten the promised inside information they discussed nearly two months earlier. The policeman grudgingly admitted to himself that he owed Frank a favor, so, when their conversation ended, he picked up the phone and made a call. He heard someone on the other end say, "Garrison Police Department."

"Officer Dunnard," he shot back, "Forrest Creek P.D. Is captain Russo around?"

"Hold please," the voice said.

His friend was on the phone in less than a minute, "Hey, Dunnard, what's up?"

"Hi Dom. You guys investigating the assault on those kids at Garrison Mountain?"

"Yeah, it's been almost two months, and no one's in custody. Harry's kid was stabbed and he wants the kid who did it. But his son and the other two hardly gave any description, just 'a big kid and a skinny kid.' Cripes! Don't they want us to catch 'em? You got a lead?".

"Maybe." Dunnard probed. "But I hear you already gotta suspect, my side of the tracks."

Russo considered this inquiry for a moment. "We got witnesses who saw two boys and two girls on bikes leaving the scene. One of them was a big kid. And a bus driver who saw four kids on bikes matching the description riding down the highway, heading towards Forrest Creek."

"And kids on bikes," Dunnard said, "don't go more than ten miles, so we're on your radar."

Russo said, "Right. You also got a high school football star with a rep for assaults, who came from a place where maybe he did some bad deeds, but I guess there was no evidence. Course, we're not supposed to talk about that."

"Sounds like a stretch," Dunnard said.

The captain sounded frustrated. "We're still diggin', doing some interviews, matching bike tire marks. You know Harry's kid had surgery. They took out his spleen. We want to nail the perps. What's your interest?"

"I know the counselor whose son's a suspect," Dunnard answered. "I don't think his boy did it. Could you sit tight for now? Don't charge the kid? I'm doing some interviewing myself."

"I heard about that lawyer. Piece of work. Well, sure. We got nothing hard anyway. Call me if you get something," the captain ordered.

"You bet. You'll be the first to know," the subordinate officer replied, and hung up.

At every opportunity, whether patrolling a high school sports venue or stopping for coffee at the luncheonette in town, officer Dunnard informally questioned the kids. He would challenge them, "Hey, who can ride their bikes all the way up to Garrison Mountain?"

So far, he had no leads.

CHAPTER 30

Tim was holding my legs as I finished a "wall walk" on the side of my house. "You're gonna kill yourself," he said. The sky was nearly dark, the early November air crisp. Tim asked, "The stuff you do on the lawn, the 'backwards bear crawls,' 'crab walks,' and piggy back sprints, they do all this stuff in wrestling practice?"

"Oh yeah," I said, "and more. But sprinting with you on my back is my own invention."

"So why do you redo these insane workouts every night?" Tim asked.

"I don't do it *every* night." I replied. "Look, wrestling is really tough, and there are guys with a lot of experience who've built up their endurance. Most guys lose their first year out. I'm not going to be a loser."

I didn't try to explain the messy thought process behind my drive to win. It came from realizing that I might fail to explain consciousness. That would leave me with no certainty there was a God and no spiritual meaning for my, or anyone else's, existence. On the other hand, even if I could not prove to myself that there was a spiritual world, I was inspired by my mother, who, though gone from this life, burned affectionately in the minds of many. It was a kind of immortality. So, I intended to make my life meaningful. To exit the stage of life a bright flame, like

Achilles or Edison. When the time came to part this world, I wanted to leave my identity indelibly stamped on the collective mind of the living. That meant winning, setting records, making great discoveries. Losing would truly make me meaningless.

Tim said, "Come on. You're good, you made the JV team! I don't see how you can lose. Look at you! You're gonna crush the other guys."

I was running back and forth across my backyard on all fours. I panted, "You should see some of these wrestlers. They're pretty serious." I got up, grabbed Tim's arm, draped him over my back, and sprinted across the yard, back and forth, over and over, until my legs buckled and we toppled to the ground.

Tim laughed. "You're nuts man, just plain nuts!"

Having trained for months, I looked forward to our first match. Our Northern Catholic Lions would be hosting the St. Bonaventure's Ironmen. It was a cold, clear November Saturday morning. Tim rode with Dad and me to the match. "Stephanie's coming later," he said.

My father asked, "Do you know who you're wrestling?"

I said, "The Ironmen don't have a JV heavyweight, so the coaches agreed I'd wrestle a Junior who's on the varsity team. The match won't count officially. They thought it'd be good practice for both of us." I was not happy about this.

Tim said, "You're gonna kill him anyway."

I told him, "The kid's supposed to be really good. They call him 'The Vice.'"

"Well, good luck," my father said. "We'll be rooting for you."

As we emerged from the Lions' locker room, I glanced at the stands. Only a few family members and a number of senior wrestlers showed up to support the JV players. My father, Tim, and Stephanie sat midway up the stands on the Lions' side and waved.

When my match came up, a few senior wrestlers clapped and called out.

"Come on, Alan!"

"You can do it."

"Show em what you got, Alan!"

My coach stood next to me. He said, "Do your best, show no pain."

In less than one minute, "The Vice" took me down. I managed to escape, but he took me down again. At the end of the first period, I was losing 4-1. I was talking to myself. *He won't get my leg again. I've got to get position.*

In the second period, The Vice took me down again. I had another escape, but the intense grappling was draining my strength. By the end of the period, I'd been caught in a few precarious positions. Then, thirty seconds into the third period, with a lightning-fast move, the Vice pinned me. My face slammed to the mat. I got up slowly, a mat burn on my forehead, a small amount of blood trickling from my nose.

In the locker room my JV and varsity teammates slapped me on the back, "Hey, man don't look so glum. You wrestled varsity and hung in there!"

The coach came in. "This was a good showing first time out. You guys did a good job. Alan, this will be a good experience, trust me." He left.

I was looking down. "I lost. Got pinned for chrissakes."

One of the seniors said, "He needs re-calibration, right, boys?"

Another smirked, "Heh-heh. Yeah, damn right!"

A third picked up the cause. "You're coming with us to the Ale House, no more lame excuses."

I had no interest in the varsity tradition of riding across New York's state line where it was legal for eighteen-year-olds to buy alcohol. "But my dad drove me and my friends—"

"No more of that shit," one said. "I'll tell your dad the team's taking you out to cheer you up, OK?"

I could see their intent expressions. It was no use to argue. "I'll talk to them," I said.

I showered, got dressed, and went into the gym. Stephanie stayed up in the stands. Dad and Tim came up to me. "Hey, no biggie. You'll beat that guy next time," Tim said.

Dad said, "I thought you did pretty fair, wrestling a varsity player, first competition. You OK?"

I said, "Yeah. I guess I'm not as good as I thought. I mean I was pinned."

Tim sighed, "You just started. You told me experience matters. The kid you wrestled has two years' experience. Don't sweat it."

"Yeah, OK" I said. "Look, I hope you guys don't mind, the team wanted to take me out to cheer me up."

Tim looked at my father who said, "Sure. I'll leave the door open. Don't get home too late."

Tim added, "OK, I'll talk to you tomorrow."

In the Ale House parking lot, I sat with four teammates on the hood of a senior's green Pontiac. The seniors challenged one another to "shotgun" cans of beer. One of the varsity players demonstrated for me. "Hold the can like this, use the can opener to make a hole at the bottom, here. Put your mouth over the hole and pop the lid. Don't try to swallow, just keep your throat open cause, *pow*, it's gonna go right down."

I drank three cans of beer. Some of the muscle aches and disappointment dissolved. Over the next few hours, I laughed at some crazy wrestling stories, ate pretzels, and downed a few more beers. It was around ten p.m. when the green Pontiac pulled up in front of my house. When I stepped out of the car the ground was rolling under my feet, like I was walking on a water mattress. It suddenly occurred to me how lucky we were that the driver hadn't crashed. The house was quiet, my father asleep. I climbed the stairs and dropped into my bed with my clothes on.

On Sunday morning, I managed to get cleaned up and dressed without raising Dad's suspicion. I left the house to have breakfast at John's. Tim met me at John's driveway. Without thinking it through, I confided in Tim.

"You? You went out drinking?" Tim asked. "Are you fucking kidding me? What, are you trying to turn out like my father? Because you lost a match that no freshman could have won?"

I tried to explain, but Tim was too angry and stopped listening.

"No. I don't want to hear it," Tim said. "I don't fucking believe this." He left.

I failed myself, my team, and my best friend. I was in no mood to meet with John and be reminded of my failure to explain consciousness. I walked home sulking. My life was spiraling into a meaningless pit.

The following week we wrestled the St. Mary Spartans. Dad had to go up to Ona's for the weekend to help her fix a leaking pipe. One of the seniors offered to drive me to the match. Tim was not coming. I was unable get ahold of him all week.

Despite getting pinned my first time out, I won my match on points in three periods. In the locker room the coach told each kid on the team what they had to work on in order to improve. He appraised me last. "Son, you OK? Cause you looked like crap out there. I thought that giving you your toughest opponent in your first match would get you on the road to being a real champ." He looked at his other wrestlers. "This goes for all you guys. I don't want anyone on this team who's not giving the Lions one hundred percent. Mentally and physically. We show no pain and never surrender! Go play football if you can only give ninety percent." He turned back to me. "I want you to think about whether you want to stay on this team or not.

If you do, I want to see someone who believes he's a winner on that mat every match. Understood?"

I froze. I just croaked, "Yes sir." The coach left. My confidence reeling, I thought, *I won the match, but I know I looked like crap. What am I supposed to do? Shit, he might kick me off the team. I can't practice any harder. I am giving one hundred percent. Aren't I?*

One of the seniors came up to me. "Come on, we're heading up to the Ale House. We'll talk about next week."

"Yeah, sure, but whoever is driving doesn't drink," I said, recalling my last ride home.

"OK, OK," the senior whinnied a laugh, "I'll just have one beer."

This time the Ale House provided no absolution. I was confused and unsure how to emerge from my funk.

On the ride home, two guys were hanging out the rear windows singing and joking. Although the driver only did drink one beer, he was swerving playfully on the road. We passed the "Welcome to Forrest Creek" sign and heard a siren. Lights flashed behind us.

"Oh shit!" the driver said, pulling to the side of the road.

The policeman walked up to the driver's window and barked in a gravelly voice, "License and registration." When the driver handed him the documents he continued, "You boys been over the state line? You know some kids go up there to get alcohol." He looked at each boy, sticking his head in the window and sniffing for any sent of liquor.

"Yes sir," the driver said. "But it's legal in New York."

"Maybe legal for eighteen-year-olds. All of you eighteen?" the policeman said. "You know it's against the law to drive drunk?"

"Yes sir," the driver replied. "I'm not drunk."

"OK, everybody out of the car," the officer said.

He put the driver through some tests and, convinced he was not drunk, he said, "You're not from Forrest Creek, huh?"

"No, sir," the driver said.

"OK, back in the car. How 'bout you boys, got ID?" the policeman asked.

We showed him our driving permits or school IDs. He looked at them closely, asking each of the other guys to get back in the car, until he got to me.

"You're from Forrest Creek? Go to Northern Catholic?"

"Yes, sir," I answered.

The officer said, "Do I smell alcohol? You're under aged to drink anywhere in this country. You know that?"

My heart was pounding. Nightmarish scenarios were running through my mind: being arrested, getting kicked off the wrestling team, thrown out of Northern Catholic, losing the trust of my father, losing my friends, and losing any chance with Emilie.

"Yes, sir," I said.

"Look, I'm not gonna arrest you. But I'm gonna give you a warning. That means I'm gonna let your parents and your school know there could be a problem," the officer said.

"My mom's gone," I informed him. "She was in an accident last year."

The policeman looked back at my ID.

"The music teacher?" he asked.

"Yes, sir," I replied.

"I'm sorry. OK, maybe I won't trouble your dad this time. But I'll have to notify your school, since it's so close to the New York border, you understand?" The policeman's voice softened. "I want to ask you a question and I want the truth, understood?"

"Yes, sir," I said.

"Do you or your friends ride bikes to other towns?" he asked.

I was puzzled. "Well, yeah, we do."

The officer continued, "Ever rode to Ridgewood? Lodi?"

"Yes, sir," I said. I had no idea why he would ask these questions.

"How 'bout the parks? Been to the park at Garrison Mountain?" the policeman asked.

"Yeah," I said, then I understood. I stiffened. The officer just smiled.

"OK," he said, opening the car door to let me climb back in. "Now you boys behave yourselves. You only get one warning. Oh, and if you boys or your parents need to get in touch with me, I'm officer Dunnard."

CHAPTER 31

The following week, on Wednesday afternoon, Rich got on my case. We were walking to our bus for the ride home when Rich said, "Tim told me what you did. You're acting like a fuckin' asshole. I didn't know I had a friend who was such a wimp. You got pinned. So fuckin' what? You're just gonna give up? You shot your tiny wad?"

We sat next to one another in the middle of the bus. I got a tongue lashing from Rich. That's when it occurred to me that maybe I had mistaken a physical challenge for what was really a mental challenge. Maybe intentions mattered. Maybe that's what the coach was saying: *I want to see someone who believes he's a winner.*

I was thinking about this on the way home from school while Rich and some of the upperclassmen entrenched in the rear hurled taunts and insults at one another. The bus was on its way to pick up some girls at the Sacred Sacrament Academy because our two schools shared a transportation contract.

"You've got half a dick," Rich called back to one of the juniors. "That's why your girlfriend was at my house last night." The bus rolled into the SSA parking lot.

I was looking out the window, smirking. I saw the girls in their gray uniforms, regimented into lines and patrolled by the Sisters of the Sacred Snatches.

A senior from the back of the bus yelled back, "Rich, we all know you can only get it up for your *girlfriend* sitting next to you." Laughter reverberated from the back of the bus. "Yeah, you only have eyes for Alan. You've been sticking it up his butt!" another exclaimed.

As the girls boarded the bus, Rich opened the window next to his seat and looked toward the back of the bus. "That's about as funny as this," he said. Abruptly, he pulled down his pants and stuck his bare ass out the window.

For a moment everyone was quiet and only a few upperclassmen could be heard sucking in air. Then, as if something had frightened a cage full of chimpanzees, the bus erupted with raucous hooting and laughter, and the bus rocked as boys jumped on one another, slapping backs and pointing at Rich. They didn't hear the freshman in the front of the bus yell, "Incoming! Nun!"

I saw the veiled figure round the front of the bus to investigate the commotion. "Get down!" I said to Rich. "Nun." I pointed.

It was too late. As the bus pulled out of the parking lot, we all saw the nun's face change from disbelief to horror to anger. She pointed a bony finger at Rich's waning moon. Rich pulled up his pants and sat down quickly. He blushed and just said, "Shit."

The next morning at school an announcement summoned all the students on our bus to the principal's office.

"LINE UP!" the ex-marine disciplinarian Brother Richter barked.

I thought, *Man, he's pissed off.*

"Every one of you will be expelled! I will not allow the good name of this school to be tarnished by one delinquent if I have to expel the whole lot of you! Do you understand me?"

We mumbled, "Yes, sir."

Brother Richter bellowed, "DO YOU UNDERSTAND ME?"

"YES, SIR!" we shouted.

"Good," Richter replied, "because if the young man who thought it was a good idea to stick his skinny ass in the face of a sister of the sacred sacrament doesn't admit to it, this school will be done with all you sacrilegious misfits!"

The air was still. Then Rich stepped forward. His eyes reddened, his voice cracked. "It was me, sir."

"You, in the conference room," Richter barked. "Everyone else dismissed for now. But I'm not through with the rest of you for your antics on that bus! Alan, you stay for a moment."

Rich turned from the conference room door. "He didn't—"

"In there." Richter pointed. "Enough from you!" When the conference room door closed, I stood face to face with the disciplinarian. "I don't know all your circumstances," he said, "but I've heard some disturbing things."

I felt my cheeks warm and my stomach squirm. I thought, *The police called about us drinking. Oh man, my dad will be mad if I'm kicked out of here for that.*

Ricther continued, "We'll be discussing what action the school will take at the board meeting. They usually do not excuse dishonorable behavior or breaking the law, but I'll argue against expulsion at this time. In the meantime, I think you should re-examine who your friends are and whether they're worth losing the opportunities that this school can provide for you. I think you're a good young man, but young men can make bad choices that ruin their lives. If the board does decide to keep you, I can guarantee you this, if I hear one more story that you have engaged in, or are in the company of others who engage in, behavior that reflects poorly on this school, then you will definitely be gone. Clear?"

"Yes, sir," I said weakly, looking down.

"I want you to have your father call me to set up a meeting," the principle said.

My head snapped up, my arms and legs froze. "*What? When?*"

"Just have him call me. We'll decide the details. Now go," Richter commanded. He spun around and stomped into the conference room, closing the door behind him.

The next day, Friday afternoon, my father left work early and drove to the high school to meet with Brother Richter. When he came home, we had a late dinner. I waited to be castigated and punished. What happened was almost worse. He spoke one sentence, telling me that he was dis-appointed in me and that we would talk about what Broth-er Richter said in the morning. He was quiet the rest of the evening.

What a difference a year made. When my mother died, my relationship with my father was practically hostile. Back then, I thought he repeatedly put me down for my religious beliefs. I was certain that his demands exposed a distaste for who I was, his military manner rejecting a wayward recruit. Maybe pride and anger clouded my judgement. Things changed since my mother's funeral. The turning point was when he and I went hunting at Ona's. He confided in me and explained why he was an atheist and how his parenting was his best attempt to pre-pare me for whatever challenges the world would throw at me.

Following his conversation with Brother Richter, I knew my relationship with my father had grown because it really hurt to hear that he was disappointed in my be-havior. It wasn't the pain an adversary could inflict; it was the deep pain only a loved one could exact.

I had disappointed a few people who were very im-portant to me. The choices I was making were preparing me to become a nobody in Palookaville. I went to bed con-fused and hoping Rich and I would not be expelled the way Tim had been.

Over breakfast Saturday morning, my father told me about his conversation with the principal.

"He wanted to know if I had any idea why your grades were slipping, why you'd go drinking with some seniors. I had no idea these things even happened. I told him good adolescents sometimes have to find their way. I said that you seemed to be obsessed with winning your first wrestling match and getting pinned was tough to handle, that your reaction probably had something to do with Mom's passing, the difficult religious questions it raised, which I've not been much help with. Sound right?"

It was a pretty insightful analysis. "Yeah," I said. "I'm really sorry. I was just stupid."

"Brother Richter told me a story. A few years ago he had a boy, good athlete and student, who lost a parent his freshman year. The boy questioned his faith, began taking drugs. He overdosed his junior year. Brother Richter choked up telling me this. He made it very clear he would help you anyway he could, but he said he must protect the reputation of the school at any cost. He said the school is giving you one more chance."

I was relieved to hear I wouldn't be expelled. *Thank you*, I mouthed, though the principal couldn't hear it. "Did he say anything about Rich?" I asked.

"Oh yeah. He told me about Rich. Why in the world would Rich do that?"

I shrugged.

"Well, Rich was almost certainly going to be expelled. Apparently, Father MacKristin did some investigating and found that Rich had some problems at home. He argued that his teachers should try to set boundaries, which the priest thought were not being set at home. He argued strongly that the school needed to help your friend believe he could succeed, not expel him and 'leave him to the random forces of society.' The school agreed to give him one more chance too."

I said, "I'll change, you'll see. I know what I have to do."

And I did know. It came down to what the coach was telling me when he said, *I want to see someone who believes he's a winner on that mat every match.* Until I figured out what that meant, I had it wrong. Sure, winning mattered, but what was more important was that I never gave up *believing* I could win. Strange, right? I mean, when you have a new idea, there is no evident change in your body or surroundings. Only something intangible and invisible changes: your mind. I started to *believe* I was a winner, and that season I didn't lose another wrestling match. Moreover, that spring, my academic performance skyrocketed as a result of a little outing that Dad arranged. John came with us, and I'm sure he'd agree, it was an experience that changed both of our lives.

*****

In mid-November, Frank Bellcon was in a meeting with a senator and a federal judge when his secretary interrupted. "There's a call you were waiting for?" she said.

Frank said, "Excuse me one moment," to his clients, then turned to his secretary and said, "OK, put it through." Frank picked up the phone. "Yes?"

"Dunnard. I might have something for you, but I gotta check the P's and Q's. Just wanted you to know, Captain Russo of the Garrison Township PD is putting their investigation of the August assault on hold while I look into things."

"Thank you, officer," Frank said, "I appreciate it." He hung up.

Dunnard and Captain Russo kept in touch, but the assault on Garrison Mountain remained a cold case. The police officer whose boy was stabbed also kept in touch with Captain Russo. He wanted justice. But his son and the other assault victims from Garrison Mountain did not seem very interested in the police finding the perpetrators. If anything, they were uncooperative. So Captain Russo was happy to leave the case in limbo, though a few months later he followed his instincts and made a couple phone calls.

In late March 1969, Bellcon was summoned to the principal's office. With an unblinking stare and a crooked, confident smile, he sat across from the school's disciplinarian and said, "Mr. Vandike, I didn't know Molly was your niece. Why shouldn't I talk to her? I think she likes me and—"

The principal stiffened. "You stay away from her because I'm telling you to."

Something's off, the burly student thought. *What's he thinking?* "I'm sorry," he replied. "I haven't done anything wrong. She likes talking to me, so I don't think I'll stop. Are we done?" Bellcon stood.

"I'm warning you," the principal said, glaring, "this isn't Dargton." Bellcon turned his head to stare at him. The principal added, "I hear small towns like that have unsolved crimes. Rapes, murders, disappearances. Nobody would stand for that in Forrest Creek. It won't happen here."

Now the suspect understood. *Those fucking rats in Dargton,* he thought. *They were supposed to keep their traps shut. Who did they tell? When I find out—.* "What are you talking about? Dargton is a great town," Bellcon retorted. "I didn't hear of any crimes, and the folks were friendly, like here. Who told you this stuff about Dargton? Maybe I know them."

"That doesn't matter." The principal's voice wavered.

"You've got the wrong idea," Bellcon protested. "You're missing some very important information that I think you should hear."

"What information?" Vandike growled.

"May I use your phone? It would be best if you heard it from the source." The principal frowned. His student added, "You want to get the whole story, don't you?"

"OK," the principal said skeptically, "make your call."

Bellcon dialed. "Hello, Dad?" he said. "I'm in Mr. Vandike's office. He thinks that I was involved in a crime or something in Dargton. I don't know. I'll put him on." Bellcon handed Vandike the phone. He was pleased to see the man looked nervous now.

"Vandike," the principal said into the phone. He listened for a moment, then said, "Your son has been involved in a number of assaults in neighboring towns—. Only bullies? Yes, well that's another matter. I am aware of crimes that were not fully investigated in Dargton—. I didn't accuse your son—. I don't recall where I—. Yes, I heard about a gag order—. No, I haven't informed the authorities—. Then I'm what? Aiding and abetting? Now you just—. Yes, I remember the assaults at Garrison Mountain. As a matter of fact I got a call from Captain Russo—. Did you say *our* police force? They are? I see. Yes, I'll wait until the evidence is in, but I would chance losing this job to protect my kids and see justice done—" Vandike gulped. "No, I'm not a vigilante—." Vandike became pale and dropped into his chair and listened for a long moment. "How did you know that? What? Yes, I'd probably have to find a new career if I were wrong. I do understand. Thanks for your advice, counselor." He hung up the phone and looked at Bellcon. "You can go," the principal said.

The brawny student smiled. "Have a good day," he said as he walked out the door. Passing the secretary's desk, he heard Vandike's voice crackle over her intercom. "Missy, would you step in for a moment?" He watched her stand up and walk into Vandike's office, closing the door behind her.

When she saw the principal crumpled in his chair she asked, "Are you OK, Jake?"

"Missy," he said with concern, "we've known each other a long time. Have I been outta line with a student since, uh, the Jefferson school incident?"

"You were right to do what you did. I've always said that. The boy had to be stopped. That's a rare thing. Nothing like that has happened for over eight years," she said and waited.

"I know we weren't supposed to let on that we knew about Dargton. We promised we'd let the system work.

But when that Captain Russo called yesterday asking about Bellcon in connection with the stabbing and assaults on Garrison Mountain, I thought about that teenage girl who disappeared in Dargton. I thought about my niece and all the other girls here at the high school. They've been in danger for Christ's sake! All these months. What are the authorities doing?"

Missey tried to console him. "What can be done? They need evidence."

"Yeah, I guess they need a dead body with fingerprints on it. And that damn Frank Bellcon. It's just like they said. That son-of-a—. He threatened me. Brought up Jefferson. I thought that was done. Buried. But it'll always be there. If it's publicized, I can kiss this and any other teaching job goodbye. I should have listened to Marie, may she rest in peace. Well, I'm done with being silent. I want you to set up a closed-door meeting with the teachers. We're going to monitor the hallways, the campus, and every off-campus school related event. We'll enlist parent volunteers, everywhere in this town. We'll be visible and invisible. They need witnesses? We'll record everything that boy does. And if he harms my Molly, or any other kid, I'll just chance losing this job."

Bellcon walked back to class. He thought, *It's going to happen again. The rumors, the people in town turning against me, the kids staying away. The word will spread. They'll all be watching. Shit! It's like prison. I'm going to find the bastards who poked their nose into my business. Maybe there'll be a few accidents. They'll die when their house catches fire, or just kill themselves. But somebody's gonna die.*

CHAPTER 32

It was one of the weeks leading up to Easter 1969 when Dad said, "I have an idea. How would you and John like to come to Bell Labs to hear about some new inventions and see a LASER demonstration? I think they're going to make a hologram."

I had no idea what a hologram was, but it sounded cool. John was crazy excited about the trip.

On Wednesday morning April 2nd, Dad went down to the basement to retrieve two small boxes of delicate equipment that had to be returned to work. He asked me if I'd mind sitting in the back seat with John. He carried the boxes out to the car and strapped them securely onto the front passenger seat. Then we drove to John's.

We pulled up in front of the house. John and his mother, Claudette, were waiting in the doorway. John sprinted to the car and I opened the back door for him. Dad rolled down the window and called to his mother, "I'll have him back around five p.m. if that's OK?" Claudette smiled, nodded and waved. "Have fun boys!"

Driving to his workplace Dad said, "Today Bell labs has tours for college interns and family members. I made arrangements for you guys to sit in on a work group, and a short presentation in one of the labs. Then we'll have lunch, and, to finish the day, we go to the hologram demonstration."

I asked John, "You know what a hologram is?"

John smiled, appeared to consider several answers, then began, "I went to Princeton's library when I was on campus yesterday and found some helpful materials. The technical explanation is really neat, but I'd rather tell you what I think is so, ah, cool about holograms."

"OK," I said, amused that John was picking up words like *cool* from our group. Then using one of John's favorite terms I said, "Shoot."

"Have you ever heard of Fourier transforms?"

"No," I replied, frustrated that I did not even get past the first explanatory sentence.

"That's OK," John continued, "I can explain things easier. Remember the envelope your dad sent to me?"

"Yeah?"

"It was a paper by a guy named Shannon about information and messages. I think holograms become really cool when you think about them in terms of information. What do you think information is?"

I thought for a moment. "I guess it's what's written in newspapers and books. It's what's behind words, like your explanation of things."

"Not a bad start," he said. "Now, just trace your idea backwards. You read words on a page, or hear sound waves in the air that make up a word. These things are just *patterns*. Your brain creates meaning out of patterns. Patterns of ink on paper or waves of sound in air. Patterns can show up on anything that can be formed, creating in-*form*-ation."

"Clever. OKaaay?"

"Think of the information in an image, say a photograph of" —John looked out the window and saw a truck— "of that truck. When we take a photo of it, light carries the *pattern* of its image to a camera where it is recorded on film, and ultimately a paper photograph is made. In the photo each area of contrast and color from the truck is reproduced and makes a picture, right?"

"OK."

"Now there is another way to record the information in this image. Remember we talked about interference and waves combining?"

"Yeah?"

"Well, imagine a beam of light in a *pure* form, a single frequency with the waves all moving in concert, that's LASER light."

"Oh, that's what a LASER does? It makes a pure light?"

"Yes. Now imagine we split this LASER beam in two and reflect one off the truck. Call it the *object* beam. The other we direct with mirrors to a photographic film. Call this one the *reference* beam. If the object beam and the reference beam meet on the photographic film, an interference pattern is recorded."

In my mind, I was standing in the rain on the riverbank at Ona's, watching all the concentric waves on the water's surface combining and creating beautiful patterns. Then I imagined the pure light waves reflected off the surface of the truck and crossing paths with the light waves of the reference beam, their waves combining, interfering. I tried to visualize the interference pattern frozen on a square sheet of photographic film. I said, "So that's a hologram?"

"Yes," John said. "Now, a photograph records information very differently than a hologram. Remember, one spot on our photo represents one spot on the truck, just like you would paint a picture. But a hologram is created by the *waves* of light reflected from each spot on the truck. Imagine where a *wave* of laser light strikes one spot on the truck; the reflected wave, expanding from that spot, then passes over the entire photographic film. This happens at every spot on the truck. So, *every* spot on the hologram contains light reflected from *every* spot on the *whole* truck! Some people say the hologram records *the whole in every part.*"

"So what does a hologram actually look like?" I asked.

"If you look at the negative, it looks like a random pattern of spots and clear spaces, made by the peaks and troughs of the interfering light waves on the photographic film. But, if you shine the reference beam through the film, on the other side you'll see a three-dimensional image of the truck! The hologram reproduces the interference pattern that passed through the film."

"Wait," I said. "You still see the truck, but you're saying the *pattern* can be stored in two different forms. Photograph and holograph," I repeated slowly, trying to get his depiction to sink in.

"Exactly!" John exclaimed.

I still didn't get it. I thought more explanation might help. I asked, "OK, and what's this Fourier thing?"

"Ah, well. It's sort of a mathematical way of looking at the differences in these two patterns. Let's call the photo 'spatial information.' Each spot on our photograph exactly reproduces a similar spot from the truck. A dark spot on the truck is a dark spot on the photo. Fourier, on the other hand, is a mathematical operation that can take the entire image of the truck and transform it into the exact set of interfering waves that would recreate the *whole* image. A whole image in the form of interfering *waves*, so we call it *frequency* information"

"Kinda like the hologram?" I observed.

"Kinda," said John, using my word. "Fourier equations show how spatial information is translated into frequency information. Now, holograms are not only cool because they make three-dimensional images, they have other amazing properties, like if you cut our truck-hologram into pieces, each piece would contain an image of the entire truck!"

"Whaaaat?" I said.

"It makes sense," John replied, "because if you think about it, information from every spot on the entire object is recorded at each little spot on the film in the hologram. And the wave-interference information lets you record an extra dimension, so even if the film is 2D, the image you reproduce is 3D." I was stymied. John saw my perplexed expression and said, "I think we'll have to see the hologram demonstration to get a better idea of what we're talking about."

When we arrived at the Bell Labs facility, we parked the car in a large parking lot. The main buildings had numbers, which were displayed on small strategically placed signs throughout the campus. We parked nearest to building #1. It was a long rectangular structure with an attached L-shaped wing on the other side. It had short, perpendicular extensions, which, I found out later, housed laboratories jutting out at intervals.

Dad retrieved the boxes from the front seat and ushered us through the entry check point. The guard greeted us and gave John and me temporary ID badges. Dad's office was a shared room halved by a movable metal wall. On each side stood a desk and shelves cluttered with notebooks and electrical equipment.

Dad set the boxes on his desk. "OK, here's home base. My office. Let's meet some people and see what they're up to." He took us to one of the labs where two researchers gave us demonstrations of their work with speech recognition and rudimentary computer graphics for making movies. "How cool is *this*!" I said. John's eyes sparkled, he grinned broadly as the scientists drew on TV monitors and special pads using "light pens." Taking turns, we launched question after question at our instructors.

My father popped his head into the doorway. "Hey, guys, there's a brainstorming meeting down the hall I think you'll enjoy. Come on!"

As we walked through the hallways I said, "Man, everyone seems like they're in a big hurry around here."

Dad tooted a quick laugh. "Hoo boy! Yes, they are. Inventing is exciting, but it's also a race."

He ushered us to a small classroom where we sat at a table with two vacant chairs next to a young man and woman, who I suspected were college interns. They wore temporary ID badges. Our hosts had set a pad of paper and a pencil on the table in front of each of us. On the opposite side of the table, two scientists stood at a green chalkboard, pointing at parts of a sketched diagram. They took turns asking and answering each other's questions. A third adult, standing off to one side, was listening. He occasionally made a suggestion, and jotted down notes.

I wasn't sure what they were discussing. Terms repeated like: *UHF-analog-digital-signal to noise.* I looked over at John whose eyes were locked on the chalkboard while his hands independently doodled on his pad.

Twenty minutes later, the scientists agreed they had taken the matter as far as they could. Then John raised his hand and asked something about "Silicon-gates" and "digital signals." The scientist leaning against the table made a throat-clearing like laugh and looked over at his colleagues as if to say "I told you so," and replied, "I think that's where this will be going, young man." He seemed about to introduce himself to us when John spun his pad around, and slid it across the table.

"Would this work?" John asked.

Just then Dad appeared at the doorway. He must have seen the three scientists concentrating on John's notepad. No one was speaking, so he said, "Time for lunch, boys!"

We grinned at each other and shot towards the door. As we were leaving, I looked back and heard one of the scientists say, "That'd be an order of magnitude smaller in size with greater capacity."

"For Pete's sake," another said.

Dad led us over to building #2. We walked down a glass enclosed spiral staircase Dad called "the bird cage" to the cafeteria. We were swept up in the excitement that seemed to permeate even the dining area.

"What were those guys talking about?" I asked.

John paused, "Someday people will carry phones around, like a watch. Phones won't need to be plugged into walls with wires. Imagine that. Being able to talk to anyone, anytime, from anywhere."

"Jeez," I said. "Will watches have a tiny TV picture of who you're talking with, like the one Dick Tracy has?"

John laughed. "Probably!"

Dad smiled. "That's not all, guys. Let's finish up. I don't want you to be late for the LASER demo."

We wolfed down lunch, then we followed my father to a conference room. It was arranged with fifteen folding chairs facing a table flanked by two engineers. Behind one of the engineers was a blackboard covered with diagrams similar to some John had drawn in his basement. I walked up to the table and looked closely at the equipment set out on top. At the far end, a four-foot-long rectangular metal box about two inches high and wide sat on small metal blocks. It had closely spaced elliptical holes across the top. I figured this was what emitted the laser beam since a sticker on the side of the box warned against looking directly into it. On the near end of the table, a number of little pedestals, topped with various devices, were carefully arranged. One of the pedestals held a square plate that our instructors would later explain contained the photographic film for making the hologram. Perched on top of another pedestal was a statuette. I recognized it, *The Thinker* by Rodin, a naked man sitting and leaning forward, elbow on knee, with his chin supported by the back of his hand, apparently deep in thought. John and I found seats in the second row and the room filled with guests.

When everyone was seated the engineers introduced themselves and began to explain that the acronym "LASER" stood for *Light Amplification by Stimulated Emission of Radiation*. They rehashed what John had told me in the car about pure or *coherent* light and used the blackboard to explain how laser light could be used to create interference patterns. Then they began pointing to each device on the table, explaining the purpose of the beam splitters, lenses and mirrors and, finally, the photographic plate. They traced the path the laser beam would take. The first step was splitting the beam into two so that one, the "object beam," would reflect off the statuette, and the other, the "reference beam" would reflect off a mirror. The light from these two sources would converge on the photographic film and imprint an interference pattern.

One engineer darkened the room. Another placed a photographic plate in position, removed its metal cover, and turned on the laser. I could see the thin straight lines of pure red light, perfectly aimed and focused by the optical hardware. One beam illuminated *The Thinker;* the other reflected off a mirror aimed at the photographic film. In less than a minute, the laser was switched off. A technician put the hologram in a case and went to develop the film and the lights came back on. The engineers explained how shining the reference beam through the interference patterns in the film would recreate the pattern of light that was reflected off the statuette. "And so the statuette will be seen in the film just as if you were looking directly at it, in three dimensions!"

The technician returned with the developed film and invited the guests to take a look at it under a microscope that had been set up on the table. When it was my turn, I peered into the eyepiece and saw a honey comb of shadowy lines. To the naked eye the film looked blank. John looked into the microscope next. He hummed a brief laugh with his mouth closed and just said, "Cool." When the audience was re-seated, the lights went down, the laser was turned on, and one of the engineers showed the guests how to hold the film up to the reference beam and view the hologram. One by one the visitors came up to the table, took the film, and looked at the image. Some of them gasped. One remarked, "I can see around the sides of the figure in the film. How is that possible?"

When it was my turn, I stepped into place and took the film. I moved it across the reference beam and saw the three-dimensional image, as if I were looking through a small window at *The Thinker*. I turned to John who enjoyed seeing the utter amazement on my face. John said to the engineer, "Can you show him what happens if you cut the film in half?"

One of the instructors smiled. "I'll do one better," he said. He picked up a pair of scissors and cut the film into four pieces. He handed one piece to John and one to me.

We ran our pieces over the course of the reference beam. We were still looking at the *entire* statuette, though through a smaller window. We had to move the smaller pieces of film around through wider angles, but we each saw a duplicate of *The Thinker* in three dimensions.

I felt lightheaded. *How can I be seeing a three-dimensional image?* Memories flashed through my head as my brain tried to connect the dots between what I had just seen and any prior experience. But there was only one thing I could think of: when I told Dad about faces created by ripples on the river at Ona's. I asked him if there could be something going on below the surface, something important. He gave me the book, *Flatland*. The book described what it would be like if there were dimensions around us that we did not experience. After I read it, I imagined tiny "flatlander" scientists living on the river's surface, unable to experience the water below them, and trying to understand the effects of the undercurrent.

I began to imagine new tiny flatlanders whose whole universe was the surface of the hologram. They were completely unaware that the surface they lived on was projecting another dimension. A dimension they could not experience. I wondered if there could be other dimensions, ones that were unmeasurable, inaccessible to humans. I felt like I was falling down the rabbit hole.

In my mind's eye, I saw myself standing in the rain, looking at patterns of ripples on the river. Above the ripples a ghostly image of "The Thinker" loomed above the tiny scientists floating on the river, who could only experience what took place on the surface of the water. I recalled what John had said about holograms, *the whole in every part,* and The Thinker in my vision shattered into hundreds of tiny clones. I thought, *There is so much I don't understand, so much that could be hidden, even from these brilliant scientists. What about consciousness?*

Overcome with wonder, I looked at John, who had been holding his hologram up to the reference beam.

Suddenly, as if struck by a spell, John's hand dropped to the table. He froze with his mouth partly open, and stared with an indifference to his surroundings. Discretely, I moved closer to him, bumped into him gently, and said quietly, "Hey, John, everything OK?" No response. "John, hey, this is pretty cool, right?" Nothing.

I was about to grab John by the shoulders and start shaking him. Slowly John turned his head. He looked through me with a dreamy expression. "I just had the most incredible thought. Intuitive really. It couldn't be, but maybe. It would be the most amazing...," His words trailed off.

"Are you OK?" I asked.

"Yes," John replied, but he did not move. He seemed to be in a trance. The demonstrator began to look concerned. I smiled at him. "He's fine. We'll just go back to our seats. Come on, buddy." I put my arm across John's shoulders and led him, like a narcotized blind person, back to our seats.

When Dad showed up, he said we'd better head home before rush hour. Leaving the conference room, John became more engaging and animated. I asked, "What was that all about?"

John smiled. "An idea. Something that will take a very long time to figure out. If it works, I'll tell you about it."

Imitating John, I rubbed my chin and said thoughtfully, "Hmmm, I'll have to think about that." We laughed and pushed and teased each other as we walked to the parking lot.

"You should have seen your face at that demo," John threw his head back and laughed.

"My face? My face? What about your face?" I shot back.

On the way home I sat in the front passenger seat, but for most of the trip I was turned around, facing John, who was sitting behind my father. We talked practically non-stop about what we had experienced and our speculation about how technology would transform people's lives in the future. Having unleashed our imaginations, Dad grinned the whole way home.

CHAPTER 33

On Wednesday evening May 28st, 1969, the week the school year ended, the phone rang. It was Tim. He said, "Hey, man, how's it going?"

"Fine," I replied, "What's up?"

"Oh, nothing," Tim said, sounding unusually euphoric. "I'm just checking in on ya, making sure you're doing your homework," he snickered.

"Tim, you been smoking something? You sound high."

Tim laughed. "No, man. I thought I'd pass along something a little birdie just told me. Emilie broke up with Andrew!"

"What? You're shittin me! When—"

"Swear to God," Tim cut in, "Steph just told me. I think she let it slip out by mistake. They broke up three weeks ago. Sounded like Emilie didn't want anyone to know, so no one would bug her about it. Andrew didn't tell anyone either."

"This is great!" I said. "But three weeks. Somebody's gonna ask her out."

"Yeah, I think you better make a call. Like now."

"Yeah, uh, thanks, Tim."

"Hey, Alan?"

"What?"

"Take a breath before you call, K?"

"Yeah, right." I hung up.

I paced around the kitchen. Then I went out to the backyard and walked in a big circle. Finally, I went to the phone, took a few deep breaths, and tried to focus. I wanted to sound calm, cool.

"Hello?" Emilie answered.

A lump of word choices crowded my vocal cords. I cleared my throat. "Hi, Emilie, it's me, Alan."

Emilie's contralto laughter sang through the phone. "Of course it's you, Alan. How are you?"

I joked, "Me, Alan, am fine."

Emilie laughed again, and I became relaxed and hopeful in those rich musical notes. She said, "Mom and I were talking about you yesterday. The last time you were here, *months* ago," she teased, "you gave her some good advice on an art history paper she had to write. She was counting on you for more help, but you've been a stranger again."

"That's what I'm calling about, actually. Are you guys going to be around Saturday? I could drop in."

"Uh, Saturday I have softball tryouts," Emilie said, and my hopes began to fade. "Why don't you drop over after tryouts?"

"Great, sounds good. I'll see you then."

I hung up the phone, went out to the backyard, and began running in a wide circle, hands triumphantly above my head. I did a few somersaults and then lay down on the ground looking up at the sky. When I sat up, I saw my neighbor Mr. Wayne at his kitchen window, looking at me with his mouth open, as if my head had fallen off. His wife appeared at the window and smiled. I waved, and she gave me a thumbs up. She knew it was spring.

It was Friday, May 30th, the last day of school, when some teachers held exit interviews Following a half day of classes. I went to the office for my appointment and knocked.

"Enter," came the familiar voice behind the door.

I stepped into the small office. Overcrowded book shelves covered three walls. Stacks of papers lay everywhere. A large window overlooked Northern Catholic's sports fields.

"Ah, Alan. Saved the best for last," said Father MacKristin. "Please, sit."

I sat in the club chair across the small mahogany desk from the priest.

He began, "I traditionally interview each of my students near year's end, find out what we did well, what we can do better. Before we start, do you have any questions or comments about my class or the school in general?"

I smiled. I had developed a friendship with the priest who loved science, wore civvies, and allowed only students who aced his class to call him "Jim."

"I want to thank you again for helping Rich. That was pretty great. And I loved your class. Nothing I'd change. I'll miss it."

"Well, now that we've gotten the formalities out of the way, let me say that we were worried about you for a while. We've seen some good young men choose the wrong path. But you really turned things around. You're back on top with your grades, and you set a school record in freshman wrestling, despite being *pinned* in your first match, no?"

I heard the emphasis on "pinned." I recalled how I had lost confidence and acted foolishly. "Yeah, well..." I said and paused, embarrassed to go on.

With a melodramatic flare he asked, "What made you rise out of the darkness?"

"You, my friends, my dad. You all made me see that intentions matter. I learned *intention* is like potential energy. It hasn't done anything *yet*, but it has to be counted as part of the total recognition we earn by our accomplishments."

"Ah, a scientific analogy. Well said." The priest smiled. "Which brings me to my evaluation and my earnest questions." He paused. "The paper you wrote, *What's the Matter with Omniscience?* Did you have help writing it?"

"My friend John helped me. Especially with the math," I said. "Why?"

"Remarkable," the teacher confessed. "We discussed Descartes' mind-body dualism in class, but I think what you are saying here is quite different." Father MacKristin picked up my paper from his desk and read something to himself. "The duality you speak of. You make an analogy with quantum mechanics?"

I grinned. "Yeah, I've been trying to convince John about that too. Here's what I'm thinking." I leaned forward. "Quantum mechanics teaches us that the smallest physical building blocks are both particles *and* waves. One completely different from the other, what physicists call a *duality.* John says experiment after experiment confirms this."

"How can a fundamental particle of reality be *two* different things?"

"Ah hah!" I exclaimed. "Let's talk John's perspective for a minute. Take a hologram. Ever see one?"

"No. I've read about them. Fascinating," Father MacKristin said.

"We start with information," I began. I slid a statuette of Thomas Aquinas from the side of the priest's desk to the center. "The information we need to recognize this figure comes from the pattern of light it reflects, right?"

"Yes, agreed."

"We could record that information on film as either a photograph or a holograph. I can tell you that the two negatives look very different. So which one correctly records the image of the statue? Answer: they both do. It's probably not the best analogy, but the point is that the essential information we need to recognize this statue can be in *two* very different forms. Like a duality. Now, imagine reality is like these two negatives. It can be understood as photographic or holographic. Information that can be in two completely different forms at the same time."

Father MacKristin stared at the statuette. "A particle *and* a wave," he mused. "Information, a duality. Interesting. And in your paper, the duality is between consciousness and matter?"

"Like I said to John," I replied, "mathematics shows us that particles of matter can be in two very different forms at the same time. So why can't they have an external, physical expression *and* an internal awareness? Not like Descartes thought, not two different things: mind stuff and matter stuff. *One* thing with a *dual* expression. A single coin with two sides, physical information on one side, and information *aware of itself* on the other."

"But," Father MacKristin sounded skeptical, "as I asked in red pen on your paper, you're saying that even subatomic particles would have a conscious side?"

"Look, let's do this little experiment I do with John. Close your eyes."

"Please?" the priest said.

"Seriously, close your eyes," I repeated. Once the cleric closed his eyes, I went on. "Now you see nothing. Try imagining you smell nothing, taste nothing. Imagine your skin is so numb you can't feel your arms on the desk, the pressure from your chair, the temperature of this room. You're floating in space. When I stop talking, imagine you hear nothing, and then imagine all your memories gone, and completely stop thinking. Open your eyes when you can tell me what's left of your consciousness."

The room went silent. The priest's face relaxed. It was a long minute. Then he opened his eyes and said, "Being. There was just, being."

"You see, there are different levels of consciousness," I offered. "Maybe an electron has the smallest level. Maybe the atoms and molecules that make up the brain bring together their tiny amounts of consciousness in a way that creates *human* consciousness, similar to the way life emerges when the atoms and molecules making up the chemicals of life come together. The ingredients of a complex soup producing something amazing and unexpected."

"Where did you ever come up with this idea?" the priest inquired. He smiled and shook his head with an honest affection that was almost embarrassing.

My face flushed a little. "Listening to John's lectures about the weird way particles move— like they have choices to make to get to their destinations— it seemed to me the brain works in a similar way. I'm not saying that a quantum particle thinks about where it wants to go, but it struck me as strange that there was this similarity. So I asked myself, 'If brains have a human consciousness, what do quantum particles have?'"

"At the end of your paper," Father MacKristin asked, "you talk about *entanglement* and speculate that if all the fundamental particles of matter were connected, then your material-mental duality idea suggests an omniscience. If you're correct, a scientific basis for a cosmological consciousness?"

"Yes," I replied, "but I've got to learn a lot more about how the brain works, and John has to figure out a lot more about how the universe works, to believe it's possible."

"This John, he sounds pretty amazing," the priest commented.

I grinned. "Ohhh yeah."

"It's a wonderful idea though," the teacher said. "I like it. You certainly deserved your grade."

"Thanks, Jim," I said.

"Perhaps this idea could help an old acquaintance of yours." Jim went on. "Father Curtain is having a crisis of faith. Some personal tragedies have dragged him into the darkness. He always had great respect for you and your family. I wonder if you would talk to him? Tell him your experience with the darkness and your ascension into the light with this wonderful idea."

Father Curtain? Crisis of faith? It didn't seem possible. "I didn't know," I said, wondering what possibly could have happened. "I'd be happy to talk to him, but I don't know how I can help. I stopped believing what he was teaching. I don't even know what I believe yet."

"Just explain it to him, like you explained it to me," Jim said. "Tell him how you and your friend conceived this intriguing idea. Coming from you, knowing your personal adversity, I think you might be his perfect good Samaritan."

On Saturday May 31st, Tim called and asked if I wanted to go with him to the park and watch Stephanie and Emilie tryout for the girls' softball team. The girls were out on the field when Tim and I walked out from the wooded path behind St Peter's school. We took a seat in the stands. Girls from eighth and ninth grade were showing off their skills under the selective eyes of the high school's baseball coaches. During a few weeks of practice, fifteen girls from each grade would be invited to play in an annual rivalry, the Forrest Creek's girls' charity softball game. Proceeds went to various charities. When the girls finished, Tim left with Stephanie, and I walked Emilie home. We talked about who the best players were. Of course, I told her she was one of the best.

When we got to her house, Ada was excited. "Hi, Alan." She turned to Emilie, "How did it go?" she asked, looking at the patches of dirt that covered her daughter from shoulders to sneakers.

"Good. It was fun," Emilie replied. "There are lots of serious players. But Steph and I weren't sent home, and half of the girls have been cut already! Alan said we looked like the best players, but I'm sure he's lying!" She laughed.

"Wonderful!" Ada responded.

"And," Emilie added, "I've been meeting some of the high school girls. They're nice. Maybe some of them will be in my home room next year."

Then Ada's expression turned serious. "Ah, that reminds me. There's something I need to talk to you both about."

Emilie filled a glass with lemonade from the fridge and sat down. "What's the matter?"

Ada looked at me and said, "It will take a little time. Alan, can I invite you to dinner? Emilie can get cleaned up, and we can have a conversation?"

"Sure," I said.

Ada told me to come back at about seven p.m.

*****

It was a Saturday afternoon, and the weather was perfect. Yet Bellcon found himself fighting the nausea that usually accompanied his encounters with Molly. Some morsels of her information were valuable, so he smiled and allowed himself to suffer through the prattle. Months ago he'd found out he was a suspect in an assault at Garrison Mountain. His father had asked him to "lay low" for a while and be careful not to get in any trouble. He had put a hold on his plans to embarrass Andrew and get acquainted with Emilie. Now Molly made him see that he'd need a whole new strategy.

Molly said, "Yup. A couple weeks ago. She broke up with Andrew, just like that. She told me at the softball tryouts today, but I'm not supposed to say anything. He's not a bad kid. You think she did it because he's older and going to college?"

"Don't know," Bellcon mused. "Maybe she has another boyfriend."

Molly puckered her lips, thinking. "She's always hanging around with Stephanie and that boy Tim. My mom says that's being a third wheel. You think she's a third wheel?"

Bellcon forced a raspy laugh without changing his serious expression. "What about that other kid? The one whose mother was killed?"

"Oh, yeah." Molly blinked. "Alan? Ya know what? He was at the tryouts! I think you're right. Wait till the girls hear this. Some of them wanted to get their claws on that boy."

Bellcon grinned at her. He was already contriving a new plan to have his way with his eighth-grade pin up girl. "Don't get those poor girls depressed, Molly," he said. "If

Emilie is going out with Alan, maybe it won't last very long. Strange things can happen."

Molly smiled and rolled her eyes. The metal between her lips shined, as though she were just asked to the prom. "Ya think so?" she asked.

"Oh yeah," Bellcon answered. "I know so."

CHAPTER 34

On Saturday evening, Emilie led me up the stairs to their kitchen. On the table I noticed a vase full of blue irises and white tulips. I felt a slight shiver. "What are the flowers for?" I asked.

"That's my dad. He likes to surprise us once in a while. Irises are my favorite; my mom loves tulips. He's away on business for a few days and had them delivered."

We sat at the kitchen table. I said nothing about my mother's love for irises, but occasionally found myself glancing over at them. Ada set out food, a middle eastern chicken dish, rice, pita bread, and a salad. She sat down, and the three of us began passing plates.

"OK," Emilie said, "what's the big secret?"

Ada said, "The high school principal called me. He warned me about something. Actually, it's something Marie had told me about." She nodded towards me.

"Alan's mom?" Emilie interrupted.

"Yes. You know she was the guidance counselor," Ada said. "Well, she and a few senior staff people were given confidential information. She only told me about it in case there was still a danger when you went to the high school. Marie said there were authorities investigating the situation, but they were having a difficult time obtaining hard evidence to prosecute. Mr. Vandike wants to form an army of parents to protect our kids."

"What are you talking about? What danger?" Emilie asked.

I said, "My mom never said anything to me."

Ada cleared her throat. "There is a boy at the high school. He transferred here from a small town in the midwest. A teenage girl disappeared around the time he transferred. At first her father was a suspect, but later he was found beaten to death in his home. The police said it was a robbery. The district attorney, who thought this boy had something to do with the girl and her father, was investigating when he was swept up in a scandal that landed him in jail."

"Wait," Emilie interrupted, "the district attorney went to jail?"

"That's right," Ada replied, "and a gag order was issued by a judge, so no one could speak about the case."

"*What*?" Emilie said, wide-eyed. "How could such a thing happen? How come this kid is not in jail?"

"Who is this kid?" I asked.

Ada said, "His name is Bellcon."

Emilie and I looked at one another. I remembered how Bellcon had looked at her in the football stands. My face began to burn. Emilie's face instantly went pale. Her mouth dropped open. "Oh my God," she said.

"You know him?" Ada said in a low voice.

"He's a football player at the high school. I, uh, I've seen him at games."

I didn't want to scare Ada. I said nothing, but I began to think of how this threat would need to be eliminated. The kid was scary, no doubt, but something had to be done.

Emilie added, "Sometimes I had the strangest feeling, when he came off the field, like he was staring at me."

Ada sucked in a breath. "The principal is right. This has gone on too long! He wanted to assign parents to watch this boy. To make sure we'll have evidence if he does anything."

"I've got to tell my friends," Emilie said.

"We can't tell too many people, Emilie," Ada said. "Mr. Vandike said we have to be very careful talking about this publicly. We have to think. If Bellcon's father finds out, he can pull strings. We are too familiar with this kind of thing. The police, judges, even the government can become a tool for the criminal."

"We haven't done anything wrong," Emilie replied. "This isn't Nazi Germany!"

Ada sat up straight. "We can't be naive."

"We can't do nothing!" Emilie exclaimed.

"Emilie's right," I said. "Other people have to know about this. As many as we can tell who we can trust."

Ada said, "We will also talk to Dad. He knows some people. We may have some strings to pull too."

"Mom," Emilie interjected, "there are no strings to pull without evidence."

"The plan makes sense," I said. "As many people as possible keep a close eye on this kid. Something happens, we share any evidence. I've got to warn Tim. He always stumbles into people like this. And what about Steph?"

Emilie replied, "I'll tell her Monday night. We invited her to dinner after softball practice. We can have a private conversation."

"I'll see Tim at John's tomorrow. I'll talk to him when we're alone," I said.

"What about John?" Emilie asked

"I don't think he'll have a problem. That kid hardly ever leaves his house, unless he's at school."

"It's settled then," Emilie said.

We finished eating and cleared the table. Ada looked satisfied, she thanked me for coming and excused herself from the table. Talking with Emilie, the time passed quickly, the sky darkened.

Emilie said, "Steph and Tim have told me about your heavy scientific discussions at John's. You guys like to talk about the universe and astronomy?"

"Yeah," I laughed. "We get pretty carried away."

"Well," Emilie asked, "want to see it?"

I was confused. "See what?"

"The universe," Emilie said, as if it were in her pocket. "You should see the view from our deck in the backyard. There are no lights back there, and on a clear night it's pretty impressive. We see lots of shooting stars."

"OK, cool," I said.

We walked through sliding glass doors out onto the deck and sat next to one another on two patio chairs. We looked up into a cloudless sky. There was no moon. I gasped, "Oh my God. I've never seen so many stars. See that?" I touched Emilie's arm with one hand and pointed with the other. "That's the Milky Way. It looks like a white cloud, but every tiny white dot is a star."

Emilie touched my hand. She said, "I love looking at that sky. It makes me feel everything is right somehow. Is that strange?"

"No. Not at all," I said, looking into Emilie's eyes. Her black pupils, large in the dark, were rimmed with hazel-green. They were pools I waded into, before realizing the undertow. I leaned towards her. We closed our eyes, and our lips met.

The eternity of the sky above us, the allure of Emilie's eyes, and our communion exploded into my brain like the birth of a new universe. I was enveloped by an awareness, deep, endless, and uncoupled from any of my senses. For an instant, I knew no boundaries. Emilie and I were one. We were the universe and the universe was us. From a distance I could hear Emilie calling, "Alan? Alan, you can open your eyes."

I did not want the moment to ever end. Reluctantly, I opened my eyes.

"Are you trying to be dramatic?" Emilie teased.

"Did you feel that?" I asked.

"Yes." She smiled. "It was nice."

"That's what it must be like. Being in the river."

"What? Is that supposed to be a compliment?" Emilie demanded.

"I mean the river below. We are all the ripples on the surface. I mean, oh boy, this is going to take a while to ex-plain," I said, flustered.

Emilie folded her arms over her chest, "Well, then you had better get started."

I had talked with Emilie about her strong faith, and I admired how she had thought through some tough questions about God. So I began by telling her how, when my mother died, I wanted to prove to myself that there was a God, an afterlife. The key, I felt, was to understand consciousness. I told her about my experience at Ona's, the raindrops on the river creating superficial ripples and interference patterns, while the water below was invisible. Just as the surface of a river has a hidden depth, I explained that I thought it was possible that the stars, the planets and our brains were made from a substance that, like the river's surface, had a deeper and inaccessible level. Underneath the substance of fundamental particles was sentience. To demonstrate a particle's fundamental awareness, I had Emilie do the same experiment as Father MacKristin.

When she opened her eyes she said, "Just *being*. That's what I felt. And you're saying when you kissed me it was like wading in the river, connected to everything?"

"Yes," I replied.

Emilie looked up at the dark, impassive sky. "I like your explanations, they're about things I've taken on faith. You think there is a unified awareness? A river running through the universe? How would that be possible?"

I briefly described how the image of a hologram could not be cut into pieces, how the information on it was unified. I added, "I'm still trying to figure it all out."

"But could science, I mean their theories, describe such things?" Emilie asked.

"That's what I'd like to know."

"Alan," Emilie said enthusiastically, "you've got to do this. It's so much like I've thought. God being everything, and everyone being connected. It's one of the most beautiful ideas I've ever heard. Promise you won't stop believing and won't stop searching until you find the answer."

"OK. You really like this crazy idea?"

"Oh yes," Emilie replied, her eyes seeming to glow in the dark.

She leaned into me and kissed me deeply. The river engulfed us, and our stubborn corporeal boundaries dissolved into its clear, fathomless waters.

CHAPTER 35

When I woke up Sunday morning, I felt reborn. Things had changed. Even my room looked different. I had an impulse to call Emilie, to be with her. There was a strange new emptiness in my chest without her, and, to fill the part of myself that she had taken or that I had given her, I knew I would have to be with her. First, though, I had other obligations. There was breakfast at John's, I had to warn Tim about Bellcon, and later in the afternoon, I had an appointment with Father Curtain.

When breakfast at John's was winding down, Tim turned to me in front of Hip and John and asked with a smirk, "Anything new with the love life?"

I told them sheepishly, "Yeah. I'll probably be going out with Emilie now."

Tim laughed. "Probably? Oh, I get it. A quantum mechanical sorta love, huh?"

They all laughed. Hip said, "You guys make a great couple. Emilie is smart and cool, but she's a tough cookie."

"Yeah, Alan," Tim added, "she'll be mopping the floor with your weak-ass mug."

The boys laughed again and I said, "You've probably got that right."

We all headed for the stairs to leave when John tapped me on the shoulder. "Hey, can I talk with you for a minute?"

"Yeah, what's up?" I called to Tim, "Hey, Tim, wait up for me outside, OK?"

I turned my full attention back to John. "OK, got a new paradox or something?"

"I wanted to let you know, to tell you..." John paused.

"Come on, man," I said, laughing and pointing to his head. "There's something in there that wants to come out."

"Yes, well, uh, I just wanted to say, uh, maybe someday I'll be lucky enough to talk about a relationship like yours. I just wish you and Emilie the best of luck." John responded.

I could tell John was holding back something. Like the times during our meetings when he'd say something like "Don't let others tell you what to think," then he'd look at me as if hoping I'd understand something he didn't want to explain. I figured sooner or later he would clue me in. I grinned. "Thanks, man, I appreciate that." I gave John an affectionate slap on the back.

I headed out to tell Tim the news about the monster of Forrest Creek and to swear him to secrecy. When I finished filling him in, he whistled and just said, "Holy shit."

In the afternoon, I waited in the rectory study. The secretary's words concerned me. "Try not to upset father," she said. "He was just released from the hospital last week." I looked around the room, recalling the priest's impassioned defense of his strong faith. I wondered, *What happened?*

"Hello, Alan," Father Curtain said, entering the room looking pale. "So kind of you to come. You look well. How is your father and your grandmother, Grace?"

"They're all doing OK, Father," I said, standing. "But how are you?"

"Did you hear what happened, Alan?"

I shook my head.

"It was terrible. Senseless. Like what happened to your mother," the priest began. "I've thought about our conversations a lot. Now I understand the chasm between the sufferer and the sympathizer. When your mother died you said you did not ask *how* God could let horrible things happen, but *why* He would let them happen, yes? And I too found there was no answer. When He could have stopped the thief or sent a good charitable person to help my sister or done a thousand other things to stop what happened. Her car had broken down on a highway and a robber killed them. Her and her beautiful little daughter." His voice cracked. He paused, sighed, and continued. "At first the alcohol was to numb the pain, stop my incessant questioning. They put me in the hospital's psychiatric ward, and it helped with the recovery of my mind, but I'm afraid my faith, it's gone." He looked down, putting his right hand on his forehead.

"You're right," I said, "the last time we spoke, it was hard for me to believe in God, the God I was taught about in church."

Father Curtain looked up, curious.

"The only thing that seemed reliable," I went on, "was science, and I decided to find out if science could describe anything that we might call God."

"And?" Father Curtain asked. "You look like you've discovered something."

"There may be something. I'm not sure yet," I answered.

"Will you tell me about it?" the cleric asked. "I'd be grateful."

"It's a long story," I warned.

"Please," said the priest, "it would be of great interest to me, coming from you."

I told the whole story to him. How my ideas developed: from the ripples on the river at Ona's and lessons from John, to the explanation of a hologram. When I had finished the priest observed, "Suppose there is this Omniscience pervading the entire universe. I guess we could refer to it as God. But would it just be an awareness? A being that does not judge, unable to intervene? Unable to stop the horrors men visit upon one another?"

I recalled what Emilie had once said. I explained, "Men have free will, Father. We can't have both free will and a God that intervenes. And I believe John is right when he says we are the only judges, and each one of us must take responsibility for our actions. Our choices define what kind of person we want to be."

"And the innocents," the priest asked painfully, "cut down by remorseless killers without ever knowing much of life?"

Again, I remembered what Emilie had said. "Yes, the world is broken. We are a part of it, and there are things we can fix. But our consciousness, our life is a precious gift that has been lent to us. One day, we can't know when, we'll have to give it back."

"So, we're on our own on this Earth?" Father Curtain said softly. "Doesn't sound like a promising belief to inspire faith."

"There may be something else though," I answered.

"What is that?" the cleric asked.

"If we get our consciousness from the same stuff the universe is made from, then everything, and all of us, may be *connected*, like quantum particles. We're all entangled with that cosmic consciousness," I said. "If that's not cool enough, think of how special it would make each of us. We are tiny beings where the universe becomes aware of itself. It creates an impression in our minds. That puts the universe in each one of us."

"Like that hologram?" the priest mused. "The whole in every part?"

"Yes, Father. But most amazing, the things we do can *change* the universe."

"Interesting, I'll have to meditate about it some more. Thank you for sharing this with me. You worked with John on these ideas? I'm impressed with John too. He's a very intelligent young man. When his parents came to me for help, I talked with him. But it was hard. I guess I just don't understand homosexuality—"

"What?" I interrupted. "What did you say? Homosexuality?"

"Oh, my goodness," the priest said with surprise. "I thought you would have known by now. I'm sorry, I didn't mean to be the one. John said he was going to... oh dear. Please don't treat that boy harshly. He deserves to be treated kindly. He's simply misguided."

My face flushed. I was being smothered by emotions. Among my male friends, homosexuals were loathed. I had an impulse to get out of the rectory, to get outside where I could breathe again. I knew I had to say something to appease the priest. "I'm sure I would have found out soon. Don't worry about it. I wouldn't harm John." I stood up to end our meeting. "I'll let you know if I make a breakthrough with these ideas. I hope you get better quickly. People need you."

The priest stood, shook my hand, and said, "Thank you, my son. I've really enjoyed our conversation."

"I have too," I said. "Take care now."

Father Curtain watched me disappear through the doorway.

My head became a jury box, filled with indecisive jurors. They could not deliver a verdict on John. Was John a deviant homosexual, as homosexuals were viewed by my friends? Did he betray us by not revealing his secret? Did he fantasize sexually about me or my friends? I liked John a lot. From that first day of school when he said "We will be friends," a piece of John had grown in me. He helped me understand that logical rules organized the universe, not malice. There was a beauty in his view of the world, which expanded into the void left in me by the loss of my mother. It grew larger and surrounded me, like a shell protecting an embryonic child until I was less vulnerable. He was light in the darkness. He made sense of things. I'd never have learned the things he taught me. I owed so much to him. Homosexual? I wondered if I could ever feel like John's friend again. I was confused and near tears. My only decision was not to tell anyone about this. I knew how cruel kids could be.

CHAPTER 36

Fortunately, I had arranged to work over the summer for my neighbor, Mr. Wayne. He owned a trucking company, and it was hard work, driving in with him at six thirty a.m. and loading trucks with heavy boxes all day. So starting work on Monday was a welcome distraction, though what to do about John haunted me while Mr. Wayne drove me home late Monday afternoon. When I opened my front door, the phone was ringing. I answered it.

"Hello?"

"I think I fucked up," Tim said, sounding worried.

"What do you mean?" I asked.

"I went to meet Steph today at the luncheonette. I walk in and, shit, she's sitting there smiling and talkin' to that fuckin' murderer!" Tim replied.

"*What?* Didn't she know?"

"Emilie was going to tell her tonight, remember? But I figured I'd meet her at lunch, where we could talk and I could warn her. That scumbag must have followed her there. He must have introduced himself and sat down. Steph was all smiles, telling him about their softball practice. Damn!"

"What did you do?"

Tim was quiet for a moment. Then his voice was calmer. "Well, I sat down. He said his name. I told him I knew who he was. Then I figured, you know, I couldn't rat him out right there—"

I cut in, "Thank God."

Tim continued. "I just started asking him questions, like I was interested. 'Where are you from?' I said. You know he wouldn't say. He kept answering me with questions, or saying 'That's not important.' So finally, I says, 'Around here it matters where you're from and what you've done.'"

"Oh crap," I said. "What did he say?"

"He, uh, asked me outside for a minute. We went into that little alley on the side of the building. Ha, I thought he was gonna strangle me. You should have seen his face. He's a killer all right. He says 'You got something you want to say to me? Something you think you know about me?' I asked 'Maybe there's something you don't want to tell us?' He says, 'Everyone's got something they'd rather not talk about. Maybe it's a father who's a drunk, who did something really bad.' I don't know where that fuck came from, but I was really pissed. I said, 'So, you know all about me. Guess it's time for me to find out about you, call my friend in that little town you came from.'"

"What did Bellcon say?" I asked.

"He says, 'Be careful, it can be very dangerous poking your nose into other people's business.' And I say, 'Maybe it can be dangerous not to.' He got right in my face, Alan. Tried to scare me, and says, 'You'll regret it.' Can you believe that?"

"And what did *you* say Tim?"

"I said, 'I'm not afraid a' you.' "

I shook my head, "Jeeezz-us!"

On Saturday morning June 21st, Rich and I were playing tennis. The sky was clear, the shadows long, the park soundless except for bird songs and the rhythmic thuds from a tennis ball reversing direction on our racquets. It was the week before Forrest Creek's girls' charity softball game.

"They've been practicing three times a week for almost a month," Rich was saying. "My sister could play for the damn Yankees by now! The game is next week. Why another practice this morning?" He bounced a ball in front of him. "Losers. What time is their practice?" In slow motion, he lofted the ball above his head. (*Thud*, soft serve.)

"Didn't Steph tell you?" I asked. (*Thud*, corner shot.)

"I forget half the stuff Steph says," (*Thud*, top spin return.)

"It's at nine," (*Thud*, net ball.)

"Nine a.m.? Why so frickin' early? I had to get up before the damn milk man, so you could go to their zillionth practice?" Rich asked, pulling another ball from his pocket.

I laughed. "That your excuse for the lame serves?"

Rich smiled, eyed the center line, and fired a serve that blew past me before I could extend my racket. "Like that one?"

"Oh yeah!" I said. "Holding back on me, you lazy dick? Come on, play hard for thirty minutes, and then we'll go watch the girls practice."

*****

It was one week until the girls' softball game. Bellcon sat watching the boiling river rapids under suicide bridge. He had done his homework and chose his blind well. He knew he would be invisible. The woods and heavy underbrush completely blocked the view from the softball field, which was thirty yards away, down a tiny winding path. He had set a towel and dry clothes on a rock nearby. The widest part of the river was a stone's throw away. Water rushed under the bridge and sounded like a jet engine as it flowed around river rocks and gushed past the "HAZARD!" sign planted in front of the low-head dam. He had heard stories of the guy who jumped off the bridge after losing everything in the Great Depression. The powerful falls had swept his body into a rocky crevice on the river bed. The body was not found for a month. An unlucky kid was also swallowed by the river. He had slipped on a rock while fishing under the bridge. His body was trapped for weeks in the river's jaws.

Then there was Molly, who told Bellcon a rumor that Tim tried to kill himself at this very place, but was saved by Father Curtain. "Everybody knows that," she had said. She also told Bellcon about her softball practices and about some of the girls whose boyfriends came to watch. Like Stephanie and Tim.

Bellcon had come early to two other practices. He did not sit in the stands. He watched from a distance. Both times he was surprised to see Tim also arrive early and head down a path that cut through a wall of trees at the perimeter of right field. The path led to the river, just upstream from the rapids under suicide bridge. He wondered if Tim still contemplated suicide. The thought made him smile because if Tim drowned in the river, the town would know the rumors were true and Tim just finished himself off.

Bellcon looked at his watch, then looked towards the path that cut through a wall of trees and underbrush and led to the park's recreation area. The kid was a little late. The predator knew this would be risky, but he was sure it was Tim who had been spreading the truth about Dargton, which threatened to ruin everything. Tim had said he had a friend in Dargton. Bellcon thought this was probably bullshit, but Tim seemed to be getting information from somewhere. In any event, Bellcon knew he had to nip this in the bud. Something else angered him. In the back of his head Tim's voice played like a broken record. *I'm not afraid a' you,* he heard over and over. He thought, *You wanted to end it all right here. Everybody knows that. It would have been good for you. It would have been good for me.*

Some twigs snapped, bushes rustled, and Tim came walking down the path, towards the river.

When she did not see Tim in the bleachers, Stephanie guided Emilie towards the path that led to the river while they continued their conversation. Behind them, the softball team began to take positions across the outfield, warming up.

Walking into the woods on the path, Stephanie said, "They went to the courts around eight."

Emilie laughed. "Alan told me your brother said only losers get up early on Saturday mornings."

"What did he mean by that? We're up."

"I think that's what he meant!" Emilie giggled.

Stephanie stopped and cocked her head. "Do you hear that?" Some muffled sounds came from ahead. The girls picked up their pace and rounded the last turn. Stephanie froze. Tim was struggling with Bellcon at the river bank. He held Tim from behind, with one hand over Tim's mouth and the other wrapped around his torso. Tim was trying to kick, elbow, and punch him.

Emilie grabbed Stephanie's arm. "Scream, Steph, scream!" she ordered. "I'll be back." She took off in the opposite direction.

Stephanie's scream sent birds flying and nearby wildlife scurrying for safety. At that same instant the two boys fell into the river. They seemed to be thrashing under water near the river's edge. Bellcon's head popped up. His right cheek was reddened and blood trickled from the corner of his mouth.

Bellcon called out, "*Steph, help me*! He's trying to kill himself."

"*What?*" Stephanie shouted, mouth agape. She walked towards the water. "*Pull him up! Pull him up!!*"

Bellcon's head disappeared under the water for a moment, and the struggling seemed less tumultuous. His head popped up again. "I can't. He's holding on to a rock!"

Stephanie stepped into the river, confused. "*Get him up!* You've got to—"

The beast of Forrest creek sprung from the water like a crocodile reaching out for her. But as he reached for her shirt, he heard "*Stop!*" and froze. Bellcon spun around. Emilie was walking briskly at him.

"*Get away from her!*" she commanded, eyes ablaze and defiant. "Steph, get Tim, *quickly!*" she yelled and raced into the water to help. The demon moved toward her. She glared at him. "Life in prison, or the electric chair, which will it be, kapo?"

"You've got it all wrong. I was only trying—" Bellcon said.

Emilie and Stephanie dragged Tim's limp body up onto land. Emilie rolled Tim onto his back. Stephanie said, "He looks blue. He's not breathing." She remembered the manikin in life guard class, and she began CPR.

Bellcon moved closer.

Emilie said, "All these witnesses don't have it wrong." She yelled out, "*Giirrrrlllls?*"

From invisible places behind bushes all around them, voices erupted.

"We saw what you tried to do!"

"You tried to kill him!"

"Murderer!"

"I saw it!"

"Me too!"

"And me!"

"You were drowning him!"

Emilie said to Stephanie, "I sent one of the girls to call an ambulance, and," she looked at Tim's assailant, "Molly should be at the police station by now. She took one of the bikes."

Bellcon's face was expressionless. His voice monotone. "Since you all seem to have the situation under control, I'll go. But you've got me all wrong." He walked out of the water, retrieved his dry clothes and towel, and walked down the path.

A siren in the distance was getting louder. Tim coughed and spit up some river water. Stephanie began to cry.

Emilie stood unflinching as she watched Bellcon depart.

When Bellcon arrived at his house his anxiety turned to panic. Two black sedans were parked at the curb. At first, he thought Molly had convinced the police to pick him up. Official looking men in dark suits and ties were carrying sealed boxes out of his house. Something was very wrong. He ran to the front steps and went inside. One of the dark suits was standing behind Frank, putting him in handcuffs. "*Dad! What's going on?*" he asked his father.

"It's OK, son, just a technicality, I'm sure." He turned to the dark suit. "Can I have a word with my son? In private?" The man considered this as he snapped the metal cuffs on Frank's wrists. He looked past the door to the study and saw no windows. Large framed photos hung on the walls:

Frank standing with Spiro Agnew, another with the N.J. governor. "In there. Five minutes. I'll be right here." They went into the study. Frank's son closed the door. "What the hell is this?"

"Your mother," Frank began. "I think she wants to put us both in prison."

"What?" the boy asked.

Frank explained. "She's got an FBI boyfriend. Convinced them to run a sting on me. Got me laundering money for a senator and bribing a federal judge. It will be tough to work a plea deal."

"Shit, what am I going to do?" Bellcon asked. "I had a little problem with a kid and a girl. There are witnesses."

Frank showed no emotion. "You know what will happen to you now, don't you?"

Bellcon spat. "That fuckin kid. I want to—"

"Shut up!" his father commanded. "Admit to nothing. Remember what we planned if this happened. Your little vacation?"

"Shit. That?"

"Yes, you'll do it, *now*. There's an officer Dunnard who will help you." He told his son to pick up the phone, dial a number, and hold the phone to his ear. "Good afternoon, Officer." Franks' voice was calm. "I wanted to tell you that I will be unavailable for a while. My son is making arrangements to take a vacation, and I wouldn't want his plans to be, ah, interrupted. As you know, there are some people who'd like to put him away without evidence of wrongdoing. Would you be kind enough to watch out for him, and give him updates on the Garrison situation? I assume there's no new information?"

Although it wasn't public knowledge, five days earlier the Garrison case had been shelved. Two of the "victims" were involved in the armed robbery of a liquor store. The stabbed victim apparently had an epiphany following the Garrison affair and joined the Peace Corp. Charges had been dropped. But Dunnard simply said, "Nothin' I heard."

"OK, so would you come to my home later to meet my son?" asked Frank.

"Sure. No problem. See ya later," the officer replied, and hung up.

The door opened, the dark suit came in and led Frank away.

"Do it, now!" Frank called to his son from the front door.

CHAPTER 37

Rich and I were leaving the tennis courts. We saw Molly on a bicycle peddling frantically down the narrow park road towards us.

"Hey, Molly," Rich called out, "are you guys practicing or what?"

She did not slow down. As she got closer, she panted, "He, he's gonna kill him. Got to get the police!"

"*What*?" I asked. "Who?"

As she passed, we could see the panic on her face. She blurted, "Bellcon. Tim."

We looked at each other, then ran to our bikes and covered the mile distance to the baseball field. An ambulance was pulling out of the parking lot, lights flashing. A group of girls huddled near first base, all talking at once. One of the girls saw me and Rich and ran towards us.

"Oh my God, they were back there, the path to the river, and Stephanie saw them. He's a violent kid. Who knows what set him off?"

"Stephanie?" Rich asked.

I said, "Slow down. Who was back by the river?"

"Bellcon!"

"Whoa!" I said. "What did he do?"

"He held Tim under the water. Stephanie had to revive him. Bellcon wanted to drown them. Stephanie too! But Emilie told us to hide in the bushes, so we could be witnesses. You should've seen his face."

Rich looked around, alarmed. "Where's Steph?"

I knew something like this was coming, but a chill went down my back and a fire broke out in my stomach. "Is Tim OK?"

"They all went in the ambulance," the girl said, "Tim, Steph and Emilie. Tim didn't look good."

I gulped. "Emilie too?" My face felt cold and a shiver went through me. My first impulse was to jump on my bike and get to the hospital, but this urge was overridden by some primitive regions in my brain.

Rich said, "Why would that big fuck—"

I broke in. "Where's Bellcon?"

The girl said, "He left. I don't know. But Emilie said I should tell you they're going to be OK and not to do anything. She wants you to meet her at the hospital."

I walked to my bike. Rage was growing inside me. "Where are you going?" one girl asked.

They all stared at me as I rode off. Out of the corner of my eye I thought I saw Rich stomping over to the bat bag near his bike.

I stopped a few houses down from Bellcon's and watched as men in dark suits escorted his handcuffed father into a black sedan and drove off. His son stood at the curb and turned towards the house. I peddled quickly to his driveway. I slammed on the brakes, skidded, and called out, "Bellcon!"

The large figure turned, saw me, and mumbled, "Aw, shit." He looked around suspiciously and began walking to his backyard. "What do *you* want?" he asked.

I set my bike down in the driveway. "To make things right," I replied, following him to the back of his house.

"What's that supposed to mean?"

"You tried to drown my friends."

"I don't know what you're talking about. Your friend Tim tried to drown himself, again. I was trying to help," Bellcon said, walking into his backyard, his head turning and eyes darting probably looking around for witnesses.

"Let's cut the crap," I shot back.

The monster smiled. "I don't know what you're so upset about. Your friend tried to kill himself once already, and why would you worry about him? His father killed your *mother!*"

At that instant we sprinted at one another.

Bellcon lowered his head for a quick take down, but I had gotten lower. We collided, knocking each other back. Bellcon threw a right hook, I ducked under it and came up with a right upper cut connecting with his ribs. When Bellcon involuntarily lowered his left elbow to splint the area, I swung my right elbow at his face. Bellcon dodged the blow, wrapped his arms around my waist and lifted me off the ground, twisting to his left to throw me on my back. I swung my legs out, planted them, spun and got Bellcon in a head lock. Our arms and legs became entangled as we used the power in our backs and legs to gain advantage. We toppled to the ground, and Bellcon was able to roll on top of my chest with his legs clenched behind mine. He caught me with a vicious elbow to my left cheek, my head bounced off the ground, and I was stunned for a few seconds, long enough for him to unload a barrage of fists and elbows to my face. An encircling fuzzy darkness threatened to choke off my vision. Through the small porthole of sight I had left, I saw Bellcon rearing up, right fist ready to come down with all his weight and strength on my face. Then, it was like a switch clicked, a bright light brought everything into perfect clarity, Bellcon's movements looked slow. I shot my right hand up, the heel slamming into Bellcon's Adam's Apple. Bellcon drew his hands to his neck, wheezing and unable to take a deep breath.

Nearby a voice said, "Don't fucking move, asshole."

I looked towards the familiar sound. Rich was in a stance, his hands by his right ear gripping a baseball bat, and Bellcon's head was in home run alley. The lawyer's son sounded like he was breathing through a tiny straw in his neck. He docilely held up his hands.

Two seconds later another voice, from the corner of the house, said, "OK, DiMaggio, drop da bat and move away."

We all turned to see officer Dunnard, aiming his pistol. Rich dropped the bat and put his hands in the air.

I breathed a sigh of relief. "Officer, this one," I nodded at Bellcon, "tried to kill my friends."

Bellcon was rubbing his neck and breathing erratically. "Bellcon, over here," Dunnard said, holstering his weapon.

"Your father wasn't kiddin. They really do want to ruin your vacation."

I got to my feet slowly. "What?" I said, pointing at Bellcon, "He's the one. Didn't Molly tell you? Isn't that why you're here?"

Dunnard replied, "Don't know no Molly, but Mr. Bellcon warned me about you guys. Hey, you're the Garrison Mountain kid, aren't ya? Yeah. OK, you and Mickey Mantle here are coming with me. I need to ask you some questions. Get in the car."

Rich and I were locked in the backseat of the patrol car. Dunnard turned to Bellcon, "Promised your dad I'd keep the vermin away until you left for vacation. I don't know what these kids are talking about, but if I were you, I'd skedaddle."

"It's a misunderstanding, officer," the counselor's son said. "I was trying to help this kid who tried to kill himself in the river for the second time. I think these guys are out to get me."

Dunnard's eyes narrowed. "Yeah, sure. Like I said, I promised your father. Hey, where is he?"

"He had to leave town for a few days. Giving some testimony or something, said it was a technicality."

"OK," Dunnard said, walking around to the driver's side of the car, "best to just get outta here. Know what I mean?"

"Yes sir," Bellcon said politely. Then he bent down and looked into the back seat, turning his body, so only Rich and I could see him. He smiled, pointed at me, and mouthed the words, "Tim, and Emilie," and he cut a line across the base of his neck with his index finger.

CHAPTER 38

It was a hot morning in early August, 1969. The windows across from the kitchen table framed the wild flower gardens and backyard woods. A short walk from the front door, down a gravel access road, white dunes led to the ocean. The Hampton beach rental was perfect for the clients that Emilie's father, David, had entertained over the summer. Now Emilie, her parents, Stephanie, Tim and I were sitting down to breakfast.

"This is so great," Tim said, his voice subdued since his near drowning. "Thank you, guys, for inviting me."

"Me too," Stephanie said, excited. "I can't wait to get to the beach."

Having been to the house several times, I said to David and Ada, "It's been a great summer. I can't thank you enough." The facial swelling and bruises inflicted by Bellcon were long gone.

Ada put out plates of Pita bread, assorted cheeses and Danish. "It's our pleasure to have you all here with us. The best part of life is the part we share with friends," she said.

Emilie began filling everyone's mugs with coffee.

"Yeah," Tim said, "someone might not be sitting here if it weren't for good friends." He smiled and nodded at Emilie and Stephanie.

"We're happy you're here. And you're all welcome anytime," David said. "I don't want to put a damper on the conversation, but has anyone heard anything at all about the Bellcon boy?"

We all shook our heads. Stephanie put some cream in her coffee. "I'm glad he's gone."

I said, "If I see that kid again—"

"You promised you'd call the police." Emilie cut me off, concerned. "As I recall, you didn't look so well after your first meeting. And that policeman warned you to stay away from him."

"He told me not to go looking for him. But if I run into him again, he'll be the one not looking so good," I responded.

"Alan," Ada spoke up, "enough of that thinking. He's a killer. You should not confront him alone. Your father told me he talked to you?" She looked at her husband. "I spoke to Michael after he picked Alan up from the police station that night. He was furious. He wanted to hunt that boy down himself. But he gave it some thought, and then what did he say, Alan?"

"He said we should avoid confronting him and help the police and courts put Bellcon away. Boy, he was mad that night. I've never seen him so angry. He still calls that cop almost every day."

"So do we," said David. "I'm glad Bellcon won't be around when Emilie starts her freshman year. It's just strange how he disappeared. Well, I didn't mean to darken our day. I apologize for bringing it up. What do you all say we pack some lunches and head to the beach?"

"Yes!" Stephanie squealed, and everyone laughed.

We ate breakfast. Ada shooed everyone out of the kitchen so she could clean up. "Everything for the beach is in the shed out back, except for the towels. They're in the closet at the top of the stairs."

Heading for the second-floor bedroom we were sharing, Tim and I each grabbed a beach towel as we passed the closet. We entered our room and began changing into bathing suits. I pulled my suit and a shirt from my suitcase and told Tim, "They've got some great stuff for the beach in that shed. Stuff for paddle ball, skim boards."

Tim had pulled a large knife from his suitcase and began rolling it up in his towel. It was the knife from Garrison Mountain. A chill passed through me as I remembered that day in the park. I asked, "What's that for?"

"I take it whenever I leave the house now," Tim said calmly. "I call it Duggie. Duggie's gonna come with me from now on. Anyone wants to take me down again, they're gonna have to go through Duggie,"

"Jeez, Tim, does Stephanie know about Duggie?"

"Yeah, she's OK with it. I don't know, maybe it'll help, maybe it won't. But I'm not gonna let anyone do it to me again and get away without payin' a price."

"OK, I get it. Sure. But can we keep Duggie wrapped up in the towel? He might freak some people out."

Tim laughed. "Yeah, he has that effect on people. I always keep him hidden."

I gave a small sigh of relief. "Good. Let's go."

When we finished dinner that evening, the four of us headed back to the beach with Duggie secured in a beach bag. We talked together until nightfall, dug a pit in the sand and made a small fire. We pulled our blankets far to the opposite sides of the pit, so couples could have some privacy.

Emilie lay down on the blanket next to me and looked up into a clear, moonless night.

"God, it's so amazing," she said.

I looked up, "How could we ever understand how big it is?" I asked. "You know, light, traveling at one hundred and eighty-six thousand miles every second, takes eight minutes to get from the sun to Earth. It takes light over five hours for it to reach Pluto! And from one end of our galaxy to the other, it would take light, traveling at that ridiculous speed, one hundred thousand years."

"Wow," Emilie said.

"Even more amazing? There are many other *galaxies*," I mused.

"They've figured out so much, I wonder what we'll learn in the future," Emilie said. She whispered, "I've been thinking about what you told me about John. Tell me again, why did you stop meeting with him?"

I said, "OK, but keep your voice down. I haven't told anyone else about it."

"I'm whispering if you haven't noticed. So?"

"It's too weird," I whispered. "He's homosexual."

"And?"

"Everyone thinks they're deviants, queer. Unnatural. It gives me the creeps to think about."

Emilie replied, "His intelligence is deviant, queer, and unnatural, and you seemed to like it."

"What? Yeah, but—"

"But what?" she fired back. "Did he hurt you or anyone else that you know of? Wasn't he your friend?"

"Well, no, uh, yeah, I mean—"

While my mind tottered, Emilie pressed on. "Oh, I see. You're just going to drop your good friend because everyone else is telling you how to think? Is that it? From everything you've told me, John is as good a person as he is smart. All of a sudden he's a bad person because he's homosexual? Maybe it's not a choice. Maybe it's natural for him. Anyway, what do you care? He's not asking *you* to be homosexual, is he? Are you afraid of him? I think you need to go back to that boy and apologize!"

"*Apologize*?" I said.

"Yes! What harm did he ever do to you? But you, you stripped him of your friendship. He really liked you, and I'll bet that hurt him. You've even told me how special he is. When will you ever, ever meet someone like him again? Maybe your friendship with him is destiny? I mean, who on this planet would be better to help you with your big question? Who, Alan?"

"You mean consciousness?" I asked sheepishly.

"Yeah," Emilie said, righteousness in her voice, a dare in her eyes.

"When you put it that way..." I said, smiling and letting the words hang, tempting her mind to complete the sentence. I reached over and put my hand behind her neck.

She gently brushed my hand away. "Well?" she demanded playfully.

"I'll call him as soon as we get back, OK?" I replied, pulling her over me. She laughed.

We toyed with each other's bathing suits for a few minutes, then we rolled. The sand was cool, our skin was hot, the sky was deep.

*****

"Yes. Yes, thank you, I'm happy to hear it!" Frank Bellcon was talking into his speaker phone, smiling. He had known what the caller would tell them. It was nearing the end of August, a deadline set by his secretary, who sat across the desk from him. Whether she stayed or left him hinged on this conversation, so he had asked her to sit in on the call with him. "And I want to thank the FBI for their daily vigilance to make sure our public servants stay honest." He hung up, looked at his secretary, and said, "There, you see, case closed. Boss exonerated. You stayed with me these last few months, and I want to show my appreciation." He reached across the desk and handed her an envelope. She opened it.

"A raise?" She smiled, "you already gave me a generous bonus to stay on."

Frank held up the letter of resignation she had written two months earlier. "May I tear this up?" he asked.

She giggled. "Yes, of course. I'm so happy this has turned out OK. But I still don't understand what all the fuss was about. I mean, it looked serious. When you were gone for a week, I thought, uh—"

"I know it's confusing," Frank said, looking relaxed and confident. "Let me explain it this way: when that judge and senator came to the office, I knew immediately they were up to no good. I kept careful notes to show the authorities exactly what illegal activities the two of them were up to. I had no idea that the FBI was also investigating them. The FBI thought I was involved with the judge and senator's scheme, but once I shared my notes and explained my intention to expose these crooks, they realized I couldn't, er, shouldn't be prosecuted."

"You were like an undercover detective," she said.

"Exactly!" Frank said happily. "Now, one more gratifying item to take care of." He picked up another envelope from his desk and thoughtfully looked at both sides. "Please get officer Dunnard on the phone."

"Yes sir!" she said with rediscovered pride in her voice. She left for a moment, the intercom crackled, "Officer Dunnard is on the line."

Frank picked up the phone, "Hello, officer," he began brightly.

Dunnard interrupted. "Listen, Frank, you gotta give me something about your kid—"

Frank cut in, "Well that's why—"

Dunnard just continued, "I'm takin' a lotta heat for not bringing him in for the river incident. It's been two months, Frank, you still don't know nothin'?"

"But I'm—"

"You know," Dunnard cut him off, "the parents call me every frickin day, and one of them knows the mayor. The mayor's callin' me for chrissake! Your kid's accused of trying to drown someone. There are a bunch of witnesses!"

"Look, would you please listen?" Frank waited.

"Yeah, sure. Whadda ya gotta tell me?"

"First, like I've told you, the press, the mayor, and those kids were out to get my son. He was only trying to help."

"Yeah, right," Dunnard said, sounding unconvinced. "But there's an investigation. This is an open case. If he's innocent, he's got nothin' ta hide, OK? You know the drill. They're gonna find him, and I'm gonna help them find him. I ain't abettin'."

Frank spoke slowly and calmly. "I've always appreciated your good work. That's why I called you first, as soon as I got word. I just received a letter from my son."

"*What*? Where is he?" Dunnard asked excitedly.

"Vietnam," Frank answered.

"Vietnam?" Dunnard asked, sounding confused and disappointed, as if he'd just been reassigned to Hoboken.

"He turned eighteen and enlisted," Frank said, proudly. "Sure surprised me! These kids just grow up one day and start acting responsibly. After boot camp he was sent to the front lines. He's in the jungles defending our country, and apparently he's already been decorated."

"Vietnam?" Dunnard repeated in a fog.

"If you'd be kind enough to tell your captain and the mayor," Frank continued, "I'll tell the presiding judge. Just so happens we're golfing today. I assume this information will at least put the investigation on hold? And I hope it gets you off the hook. You're a good man."

"Yeah, yeah. Thanks," Dunnard replied and hung up.

Frank leaned back in his leather chair, looked up at the ceiling, closed his eyes, and smiled.

CHAPTER 39

Tim's voice echoed back over the phone. *"Vietnam?"*

"Yeah, that's what she heard," I replied.

"How did Emilie's dad find out?" Tim asked.

"He knows the mayor," I said. "I guess bankers hang out with the upper crust, you know?"

Tim was dumbfounded. "They took him in the military? Didn't they know the police were looking for him?"

I was at a loss myself. "Word is, the district attorney talked to a commanding officer weeks ago, then he decided to drop charges."

"What? That son of a bitch tried to kill me, Alan. He beat the shit out of you. He's killed other people in that little town he came from. Are they fuckin' kiddin'? The kid's a killer!"

"Yeah," I said, "and now he's being trained to be better at it."

"Holy shit, he can't get away with this," Tim said. "He'll come back and keep killing people."

"Let's hope he doesn't come back," I said. I thought of Bellcon's threat to kill Tim, Stephanie and Emilie. "Look, Tim, we're not going to let this go. Like Emilie and Ada say, we've got to stick together to get this guy. Emilie said her dad's talking to people in high places too."

"Man, this is bullshit!" Tim said.

"You're right. We'll figure something out. Hey, you around Sunday? I talked Emilie into coming to meet John."

Tim said, "Haven't been to John's in a long time, the summer n' sophomore year n' all. I'd like to hear what he would say about all this crap."

"I don't plan on telling him."

"I can't go anyway. I promised Steph I'd go with her to her grandma's big birthday party Sunday. But definitely next time, huh?"

"Yeah sure," I said.

Tim calmed a bit. "Cool. Let me know if John talks about any crazy new theory, like the universe is slowly turning into a pile of shit or something,"

"It wouldn't surprise me, man. Later," I said and hung up.

On Sunday morning, Emilie and I walked to John's house.

"What did he say when you called him?" Emilie asked.

"He was just, uh, John." I said.

"Meaning?"

"I told him I was sorry I stopped visiting. That I needed to get my head on straight." I shook my head and cleared my throat with a laugh. "He just said 'OK, have you learned anything new about consciousness?'"

"That's it?" She seemed surprised. "He just said OK?"

"Yeah," I said, "like we hadn't seen each other for one day, like no hard feelings."

"So why do you insist I come with you?" Emilie asked.

"I want you guys to meet. You'll really like him. Nervous?"

"Why would I be nervous? I'm not his type," she said with a mischievous grin.

I said, "He's a bit intimidating. Intellectually."

"We'll see about that," Emilie countered, as we reached the front door and I knocked.

Claudette, John's mother, answered the door, smiling, unable to conceal her delight. "Hello Alan! And this must be Emilie. My, you are a beauty! Welcome, please come in. John's downstairs. He's very excited. There are doughnuts on the table."

When I reached the bottom of the stairs, I saw John sitting at his workbench with a pen in his hand, head lying on an open notebook, and eyes closed. Two other large notebooks were stacked next to him. He appeared to be sleeping.

"Hey, John," I called out. There was no response. I looked at Emilie and smiled. "*John!*" I barked.

John sat up and turned towards us with wide eyes and an expression like he woke up on the wrong planet. He blinked, took a deep breath, and said, "Ten-twelve, oh my, I'm sorry I was, ahem." he hopped off his chair.

I looked at my watch, it was ten twelve a.m.

John moved towards me quickly and held out his hand. "It's good to see you, my friend," He turned to Emilie. "Alan told me he was bringing 'a girl.' How modest. Now I finally know what Lord Byron meant by 'She walks in beauty.'"

Emilie smiled and held out her hand. "I've heard so much about you. It's a privilege to meet you."

John shook her hand. "No, no, the privilege is all mine. I apologize for my trance when you arrived. I was working on something, uh, captivating."

"Yeah," I said smiling, "and top secret."

"For now," John said, "But since you already know one of my secrets, and you're still here, perhaps I'll share this one with you too." He pointed at his notebooks. "But first, let's sit down. I'd like to hear about the progress Alan mentioned."

Emilie looked at me. "Oh? He hasn't told me. Something new? I'd like to hear this myself."

"It's just some stuff I've been thinking about recently," I began. We each took a seat, I continued. "OK, we really don't know how the brain does it, but we'd all agree that somehow consciousness is created in the brain, right?"

"I don't know where else it would come from," John said. Emilie nodded.

"Right," I said, "and the brain is a collection of electrically active cells called neurons. There are billions of them. They act like microscopic wires, batteries, and switches. So consciousness must be associated with electricity. Somehow, the way electricity moves through this tangled mess of neurons makes consciousness."

"Did you figure out how?" Emilie asked, her eyebrows rising.

"Uh, no," I said. "But two things occurred to me about this. One: what we experience starts out when something simulates our senses. For example, light reflecting off of you enters my eyes and activates my retinas, or sound waves from your voice hits my eardrums. Then nerves send electrical signals from these sensors to my brain, which creates an experience. Think about that. The *only* experiences our brains can create come from these sensors. We're getting second hand information and guessing what the world outside of us is made of."

John said, "So what happens outside of our bodies becomes just a story told by our brains."

"Yes!" I said.

"Wait," Emilie said, "I'm not sure I understand your point."

I explained. "Consciousness is a language of the brain. A different kind of language, not the process of translating information into symbols, it's the process of transforming information into experiences. Everything we are aware of is the result of brain cells working. I see and hear you standing in front of me. I can reach out and touch you. But everything each of us knows about one another, and the world around us, is simply electrical patterns that represent experiences, a model of reality assembled by —and imprisoned in —each of our brains. If the brain didn't create a model of the world, we'd only be aware of our retinas being stimulated by light, or our eardrums vibrating."

"Hmmm, then what about dreams? Things we imagine?" Emilie asked.

"Our brains can use stored information to create a fictitious experience," I said. "Like dreams or hallucinations. Since it's all the same process, sometimes people can't tell hallucinations from reality."

"It's kind of a depressing thought," Emilie observed. "Our thoughts are prisoners, and we don't know if we're hallucinating?"

"Let's not jump the gun," John interjected. "OK, so let's say for a moment that electrical patterns moving around the brain create our conscious experiences, one of the brain's natural languages. But the brain can learn other languages too. We can teach it English for instance. Then *my* brain can communicate with *your* brain, and we can compare notes on our observations. It would be unlikely we're hallucinating if we're all seeing the same thing. And there is an objective language we can teach the brain: mathematics. Used correctly, it can give us a more accurate way to understand things around us."

"So, you see, Emilie," I offered, "by working together we can see things more clearly. There's something else, something really cool about this. Everything we know— a lifetime of collected experiences—makes up our picture of reality. By observing the universe, the brain creates its own *personal* universe. And here's the thing, I've gotten to know you and John. You've both changed the patterns in my brain, become embedded in the thing that creates my reality. So you both will always be part of my universe."

"Hmmm," Emilie replied, "that's a nice thought."

"OK, here's the second thing," I continued. "I'll get to consciousness in a minute, but first think about a unit of *life,* a cell. It can make its own energy, assemble the compounds it needs to sustain itself, and reproduce. No one would guess that such a thing would emerge from a soup of chemicals."

John said, "You're not going to try and explain life with electrons and protons, are you?"

"No," I said, "just the opposite. Life results from the *interactions* between so many different ingredients that it *can't* be explained by its parts. The behavior of one cell depends on what all its parts are doing, and you can't understand why it's alive if you just know what each part does. Imagine a cell with a vital factor, call it *molecule A*. Molecule A will influence the roles played by thousands of other vital components in the cell, and they will all influence molecule A and one another! What we see as life is the sum of *interactions* between all its parts. The cell lives as a whole, like a hologram. You can't understand life by its parts. A hologram's three-dimensional image cannot be broken into pieces. It exists as a unit."

"Hmmm...how does this apply to consciousness?" Emilie asked.

"Think of the human brain as a unit," I said. "It is built from atoms, molecules, cells. Its peculiar behavior emerges from all the many parts interacting with one another to form complex electrical patterns. That's the physical description, but I think there might be a duality here. John explained the duality of a single subatomic unit, behaving as both a wave *and* a particle. You would think particles and waves are entirely different things, but it's an example of how one thing can be described in two ways. Well, what if the brain's atoms, molecules and cells could also be described in two ways, not only as physical things, but also as the tiniest fragments of self-awareness. Maybe all the interactions between these building blocks of self-awareness create a whole human consciousness. Then the brain can be described objectively: by chemical or electrical patterns, or subjectively: by what it's experiencing. Sort of a duality."

Emilie and John stared at me blankly.

"How 'bout this," I said, "what if I hook you up to a machine that reproduces the exact interactions between your brain cells when you listen to Beethoven's Fifth symphony. When I turn the machine on, you wouldn't know whether you were hearing the symphony on the radio or if my machine was creating your experience. There are only two ways I can describe what goes on in your brain: the physical interactions or the experience; what the chemicals and cells were doing, or the symphony you heard. An *external* and an *internal* description of the same thing. A duality."

John smiled, "We've talked about this. It's a bit circular, isn't it? Saying my experience sitting here is the electrical pattern in my brain, and the electrical pattern is my experience. We agreed that somehow those patterns are related to consciousness. The question is, how? And this sounds dangerously close to what Descartes said."

"Not quite," I replied. "He said there were two kinds of stuff in the world, mind stuff and material stuff. A dualism of two different kinds of things. The problem was that there was no way to make these independent things interact. It didn't work. What I'm saying is, what if the material stuff *is* the mental stuff, not a *dualism* but a duality? I'm not saying the chemical and electrical activities in your brain are *related* to consciousness, I'm saying they *are* your conscious experiences, just described a different way. A duality of sorts."

"Particle *and* wave. Electrical pattern *and* consciousness, is it possible?" Emilie mused, looking at John.

"Well," John said, "dualities concern equivalent solutions that come from different mathematical frameworks. I don't think—"

I cut in. "Look, there are measurements and there are experiences, you can't have one without the other. Maybe they're the two sides of one coin. We're talking about an *experience*! Are we going to get hung up because it's not a measurement?"

John replied, "No, but then every experience is confined to the chemistry of one person's brain. One day scientists might know what every neuron in your brain is doing when you listen to Beethoven's symphony, but they won't *hear* what you're hearing."

"So?" I said.

"So," John shot back, "we can't *measure* someone else's experience, and without measurement we can't call it a scientific explanation. And why would electrical patterns in the brain be the only place we find consciousness? Why not in a light bulb?"

Emilie answered, "I think I see what Alan's saying. Maybe there are different levels of consciousness. He made me do that experiment where you close your eyes and shut down all your senses and you're only aware that you're here. Maybe a light bulb or even an electron has a tiny shred of awareness. How would we know?"

I sat up. "Maybe the electric charges around nerve cells are also tiny amounts of awareness. They could be organized by billions of brain cell interactions to create something unexpected, a unit of human consciousness. Like the chemistry of a cell creating a unit of life."

Emilie and I looked at John, who responded, "You're fine tuning your 'sit-in-a-chair and turn off all your senses' experiment? Human experience emerging from adding together bits of awareness that are part of atoms?"

I leaned toward John, "Awareness isn't a part of the atoms and molecules. The bits of awareness *are* the atoms and molecules, described in a different way."

"It's an interesting hypothesis," John added. "There are a few sticky points I see if you're right."

"Like what?" I asked.

"If this is true, then brains are like computers, and consciousness would have nothing to do with our decisions. Consciousness would only be a *bystander* to brain operation, like heat coming off a computer. And a computer, a machine, has no *will*."

Emilie's face dropped. "You mean like no *free* will? That's not good. We're just machines?"

I interrupted. "Hold on. I thought about this a little. So what if the brain is just a machine making decisions? If it weighs its options, the same way a consciousness would, what's the difference? It's not like the brain is some man-made machine. It's incredibly complex and, as I've said, if it behaves like a quantum particle, then it may freely choose between options, which would be like free will."

John and Emilie looked at each other. John said, "It's a good idea. I'll have to think more about it, but keep looking for evidence to back your model."

Emilie smiled and nodded, "I think it's going to be amazing when you're done perfecting it!"

Then John said, "Now I'd like to just mention what I've been working on. I've got to thank Alan for giving me a, uh, cool idea."

"I did?"

"You remember your observations at your grandmother's house, at the river?"

"Yeah?"

John said, "You imagined a group of scientists that were stuck living on the surface of the river, unable to experience the deep water below them. Trapped in a two-dimensional reality. Well, when we went to the hologram demonstration I began to wonder, what if we're like the dots on the hologram film? Suppose we're living on that two-dimensional surface while there is a larger reality, a more multi-dimensional reality. It occurred to me that additional dimensions could bridge some of the unsolved problems in physics. I began thinking about the information on the hologram as tiny dots and clear spots, like 1's and 0's, binary digits, and how multi-dimensional images could be projected from that pattern. A mathematician at Princeton has been helping me to look for solutions. I've been successful at learning a lot of interesting mathematics and finding many models that don't work." He laughed and pointed at the used notebooks on his workbench. "But I have reasons to believe that I'm on the right track, and there are interesting implications."

"Like?" I asked.

"Like, space and time are not things," John replied. "They can be reduced to information and are ultimately unnecessary concepts. The universe may be modeled as a single multidimensional block of interrelated binary digits that ebb and flow through registers in the medium of reality. The ebb and flow are caused by the medium's built-in algorithms. These natural algorithms are the laws I'm interested in finding."

"What?" Emilie said. "No time, no space? How could we describe one thing happening after another without time?"

John explained, "I think we're going to learn that things appear the way they do because we're stuck in a four-dimensional reality, and there might be many more dimensions out there. Just think, the three-dimensional image of a hologram looks completely different than the film it came from. As for time, think of it like this." John took a piece of paper from his desk and drew a spot in the center, then a spot at either end. "Imagine you're living on this two-dimensional piece of paper on the spot in the middle, which is what you think is the present. The spot on this end is the future, the spot on the other end is the past. You feel like the past and the future are distant from you, the future is ahead of you, the past is behind you. See?"

"OK," Emilie said.

"Now," John continued, "by folding this two-dimensional paper in a *third* dimension, I can—" he folded the outer ends of the paper to the center, so the three spots overlapped.

"Connect the past, present, and future." Emilie clapped. "That's pretty neat!"

I asked, "You said the universe might be one block. What's that mean?"

"One block," John said, "a single thing. Like a hologram, all its parts inter-related and inseparable."

I grinned. "Kinda like what we were saying happens with consciousness. Each of our minds is like a spot on that hologram. Every consciousness contains a whole universe that becomes inter-related and inseparable from others. You're in my universe and I'm in yours."

"I love these ideas! I wonder if it's all true," Emilie said.

CHAPTER 40

O ver the next few years, after Emilie met John, it seemed as though my life and the lives of people around me blossomed like flowers in Eden. Before I graduated high school, Emilie and I started an organization called *Let's Cultivate the Garden State*. It was her idea and we had lots of help from her parents, Dad, and Father Curtain. The organization coordinated shipments of food donated from restaurants and local farms to food banks throughout the state. We won the New Jersey Adams Community Service Award. There was even a long article in the local paper about each of us and the organization. Jim, as Father MacKristin asked us to call him, said that making Father Curtain an administrator of L.C.G.S. had been a great idea. It helped Father Curtain regain the self-confidence and the faith he needed to lead his flock again.

I graduated from Northern with some academic honors, came in second in the state in wrestling and was accepted at Cornell with a little help from John and Jim. Jim helped me to rewrite my *Science and Religion* paper and suggested I submit it with my Cornell application. The new title was *The Science Behind the Mind Body Problem*. In the paper I tried to combine my thoughts about consciousness with speculation that the brain operates in a way similar to the way holograms are formed. I found the brain-hologram ideas in a book by Dr. Pribram, which John had brought me from Princeton's library, called *Languages of the Brain*. John had helped me with the math, of course. My first year at Cornell went quickly, the second year was whizzing by as well.

Emilie graduated valedictorian from high school. She was accepted at Syracuse and enrolled in their liberal arts program with plans to emphasize public policy and civic service. The two of us had become amateur chefs and, whenever we had the opportunity, we cooked dinner for my dad and a few guests at my house. Jim came to a few dinners. He and Dad (a devout atheist) had become good friends.

John went to Cal Tech to work under Feynman. Surprising? Not really. He planned to come home when he could, and we agreed to have "breakfast at John's" when he did.

Tim and Stephanie were going to Binghamton University, Steph to study nursing and Tim graphic arts.

Everything seemed to be going great.

As spring break approached in late March 1974, Emilie was completing her first year at Syracuse and my second year at Cornell was wrapping up. My schedule in engineering was heavy, and the one elective I had signed up for, a graduate philosophy course on the mind-body problem, was more work than I bargained for. I was stressed out and not looking forward to final exams. Something else weighed heavily on me. It was time to call Emilie. I usually called her from school on Saturday nights. This call was a bit different. For one thing, I hadn't seen her for a while. We hadn't been able to coordinate our schedules for five months. Ordinarily we'd both plan a visit home every month or two. As I began to dial, I felt a knot form in my stomach. For the past three weekends, Ada got on the phone and told me that Emilie was not at home.

David, Emilie's father answered the phone.

"Hi, it's Alan. Is Emilie in?"

"Hi, Alan. How's Cornell?"

"It's great. Profs are great, people are fun. A lot of political stuff right now on campus. I think Emilie would enjoy it. But it's getting busy. I'll have finals after spring break."

"I'm sure you'll do fine. Uh, Emilie and her mother are on a road trip to New England," David said, voice strained. "I'm sure she'll want to tell you all about it. She asked me to apologize that she missed you again and to tell you she needs to talk to you. She said she's looking forward to seeing you during the break."

I felt a slight chill go through my body. "Yeah, sure. Uh, tell Emilie I'll be home on the twenty-second, next Friday night. I can come over then."

"Sure, son, take care. Bye."

I felt a bit nauseated. My heart missed a few beats. I thought, *Something's happened. Doesn't she feel the same way I do anymore? Did she find someone else at school?* I had heard many stories like that, but how could she love someone else? I had to be practical. She was avoiding me, and her father said, *She **needs** to talk to you.*

With a mountain of academic work to climb over the next week, I began to prepare myself for my next meeting with Emilie. I imagined Emilie wanted to give me the news face to face. Although I felt one conversation away from being crushed, I knew I only wanted her to be happy. I thought, *If she would be most happy with someone else, then so be it.*

When my ride dropped me off for spring break, I grabbed my sea bag from the trunk, waved, and faced my house with trepidation. I was imagining a life without Emilie, a destiny obscured by a fog of uncertainty. It was Friday afternoon, and, following dinner with my father and Ona, I was meeting with Emilie.

The dinner conversation was taken up by Ona. I offered only a brief update about school. I'm sure Ona could tell something was going on with her grandson that he did not want to talk about yet. So she filled the airways with quirky news about her neighbors. When dinner was finished, Dad said, "I hope seeing Emilie tonight gets your spirits up. You're on a break, lighten up!"

"Yeah, you're right. Sorry, Dad. Might be home late. Mind if I take the car?"

He tossed me the keys. "All yours."

I drove to Emilie's. When Ada opened the front door, her face was pale. She seemed to move stiffly. "Hello, Alan! So good to see you!" She hugged me. "I hope your studies are going well?"

"Good to see you," I said. "Yes, I think things are going fairly well. Heard you took a trip up to New England?" "Yes, yes. Emilie will tell you all about it. She's upstairs in her room. Please go right up."

I thought this was odd. I'd never been to Emilie's room, but I was anxious to get this over with and went up the stairs.

I knocked gently and opened the door to find Emilie, apparently just out of the shower, with a towel on her head, wearing a robe and blue jeans. Her face was pale. She smiled, stood, and said, "Hi, Alan!" Her embrace and kiss were quick.

"Please sit down. I've got so much to tell you." She motioned to a chair beside the bed. I sat down. "First, I'm so sorry I wasn't around when you called. So much has happened. But I had to think things through. It was so, unexpected."

I could see she was struggling. I interrupted. "Listen, Em. I want you to know that if there's someone else, that's OK. Whatever makes you most happy in life. I'll always love—"

Emilie frowned for a moment, not understanding what I was saying. Then she sat up straight and cut in. "*Alan!* Oh my God. You thought? Oh, dear. I am so sorry. There is no one else! It's you I want to be with, forever. Don't you know that?" She took my hands and looked into my eyes. "Only you."

"Well, what then?" I said, smiling.

"I have leukemia."

"You have *what*?"

"Leukemia. It's a cancer of the blood called AML. My mother took me to a doctor in New York at Columbia. I had to have a bone marrow biopsy. We got another opinion in Boston, but I started the chemotherapy a few weeks ago." She removed the towel from her head revealing a nearly bald scalp with a few wisps of hair.

I held back a gasp. "Why didn't you tell me what was going on? *I should have been here!*"

"No. You should have been right where you were, in school not thinking about this. Now is the time to talk about it, on your break," she said firmly.

"I don't, I mean, are they sure?" I asked. "Aren't you too young to get this?"

"They're sure. We've been to two top hospitals. My tests were reviewed by excellent doctors."

"But it's curable, right? You're getting the treatment?"

"They say I'm responding and might go into remission. That's when they don't see any cancer cells in my blood anymore. But you have to understand, even if I go into remission there's a possibility I might have to go back for more treatments."

I was confused. "If there were no cancer cells in your blood, why would you have to go back?"

Emilie looked down. "The cancer often comes back."

Shocked, I asked, "Then what do we do? There's got to be something that works."

"We fight, Alan. We keep fighting till we beat it. We throw everything they've got at it, no matter how hard it gets," she said with conviction. "Are you ready to fight with me?"

I said, "Of course I am. We're gonna beat this cancer, I know it."

"OK. Then I need you to make some promises to me," Emilie said.

"Sure. Anything."

Emilie smiled. "There will be no compromises. I've thought about this a lot. We'll talk about the promises tonight and never again. Agreed?"

"OK," I said.

"First, you will not take time off from school unless I ask."

I stood up. "But—"

"Promise?" Emilie asked.

"I shouldn't have agreed to this," I muttered. "Uh, OK."

"Second," she said, "promise you will continue to meet with John and work on those incredible ideas." Her eyes sparkled. "I don't want you to ever give up trying to understand consciousness. Maybe, well, I hope you'll even find God in all that scientific stuff. I think you're close to something wonderful. Remember what you said about how the brain creates a whole universe we each carry around, and how, since we met, I'll live in your universe and you'll live in mine, forever? It's helped me deal with my diagnosis."

"Really?" I said. "Great. OK, promise."

"One more. But it's a couple of promises rolled in one. I know we'll beat this cancer, but it's made me realize that we all die someday. If I ever die before you, I want you to promise that you will find someone you can love, and have a happy life."

I was caught off guard. "Hey, Em, we don't have to—"

"And," she cut in, "I'd like my ashes sprinkled over the Atlantic, where I've had such great memories. If you need to feel my presence, take a dip in the ocean. Do not bring flowers to some memorial. Now promise, and we won't speak of this again." Her eyes glowed with determination.

"OK," I said, admitting defeat.

"Good. Now, I have to go to the hospital in New York tomorrow. Do you want to come along?"

"You bet I'm coming," I said.

"I'll be staying for a few days. You can drive into the city and stay for visiting hours. There's a parking garage at the hospital. If you visit, bring a book. It's boring." She patted the bed next to her and smiled.

I looked around, expecting adult supervision. But Emilie reached over and put her hand behind my neck, pulling me over her on the bed. Our bodies and limbs wrapped together, each universe entangled with the other. We kissed recklessly.

On Saturday morning I told my father and Ona about Emilie. Although I was up half the night thinking about Emilie's diagnosis and couldn't decide whether to be confident or scared, I answered the concern on their faces by saying, "She's going to be OK. The treatment is rough, but Emilie won't quit. She'll do whatever it takes."

I called Ronati's florist and ordered a bouquet of irises.

CHAPTER 41

Ada, Emilie, and I made our way to the hospital room. While Emilie was being prepared for her chemotherapy, her nurse asked us if we knew the isolation protocol.

Ada said, "I could use a review, and it's Alan's first time."

"OK," the nurse responded cheerfully. She explained, "Since Emilie's immune system and ability to fight infections will be weakened by the chemotherapy, everyone needs to take precautions to keep germs away from her. Always wash your hands when you enter the room. Here are the disposable gowns. You put them on like this." She helped Ada put one on. "And wear these masks when you're in the room." She held up a surgeon's face mask. "Emilie cannot have fresh fruit, vegetables, or flowers in the room, or food prepared outside the hospital. We do not allow visitors who are ill, even a minor cough, to visit."

Whether it was the smell of the hospital, the closeness of the room, or the words of the nurse, I had the urge to grab my girlfriend and run out of there. Confidence deserted me. I was terrified. My knees nearly buckled as the gravity of her condition became clear. I could not let Emilie see the fear that turned my face pale. "I guess kissing is out of the question," I joked nervously.

The nurse laughed. "Yes, for now." She turned and left.

"I told you it would be boring." Emilie smiled. "Did you bring a book?"

I had a plan to divert our attention from Emilie's illness. I said, "Yeah, but I also brought this paper I'm writing for my mind-body class. Thought you and Ada might be interested and give me some ideas."

"I'd really love to hear it," Ada said. "What's it about?"

"Well, I've been trying to find out if God could be described with scientific theories, which led me to try and understand consciousness. I put my most up-to-date ideas in this paper, *The Case for Universal Awareness.*"

"Sounds interesting," Ada said. "You're going back to school soon, no? You think it's enough time to explain it to me?"

"I'll start today and cover as much as I can. Tell me what you don't understand, and I'll be able to write better explanations. When I come back for the summer, I'll show you the finished product, OK?"

"Deal," Ada said.

The nurse walked in and started Emilie's I.V. fluid. She attached a bag of chemotherapy. The poison, engineered to kill all the fast-growing cells in Emilie's body, trickled into her veins.

I read from *The Case for Universal Awareness.* As always, Emilie loved talking about these ideas. Ada was attentive and asked many questions. It definitely helped to draw our attention away from the war being waged in Emilie's blood. I explained the key points: information was pattern in some medium; dualities were coincidences when two different patterns in two different media could represent the same reality– like an electron described as a particle and a wave. I divulged my guess that consciousness was a duality, which could be described either as chemical and electrical information in the brain or as experiences. I went on to talk about holograms, emphasizing their property of *the whole in every part*, and tried to summarize Dr. Pribram's ideas that some parts of the brain handled information like holograms. I voiced my speculation that these areas in the brain, the ones with holographic characteristics, were the ones responsible for human consciousness. I offered the crux of John's idea: the entire four-dimensional universe we are familiar with is actually a duality that could also be described as a hologram with many more unseen dimensions.

Finally, I summed up by trying to tie these two dualities together. "So, if the brain organizes its chemical and electrical activity in a holographic way, creating human consciousness, what is created if the entire universe is organized by a holographic principle? Omniscience?"

When I finished Ada said from beneath her mask, "You know, I'm familiar with holograms, as an artist. I didn't understand how they were made, or this idea of a duality, but do you think it's possible?"

Emilie said in almost a whisper, "Isn't it a wonderful idea, Mom? It's like God is in us, and we are in God. Like holograms, *the whole in every part*. I love it."

She looked so weak.

Ada asked, "But if 'God' just means the universe is aware, how do we learn good from evil?"

"Each of us," I replied, "has to decide good from evil, choose how to live. Try to right wrongs."

Ada frowned. "But wouldn't God step in when powerful evil people begin mass killings, torture?"

I looked at Emilie and repeated what she had once said. "Yes, there is evil. But some people believe the imperfections of this broken universe make it more perfect, because we can fix some things. We can make choices. If God could step in, we wouldn't have choices. We can't have it both ways."

Emilie smiled weakly, "I *am* in you. I am..." She nodded off.

A few days later I stopped by Ronati's and picked up the bouquet I had ordered and brought them to Ada. She put them on a table outside the sliding glass patio doors, so Emilie could see them when she returned home. It reminded me how frail our patient was. I reluctantly returned to school. It felt like this was a time when Emilie needed me the most. But was it? I mean, what could I do other than act strong and confident when I was with her? Eventually, I learned that after Emilie returned home, she got weaker, and suffered from mouth sores, dry heaves and diarrhea before beginning a slow recovery. I could have insisted on staying with her, but she would never have allowed it.

Despite my absence, Emilie made it through the spring. She recovered the weight she had lost and regained her strength. Her hair grew back. By late June we were enjoying the summer, often making the trek to the Long Island beaches.

I became more distracted and excited when Tim told me he was going to give a talk to the community in July about adolescent suicide. Father curtain had been encouraging him, and he finally agreed. There was a short article about it in the local paper. It was our hot topic of conversation for weeks.

I focused on anything else going on, trying to push the question of Emilie's health to the back of my mind, where it was less daunting. Then, bad news. Emilie's blood showed a few abnormal white blood cells. She was going to need chemotherapy again.

*****

In mid-June 1974, Bellcon leaned back in his chair, frustrated. At one thirty a.m. the smoke-filled pub, menacing patrons and the seedy Los Angeles neighborhood looked like a scene in a violent movie. He sat at a table furthest from the bar with his Vietnam brother-in-arms. They had returned to the states when Paris Peace Accords were signed in 1973, technically ending the war.

"You saved my life," his sergeant said. "More than once. I'll help you find a good job anyway I can, but you've got skills. You've looked into the military? Black ops? Private sector? There's nothing?"

Bellcon's large frame was concealed in the army jungle jacket. Through a bored expression he replied, "Nothing interesting. Listen, we've been through a shit storm. You backed me up, above and beyond, Sarge. But I've got to ask you not to say anything we did over there to anyone, especially my uncle Don. I was talking to him about a job in LAPD. I think you spooked him."

"Fuck, man," the sergeant said. "I'm sorry. I figured he's an LAPD cop, a captain for chrissake! He's gotta know the score, don't he?"

Bellcon said, "Hey, what we did in those villages, we got the information we needed. We saved American lives. But look what the papers are saying about some of our guys. They don't get war. Papers make it sound like we were slittin' throats and blowing shit up for fun! Like it wasn't about finding fucking tunnels and catching Cong. Hell, I don't think my uncle would get it."

"Damn, I'm really sorry. I just wanted him to know what a great soldier you are. When I sent you to recon a village, it was like sending a one-man intelligence operation. We were lucky to have you, brother."

Bellcon smiled, recalling the excitement, the pleasure of all those pleading eyes. "Yeah, thanks," he said.

"Listen, I gotta go." The sergeant stood up. "But you got my number. And if anything turns up, I'll call ya."

"Sure, thanks, Sarge"

His sergeant paid for their drinks and left. Bellcon hit the john to empty the distilled hopes he had been drinking from shot glasses and mugs all night.

He stepped out into the cool, desolate night and walked down the block. When he turned a corner, he saw his sergeant surrounded by three wild-eyed thugs. One brandished a large knife. Another turned to face Bellcon. "Hey, captain, how 'bout you? Gotta couple a bucks to spare?"

Bellcon tried to look terrified to pacify his enemy. "I'm not a captain. You fellas have the wrong guy." He slowly made his way closer to the thug with the knife and kept talking. "I've got some money. Please take it and just let us go." He made his hands look shaky as he reached for his wallet. The thug with the knife smiled, then turned towards Bellcon, and the others closed in.

Sarge saw the familiar look on his corporal's face. "Bellcon, don't—"

But it was too late.

The following morning, around noon, Bellcon was having coffee at the kitchen table. The back door opened and his uncle Don, in full uniform, walked in.

"Morning," Bellcon said. "Home early?"

"I was passing by, thought I'd get another cup of coffee," his uncle said. "Any left?"

Bellcon pointed with his cup. "Sure. Half a pot."

"Mind if I ask where you were last night?"

"Sarge brought me to some bar, why?"

"Was it anywhere near MacArthur Park?"

"Was there a problem?" Bellcon asked.

"Two guys were killed near there. Another one's in the hospital and probably won't make it. Bad head injury. They've all done time, have long records. Bad dudes."

Bellcon smiled. "Sounds like someone did the city a favor."

His uncle's face hardened. "One guy's neck was snapped. He didn't fall out of a building, and there were no stairs around. The other guy had a small stab wound in his neck. The coroner said it was just above the vocal cords. Seems the guy drowned in his own blood. We've never seen anything like that, even in L.A. It sounded like the stories your sergeant was telling."

Bellcon returned his uncle's stare. "You don't think? Hey, we're back in the states. We know the difference between enemies and criminals. Sarge made half of that stuff up to show you I was a good soldier and could be a good cop."

His uncle's shoulders relaxed slightly. "Like I said, a job offer is not up to me. I put in a word. We'll see." He turned to leave.

"Hey, uncle Don, can I make a call to my dad?"

"Yeah, sure. Just keep it under ten minutes. The long-distance charges aren't pretty."

Bellcon picked up the phone and dialed. "Hello, Dad? Fine, everything's OK—Yeah, still in L.A. I'm thinking about coming home in July— Look, the LAPD has my application—Come on, it won't stir things up. It's just for a weekend. Nobody'll even know I'm there. I'm going to stay with Stan— Yeah, my alibi—What? —Oh, I saw there's a get together with some old high school classmates in the paper you sent, and I just wanted to say hi to a few old friends."

There were really only three old acquaintance he wanted to settle with. The three people he could thank for being uprooted, dropped in the shit-hole jungles of Vietnam and nearly being killed more than once. Now there was an opportunity.

His father had been sending him copies of the local paper for months. The most recent *Forrest Creek Weekly* had an article on the third page that told of a local kid who would be speaking to middle school and junior high students about teen suicide. It was Tim. He was going to share his personal experience at eight p.m. at St Peter's auditorium on Sunday, July seventh.

Bellcon thought, *All that talking Tim will be doing might dredge up bad memories. Make the kid suicidal again.* The article also mentioned that Tim was the victim of an attempted drowning five years earlier. No one had been charged. The case was sealed, but some parents in town were trying to have the case reopened. *Those bastards knew I could've been killed in Vietnam,* he thought. *Now that the war is over, they're out to get me? After what they put me through?*

His memory flashed back to a college professor, a Viet Cong sympathizer, pleading for his family. The man's wife and children were locked in an old automobile, coughing. Exhaust from a hose that had been shoved into the tailpipe billowed out the other end, which was set through a partly open back window. He had heard of folks committing suicide that way and the parking lot at St Peter's school was the perfect place. Desolate. Bordering the woods.

Bellcon had incipient plans to deal with Alan and Emilie too. Though they were a bit more complicated. A few months earlier he had read a large article in the *Forrest Creek Weekly* about those two, their parents and a priest.

They had created an organization in N.J. that was expanding into N.Y. state. Bellcon learned that Alan's father, Michael, was a decorated paratrooper. If he was anything like his son, he would be a pain in the ass once Alan was delt with, so the plan had to include Michael.

Assets Bellcon acquired in Vietnam would be put to good use: he knew how to fashion simple timed detonators; he also had become familiar with a new drug used in the M.A.S.H. units called Ketamine, a sedative that split people's minds from their bodies. It made patients cooperative, even with painful surgeries, and could also cause nightmares. *That's a drug I've got to have*, he had thought when he heard about it. Hanging around mobile surgical units, he had carefully observed how the drug was administered and had asked doctors about the effects of different doses. They were happy to educate him. Then, in the sometimes-careless process of troop withdrawal, Bellcon stole a few vials of Ketamine and some syringes. The sedative would work perfectly to stage a few fatalities without any suspicion of foul play.

His plans for Tim, Alan and Michael gave him a good feeling, what normal people would describe as pride. But when he thought about meeting Emilie again, he felt aroused.

Stan invited Bellcon to stay with him when his friend mentioned he was coming to town. Stan had a two-bedroom apartment in Forrest Creek. It was about a half mile down the road from St. Peter's school. He felt a strong bond with his high school buddy and was happy to have another Vietnam vet stay for a few days. Stan had sustained a spinal injury in the infantry that left him less of an asset and more of a liability on the battlefield. He was medically discharged from service and on disability, but he got around OK. Since he did not use his car much, he encouraged Bellcon to borrow it.

Tim was giving his talk in one week, and already Bellcon had driven Stan's car several times through the St Peter's parking lot, past Emilie's and Alan's houses and around town, trying to get a fix on his target's habits and noting travel time between each place. He knew where he would find Tim on Sunday. But his plan called for coordinating Emilie's and Alan's locations. He needed to figure out a way to meet Emilie alone. He also needed to get Alan to go somewhere away from his house, but then return home at just the right time, while his father stayed at home.

On Saturday, Stan asked Bellcon if he wanted to go to a bar the following evening with a few guys. Bellcon reminded Stan that he did not want anyone but a select few to know he was in town. "You know there are folks who are trying to get that drowning case reopened. And who knows what else they'll try to pin on me," he said.

"I can't believe. After all these years?" Stan said. "Yeah, you're probably right. But how did those scumbags get away with accusing you of that shit? You were trying to help, right? That kid tried to drown himself. Don't it matter now you're a war hero n' all?"

"The world's full of evil people, man," Bellcon said. "Jealous, evil people. But we won't let that stop us from having fun. Tell you what. Let me borrow your car tomorrow. Got some people I need to meet for a few hours. Meet me in the parking lot afterwards, and we'll head into the city for a few beers. I'm buying." He told Stan what time to be there.

Early Sunday evening, Bellcon parked across the street from St. Peter's school. From the back seat, he took the coiled garden hose he had brought. He walked quickly across the street, past the auditorium entrance, to the far, back end of the parking lot. He stepped into the woods and waited.

Bellcon looked around. He had figured no one would hang around this corner of the parking lot. He thought, *Perfect, no witnesses.* He wore a black T-shirt and dark jeans. When the sun set, he would become more invisible. He paced the wooded perimeter of the parking area. There was a twenty-minute period when cars pulled in, at first steadily, then sporadically. The cars were parking on the other side of the lot, close to the school, near the auditorium entrance. He watched parents escort their children into the building.

Bellcon had brought a few syringes prefilled with Ketamine and hid the left-over vials and needles. He thought about the choke hold he would use that would only take seconds to knock Tim out, without leaving a bruise. Tim wouldn't be unconscious for long, but then there would be the Ketamine injection into Tim's armpit, where a coroner would not likely find the site. The sedative would keep Tim immobile, seated in his own car, as the garden hose channeled exhaust into the cab. It would be an obvious case of suicide.

Tim pulled his 1967 white Chevy Impala into the school parking lot. Out of habit, he parked in the spot he had used for Sunday Mass. It was away from the other cars, near trees lining the entrance opposite the auditorium. Tim took the keys out of the ignition. He reached across the passenger seat and opened the glove box. The large combat knife he called Duggie was there. He briefly thought about strapping Duggie to his leg under his pants as he usually did. But he couldn't imagine he'd be threatened by people attending his suicide talk. He closed the glove box and headed into the school to discuss suicide with the audience.

CHAPTER 42

All of us were excited when we first heard that Tim would be speaking to the community about adolescent suicide. I marveled at the kid's development over the years. He had grown to a stage where he volunteered to stand in front of strangers and reveal his deepest insecurities, flaws, and vulnerabilities from the past. Tim said Stephanie cried "tears of pride" when he gave her the news, and Rich was very supportive. Both of them were disappointed that they would be away on a family vacation during Tim's presentation. I had mentioned Tim's talk in a letter to John, and John sent Tim a long note praising him up and down about what a great thing he was doing. Hip was moved by Tim's event and said he hoped Tim wouldn't mind if he didn't attend. He said, "It's in the past and too sad." Emilie told Tim that the hardest thing anyone could do was to confront evil, whether it was in the ideas to destroy yourself, or in the people or groups with ideas to destroy others. She said her grandparents would have been proud of Tim. That one really got him pumped.

On Sunday evening, the night of Tim's talk, I called Emilie to check in on her. She had looked fine when I stopped by in the afternoon, though she'd lost her hair again from the chemotherapy. I knew she wasn't feeling great because she called Tim and said that she wanted to attend his talk but asked if it would be all right if she sat this one out. I told her I'd take notes, and Tim and I would drop by afterwards. Her parents were away for the weekend.

I got to St. Peter's later than I intended. Tim was already inside, and I had about two minutes until he was scheduled to speak. There were probably a dozen cars in the lot huddled near the auditorium entrance. I parked next to his Impala on the other side of the lot and rushed inside.

*****

Bellcon saw the white Impala as soon as it pulled into the parking lot. He couldn't believe that Tim parked so far from the auditorium. Then, in another stroke of great luck, Alan pulled in and parked next to Tim's Impala. He saw Alan get out of his car alone. Emilie apparently had not come. A complete plan instantly crystalized in Bellcon's mind. He ran through the trees, which bordered the side of the school opposite the auditorium, and across the street to Stan's car. He jumped in and drove to Emilie's.

At the bottom of a gully behind Emilie's house was an access road that led to a public works building. Bellcon parked on the deserted access road. He grabbed the fake parcel he had made, along with a pre-filled syringe, and raced up the hill to Emilie's backyard. It was still light out, and he peaked through several back windows. No activity. It was difficult to tell if anyone was home. He recalled that when he was casing Emilie's house two days earlier, a car was in the driveway and the garage door was open. The garage was completely filled with boxes. So when he peered around the corner of the house, he was happy to see there was no car in the driveway. Perhaps her parents were out. Furtively, he went to the front of the house. The street was empty.

He quickly placed the parcel by the front door, rang the bell, and hid in the bushes to see who answered the door. He kept the syringe in his right hand. When Emilie appeared, he felt a rush of excitement. He wondered why she had a bandana wrapped around her head. He waited for her to open the screen door and step outside to pick up the package. Then he sprang out of the bushes and put his left hand over her mouth. He got behind her with his right arm wrapped around her torso, and pulled her back into the house. He quietly kicked the front door closed. There were no sounds in the house. The two of them were alone.

"Hi sweetheart. Happy to see me?" he whispered.

Emilie struggled weakly. She felt a pinch under her left armpit and lost consciousness.

Bellcon slung her over his shoulder. She was light. He went out the back sliding glass doors and raced down to the car. *Piece of cake*, he thought. He put her across the back seat and drove to Alan's house.

Parking down the street from Alan's, he pulled a baseball cap visor low on his head and took another pre-filled syringe. He opened the trunk and took out Stan's toolbox and the carton with the alarm clock gizmo he had constructed. He walked up the front steps and placed the carton outside the front door. Then, stepping to the side, out of view, he rang the bell. He'd only need the element of surprise for a second or two.

Michael opened the inner door, looked on the porch and opened the screen door. He stepped outside to inspect the package. Bellcon spun around, catching Michael's neck in the angle of his left arm, squeezing the carotid arteries shut and pulling him into the house. If he had not passed out, Michael would have felt a pinprick in his left arm pit.

Bellcon put Michael in the bedroom. He grabbed the box he had brought and quickly went down the stairs off the dining room. He did not want to flip a light switch on or off, so he was happy to find the basement illuminated by six large above ground windows.

The basement was partially finished. The walls were decorated with framed posters of Broadway shows and pictures of symphonies. At the far end was a small room enclosing the furnace. A central area had four small tables surrounded by soda fountain chairs, each under a pendant lamp. One had a few small boxes stacked on it. *Perfect*, he thought.

He put his box on one of the tables, used a box cutter to slice open the four sides, and flattened the cardboard. He crisscrossed a single piece of kite string under the table and tied rubber bands at different points on the string. Very carefully he looped the rubber bands over the hammer on the alarm clock detonator. When he was satisfied the device was stable, he attached the modified match stick and striker strips. He left a note, written on toilet tissue, hanging from the pendant lamp, and went to the gas furnace. He loosened a few pipe connections and adjusted them by the hissing sounds. When the house blew up it would be attributed to old pipes. It was not that uncommon.

He got back in the car and drove to St. Peter's to con two old pals. He parked Stan's car at the far end of the lot, close to the wooded trail. He ran to the river and disposed of the syringes he'd used so far. Then he ran back to his car. He didn't have to wait very long.

CHAPTER 43

Tim was sitting in a chair on stage with only a small tripod table and a glass of water next to him. Parents, sitting with their teenagers, were spread out over half of the auditorium. Father Curtain was in the first row. As I sat, Father Curtain stood. He talked about the difficulties of being a teenager: encountering problems related to acceptance, peer pressure, and bullying. All this while a young person is trying to figure out who they are, who they love, and what their place in the world should be. He mentioned that as a boy, he was made fun of for wanting to be a priest and how his faith strengthened him. Then he introduced Tim.

I was surprised that Tim held nothing back. He talked about the rages of his alcoholic father, and the burden of his classmates' daily derision. Without mentioning names, he gave specific examples, including some of his fights with a much bigger kid (Jerome). When he talked about how nauseated he felt going to school each morning and then how afraid he felt coming home every afternoon, I saw some of the mothers wiping their eyes. He explained how a feeling of self-hatred grows in you. How you realize that you will never be good at anything, never be successful, never be more than a burden to your friends. In a soft voice, with everyone perfectly still, he gave a dramatic account of jumping in the river and the friend who wouldn't let him go. Nodding to Father Curtain, Tim thanked him for his life changing and faith restoring interventions.

I sat in my seat and waited for Tim to answer a few questions and for Father Curtain to invite any child or parent to call on him at any time for help. The audience left. Father Curtain shook Tim's hand and went out a side door. Tim and I walked out to our cars together. A red glow on the horizon marked where the sun had set. Only our cars, at the far end of the lot, and one other, parked near the woods, were left. Briefly I wondered why there was a car parked there. *Probably kids making out*, I thought.

"That was a pretty amazing talk," I said.

"Think so? Hope I never have to do that again," Tim said, looking drained.

I was looking over the top of my car at Tim. "Maybe tomorrow—" A black shadow flew around the back of his trunk and enveloped him. At first, I didn't understand what I was seeing. Then an arm wrapped around Tim's neck, another held a metallic object in front of his face. From under a dark baseball cap, an unmistakable voice said, "Don't do anything stupid, Alan. Your girlfriend is in a safe place and Tim will be OK if you do exactly what I tell you."

It was Bellcon. Tim stopped struggling when he saw the box cutter. Bellcon's other arm was a vice around Tim's neck.

A wave of heat spread across my entire body. Recognition of the enemy and his words made tight coils of every muscle in my body. Somehow, I resisted pouncing on him. "Where is Emilie?"

"In a safe place." Bellcon smiled. "Just do what I tell you—"

"This is between you and me. *Let them go!*"

"I will let them go, champ. But first I want you both to agree that you'll get the parents to stop trying to open the case on that little drowning thing between Tim and me. Forever. And one other thing. I need you to pick up something for me." He glanced at his watch.

Tim said, "Don't do it Alan. Turn him in. This bastard needs to burn in hell!"

"I'll only agree once I'm convinced Tim and Emilie are safe," I said.

Bellcon smiled confidently. "Afraid you don't have a choice, champ. Listen carefully. A package was delivered to your house," Bellcon said, speaking slowly. "I happen to know it was delivered today. Your father probably put it in your room, or maybe in the study. Don't try to figure out why my package was delivered to you, or why it's so important that I have it right away. Go home. Find it. I want that package *now!*"

He looked at his watch again, as if he were stalling. It all made no sense. A package? Delivered to my house? Something *he* wanted? Was it drugs? A weapon of some kind? I looked at Tim who shared my expression. Bellcon saw the questions written on my face.

"You'd better hurry. You only have six minutes to get me what I want. I'm not kidding. Six minutes if you ever want to see Emilie again."

I saw death in his eyes. A chill ran through me. I jumped in my car and sped to my house.

As I drove, I wondered if this was a trap, an ambush of some sort. I parked around the corner and ran behind my neighbor's houses to our backyard and our large dining room bay window. I peered inside. The house was quiet and still. Where was my father?

I entered through the back door. The smell of gas was overwhelming. *What the hell was going on?* I pushed the questions out of my mind. I had to find that package fast. Running through the kitchen and dining room I did not see any parcel. The basement stairs were to my left. Since my father often put deliveries from work on a table in the basement, I ran to the stairs and almost instinctively flipped on the light switch. *Wait, the gas!* I thought. A tiny spark from the switch, and the house would have exploded. Luckily, enough sunlight from the evening summer sky spilled through the basement windows.

On one of the tables in the basement here was a cardboard box, cut open and flattened. In the center of the strips of cardboard was what looked like an old double bell and hammer alarm clock with strings tying it down to the table. Is that what Bellcon wanted? A tissue paper note hung from the lamp. *Save your dad?* Then I understood.

I looked at the odd device on the table. Attached to the hammer on the alarm clock was a sliver of coated wood that looked like a large match stick. Alongside the match were striker strips. Multiple thin rubber bands were looped over the match stick and tied to a long string that crisscrossed under the table. They were carefully counter balanced, so that cutting any string or moving the clock would strike the match. The clock showed about one minute until the match-hammer vibrated on the striker strips, and the house exploded.

I ran up the stairs. "*Dad! Dad!*"

He was half on his bed, moaning. I grabbed his arm, slung him over my shoulder— the way I used to train with Tim for wrestling— and ran out the back door. I was about twenty-five yards into the green space behind our house when a flash and the loudest noise I ever heard came with a concussion that knocked me to the ground. Pieces of brick, wood, siding and shingles rained down on us. I looked back. Only half of the brick walls were standing. Everything else was gone. My father looked drugged. His speech slurred. He asked, "Alan, where are we?"

"It's OK, pop," I said. "It's going to be OK."

Mr. Wayne, my neighbor came running out of his house. He yelled, "*Good God, Alan, are you guys OK? What the hell happened?*"

"It was a gas explosion! Listen, call an ambulance for my dad! I'll be right back."

I sprinted to the car thinking, I could have flipped the basement light switch on and been blown to bits, or if I had gone through my front door, I would have wasted time going up the stairs off the living room to my bedroom looking for Bellcon's package. Then back down the stairs to the study. I would have seen my father in his bedroom and tried to revive him for information about the parcel. I probably never would have made it to the basement. Even if I had, Bellcon's note would have made me take time to try and save my father. One way or another, we both would have been blown to smithereens. I sped back to St. Peter's, hoping I would not be too late.

*****

Bellcon kept Tim's neck in the choke hold. He looked at his watch and ignored Tim's questions and accusations. A few minutes passed. There was a thunderous deep rumble. Tim said, "What the hell was that?"

"I'm afraid," Bellcon said, "there was an accident. Your friend Alan was just blown up in his house."

"*No!*" Tim shouted, kicking and twisting.

Bellcon took pleasure in telling Tim what was going to happen next. "And now, it's time for you to finally be successful committing suicide. All that talk about suicide tonight must have inspired you. I saw you coming out of the auditorium tonight, you looked pretty depressed to me."

Tim flailed wildly, but Bellcon tightened his grip and lifted Tim off the ground. Tim tried to yell, but his voice box, clenched between strong arm muscles, produced only a raspy whisper. "*You bastard! You won't get away with this!*"

"I want you to know," Bellcon said softly, "that while you're dying in your car, I'm going to play with Emilie for a while. Then I'll carry her to the bridge and dump her in the river. She'll get sucked into the Chomp. They'll never find her body."

"*You fucking bastard!* Let me go—" Tim pulled at Bellcon's arm with all his strength. There was a pinch in his right armpit. He kicked and struggled and knocked the last syringe out of Bellcon's hand. Relaxation spread over him. He felt like he was floating above Bellcon, though he knew Bellcon was putting his body in the front seat of his car. Something was terribly wrong. Yet there was nothing he could do about it. It was like he was looking down from above watching the lap seat belt being strapped over his body. The keys were taken from his pocket and the car was started. He wanted to sleep.

Bellcon closed the car door. He bent down and picked the syringe up off the ground. He saw that less than half the intended dose had been injected when Tim jarred the syringe out of his hand. He looked at Tim and thought, *I put a big dose in that hypodermic. He looks zonked from what he got. He'll be dead soon anyway.* He sheathed the syringe and put it in his pocket. Then he took the garden hose and put one end into the exhaust pipe and threaded the other into the partly opened rear window.

Bellcon walked about forty yards to his car, near the trail that went through the woods and led to suicide bridge. He pulled Emilie out of the back seat and laid her on the ground. She was awake but groggy "Where? What?" She mumbled.

The bandanna tilted on her head and Bellcon looked at her quizzically. He slid the bandanna off. "What the? You shaved your head?" He laughed. "Hey! You don't look half bad!"

He started to unbutton her blouse.

CHAPTER 44

I parked the car across the street from the school hoping that Bellcon and Tim were still in the parking lot. Praying I could catch Bellcon by surprise, I ran through the trees, lining the side of the school opposite the auditorium, until I saw Tim's car. I could hear the engine running. There was a shadow moving towards the car parked in the back of the lot at the edge of the woods. It must have been Bellcon. No one else was around. When I got close, I saw Tim in his car staring out the front windshield. Under the cover of nightfall, I slipped to the driver's side of Tim's car and saw a hose from the exhaust pipe going into the rear window. Quietly, I pulled the hose out of the window, opened the car door and unbuckled Tim. "Tim, you OK?"

Tim was awake. He sat motionless. His eyelids undulated, refusing to close. "Alan? Am I dead?"

"No buddy. You're gonna be fine."

"He drugged me."

I left the car running for some cover noise and for the getaway I planned. Quietly I said, "Stay in the car. *Wake the fuck up!* We gotta get out of here and find—"

I looked at the car near the woods. Bellcon was dragging something out of the back seat. Was it a body? Was it Emilie? I prayed she was alive. I *willed* her to be alive.

There was an explosion inside me. I never felt anything like it. Suddenly my bones and muscles felt like they were made of steel. I was invincible. I had no fear, and I was filled with hatred. I began running toward Bellcon. I saw it *was* Emilie beneath him. His hand was on her blouse. There was no doubt in my mind that I was going to end him.

When I was about ten feet from Bellcon he looked up. For one second, he stared at me with a blank expression, then his eyes grew wide. I dove, crashing into him and knocking him to the ground. He wrapped his legs around my torso and rolled, getting on top of me. His fists swung wildly, but I dodged them and they only glanced off my head. The power I felt was incredible. With one arm, I turned his body. I rolled and stood up with Bellcon's legs still wrapped around me. Roaring, I brought my fist down, like a hammer on his chest. Once, twice. He fell to the ground and started to get up on all fours. I jumped on his back. My left arm shot under his and secured my right arm, which I wrapped around his neck, the way he had done to Tim. I began to squeeze. All I could think was, *Die you son of a bitch!* And I was happy to hear him gasp for air. His body seemed to be relaxing. His hand went to his pocket. Then, as he went limp, I felt a pinch in my left leg.

My head felt fuzzy. My limbs felt like they were slipping away and the two of us collapsed. My full weight dropped on top of Bellcon the instant I passed out.

CHAPTER 45

I don't think I was out for very long. When I came to, Tim was helping me off the ground. He pulled my arm over his shoulders and was walking me towards his car. My body was next to Tim, but my mind seemed to have leeched out over the entire parking lot. I saw Bellcon crawling slowly on the ground. Emilie was no longer there.

"Wait, wait. Where's Emilie?" I drawled.

"Come on, Alan. We gotta get out of here, *fast!*"

"But—" I protested.

"*Emilie's in the car!* She's waking up. Now *hurry!*"

Tim's engine was still running. He dropped me in the passenger seat. His large combat knife was on the floor mat at my feet. Tim ran around to the driver's side, jumped in and drove out of the parking lot with his head lights off. Once on the street, he turned the lights on and drove away.

I was becoming more alert, my mind finding its way back into my head. I looked in the back seat. Emilie sat with tears on her cheeks. "Are you OK?" I asked. She looked pale and weak.

"Yes," she said softly. "Just tired. Remember, I was the one who didn't want to go out tonight." She smiled, joking. I wanted to hug her.

"What the fuck was that explosion I heard?" Tim asked.

Still a bit drugged, I said too matter-of-factly, "My house blew up."

"*Holy shit!*" Tim said.

"*Alan!*" Emilie said. "Thank God we're all alive."

"It's OK, I got my dad out. Bellcon opened a gas line and set a timer. *Hey! what about Bellcon!*"

Tim said, "We've got to talk. I think I killed him."

"I saw him crawling on the ground!" I said, looking at Emilie.

We arrived in front of Emilie's house. Tim said, "I told Emilie part of the story. She said we could come here and talk things through."

"Let's go inside," Emilie said. "My parents will be home soon, but we can talk in private in the study. Alan, I want you to stay here tonight. Your dad is welcome too."

We parked in front of the house and went inside. First, I called Mr. Wayne to check on my father. Dad got on the phone, said he was staying with the Wayne's tonight and had refused to go to the hospital. He told me I was invited to spend the night there and wanted to know what happened. He couldn't remember much, but figured there was a gas leak and somehow it made him feel drugged. He said he was going to arrange for us to stay in a hotel until we could rent an apartment. "It's a miracle you got us out of there, son. How the hell did you do it?" I told him we'd talk about it tomorrow and that I was staying at Emilie's for the night.

Once in Emilie's study, Tim explained what happened. "I saw you running towards the car parked near the woods. I knew it was Bellcon. Got Duggie out of the glove box. I was still a little shaky. I was running to you. I saw you drop on top of him. Guess Ballcon stuck this in your leg." Tim pulled a syringe out of his pocket. "Bellcon rolled you over just as I got there. I couldn't stop myself, and I fell over you. Came down hard on Bellcon. I was holding Duggie with both hands. The knife went right into his chest! I pulled it out. Bellcon had this weird look on his face. He started to get up. Fell and started crawling. Emilie was more awake. We grabbed the bandana. I helped her get to the car. Then I helped you. What am I going to do?" Tim asked me. He looked distraught.

"OK," I said. "So we don't know he's dead for sure."

"The knife went in, man. I think all the way," Tim said.

"Look, say he is dead, just say, what do you think we should do?"

"Oh man," Tim said, "his father and the police are gonna want to hang somebody for this. His father will say the three of us planned to murder his son ever since the drowning incident and you guys are my only witnesses."

Emilie looked at me. "Tim's right. I'm sure that creep could find a few people who'd testify that you guys said you wanted to kill that kid a few years ago. And maybe he'd even plant some evidence in the parking lot."

"But Bellcon has a reputation. We shouldn't go to the police with this?"

Tim shook his head.

Emilie said, "I'll bet Bellcon's father has helped his son get away with murder more than once. His friends in the courts and police departments have allowed his twisted justice. I wouldn't trust their judgement. The only reason Bellcon came here was to get the three of us. And wouldn't each of us have killed him to save the others? We are responsible for whatever happened. But I think we all agree that if he's dead, the world is a better place. Do we think we've done the wrong thing? Do you want to go to the police, Tim?"

"No Way," Tim said. "But what are we going to do?"

Emilie said, "What's the right thing to do? If he's dead, it's done as far as I'm concerned."

My head was clearing. "I think Emilie is right. Let's just sit tight for a few days. The parking lot was empty. Nobody saw what happened there tonight. Tim and I left after his talk. We planned to check on Emilie. I had trouble starting my car, so I left it parked across from the school and drove with Tim. We came to Emilie's, and I borrowed Tim's car to run home and get a book I wanted to lend Emilie. When I opened my door, I smelled gas and ran my father outside before the house exploded. Dad and I were just lucky. I left Dad with Mr. Wayne to go back to Emilie's, return Tim's car and check on her. Emilie never left her house tonight. That will be our story. For all anyone knows Bellcon was involved in a drug deal that went bad. That kid is a killer who keeps getting away with murder. If he's dead, we've probably saved a lot of lives. And we were defending ourselves. OK, Tim?"

"If he's dead, I'm not sorry I did it," Tim said.

I put my arm on my friend's shoulder, "We've all got to stay calm. We'll keep what really happened tonight to ourselves. Nobody else will know." While I was saying this, the front door opened and Emilie's parents, two more alibis, walked in.

*****

Bellcon was face down on the ground, trying to crawl, when Stan got to the St. Peter's school parking lot at the designated time. He had just missed the white Chevy leaving. His car, which Bellcon had borrowed earlier, was the only one in the lot. It was parked near the wooded trail. Stan sprinted to his friend. *"Bellcon! What's going on?* You OK?" He turned his friend over. There was blood on his shirt. His buddy stared up at him, his mouth working without sound, his eyes vacant. Stan pulled his friend into the back seat of his car.

He reached into Bellcon's pocket, got the keys and sped to the Forrest Creek hospital one mile down the road. Stan's car careened into the ER entrance. He sprung from the car and yelled for help. A nurse and an orderly came running out of the entrance. Stan pointed to his back seat. The nurse looked in the car and barked, "Get a stretcher!" She reached into the backseat and felt for a pulse on the wounded man's neck. *"Come on, come on!"* she urged.

A physician and two orderlies wheeling a stretcher came running out to the car. They pulled the patient onto the stretcher and rushed him to a treatment room. Stan was at their heels. A second nurse materialized. "No pulse," she exclaimed. The trio worked frantically. The victim's shirt was cut open, revealing a stab wound. In seconds, EKG leads were placed. "I can't get a pressure," one nurse said, pumping a blood pressure cuff, while the other nurse tried to start an I.V.. The physician quickly studied the chest wound, looked at the EKG monitor, then took out a pen light and examined the patient's irises. While still intently looking at the eyes, he rocked the patient's head from side to side.

"He's gone," the doctor said solemnly.

Stan wailed, "*Nooooooo!* Don't stop! You can't!"

"I'm sorry, son," the doctor said sadly. "There's nothing we can do. Are you related? Can you tell us his next of kin? We'll have to notify them, and we'll have to talk with the police."

Stan fell into a chair, put his face in his hands, and began sobbing and shaking. He kept repeating, "What happened? What happened? What happened...?"

CHAPTER 46

My father and I had to stay in a two-bedroom apartment while our house was being rebuilt. Home insurance covered the cost, and David, Emilie's dad, got us preferential treatment from a developer who was a bank customer. A few shopping sprees replaced our day-to-day necessities. The greatest losses were sentimental items. A few months went by, and life became a new normal.

Emilie had taken her chemotherapy, gotten sick again, but then rallied over the summer. Repeating a familiar recovery, she put on some weight, her hair was growing back and there was color in her cheeks. This time she seemed even more supercharged with energy, and her eyes were more luminescent than ever. We both returned to school.

In September, I moved into the apartment at Cornell I would share with another student. The landline phone, which I only had to share with one other person, was a luxury. It helped me stay in close contact with Emilie. Though the first call I made when I got back to school was to one of my favorite contacts in Forrest Creek. After twelve rings, the old man at Ronati's florist finally answered the phone. "Ronati's."

"Hi, Mr. Ronati, it's me, Alan," I said. I knew he'd recognize my voice.

"Oh, hi, son. Sorry it took me so long to pick up. A bit busy for the end of September. Phone's ringing off the hook! Let me guess, a bouquet of irises?"

"How'd you know?" I joked. We both laughed. The old man had prepared many iris bouquets for my father.

"This for that special girl?"

"You bet," I replied, thinking about Emilie and the anniversary of my final decision to pursue her and not become a priest.

"When do you want to pick these up?"

"Oh, that's the thing. I'm up at Cornell. Could you deliver them one month from today?"

"Sure. Hey, great school, huh? Good thing you called early. Got a lot of funerals this week, but I think we can do it."

"Thanks," I said, about to hang up.

"Hey, you knew that Bellcon kid, right?" the florist asked.

"Yeah?" I replied warily.

"You know, it's been two months. They never found out who killed him. Some of the guys from the police department get their flowers here. They say the crime's a mystery. Strangest thing. I mean right here in Forrest Creek. Any of your friends see or hear anything suspicious?"

It reminded me of the secret I'd kept with Emilie and Tim. We had stopped talking about it. "Nobody's accusing anyone far as I know," I said honestly.

*****

Frank Bellcon picked up the phone in his study. "Hello?" "It's Dunnard. Still no leads. Wish I had better news." He had called Frank every one to two weeks, updating him on the murder investigation. "What about Dargton?" Frank asked. When he first received the news, he thought of five people in Dargton who wanted his son dead. He had given the names to officer Dunnard. "Nothin' there," Dunnard said. "All solid alibis."

Frank could only think of one person in Forrest Creek who had the potential to harm his son. His son said he had a tough fight with a kid before he left for Vietnam. He never said *anyone* was "tough". But the kid, Alan, had a tight alibi. It so happened that Alan's friend, Tim, had given a public talk at St. Peter's school the night his son was killed. A number of attendees vouched for that, and, along with Tim and Alan, they all recalled seeing Stan's car, the one his son had borrowed for the day, parked at the far end of the parking lot, near the trail to the river. Some offered speculation to the police that there must have been a drug deal going on. The police had similar suspicions since a small plastic hypodermic needle cover was found at the scene.

Frank thought it was a bizarre coincidence that Alan's house blew up from a gas leak that same night. But investigation showed a leaky pipe. Nothing nefarious. And Alan's whereabouts the entire evening was supported by numerous witnesses, including his father, his neighbor, Tim, Emilie, and Emilie's parents.

"I just don't get it," Frank said. "He was a big strong kid who could take care of himself. He had no bruises or internal injuries according to the forensic autopsy. There was no sign of a struggle. He just winds up stabbed in the heart?"

Dunnard sighed. "And there were no witnesses. None that came forward anyway. We've talked to Stan ten times. Said his car didn't have a scratch on it. The parking lot was empty. He didn't see anyone hanging around or leaving the parking lot. Plus, we haven't found the weapon."

The counselor asked, "What about Stan?"

"Yeah, we thought about that. Everyone confirmed he was your son's best friend. The kid was an emotional wreck at the hospital that night. They had to give him a sedative. And the timeline puts him at home when your son was stabbed in the parking lot. His parents verify that he lent his car to your son that day. And when Stan left home that night, he was on foot. A short time later, he nearly crashed his car through the hospital emergency room door, screaming for help, with your son in the back seat."

"OK," Frank said. "Stay on it and keep me updated. Thank you for your efforts."

"Sure, Frank," Dunnard said and hung up.

Frank looked at the picture perched on his bookcase. His son, with a menacing expression, wearing a football uniform. He remembered his shock and sadness when he got the call. His son, who had survived combat in the jungles of Vietnam, killed so easily in a parking lot at home.

Frank had had hopes that with a little polish his son might have matured into a powerful adult, like his father. His hopes were destroyed. His son was gone. He recalled his wife's reaction when he called her. "I'm not surprised. Thanks for letting me know," she had said, and hung up. Frank shook his head and mumbled, "What happened?"

CHAPTER 47

The weeks flew by. While I was preparing to drive home for Thanksgiving, Emilie gave me the awful news that she might need chemotherapy again. I was not in a good mood when I got home that morning, and my grandmother, who was staying over for the holiday, quickly picked up on it. Ona asked how Emilie was doing. When I told her there could be another round of chemotherapy, she and my father looked at one another, then they looked at the floor.

"She's going to be OK," I said, reassuring myself.

Ona suggested, "Why don't we have our dinner early this afternoon? You can join Emilie for dinner in the evening, and your father and I will bring my apple and pumpkin pies to Emilie's. We can all have dessert together, if it's OK with her family."

It was such a simple offer. Yet the way she said it. So natural. Optimistic. Emilie's family and mine, together, sharing dessert on Thanksgiving. Besides, it was time Ona met Emilie. "Great idea," I said. "I'm sure they would love that. But do we have enough time to get everything ready?"

Ona was already in the kitchen pulling out vegetables and assembling various ingredients. "Not if you two just stand around!" She began giving us instructions. Our moods lifted, our efforts combined into the single goal of preparing a Thanksgiving meal.

Other than a turkey, I no longer remember exactly what Ada prepared for dinner that night. I was focused on trying not to stare at Emilie, to show only confidence and a happy face. It was an effort that eased a bit when Ona and my father showed up at Emilie's, each carrying a fresh baked pie.

David answered the door. "Hi, Michael, and this must be Ona. I've heard so much about you—" he looked at the pies, "and your baking! Happy Thanksgiving. Please come in."

David and Ona exchanged some small talk, like they'd known each other for years, and we all settled down at the dining room table. Plates and cups were set out for dessert and coffee. David announced, "During our Thanksgiving feasts we always take turns telling each other what we are thankful for. I think it was Emilie's turn. Em?"

The room fell quiet. Emilie's voice was steady. "I thank God for a world where some things are determined, but others happen by choice. You can be certain the sun will come up in the morning, but not certain what I may do next. That's *my* choice."

"Unpredictable?" David said. "Ohhh, yes!" Everyone laughed.

"And," Emilie added, "I'm thankful that I became part of all of you, and you all became part of me."

When she finished her dessert, Ona popped out of her chair and, despite protests from David and Ada, began to clear the table. Ada met her at the kitchen sink. I heard Ona say, "Emilie reminds me so much of my daughter."

"Thank you," Ada responded. "Your daughter was wonderful. I loved her. You must miss her very much."

"I do. I was so lucky to have her. It's like Emilie said, Marie became part of me, and tonight I felt like she was here with me. Is that foolish?"

"No," Ada said, looking at Emilie. "Not at all."

Early on Saturday morning, the bells on the Florist's door jingled when I entered.

"Morning, Mr. Ronati," I said to the owner behind the counter.

"Hey! Hi, Alan. Home on break?"

"Yeah. I need a favor."

"Name it."

"A dozen irises in a bouquet."

The florist threw his hands up, gave a "Ho-ho," and said, "I should have guessed. Tuesday be OK?"

"That'd be fine. But I also want to arrange to pick up a bouquet every two weeks."

The florist's eyebrows went up. "For how long?"

"Tell you what, I'll pay for one in advance. When I stop picking them up, cancel the order."

The old man grumbled, "But what do I do with the one you don't pick up?"

Walking toward the door I said, "Take it to your favorite girl."

"*What?*" Mr. Ronati called out as the door jingled. "And tell my wife Alan's girl didn't want them?"

I paused in the doorway. "No. Tell her Alan's girl said, 'OK, so you love me. Enough with the flowers already!'"

As the door closed, I heard the florist yell, "*That's not a good sentiment for business!*"

Later that morning, Emilie and I sat on her couch talking. She described some amazing stories the nurses at the hospital had told her. Cases of miraculous cancer cures. I made her laugh with some odd ball occurrences at school, like the kid who fell asleep during an electrical engineering exam and failed the test. Ada walked into the room. "I hope I'm not interrupting?"

"No. Not at all," I said.

"You know, Alan, I've been thinking about your explanation of consciousness. Your ideas. I have many questions."

"Great," I said, "helps me understand what I'm saying."

Ada wanted to know details. The three of us talked for a long while about holograms, brains, and dualities. When Ada asked about entanglement and how the universe was all interconnected, I said, "Tell you what. I got a letter from John. He'll be home in two weeks when I'm back for winter break. How 'bout I ask John to come over? He can explain that better than I can, and we'll all learn something."

"You think he would come over?" Ada asked.

"Sure. Why not? He loves this stuff."

"I'd love to meet him," Ada said. "I've heard so much. He's certainly welcome."

I said, "OK, I'll write to him."

On Sunday morning, I had breakfast with Emilie. She was somber.

"It's tough, isn't it? I mean chemo again." I asked.

She said, "I keep thinking about the part of me that lives in you, before I got sick: the healthy, strong part. I feel I'm in there." She pointed to my head. "Like we're entangled particles." She stared at me and forced a little laugh-like sound. "Am I as crazy as you?"

"It's not crazy," I said. "I feel the same way."

"Always together," she said, touching my hand, her eyes sunken but luminous.

"Yes," I said. "Em, I've given this a lot of thought." I got off my chair and down on one knee. "Will you marry me?" I took a small box from my pocket and opened it. My father had given me my mother's engagement ring. I saw surprise on her face soften into a smile.

"Do you know how lucky we are?" she asked. "So many things could have happened, and we never would have met. Our parents or grandparents could have been killed in a war before we were born. We could have lived in different states or different countries. But we've had time together, to know what love really means. How many people can say that? Alan, we're already married in a way.

Entangled. Inseparable. But I won't say yes until I'm well. Remember your promise. If there's ever someone else, I want her to feel as special as I feel. Not to feel second place. We'll always be together. You in my universe and me in yours, right?"

"Yes," I said, and closed the box. "Then I'll save this for later. I know you'll be well soon."

We hugged and kissed one last time in case chemotherapy would prohibit her exposure to the infections of affections for a while. I thought about a future when we would not have to be so cautious. That's how I stayed strong, by visualizing how things would be once she was cured.

CHAPTER 48

When Emilie started chemo, she asked me not to call her until I finished my final exam. Two weeks later, as soon as I was done with the last test, I called. Her voice, just above a whisper, reminded me of what she'd been through, but I pushed any bad images from my mind and envisioned better days so I could greet her with optimism, now a practiced mental exercise. It was a late Friday night when I arrived back home. Emilie was in quarantine after finishing chemo.

On Saturday morning I picked up an iris bouquet at the florist and drove to Emilie's. Ada answered the front door. I could tell there was a strain behind her happy face. She greeted me with a hug, thanked me for the flowers and asked me to bring them around to the back deck and set them on the table, then come inside. When I entered the foyer Ada told me, "The doctors advised Emilie to stay in the house. We must keep her away from any germs. No one with even a slight cough can visit, and we still need to keep the fresh flowers outside."

I guess I expected better news, like *Hey, Alan, Emilie's all better! Cured, no more worries!* I'd convinced myself of this possibility at school, to make the situation more bearable. Each day I had chosen to visualize her amazing eyes that, at times, looked like they had harnessed the power of

rising suns. I sought strength in the memory of each en-
counter with her sharp intellect, invincible courage and
her gratitude for every minute of life.

Ada escorted me to the living room. Emilie sat in the
easy boy chair, the familiar colorful bandanna on her head.
She had been reading a book. Some of her other textbooks
were on the coffee table. She had not been to school for a
month, but she was trying to keep up with her classes.

One glimpse and reality took hold. She looked pale and
thin. I wanted to take her in my arms, hug her, kiss her.
Infuse some of my vitality into her. Swear to her that
things would turn out O.K., even though I was not sure
that they would. But I did not want her to see my fear. I
took a deep breath and willed myself to believe everything
was fine.

"Hi, Em!" I said, enthusiastically.

"Hi, Alan. You brought my flowers I see. They're beautiful. Thank you."

"Mr. Ronati said to say 'Hi'. He heard you, uh, weren't
feeling well. That guy finds out everything."

Emilie laughed softly, shrugged, and raising her palms
said, "He sure does, but he sells flowers to everyone in
town. Weddings, birthdays, babies, funerals, and he likes
to talk."

"So," she said, "how did finals go?"

"Exams went fine. Physics was a little tricky, but I think
I did OK."

Ada asked if I'd like something to drink.

"Actually, tea would be great," I said "By the way, John is in town. He can come over tomorrow if you're interested."

"That would be a nice distraction," Emilie said. "What do you think, Mom?"

"Let's see how you feel in the morning. Can we let him know tomorrow?"

I said, "Sure thing."

The next morning, I got the call. "Why don't you both come after eleven this morning," Ada said. "I'll make lunch. Oh, and bring your paper so I can ask my questions."

Later, Ada answered the door, "Well, hello," she said with a big smile. "This must be John. It's a pleasure to welcome you to our home." She held out her hand.

For a moment John stared at her hand. Then he slowly reached out, shook Ada's hand and looked up with a grin, his wide-set eyes scanning her. "Thank you," he said. "The pleasure is mine."

We found Emilie in the living room, sitting on the couch wearing her bandanna. Ada had placed her easel with colored markers on the opposite wall and flanked the couch with two reclining chairs. I sat next to a wan-looking Emilie and put my college paper on the coffee table.

David walked in. After introduced himself to John, he peppered him with questions about California, what he liked about Cal Tech and about John's family, who still lived in town.

"Well, David?" Ada asked. "Convinced this young man is not a Russian spy?" Emilie laughed.

"Sorry," David responded, "just curious."

Ada said to John, "We told David about how you and Alan started 'Church at John's' and have worked on some interesting ideas." She pointed to the paper on the coffee table. "You boys are attracting quite a congregation. Your friends, two priests, my family and possibly our Rabbi." She turned to me. "When Emilie mentioned your paper to the Rabbi, he asked to see a copy."

"Sure, I'll make a copy," I said.

"One thing must be clear," John said. "You might find personal meaning in these ideas, perhaps a religious feeling. Alan and I can offer ideas about nature, but they make no one an authority on what God demands of human behavior. Each of us must determine that for ourselves, alone."

There was an awkward silence for a minute. Then David said, "No Rabbis or priests, huh?"

To keep our discussion congenial, I stated the obvious. "We're not trying to start a religion, just understand things a little better." Emilie nodded in agreement, making an effort to maintain her posture.

"Well, professor," Ada said to John, extending her arm toward the easel. "Please tell us how the universe is like a hologram and help us understand this quantum mechanics."

John responded, "I can sketch some principles for you, but as Feynman likes to say, '*Nobody* understands quantum mechanics.'"

Ada and David looked at one another as if they were thinking, *Did we hear that right?*

John said, "Let me demonstrate how particles move, where some dualities of nature exist, then a little bit about what I've been working on."

For fifty minutes John drew diagrams, gave lucid explanations, and paused to answer questions. When he mentioned the Schrodinger wave equation and explained how a particle seemed to take its surroundings into account and then "decide" where to go, David asked, "Are you saying a particle knows its surroundings?"

John said, "No. I'm just making an analogy. But Alan is working on something you might find interesting. I'll let him explain his ideas."

Emilie had taken a short nap while John was talking, but woke up as John finished explaining how the universe might be understood as a multidimensional block of information, where every part reflects the whole, like a hologram.

Ada asked, "Could this be true?"

John replied, "It's been a tough nut to crack. But a few mathematicians are helping me and there are some promising dots to connect."

Ada turned to me. "You think your explanation of consciousness might mean the universe is conscious?"

"Yes," I said. "It would not be a consciousness as we know it. It would be very different. Each particle John talked about could be thought of as having a physical existence and an experienced existence, two fundamentally different properties, as a duality. A particle wouldn't be aware of its surroundings as we are. It might have an experience of just *being*. I believe that when trillions of these particles are organized into a complex object, like the brain, their fundamental bits of awareness compose human consciousness. And—"

Ada was excited, she turned to David and cut in. "*And perhaps if, as John thinks, the universe is a single object, like a hologram, all the connected little pieces make a cosmic consciousness!*"

"Wow! This is all, uh, heavy," David said.

Emilie and I laughed.

We all moved to the kitchen table and chatted about John's and my ideas during lunch.

When we finished eating, Emilie perked up. "You know what's really cool? Alan and I were talking: a consciousness of the whole universe would contain and *experience* all of our consciousnesses and that of every person who ever existed! And, with our choices, each of us *changes* the whole, leaving our imprint. If this consciousness is God, then God *knows* everyone's pain, everyone's hopes. God experiences being born with every birth, dying with every death. And the icing on the cake? We're individuals who define ourselves. We still get to choose where we're going—like those quantum particles— but we're part of the whole. It's true our lives are temporary, but that just means every breath is a gift. So," she said, looking at me, "you can never be disappointed in this God, no matter what happens. Right?"

At the time my mother died, I would not have agreed with that last statement. I would have told you that not even God could be forgiven for some things. But while Emilie waited for an answer, I realized my sentiments had slowly changed ever since she became part of my universe and I learned how she chose to look at things. I looked into her large green-gold irises, and her words forged new connections in my brain, connections that she had nurtured for me. I looked at John and felt certain we were right. It all made sense now. "I guess you're right," I said.

Emilie's triumphant laugh, which apparently ended our private debate, was shortened by a single cough. A smile left Ada's face as she turned to look at her daughter. "I think Emilie may need a little rest."

"Actually," Emilie said, "a nap sounds good right now." She smiled, "Thank you so much for coming, John. I think your ideas have inspired all of us. Keep us updated on your work, OK?"

"Sure thing," John said. "Thanks for having me."

I stood and said, "Yes, thanks for lunch, guys. Em, I'll call you later, all right?"

She smiled and nodded.

A few hours later I dialed Emilie's number. Ada answered the phone. "Can you believe she's still sleeping? I think she was exhausted today."

"I guess so," I said, concerned. "Is she OK?"

"I've been checking in on her. She's just sleeping."

"I'll check back tomorrow morning then."

"Yes, I think that would be best," Ada said.

The next morning, I picked up the phone and called Emilie. There was no answer. I thought that was odd and called back fifteen minutes later. Still no answer. I drove to Emilie's and found no one home. I wondered, *Did Ada forget to mention they were going somewhere this morning?* I drove back home. An hour later my phone rang. When I answered, I was surprised to hear David's voice on the line. He sounded tired.

"Alan," he said, "Emilie took a turn for the worse last night. She had a fever and a cough. We brought her right to Columbia. I'm sorry we didn't call you earlier this morning. We were so tied up with the doctors and what's going on." I thought I heard David's voice quaver briefly. "Do you think you can get to the hospital?"

For a second, I could not answer. Then I said, "I'll get there. What room is she in?"

"She's in intensive care."

My heart began pounding. I said, "OK, bye."

I told Dad what was going on. As I walked to the car for the trek to the familiar hospital parking lot, Dad said, "Probably not the time for me to be there, but I'll wait by the phone. Call me when you can, all right?"

"OK, Dad. Thanks."

I made my way to the ICU. I was escorted to a waiting room, where I found David and Ada. Their eyes were bleary, hair disheveled and clothes wrinkled. "How is she?" I asked.

Ada looked up at me, her eyes red. She hugged me and said, "Oh, Alan. She got so sick, so fast. She was weak and started having trouble breathing. She has pneumonia. They're in there now trying to help her. They said they might have to put her on a ventilator."

"When can we go in?" I asked.

David came over and put his arm around me. "The doctor said he'd come out and talk to us soon."

I was finding it hard to process the information. "Is she, uh, awake?"

Ada said, "She was in and out on the way here. She kept repeating that she loved us and you, and not to worry. That crazy girl—" Ada began to cry.

David turned his head away.

A doctor walked in and came over to us. He looked at me. "I'm doctor Olsen, and you are?"

Ada, who knew how touchy hospitals were about visitors said, "This is our son, Alan."

"Good to meet you," the doctor said. He addressed us all. "Emilie has pneumonia. The bacteria have spread to her bloodstream because the chemo wipes out both normal white blood cells, the ones that fight infection, along with leukemia cells. The germs in her blood caused what we call A.R.D.S., adult respiratory distress syndrome, which means her lungs have filled up with fluid. She began having a hard time breathing. We had to put a tube into her windpipe and use a ventilator to help her breathe."

"How are you going to get the fluid out of her lungs?" I asked.

"We support her in every way possible and hope the fluid will recede. Bacteria in the blood cause damage to blood vessels, making them leaky. That's why fluid seeps out into the lungs. It also makes it difficult to maintain her blood pressure. There are no treatments to fix the damaged blood vessels. We give her strong antibiotics to kill the bacteria and powerful medications to try and keep her blood pressure up."

"And if those medications don't work?" Ada asked.

The doctor looked deflated. "She is very sick. We are hopeful, but anything can happen."

I asked, "There's nothing else we can do?"

"I believe prayers can help," he answered. "The nurses will let you in for a short visit soon." He walked out.

We waited a few minutes, then the nurses escorted us to Emilie's room. We donned the protective garb and entered. Emilie was surrounded by beeping, blinking monitors. Her bald head and diminished frame looked lost in the large hospital bed. She was covered with the tubes and wires that connected her body to machines, giving the impression they were draining her life forces.

David and Ada went to one side of the bed. I went to the other. Ada and I each took one of Emilie's hands.

"She looks so peaceful," David said.

I leaned over and whispered in Emilie's ear, "You'll always be in my universe. I love you." I think I imagined a nearly imperceptible smile form on her lips. I straightened and began to think of a prayer. Suddenly, an alarm went off. I looked around, bewildered.

A nurse burst into the room, looked at the monitors, then shouted out to the nursing station, "*Call it!*" She turned to us and forced a smile. "Please step out for a moment, Emilie needs help."

We were briefly paralyzed by our helplessness. Then, we stepped out as doctors and nurses rushed into the room. A large dolly loaded with medical equipment was wheeled up to the doorway. We were escorted to the waiting room.

I kept asking, "What's going on?" Someone said, "The doctor will be out to talk to you."

For forty minutes the three of us spoke quietly, speculating about what may have happened, each of us trying to sound optimistic to prevent an uncontrollable chain reaction of anxiety. When Dr. Olsen appeared in the doorway, I heard Ada gasp. David stared at him, unable to form a question.

I blurted, "What happened?"

The doctor looked at me. "Her blood pressure dropped and, from the strain of fluid-filled lungs, the heart began beating erratically. Then it stopped and... we did everything we could but, I'm so sorry."

Ada collapsed into a chair, sobbing. David put his arms around her, his shoulders heaving.

I stood in disbelief, my mouth open for a moment. I looked at Ada and David, then back to the doctor. "I want to see her."

I saw the doctor's eyes redden and glaze. "Yes, of course."

The doctor escorted the three of us to Emilie's room and left. It was suddenly still and quiet, like the world outside ceased to exist. The ventilator was gone, the tubes and wires had been removed, and the flashing, beeping monitors were turned off. A clean white sheet was pulled up to her chest, it covered her body, like the cloth on a statue that had been chiseled out of marble. Her skin was unnaturally pale; her eyelids, smooth and still, shrouded those once magnificent eyes; her form was motionless and shrunken, as if the vital force it once enjoyed had made her larger in life. It triggered a powerful memory of my mother, when I knew she was no longer present in the casket that carried her body.

I took the lifeless hand, kissed a cheek. The skin had already begun to cool. I dropped to my knees and put my head down. A stinging liquid poured from my eyes and a deafening single word reverberated in my mind: *NO, NO, NO!*

CHAPTER 49

Although it was against Jewish tradition, Ada and David honored Emilie's wish and had her cremated. Their family had never been strict in their religious practices, and they belonged to a synagogue with a progressive rabbi. Emilie had given her parents explicit instructions; in the summer they would travel to the Long Island beaches and sprinkle most of her ashes in the ocean. For now, her ashes sat in an urn on the mantle.

Following funeral services, the family had returned home to sit shiva. I asked if I could stay with them for the week of mourning. I sat among the visitors, hoping my presence was as comforting to Ada and David as being with them consoled me.

During the week many visitors came to give their sympathies. Among them were my father, Rich, Tim and his fiancée Stephanie, Hip and John, my high school wrestling coach, many of my high school friends, many of Emilie's high school and grade school friends, and dozens of people from across the state who were helped by the organization "Let's Cultivate the Garden State." Father Curtain and Father MacKristin came too. The visitors all seemed to know it was proper not to speak to the mourners unless spoken to. The silences at times were long. David and Ada would talk to the visitors about Emilie's life, and everyone expressed how they would never forget her and how much they were going to miss her.

I would occasionally walk outside, accompanying some visitors when they left, as I did with Fathers Curtain and MacKristin. The two priests found it difficult to speak. They shared the pain of my two great losses, my mother and now Emilie.

"If it weren't for you and Emilie," Father Curtain said, voice cracking, "I don't know what would have happened to me. There are no words, Alan, but I like to think she was, and is, an angel."

"Aye," Father MacKristin said, "you both taught us something. Emilie changed our lives, and she'll always be with us. Like she'd say, 'Our lives are on loan, we never know when we'll have to give them back. Each breath is a gift.'"

I saw Mr. Ronati walking up the sidewalk. He stood behind the priests, listening and waiting. He watched us hug and heard me say, "Thank you. You both meant a lot to Emilie. I'm glad we're such good friends." My voice was steady, having cried down to my last tear days earlier.

When the priests left, Mr. Ronati walked up to me. "Alan, I am so sorry for your loss." He clasped my hand and seemed to tremble with distress.

I could see the old man's eyes redden. I responded, "Thank you."

"I want to tell you something," the florist began. "I heard what the priests told you and now I feel even more moved to say it. Would you mind indulging an old man?"

His eyes seemed to sparkle a little, and I hoped that letting him speak would soothe his grief. I said, "Of course, please."

"You know, I grew up with flowers. Worked in the florist when my father owned it and I was just a young boy. We'd talk about the people who came in, why they were buying flowers, the types of flowers they bought and what those flowers meant. Did you know that flowers have a meaning, a story behind each one?"

"No, I didn't," I said.

"Well," he continued, "irises are a token of the Greek god Iris. She was said to be a messenger of the gods. She would travel back and forth between heaven and Earth, sometimes leaving a rainbow behind her. I like to think irises remind us that we sometimes receive messages from God. The priests, they said Emilie was an angel. She brought a message to them: *Every breath is a gift.* I'll remember that every time I see an iris now, and I see them a lot. Don't you think it's interesting that irises were Emilie's favorite flower?"

"Yes," I said, suddenly remembering the bracelet I bought Emilie for her birthday, long ago, with the purple flowers. "They were my mother's favorite flower too."

Mr. Ronati said, "Yes, they were," his expression a mixture of sadness and hope. "I guess those angels and their messages were for you, and for all of us." He gave me a hug and walked into the house.

One year later, he told me that when my last bouquet of irises arrived at his shop, the week Emilie had passed away, he had given them to his wife, as I requested. He told her they were irises for Alan, and the story behind the flowers. She had cried. But Mr. Ronati said they would always remember Emilie for something good because, "Ever since then, my wife and I have loved each other a little more, every minute of every day. That angel is still with us."

I told him that I understood what he meant. Perfectly.

*

EPILOGUE

Alan and I have stayed in touch over the years. On special occasions he will drop in at the high school. We have a friendship that is rare and hard to explain. We are "complementary," like a wave and a particle: two sides of one coin. We finish each other's sentences, laugh, cry and search for meaning together. We are soulmates. That's probably why on one memorable visit I knew who was knocking on my door. I was sitting at my desk, which had fewer stacks of books and papers than in my younger days, gazing out the window overlooking the athletic fields of Northern Catholic.

"Enter," I called out, smiling with anticipation.

Alan opened the door, grinning. He looked from my white halo of hair, down to my latest green T-shirt imprinted with "N.C. 2012 Track and Field Champions." He laughed. "Track champs again?" Setting a vase of flowers on the desk, he grabbed and shook my hand.

"Ah, Alan! I see you've brought some lovely irises!"

"Yes," he said. "I only brought them on one other visit. Do you remember?"

I laughed and looked over Alan's shoulder. "Aye. Many visits ago. What, about 20 years? You taught me that." I pointed to a hand-made poster on the wall. It read:

Neural Wave Equation

$$iv\frac{\partial \psi}{\partial t} = \left(\frac{-v^2}{2}\Delta + U_{ex}\right)\psi$$

Schrodinger Wave Equation

$$i\hbar\frac{\partial \psi}{\partial t} = \left(\frac{-\hbar^2}{2m}\nabla^2 + V\right)\psi$$

I explained, "One equation showing how electricity might behave in the brain and another showing how quantum particles behave in space. Similar looking equations. Perhaps a little validation of an idea you had long ago. Brains behave like quantum particles, no?"

"Yes," Alan replied. "John introduced me to Dr. Pribram's ideas. I found that Neural Wave Equation in the appendix of one of his books, *Brain and Perception*. I brought the irises then to commemorate the angels that bring some light into our lives."

Struck by a sudden thought I said, "Heavens, is there something new about your ideas? I've never stopped thinking about them."

"Something old, something new, something borrowed, the flowers are blue." Alan laughed, and held out an old piece of stationary. "I'd like you to read a letter no one else has seen. A letter John wrote to me."

"Oh yes, John. So brilliant. He died too young. Tragic. There was no treatment for that awful virus back then."

He handed me the letter. I read it out loud:

"November 1982.

Dear Alan,

Maybe you'll forgive your hibernating friend for taking so long to write if I share some news. I've done it!! The math was challenging, but I'm convinced that our four-dimensional universe is a dual expression of a reality with many more dimensions. We are but spots on the flat surface of a holographic film, we cannot experience the alternate image it projects, enriched with a multitude of added dimensions. Yet, both views are correct. In a way, the equations have a simplicity, but they work from 'bits' to galaxies. It all boils down to information, the patterns we've talked about.

I realized that the theory could lead to technical advances over the next one hundred years bringing about a real military doomsday scenario. So I told colleagues the whole thing was a dead end and destroyed my notes. The world's not ready for this. It's all in my head right now. There is a part I want to share with you. I'm wondering what you'll think.

I'm hoping to make it to my parents' house early next year and can't wait to explain it all to you, to see your reaction. Here's one tidbit. Within the theory there are groups of solutions for electrical information that seem to have no reason to exist. Perhaps each group represents a sense experience, one for visual, one for auditory, etc. Perhaps you were right, my friend. Maybe we all share in a cosmic consciousness. After all, putting our ideas together, everything is either measurable information or experienced information. A duality?

When you hear what I have to tell you, we'll be the two most humble and excited humans on the planet. Really, if I died today, I'd be perfectly content. It's a beautiful theory.

Lots to talk about. Please don't discuss this with anyone!
Pastor John.

When I finished, Alan said, "Pastor John. We used to call him that when we met in his basement. He never made it home."

My eyes glazed. "No one's discovered his theory? No notes left behind?"

"No. But there is something that's come along. I'd like you to take a look at this. It's unusual to find a best seller written by a theoretical physicist." Alan handed a book to me.

I read the cover and said, "Ah, *The Hidden Reality*, it's on my list. Haven't gotten around to it."

"This copy is yours," he said. "You can read it later. For now, just read the passages I've marked off. I'd like to see your reaction."

I opened the book where Post-it notes were attached and read the marked paragraphs. For a moment I was speechless. Shocked by what I had read, as though an electric current was scrambling through my brain trying to find a familiar circuit.

"Alan, I've heard about string theory," I said, "but *serious* scientists are saying the universe may be like a hologram? And these two paragraphs: that perhaps one day physicists won't be talking about atoms and photons because the bedrock of reality is really just *information*, that's what your friend John was saying in his letter, isn't it?"

"Yes." Alan smiled.

"Sweet angels on Earth!" I said. "This is good news! Why, I can see now how science might explain a cosmic omniscience. Alan, you *must* share these ideas. I want you to write it all down. Write the story of how you and your friends developed these concepts. Write a book Alan! The characters can be fictitious to avoid any controversy. I'll help you any way I can, but you must. I can see why you brought the irises. What these scientists are saying is that you and John could be—"

Alan interrupted. "Oh no. The irises are for you. Too often we don't get to acknowledge our angels while they're still among us."

"That's nice of you lad," I said, "but I'm not a messenger from heaven. I wish I could have come up with some revelation." I felt the weight of failing to make the discovery I always thought I would. All those years challenging students, looking for clues.

Alan said, "Jim, you have been an angel to so many. Remember Rich, my friend you helped long ago? He could have been expelled, turned to drugs without your help. Instead, he became a successful businessman. In retirement, he took over *Let's Cultivate the Garden State*. It's a national organization now, feeding thousands. And you sent me to talk to Father Curtain when he was lost. *You* saved him. How many people did he help afterwards? It was *you* who encouraged me to never stop looking for the answers to my questions. And I also found out years ago, it was *you* who asked Emilie to get me and John back together. Would this conversation even be happening if it wasn't for you? You've been an angel to countless people. No Jim, these irises are for you."

I raised my head. There was some truth in his kind words. "You make an old man feel good. Thank you. I guess both of us have been lucky. We've been close to so many wonderful people in our lives."

"Yes, we have," Alan said, returning my gaze.

I grinned. "Well, if I'm an angel, what was it you boys used to say as kids? 'It takes one to know one,' right?"

We both laughed. Our laughter echoed between our universes.

Acknowledgments

This book could never have been written without the help of some very special people. A very big thank you to:

Pat Rushin for sharing his wisdom about the craft of writing and his excellent suggestions, guidance and time spent reading and rereading the evolving manuscript.

Elisa Chalem for her artistic insight, patience, help pointing out where better words and scenes were needed, sharing when she thought a character needed work, and her confidence-inspiring faith in me.

Joe Vornehm Jr. who, thank heavens, is a scientist that believes the math describing the natural world tells us something real beyond just allowing calculations, and who shared his clear-eyed understanding of some difficult concepts in physics.

James Gilchrist for his edits, valuable comments on story structure, thoughtful insights on my attempts to find common ground in science and religion, and for helping me wrestle through some tough personal theological perspectives that surface in this book.

Barbara and Bob Cariddi: Barbara for her superb editing skills, many hours examining the manuscript and revisions, and her keen suggestions that sharpened the visual imagery to bring the characters and the reader closer together. And Bob for his time reading and comments on early renditions of the manuscript.

Matt, Justin and Lindsay, for being the special people that they are, for many helpful suggestions on the manuscript, and for being patient and enthusiastic sounding boards for their dad's projects. Nancy for her patience with my writing.

"L.J." Johnson for her talent and skill creating realistic figures for the book. Marion Paganello for her helpful opinions.

These folks gave a vital boost and were inspirational for bringing the story to life.

Of course, I must acknowledge the many giants in mathematics, physics and neuroscience whose ideas my imagination blended into the soul of this book.

I would also like to thank some who are still with us, some who are not. These folks, in one or more ways, were elements of inspiration for this book including: old friends, my parents, in-laws, my brother and a few elementary and high school teachers. They are:

Thomas Pagano, Sr. & Tomaso Pagano; Fortune Pagano; Abel and Louise Garcia;

Bob Cariddi; Tom Landrigan; Rich Paganello; Elisa and Patty Chalem; Joe Vornehm Sr.; Michael Marion; Dennis Puccio; Gary Larkin; Pete Righi; Mike Sacco; Cecilia Pozo; Bradley Plohr; Mr. Peter DeLellis; Mrs. Sandborn; Father Vogel; Sister Alice; Sister Michelle, Mr. Robert Roswell; Brother Thomas.

Suggestions for further reading:

Abbott, Edwin A. *Flatland: A Romance of Many Dimensions.* New York: Dover Publications, 1992

Aczel, A.D. *Entanglement: The greatest Mystery in Physics.* New York: Four Walls Eight Windows, 2001

Blackwell, Richard J. *Galileo, Bellarmine, and the Bible.* Indiana: University of Notre Dame Press, 1991

Dickinson, Emily. *The Brain is Wider Than the Sky.* (Poem can be viewed online: search "Poem 598")

Feynman, Richard P. *Six Easy Pieces.* Addison-Wesley Publishing Co. 1995

Greene, Brian. *The Hidden Reality.* New York: Vintage Books, 2011

Isaacson, Walter. *Einstein: His Life and Universe.* New York: Simon & Shuster, 2007

Kauffman, Stuart. *At Home in the Universe: The Search for the Laws of Self-Organization and Complexity.* New York: Oxford University Press, 1996

Pribram, Karl H. *The Form Within: My Point of View.* Connecticut: Prospecta Press, 2013

Wheeler, John Archibald. *Information, Physics, Quantum: The Search for Links in Complexity, Entropy and the Physics of Information.* (Zurek, W.H. Ed.) CRC Press, 1990

ABOUT THE AUTHOR

This is Robert Pagano's first novel.

He had his childhood experiences in a blue-collar suburb of New Jersey in the 1960s. There, he explored the woods and waterways with friends, having both real and imaginary adventures. He developed a hankering for hearing and telling stories and was enchanted by some of the Romantic and Victorian poets, which sparked a fascination for the creative use of words. At nine years old, he began writing poetry and continued creative writing through college, until he became engrossed in learning about and understanding the natural world and the origins of consciousness. His writing hiatus was extended by professional responsibilities, but during this lapse, the ideas for *Irises* were brewing. He hopes to write about other ideas developed during that time as well.

When he is not writing, he loves spending time with his family, otherwise he enjoys eating a good meal, reading a good book, watching a good movie, or pretending he is exercising.

WITHDRAWN

Printed in the USA
CPSIA information can be obtained
at www.ICGtesting.com
BVHW041456180823
668707BV00002B/6

9 798986 940700